SUMMARY

He's a biker. She's a Mistress. They've always given one another what they want. But what happens when want moves to need?

Tiger walked away from the volatile outlaw biker world in which he was raised. As an alpha male, he embraces submission under the right woman's control, his strong will and intimidating demeanor adding to the pleasure and challenge.

Skye has been mute since childhood. As a Mistress, she knows communication goes far beyond words. When Tiger's past brings tragedy to him, taking more from him than he was prepared to lose, Skye's own history of overcoming will be key to bringing him back—and showing them both how much more their relationship could become.

AT HER CALL

A Mistresses of the Board Room Novel

JOEY W. HILL

ACKNOWLEDGMENTS

For every book, I find readers willing to help me navigate uncharted waters, aka topics I know little to nothing about. For this book specifically, my primary research needs were the motorcycle club/enthusiast culture and living without the ability to hear or speak in "normal" ways.

On the biker side, I offer my tremendous thanks to Lora and Bobbi. In addition to fact-checking, they gave me firsthand impressions and beautiful language to express how it feels to ride a motorcycle and experience this lifestyle fully. I appreciate the permission to use that language in more than one place in this story.

On the hearing/speech side, my sister-in-law Angie was invaluable in giving me insight into the challenges for the deaf and their perspective in a hearing world. Plus she demonstrated multiple phrases in sign language for me.

The input from both sets of "experts" made this a *much* better book—which is always the case when people generously offer their valuable time to help me get it right.

My thanks also to my brother, the awesome mechanic, who helped me with a pivotal part of the story that relied on Tiger's understanding of engines. And to Mary, my doctor friend who helped me tweak the causes and terminology for Skye's muteness.

As always, any errors that remain are my own.

A separate thank you to Katie M, for the title of this book. I know she thought there were better options, but the first time she suggested it, I had the "ping" that told me *At Her Call* was the absolute right title for Skye and Tiger's story.

Good stories in any medium inspire my work—books, TV, movies, or the man in the grocery line telling the cashier a story about his day. That said, it's rare I thank a specific TV series for an inspiration.

However, for reasons that will become clear when you reach the relevant scene, I want to say a big thank you to the Netflix series *How to Build a Sex Room*. The sexual topics were handled with sensitivity, while entertaining the viewer immensely. Go Melanie Rose!

Finally, a shout out to my readers. The BDSM romance world favors Male Dom/female sub stories, and my readers are no exception. Hell, I love them, too—it's why I have written plenty of them myself! Therefore, to read a Female Domme/male sub book, many of my readers have to trust I'll give them a story to love. The fact they make that leap of faith, plus go out and tell others it's worth the risk, is something I appreciate greatly.

Without that, the Mistresses of the Board Room wouldn't be growing in popularity the way they are. So thank you!

CHAPTER ONE

"The vultures are back, Chuck," Tiger said. "Think they know something we don't?"

Chuck squinted up at the two large birds, hunched in expectant poses on the back corner of his liquor store roof. He wiped the sweat off his brow with a forearm, his other resting on the push mower handle. "Yeah. They're thinking, 'Hot damn, this'll be the day that fat bastard will drop.' While mowing a strip of grass his wife insists on having for that spoiled poodle to take a crap."

"Can't fool me. You love Tiberius." Tiger chuckled. Leaning against a rusting metal pole of his garage's covered back patio, he lit a cigarette. The corrugated roofing provided shade from the New Orleans sun. When he and his crew were busy—which was most of the time—they grabbed a quick lunch out here on benches made of cinder blocks and planks.

Maryshka, one of his female mechanics, had stacked up old tires and put a wider piece of wood on them for a table. At the end of their long workdays it served as a place to play cards. Some of his people didn't have much of a home to go to. His garage had the things home was supposed to provide.

Tiger was glad it offered them that. But he had another place that gave him things no other did. As he took a drag on the cigarette, he stretched his shoulders, his neck. He'd been at the club just last night,

1

and his body still ached. Mistress Skye had worked him over in all the good ways.

Tiger didn't attach himself to any one Mistress; he rotated sessions among several who liked the same fluid arrangement. But Skye was stuck in his head today.

He was a big man, so most women were short to him. Skye was about five and half feet. Spiky blond hair, short on one side but long on the other, the strands artfully placed to enhance her graceful throat and frame the softness of her moon-shaped face. A good body, nice curves. She wore things to the club most women didn't. Last night it had been flowing slacks and a white, sheer blouse tied at the waist. Lace bra beneath, enough open buttons on the blouse to draw a man's gaze to her tempting cleavage.

Chunky, new age type jewelry. She'd slipped off her heels and done the scene barefoot. Casual, yet when a sub met her gaze, he saw nothing but Mistress in the glitter of her dark eyes and the set of the lush pink mouth, as if it held all sorts of commands ready to be spoken.

But they never were. Not from that mouth.

Skye was mute.

She communicated through body language, a voice app on her phone, and something indefinable. If a sub paid attention, he'd know what she wanted. What she expected. Skye didn't insist on the Mistress title, ma'am or anything else, but she left no doubt of what she was, as indelible as a fucking Mack truck parked on his ass.

Though he'd had sessions with her for a while, last night had been different. Probably why she was on his mind.

She'd started in a playful mood. Had him kneel on a mat, then move into a push-up with his arms fully extended. Trailed her fingers down his back, to the rise of his clenched ass. He wore only jeans. As he held the pose, she reached under him, cupped his cock and balls, rubbed against denim. She'd used her free hand to put pressure on his back, the other shifting to his abdomen, guiding him into a slow descent, his arms bending as he went down.

She stopped him inches from the ground. When his arms started to quiver, she'd moved to his head, her bare feet in view as she squatted. Her knees were spread to position her closer, taunting him with what lay between them.

2

He'd put his lips on the top of her foot with its daintily painted purple toenails. Then she let him go all the way down, directing his arms out straight to either side. While he lay on his erection, she stretched out on him, her soft ass in the small of his back, her body contoured to the shape of his. She braced her feet outside of his thighs, spreading her legs.

She'd stroked herself, let him feel her rise and fall as she used him as a bed, though her head tilted back over his shoulder. When she shifted it, suggesting her neck was getting tired, he risked a transgression. He brought his arms back in, lacing his hands behind his neck so she could rest her head on his biceps.

He'd relished the sound of her breathing as it became more erratic. Even lying uncomfortably on his cock, he got harder. Her desire made him ache. Other men dreamed of having a woman suck them off. His dreams were an echo in a canyon: *What can I do for you, Mistress?*

Whenever, however she answered, he wanted to fill that canyon up with his response.

She didn't bring herself to climax. Instead, she got him so hot and bothered listening to her arouse herself, he had to bite back a growl of need. Then she chose a different way to torment him.

Rising, she had him turn over. Arms in the original outstretched, self-restrained position. She lay down on him again, also facing the ceiling. With the pressure of her agile, teasing toes, she had him bend his knees so she could put the soles of her feet against his thighs, toes curving over his kneecaps. Returning to the workout she'd given him at the beginning, she had him lift her upper body and hold her above him.

It took good balance, on both their parts. And trust. She gave him both, relaxing into his hands, adjusting her feet and the arch of her body to make it work. Then she started stroking herself again.

This time it was obvious she intended to take herself over. Her shoulder blades flexed against his palms, feet shifting on his thighs. When his arms started to shake, she was so close, he wouldn't safe-word, couldn't do it. He gritted his teeth, strained, locked his muscles, and held the position until she reached peak. Until she got all the way through it, and he was sure she'd had her full measure of satisfaction.

Her harsh, erratic breaths filled up that canyon of need.

She used a two-tap signal to let him know when he could lower her. He brought her down into the cradle of his body, their torsos pressed front to back again. She pulled his sore arms around her, her hair brushing his face as she rubbed his shoulders, biceps and forearms, soothing the strain she'd put upon them.

It was an unexpectedly intimate pose, her letting him hold her like that, arms wrapped over her breasts, hands clasping her upper arms, feeling the damp heat of her smooth skin through his palms. Even as she took care of him, she was shuddering through her aftershocks, her sweet buttocks quivering against his rock-hard dick. She hadn't taken off a single item of clothing except her shoes, and yet she felt as close to him as if she were naked. He held her, breathed her in. Absorbed all the sensation she offered.

Something had been different. But the nice thing about aftercare was no one had to talk or analyze.

Then he discovered she wasn't ready for aftercare.

Pushing herself out of his embrace, she turned over and straddled his abdomen. Leaning forward, her silk-covered breasts were so close to his face he had to press his lips together to keep himself from taking advantage. Especially with those undone buttons and the lace-edged valley of cleavage so close. He swore the scent of her skin was a teasing touch on his mouth.

She reached for the chain attached to a pole behind him, a hard point for restraints. She glanced at his arms, the only cue needed for him to raise them past his head. Wrapping the chain around his wrists, she manually closed his fingers over the end of the links to hold that binding in place.

She caressed his knuckles before she withdrew, her gaze noting his reactions. She rose, moved to his feet. Another chain was brought into play, this one attached to the wall, the links long enough to reach his ankles. She wrapped them loosely, using a carabiner clip to hold the chain in place. Before she did that, she had him extend his legs as far as he could, to increase the staked-out feeling. He could free himself if needed, but the restraints reinforced a command—*you'll stay like this until I say otherwise.*

She knelt next to him. He sucked in a breath as she opened his jeans and released his dick. Reaching under the gauzy fabric of her blouse, into the cup of her lacy bra, she withdrew a condom, opened and rolled it over him, giving his thick base a hard squeeze. Her seemingly playful slap made him jump, sensation rocketing right to his balls.

His hands flexed on the chain, making it rattle. Her gaze went to it, slid back over him, a heavy-lidded look that offered him everything and nothing, because she was in control of all of it. She parted her lips, then shifted her attention back to his groin.

Fucking hell. It startled him, her leaning over and covering him completely with her mouth, sliding down. She'd teased him with oral before, but not after this much of the session had already happened. She went after him in full Mistress mode, working him, pulling on his cock like she owned it.

In this room, she did.

A Mistress could use oral as a torture. She was good at it, bringing him up and up and up. Her head never stopped moving even as she lifted a hand imperiously, one finger raised to show him he had to wait until she was ready.

When she finally turned that finger and gave him a come- hither gesture, like a martial artist inviting an opponent to unleash their best defense, his cock spurted into the latex. He gripped the chain so hard it dug into his palms, his hips bucking up, feet yanking against their binding.

She'd sat back when she gave him the permission to come, watching him hump air, her satisfied mouth still wet from sliding along his length. Seeing that was enough to keep him going, even without her touch. Yet when she added her hand on him at the end to milk out a few more intense convulsions, demanding more, he gave it to her.

After he finished, chest expanding and contracting in shuddering breaths, she released his ankles from the chain. After she gently pried open his fingers and unwrapped the chain from his wrists, she put her back to that pole and arranged them so his head was in her lap. She lifted his hand in hers, massaging the indentations in the palm. As she moved from that to a more thorough massage of his shoulders, neck and biceps, she alternated that care with occasional drifting touches over his hair and face.

He noted she seemed pensive. He wanted to make sure she was okay, but he was still too out of it. She'd worn him out. It had been a hard day at the garage, and he did something he rarely did. He fell asleep.

When he woke, he'd felt like an asshole. "I'm sorry, Mistress..."

She shook her head, faint smile telling him it was okay. After he sat up, got his bearings, and took the water she offered, she patted his shoulder and pressed a kiss to her fingers, bestowing that kiss on his forehead. A Mistress's blessing and approval.

She retrieved a black silk shawl from a hook. After wrapping it loosely over her shoulders, she tapped his clothes, folded by the door. When she left him, her lingering fragrance, like a cool vanilla ice cream, remained.

Remarkably, he hadn't craved another Mistress. Usually he'd have two or three full sessions in the same evening, with different Mistresses. Nuclear reactors could be fueled by his energy reserves. She'd proven her energy had matched his, at least for that memorable session.

Might be it was just a fluke, but things felt...different today.

Enough of that. Time to get back to work. Or to less pleasant things, because the purr of a familiar engine had intruded into his consciousness. *Shit.*

His shoulders tightened, his gut speared with the usual conflicting feelings. As Tiger crushed the cigarette out against the pole and put it in the ash container, Chuck tossed him a critical glance. "Keep smoking those, the vultures will be here for you."

"I've had my head under a car hood since I could walk," Tiger answered. "The oil and gas fumes will get me long before the nicotine."

"Or something that'll put you in a grave long before my burgers or your cigarettes. The wrong woman." Chuck sent a meaningful glance toward the parking lot.

Chuck didn't know all of his business, but he knew enough to know trouble had just pulled in.

As Tiger circled around to the front parking area, Nicole was getting out of her 1989 Jaguar XJ6 sedan. She was wearing those needle heels she liked, and looked as damn good as she always did. Her thick brown hair formed silken waves around her face, framing vivid golden-brown eyes as inviting as honey straight from the hive. Her full lips had that perpetual pouty look that made a man think of them wrapped around his cock.

Those looks and curvy body came with charisma and intelligence, and she'd put it all to good use, scoring a successful career in the porn industry. First as an actress, and then as part-owner of one of the production companies.

The wet dream body made a lot of men overlook important details, like her smarts, her drive. But Tiger wasn't most men when it came to what he noticed. Thanks to a host of memorable Mistresses, he'd received extensive reward training on why noticing less obvious details about a woman mattered.

His dick was triggered by qualities that Nicole didn't have, but beyond that, she was his brother's wife. She could do a pole dance using his cock, and he wouldn't touch her. If he needed further justification than that—and he didn't—she'd brought along the reason that put it in stone for Tiger, like the Ten Commandments.

Nicole held the back passenger door open for a six-year-old girl whose short hair had her mother's gleaming brown color. She had Tiger's dark blue eyes, a color he and his brother shared.

When the girl sighted him striding across the parking lot, she ran toward him. "Uncle Tiger!"

He dropped to a squat as she reached him. In this heat, he'd unzipped and pulled the coveralls down, tying the sleeves around his waist. Even so, he would have given her an arms' length squeeze, not wanting to transfer grease onto her, but Aubrey didn't have patience for half measures. She wrapped her arms over Tiger's shoulders, her sturdy body plastered against his chest. Then, with that rapid shift in attention that kids did, she pulled back to pet the elephant in his tattoo.

The gray tank he wore under the coveralls exposed the ink, a map of images from his right shoulder down to his elbow. A jungle populated with animals, exotic flowers, and foliage. The elephant, with its curling trunk and butterfly-like ears, was the central image.

He'd chosen a creature with a long memory, to keep fresh in his own why he'd covered the ink beneath the jungle. However, he always felt it there, branded soul deep. Just like the pain that family could inflict.

"Hello, how are you? Has Uncle Tiger fed you today?" As Aubrey addressed the image, she sent him a severe look. "Hermione likes ice cream the best, you know." No cliché name like Peanut or Dumbo for his precocious niece.

"I know," he told her gravely. "She had a quadruple scoop of chocolate in a waffle cone for breakfast."

"With Reese's peanut butter cup sprinkles?"

"She won't eat it without them."

Nicole had reached them, her heels clicking on the asphalt. Tiger squinted as the sun haloed her. "Car giving you problems again?"

"Just needs a service for a road trip. Colt wanted me to let the boys do it, but I've told him a hundred times you're the only one touching this car."

He noted the tiredness around her eyes, the tension to her mouth and slim shoulders. "Everything okay?" he asked.

She parted her lips, but hesitated. When she rested a manicured hand on Aubrey's shoulder, Tiger turned his attention back to his niece. "Maryshka's working this morning," he said. "Want to go see her?"

"Yay!" Before she could bolt, Tiger snagged Aubrey's purple top, printed with a polar bear carrying an umbrella for some mystifying reason. Kid clothes.

"What's the rule?" he asked.

Aubrey screwed up her face, sighed, but recited it dutifully. "Go in through the office, ring the bell. Wait for Maryshka. No going into the garage by myself."

"And?" He cocked a meaningful brow at Nicole, and Aubrey looked up at her.

"Mama, can I go see Maryshka?"

"Yes, you may. But stay with her until I come get you."

"Okay." She ran off after giving the elephant on Tiger's shoulder one more pat. "See you, Hermione."

Tiger stood up, cutting right to the chase. "What's up?"

"Nothing that anyone can fix." Nicole tried for weary humor, but the tone had too much pain in it. "I just wish...I wish what I always wish. That he'd done what you did. Or at least he'd come see you. I always try to get him to bring you the car or pick it up, but he'll just have a prospect do it."

Because no Fallen Angels club member would have anything to do with him. Which was fine with Tiger. It had to be, because it was better that way.

"I like seeing Aubrey," Tiger said lightly. "Stop trying to fix something that can't be fixed, Nicole. I mean it."

She looked in the direction Aubrey had gone, her dark-lashed eyes troubled. "They're about to do a lockdown again. The usual reason, some kind of trouble, and this time I said I'm not doing it, Tiger. I'm just not. I'm tired of me and Aubrey being jerked around by the bullshit between the MC and whatever they're dealing with."

"So what are you doing to stay out of harm's way?" Before he could suggest some places they could go, she waved a hand, letting him know she was on top of it.

"We're going to my parents' place in Florida for a while."

"Okay, good. I'll bump you to the front of the line and get you set up for the drive."

When Nicole put the keys in his hand, her fingers abruptly curled over his. She shifted her gaze away again, but Tiger saw her blinking back tears. Nicole was a tough woman. This was bad. Her fixed look said she wasn't seeing anything in front of her, but what was festering inside.

"When Colt and I met, I was a different person. All of the MC stuff, it's a part of him. His brothers...that's a strong thing. I get it."

Yeah, it was. He still felt the ache of it, an amputation. He'd wielded the axe that had cut off the limb.

"I love him so much," she murmured. "But Aubrey changed things. You know?"

"You coming back?" he asked.

"I don't know." She tossed him a half-despairing look. "Maybe love is just as much about knowing when to say good-bye. To preserve what memories of it you have left."

He knew that feeling, too. Sadly, by the time the "when" decision was made, the love was poisoned.

Chuck was putting the mower in his storage closet, the wheels rattling. Tiger heard the vultures take off, a heavy rush of wings that blended into the four-lane traffic noise a quarter mile from the garage. A mockingbird heralded their departure with a piercing note.

His garage was located down a dead-end side street, an ideal setting because that lack of outlet and the neighboring lots—a Hurri-cane Katrina-abandoned gas station and an empty lot populated with scrubby pines and spiky grass— gave him space. He could park his day customers' finished vehicles along the curb when his fenced backlot was full of overnights.

As his gaze coursed over today's line-up and how fast his crew was working through them, he calculated how to squeeze Nicole in and get her on the road. And goddamn, if a white van wasn't even now turning down his street to add to the load.

He took care of a lot of contractors. Because their vehicles were key to their businesses, he tried to turn them around pretty fast. He might be able to shift some other jobs to tomorrow to cover both Nicole and this guy.

The van had no company logo, not unusual. However, as it bumped over the curb into the parking lot, the sun's angle offered Tiger a glimpse of the male driver and passenger.

Their intent looks didn't say dropping-off-for-service. They said something that spiked his instincts.

Then the guy riding shotgun brought a 9mm up to a ready posi-tion, the light flashing over the barrel.

Nicole turned toward the vehicle. Tiger lunged for her, but the side door of the van slammed back. A barrage of bullets peppered out, joining those fired by the front passenger. They punched into Nicole's body, flinging her against him. As the collision knocked him onto his ass, a burning in Tiger's shoulder told him he'd been grazed or hit.

Violence wasn't new to him, but his reaction time was too goddamn rusty. He struggled to get his feet under him just as the van occupants slung a couple Molotovs. One sailed into the garage bays. The other smashed through his front office window.

Aubrey. He had to leave Nicole lying there as he scrambled for the garage, already roaring to his employees, *"Get out of there!"*

The van was spinning around, screeching away. In the part of his brain that still knew how to think during shit like this, he registered Nicole had been their target. The rest of this chaos was meant to prevent a response.

Maryshka burst out of the first bay, Aubrey in her arms. Red and Larry were on her heels, and that was everyone here this morning. Maryshka looked toward him, spiked hair glaring crimson, piercings in lip, nose and eyebrow flashing from the same sunlight that had telegraphed the front seat gunman.

Her mouth opened on a scream of protest as Tiger passed her, running into the garage. His gaze sought that Molotov, where it had smashed down, if there was time to douse the flames before...

The explosion hurled him through the viewing window between the garage and front office. Pain sliced into him in a dozen places, his skull a balloon filled with too much water, the rubber expanding without breaking, excruciating.

His head hit something, and he landed on the desk, toppled over it. Disoriented, he stared up at the ripped hole in the ceiling, the flame licking across it, sparking wiring. Glass was underneath him, cutting and sharp.

A hard jerk as he was pulled to his feet. Chuck's ham-sized hands on him. The guy huffed and puffed, but he was souped up on adrenaline, dragging Tiger's muscled body out of the office like he'd been bench pressing two hundred pounds on a daily basis.

As they emerged, Red and Larry were on top of him, helping him pull Tiger to a safe distance. They sat him down on the stoop behind Chuck's store. Aubrey was there with Maryshka. The little girl looked like she was crying, screaming, her hands clutching Maryshka's shoulders. Maryshka kept her hand cupped over her skull, so the child could only look toward the liquor store's rear entrance. Chuck's wife Kat held the door, a big-boned woman with feathered silver-gray hair and navy-blue slacks. Her cell phone was clutched in her hand as she seemed to urgently entreat Maryshka to bring Aubrey inside, which the girl did. Tiberius danced around Kat's feet, white muzzle moving in furious barking, brown eyes frightened.

Dazed and staring around him, Tiger saw what they didn't want Aubrey to see. Nicole, lying in the parking lot a few feet from her debris-covered Jag, head turned toward them. Eyes staring and fixed, her chest soaked with blood.

The world swam into squiggly lines and Tiger toppled over. Nausea emptied his stomach, and he tried to hold onto his head before it came apart. Blood was on his hands. He tried to form words. Tried to regain control.

People were gathered around him, worried. The vultures were

gone. But they could come back. They needed to move Nicole. Needed to keep them away from her. Needed...

He couldn't think. He could see, he could feel, he could smell the smoke of his garage, his business on fire. But he couldn't hear any of it.

He couldn't hear anything.

CHAPTER TWO

*M*aryshka paused on the blue and gold carpeted steps to the club's VIP lounge. The brass railing was cool under her clammy palm. Andrei's hand brushed her lower back, rested on her hip. "All right?"

"Yeah. Maybe this is stupid and I'm overreacting. It's only been a month, for fuck's sake."

"Maybe you find them too intimidating."

She snorted. "Like they don't scare the shit out of you, too."

Andrei shot her a look. "That's not very respectful to your Dom."

"But is it true?"

His wry smile answered that, but he crooked an arm around her neck and brought her against him. A tacit permission to wind her arms around his upper body and take reassurance from the strength of it. Though kind of a string bean, he was surprisingly tough.

The gesture, his understanding of where her head was at, reminded her why she trusted him enough to submit to him.

As a mechanic in an independent garage, she was in a traditional male environment. Dirty jokes, sexual innuendo, and schoolyard teasing were all part of it. If she got hurt—not unusual when dealing with engines, which could be like wild horses, hence the term horse-power—she took pride in the scars. No one had to play the damsel-rescuing hero around her.

It was the type of place her dad had run before his heart attack.

Tiger's crew were gearheads and bikers. Customer repairs and maintenance paid the bills for their shared love of modifying and restoring the same.

Tiger had employed another female mechanic for a time, but she hadn't lasted. Last Maryshka had heard, she'd found work with a corporate tire center chain, probably one with an HR department and clean waiting areas sporting a wide screen TV and the smell of Febreze. Not the heat and oil of the garage wafting in to mix with the scent of cigarettes when the guys came and went from the front office.

Her dad had showed her she didn't have to deny her girl side. She'd learned how to fix cars at his side, but he'd also taken her dress shopping for her sweet sixteen party. Even helped brush out her hair and tied the bow on the back of her dress. A man with callused hands, gruff manners and a soft heart. He'd died a year later.

She'd been left without a compass for a while, but Tiger had helped her get it back. Then she'd met Andrei. With him, she could be vulnerable. Nervous. Cry even. The first time he wiped them away after a session, he told her tears made a woman stronger.

He also didn't play at being a Dom. Which he proved now by easing her back, brushing his knuckles across her face. "Come with me," he said, taking her hand in his.

"But—"

"I will spank you in front of everyone here," he promised, in *that* voice.

She followed him, trying not to do the girly thing and bite her lip, though sometimes that turned him on, when she did it just for that reason. They didn't do Daddy Dom exactly, but they'd played on the edges when they were in the mood for it, and it was fun.

This wasn't that moment, though. She tried not to let her feet drag, because Andrei didn't issue idle threats. Public humiliation wasn't her thing, and it really wasn't his either, but he wouldn't hesitate to use it as a reminder of what he expected of her as his sub. It reinforced what she needed from him, too.

Always a circle. The give and take of what people did when they understood one another. And fuck, she'd needed what Andrei could give her this past month. She'd thought her world ended when her dad died, but violence had shown her a whole new level of what loss could be.

Nicole lying on the pavement, blood draining out of her. Staring eyes. Aubrey screaming in Maryshka's arms, fighting to go to her mother. The smell of the garage burning, a callused hand tight on Maryshka's arm as Larry dragged them away from a powder keg of flammables.

Red had stopped to hoist Nicole into a fireman's carry. Then the explosion picked them all up, threw them. Nicole's corpse had flown through the air like a ragdoll, landing her near her Jag.

That was the part Maryshka couldn't stop remembering. It should have left her alone. *She's dead, no more need to fling her around, break her. She's as broken as broken is going to get.*

She was so glad Tiger hadn't seen that part. Or Aubrey, her face pressed smothering tight into Maryshka's shoulder.

She wished she hadn't seen it.

"Baby."

Andrei's hand was on her face. She was shaking. She gripped his fingers, feeling the rough nicks from his metal sculpting. His interest in art was sort of how they'd met. Tiger liked to put together odd-looking structures from old car parts, and he had an assortment of them behind the garage. In his opinion, they were amateur stuff, but if people liked them, he'd give them away for a twenty-buck donation to the local charity jar in what used to be their front office.

Andrei had been a new customer, and had come to pick up his car. While waiting for it to be ready, he'd wandered around to the back to look at Tiger's work, at the same time Maryshka pulled in for work. They struck up a conversation and connected. Learning he was a Dom at Progeny had explained some of why she'd felt drawn to him, but learning even more about him had deepened that connection.

"I'm okay. Damn it. I'm okay."

Tiger had helped put her world back together after her father's death. She needed to do it for him. That was why she was here. She straightened her shoulders, lifted her chin. "I need to do this," she said aloud. "It will help."

"Yeah." Andrei studied her closely. "I think it will."

As they headed toward the lounge's back corner, he kept her at his side. He probably was nervous about talking to the dragon queens, as she thought of them. However, the calming stroke on her back when he reached the large round booth, and his tone as he addressed the four women there, didn't show it.

"Ladies."

A man might be intimidated by the assembled arsenal of female power and beauty, but Maryshka suspected a woman felt the impact twice over. She sure did.

The four Mistresses didn't just form a power squad here. They were top management at Thomas Rose Associates. Many people at Club Progeny used scene names, usually for two reasons. The first was to protect privacy. But TRA had been featured in multiple media outlets as one of New Orleans' top boutique marketing firms. Since the all-female executive team had been profiled in those pieces, anonymity here was a moot point.

The second reason was to provide a mental shift to get more fully into a Dom or sub identity, enhance that focus within the club walls. Several of the women used Tiger's garage for their vehicle servicing. Based on those interactions and right now, standing within target range of their uber Mistress vibes, Maryshka could vouch for the fact they didn't need a scene name to do that. At all.

Rosalinda Thomas, TRA's CEO, was sitting on the right side of the booth. She wore a black pencil skirt, blue blouse and a pair of black pumps with a blue lightning bolt and glittering starburst along the upper. Ros loved her shoes, and never seemed to wear the same pair twice. Her blond hair with black tips was cut in an artful silken bob to her shoulders. Manicured nails stroked the faceted glass of her lowball tumbler.

A magazine had once approached her with the happy news that TRA was going to be included in a spread highlighting NOLA's top ten woman-owned businesses. Ros told them to come back when TRA had earned a place in a top-ten business list that had nothing to do with her vagina. Quote, unquote.

A year later, TRA's sales and customer base landed it in the number three spot for the city's most successful boutique businesses. Hence the business news coverage that had expanded to make her and her team recognizable here.

As someone who'd fought for acceptance based on her skills as a mechanic, not her uniqueness in a male-dominated field, Maryshka appreciated that. It was also a reassuring reminder she stood in front of people who understood what it was to carve a place for yourself.

Ros's other hand was at her shoulder, linked with that of the man who stood beside her, leaning against the outside of the booth. Lawrence, her committed and collared sub. While not overly tall, he was built solid, a former Navy SEAL with steady dark eyes and an obvious protective devotion to his Mistress. The sexy alpha male also had a good sense of humor and was smart as the pop of a single tail.

She'd gotten a good spanking for observing that one night. The sexy part that is.

Abigail Rose, the other co-founder of the company, wasn't here tonight, but Ros sat with the remaining three members of the executive team. Veracity Morgan, Cynbad Marigold and Skye Sumner. Vera, Cyn and Skye.

Ros tilted her sharp chin in Andrei's direction. A smile curved her mauve lips. "Andrei, you have good timing. We were just discussing the merits of urethral sounding, and could use a male Dom's opinion."

Maryshka stifled a chuckle as Lawrence sent Andrei a mouthed, *hell no*, with a hand across the throat gesture. Ros caught it in the corner of her gaze, as Maryshka was sure Lawrence intended. She shot him an amused look.

"Obviously, a sub's opinion in this case is too biased."

Andrei cleared his throat. "I'm probably not going to be much help. Anyone who approaches my dick with a steel rod is going to be skewered with it." He dipped his head toward Maryshka, his hand on her tightening in reassurance. "But while I'd be pleased to join you ladies for further discussion and buy your next round of drinks, my sub would like to talk to you."

Four sets of eyes turned her way. She chided herself for the sudden quake in her stomach, but she admitted she was glad for Andrei's touch. Outside the garage and her brusque mechanic persona, she was actually painfully shy, something Andrei knew.

She managed to meet their gazes though, before sweeping hers down respectfully. There were protocols here, and only the Dommes could say "at ease" and relax them.

Her gaze skittered a little faster past Cyn, without shame. Cyn was a sadist Domme who scared every sensible sub, while being beloved by crazy masochistic ones. In contrast, Vera had a calm, goddess-like energy. And Skye...well, Skye was the cool kid of the group.

She sat with one leg bent, hand draped over a knee covered by flowing slacks that had a sheer layer of black over a silver satin liner. Classy but kind of bohemian. Her knit lavender shirt with a scoop neck had the outline of a silver rose printed on it. Her jewelry was a silver chain strung with a variety of overlapping charms. Maryshka recognized an ankh, a robot, and a shooting star.

Amethyst studs were in her double pierced ears, visible because Skye wore her hair cut short on one side, longer on the other, feathered over her dark eyes. Sharp, intrigued eyes, ringed in silver liner and shadowed with charcoal gray.

"What do you want to talk to us about, Maryshka?" Vera asked. Her black hair was shorn in a fade on both sides, the longer locks tumbling over the shaved area and down her back. A line of silver rings followed the shells of her ears. Her chestnut-colored skin intensified the focus of her clear gray eyes, glinting from the club lights.

Maryshka wet her lips. "Tiger, ma'am."

"Does he know you're talking to us about him?" Frost touched Ros's blue eyes.

"No." Maryshka drew herself up. "But I don't know what else to do to help him. I'm afraid for him. I thought...maybe you could give me some advice."

Tiger played privately, but Skye and Abby had evolved into his most regular club partners. And all of the women here had had sessions with him. Based on their tight relationship as Mistresses, she hoped that meant they had a pretty good grasp of his deeper layers. The darker ones.

"I know...he's your friend, same as he is for me, though we have different relationships. Maybe he doesn't need help, maybe he's okay. He went through something bad, and people need time to deal with that."

Damn it, she'd practiced this speech. *Keep it short and simple. Don't doubt yourself.* In front of her mirror, she'd told herself it was no different than explaining an engine problem to a customer. But as she'd proven on the stairs, even a month later, she was too emotional about this.

She was about to shoot Andrei a desperate look, maybe a call for a tactful retreat, when a familiar voice spoke. One she recognized from the movie *Avatar*, because she and Andrei had watched it, three times at least.

"But it bothers you enough that you want a second opinion."

Skye had her hand on her phone. Her fingers had typed as the words came forth, sounding like Sigourney Weaver. Skye had a host of celebrity voices she used.

"Yes, Mistress," Maryshka said. "He's my boss. He's still my friend, but there's a wall. Which is fine, but now he's gone behind it and locked the door. Shutting us all out. I respect his privacy, Mistresses, I really do, but I'm worried as hell about him. Since my dad died, he... he's been like that to me."

She hadn't meant to throw that in the mix. Mortified, she realized her voice had cracked. Andrei's hand moved to her nape as he firmly took over.

"It's been tearing her up," he told Ros. His expression darkened. "What happened at the garage wasn't as straightforward as the news made it sound."

The women exchanged a look. Andrei's forefinger stroked lightly over Maryshka's neck. "We had a good session tonight to help her level out and clear her head. But I think talking to someone about him will help her heart. Help bring back her focus, so I don't have to give her hell about it." He tugged her hair, shooting her a tender teasing look, with the right touch of steely Dom in it.

"A butt plug the size of your fist does wonders for focusing a sub," Cyn noted.

She wasn't joking. Maryshka had seen her do it. Andrei knew how to get her out of bad places in her head, but extremes of pain and stress were not that path for her. That was one thing coming to a club taught you. Everybody needed different things, different paths, to find that center where they could meet their own soul face to face and learn things about themselves that made life...better.

Ros glanced across the booth toward Skye. "Your call," she said.

Despite Skye being one of Tiger's regular Mistresses, Maryshka had hoped to have this discussion with all of them, or, if it needed to be just one, maybe Vera. How could she talk about something this complicated with someone who couldn't...talk? Yeah, Skye used those voices pretty well, and Maryshka didn't want to be that kind of person, but this was so hard to talk about as it was.

It didn't matter. The decision had been made. Skye was sliding from the booth as Vera stood up to let her out. The booth next to theirs was unoccupied, and Skye pointed to it.

"Would you like to share a drink with us?" Ros asked Andrei. "You can keep an eye on her while she and Skye talk."

Andrei glanced down at Maryshka. "That work?"

"Yes, Master. Thank you."

His attention shifted to Skye. Safety was an elusive thing outside these walls. But within them, there were rock solid agreements of trust and care. It was here she'd learned what the word *haven* really meant.

Andrei's look toward Skye said Maryshka was his to protect, and he required Skye's acknowledgement. It reassured Maryshka, reminding her these weren't newbie Dommes. They knew their shit. If any of the TRA Mistresses *could* help, she could trust that Skye was the right choice.

Plus, ironically, Skye was TRA's IT/Communications manager, which meant she was pretty damn good at her job.

Skye nodded to Andrei, a confirmation. Maryshka waited until the Mistress had slid into the booth before taking a seat across from her. The smaller booth was suitable for two people, the high sides buffering the club noise.

As Skye gazed at her, Maryshka felt herself falter again. Was she betraying Tiger's trust? Then she remembered Nicole's body flying through the air. Heard Aubrey screaming. Her fingers tightened in her lap.

"Do you need a drink?"

The Sigourney Weaver voice again. Smooth, a touch of compassion over a resilient core. It matched Skye's expression. The voice app was obviously a good one, but Maryshka was impressed how Skye managed to modulate the tone so smoothly and swiftly, fitting the mood of the moment. Probably a skill she'd developed through long practice, like Maryshka often knowing what an engine needed by just listening to it.

"No, but thanks," she said. "I just need to get it out. So you all heard what happened at the shop. The explosion. The shooting."

"Yes." Sigourney spoke the response Skye typed. "Tiger sent a club email, thanking everyone for their concern and saying he'll be back in when he can."

"Yeah. All's good. He's just busy figuring things out." She raised her gaze as Skye said nothing. "Sound like a trained monkey, don't I? I've said that so much the words make me nauseous."

Members didn't intrude on one another's lives outside the club unless all parties expressly said it was okay. Hell, the only reason she knew as much as she did about Tiger was because she'd worked for him before he'd figured out she was a sub and sponsored her membership with Progeny, helping her transfer over from the club she'd been driving to in Baton Rouge.

She'd about swallowed her tongue when she found out her boss, who could clear a table in a crowded bar with just a pointed scowl, was a sub. But him trusting her with that information? She'd never forget that.

Skye's gaze flickered. She made an adjustment, and now the voice was different. An assured female tone flavored with a light Southern accent. Not recognizable as anyone else. Maybe it was the voice Skye used as "her" voice, when she didn't want to borrow someone else's.

"Abby has gone by the garage. But he hasn't been there."

Abby had been the exception to that "outside the club" rule for Tiger. Sometimes they'd met for lunch. On the days Abby picked him up from the garage, the male mechanics stumbled over one another to get a glimpse of her. The woman who handled Thomas Rose Associates' financial operations had a Hollywood starlet body, catlike hazel eyes and long golden red hair.

But things had changed for Abby. Late onset schizophrenia had impacted her ability to Domme. She was also now married to another Dominant. An active Navy SEAL, Neil had served with Lawrence before Lawrence left the teams.

Neil and Tiger had worked together to help Abby fulfill her desires as a Domme, but over time she had eased out of doing club sessions, except as a once in a while thing.

"He's there," Maryshka said. "At the garage, I mean. Every day. I'm not sure if he ever leaves anymore, except to check on his place and shower."

Three of the five garage bays and the front office had been badly damaged by the explosion, but the back offices were intact. That was where Tiger spent most of his time now.

Surprise gripped Skye's expression, then sharpness. Maryshka had her attention. The Domme crossed her arms and leaned forward, cocking a questioning brow.

Maryshka took a breath. *Forgive me if I'm fucking up, boss. But I don't know what else to do.*

"He was hurt, Mistress. He can't hear. He's deaf."

Shock replaced surprise. "What percentage?" Skye typed.

"Full." At her expression, Maryshka nodded. "Yeah, they said that's rare. They also said he might get some or all of it back, but there's been no change since it happened. So I guess every day that goes by... well, you know."

She pressed her lips together. "He's not the type to wallow. I've never known him to be like that. His niece Aubrey fell and scraped herself good once when she was at the shop with us. He's a pretty protective uncle, so I expected him to get all crazy. Instead, he picks her up, dusts her off and tells her to go play. He didn't let her get all traumatized by it. That's the way he is. He doesn't overreact about things or get bogged down."

She swallowed. "I think Nicole's death and stuff from his past have combined with the hearing loss, and now he can't seem to find himself. I'm also afraid we made it worse."

Maryshka looked down at her hands, gripping one another on the table. "For a little while, we were doing a couple things in the two bays that aren't as damaged. Mostly just clean up, and trying to pull Tiger in on it. You know, he's the boss. We're used to him taking the lead, but he's not doing that."

She shook her head. "Larry's the newest on our crew, so I think he's more impatient with not knowing what's going to happen. So he goes into Tiger's office to talk about a job that came in. Just a regular who stopped by. He had a problem that didn't need a lift, so we agreed to give it a look. Even if we'd needed to send him on to a fully operational place, we try to take care of our customers. That's the way Tiger taught us."

Maryshka took a breath. "Anyway, Tiger's back office is down a hallway, but we still hear this crash, then Tiger yelling and cussing. Larry comes back looking shook up, but pissed, too."

She remembered how Red had told him to settle down and Larry had shaken him off. "Doesn't fucking matter if I shout, man. He can't hear. He got so frustrated with what I was trying to explain to him, I felt like I'd made a mistake bugging him. So I just grabbed that pad on his desk and wrote 'never mind, I'll handle it.' He put his fist through the wall next to my fucking head and told me to get out. So fuck it, I'm out."

As Maryshka summarized that for her, Skye's expression flickered with emotions she couldn't decipher. But they increased the tightness of her gut, her sense of helplessness and worry. Her short nails bit into her palms. "When Red and I came back to the garage the next day, we found an envelope for each of us. Tiger wrote out checks to cover us for several weeks' pay, and the names of two garages who've agreed to take us on as temporary help. Larry, too. Red took his check to give it to him."

She shook her head. "Tiger also put a note in there saying if we get a chance at a permanent job, we should probably take it, because he doesn't know when or if he'll be reopening the garage. That he might just take on a few regulars out at his place to pay the bills and leave it at that.

"I tried his office door, and he'd locked it. I banged on it, and he didn't answer, though I swear to God he had to feel the vibration." Maryshka fought back tears. "It's like he's just telling us all to forget about him and piss off, go on with our lives. He told me once we were like family to him, but Andrei says..." She took a breath. "He says since Tiger sees himself as head of that family, he thinks he isn't worth anything to us anymore if he can't act like that. That's such total bullshit."

She should have known Andrei was keeping tabs on her, because he was sliding into the booth, putting his arm around her. She looked at Skye through the tears that stubbornly insisted on welling up. "I mean, from who we are here, you'd think he'd realize that. Sometimes you have to let people help you, take some of the control."

"It's easier to make that decision from a position of strength. Especially for an alpha, whether male or female." Skye typed out the words in her Southern voice, even as she reached out with her other hand to squeeze Maryshka's arm. "You're a good friend. You haven't betrayed his trust. It's all right."

Maryshka sniffled. "Any advice? I don't want to go back there without a game plan. Red says I should just leave him alone for a while, and maybe so. I don't know what to do."

Skye pursed her lips, typed. "I'd like to visit him. See what's going on from a different perspective. As his friend, his family," she met Maryshka's gaze, "would you be all right with that?"

"Yeah. I think so. Just...be careful. What he did with Larry, that wasn't like him. He's not himself. I mean, Tiger will jump our asses for being slack in a heartbeat—he's a tough but fair boss. He looks like the type of guy itching for a fight, but just the opposite is true. He's ultra-careful about his temper. But right now...not so much, I think."

"Tell me the best way to get to the back office," Skye typed.

～

After Maryshka and Andrei left, Skye sat in the smaller booth for a few minutes, thinking.

Never mind.

Larry's note had made her wince. The worst two words to say to any person with communication issues. Whether the motive was a well-intentioned effort to help, ignorance or lack of patience, the subtext translated to a face punch. *It's not worth taking the time to explain it to you.*

Even worse was the deeper message. *I'll handle it, making you feel more alone and useless than you already do.*

She wasn't deaf, but so many times in her life people had talked "around" her, or avoided talking to her at all, when they realized she didn't communicate the normal way. Even when she'd shown she could capably handle a conversation with her phone and other digital methods, she'd often had to be tiresomely persistent—sometimes aggressive—to get them to engage. To stop them from retreating, backpedaling. Working around her.

Maryshka's surprise about Tiger's unwillingness to let anyone help him wasn't surprising to Skye at all. Dominants could be control freaks, but in the outside world submissives were Olympic champions of the trait. Tiger's need to go through two to three Mistresses in one night spoke to it. The man did have knee-weakening sexual endurance and a fierce need to serve a Mistress, yes. However, even as he was surrendering to that need, he was proving he could handle anything thrown at him. Proving he hadn't fallen short of his expectations for himself.

Nothing wrong with that, as long as he didn't take it down a self-destructive path in scene, and he never had. People came here for different reasons, with different needs. He could push back, be playful. Stubborn, sometimes willful. Tiger used his scenes to manage some personal demons, but he had no desire for a Mistress to take over that demon management. He kept his sword and shield firmly in hand.

He needed the submission, but he needed to experience it inside a safe sphere, which suggested out in the world he'd needed his walls. Needed to be the boss.

What Skye had found increasingly intriguing about him was how deep he could go in session. He'd recognized what parts of him it could save, and he routinely let it. But by the next week's session, that well needed filling again.

She thought of Maryshka's comment, about how carefully he controlled his temper. And what Abby had once said about him. *He knows what waits in the shadows.* Though the statement had been influenced by Abby's schizophrenia, Skye had felt the truth in it.

Every Mistress who dug into her own control issues recognized a sub who held back, not taking that full leap of trust. It wasn't a judgment on the Mistress; if a sub didn't need a soul-stripping experience, if they were good at another level, that was fine. Tiger gave and received pleasure wonderfully, and everyone went home satisfied.

Abby had been comfortable with that, and so had Skye, mostly. But as Abby had stepped back from sessions with him, Skye had found herself interested in reaching deeper.

When she'd built up a history with a sub, learned his tells, a Mistress could zero in on the less obvious ones. The last time she and Tiger had played, she'd switched it up, chosen things that exhausted the physical body, then gone after his emotional defenses, alternating offers of intimacy and care with her demands.

He'd fallen asleep with his head in her lap, a fond memory she'd revisited frequently, especially when she'd heard about his troubles.

Tiger was a confident man who'd built a world for himself he was proud of, that he operated with tremendous competence. Having it all dismantled by a terrible trauma, a violent loss, *and* losing a key sense? Yeah, he was going to flail like a drowning swimmer for a while.

Sometimes it was best for friends and family to stand back and wait it out, let the person realize they could swim out of the deep water. Or give them time to put their feet down and realize they weren't in over their head after all.

But sometimes a person would drown before they figured that out. Skye knew those flags. Maryshka's information had raised them.

She'd saved some news clips after the attack had happened, and now she pulled them up on her phone to give herself a refresher.

The murder victim, Nicole McAlister, is the wife of Colt McAlister, president of the Fallen Angels, a local outlaw motorcycle gang. The garage owner, "Tiger" Roseland, is his brother. While the attack could be gang-related, a domestic dispute has not been ruled out. Nicole McAlister reportedly visited her brother-in-law frequently, and Roseland refused contact for comment. Fortunately, no innocent bystanders were killed in the incident.

Skye's lip curled at the innuendo about Nicole and Tiger. Anyone who knew Tiger knew that was bullshit. They also hadn't done their research enough to realize Tiger was his given name, not a biker nickname.

She pulled up the news blog piece that had come out a few days later, authored by reporter Celeste Keller, who took more time to investigate sources. *Investigators have credible evidence the incident was an answer to resistance by the Fallen Angels to relinquish more of the local illegal drug trade to rival gang, the Cuidado Kings. The Kings have Mexican cartel ties and are becoming more active players in Louisiana.*

In recent years, the Fallen Angels have stepped up their drug activity, a legacy of the former president, 'Big Mac' McAlister, continued by his son, Colt McAlister.

When a sub needed something from her in session, if Skye was tapped into him the way she should be, she'd detect that need, figure out how to get him to communicate it more clearly. Sometimes he couldn't see it himself—they'd both just feel it, and she'd find her way through the maze to get them to the center of it.

In this case, the need she was detecting might mean taking her role as a Mistress outside these walls, across boundaries where she hadn't been invited.

Bringing Tiger her classic Mustang convertible for servicing was as far as their outside relationship had gone.

So send him a fucking fruit basket and a cheerful note. "*Good luck with the whole deaf thing.*" Leave it at that.

She grimaced and slid back into the larger booth. As she settled next to Cyn, elbowing her to move over, she fended off her friend's hair tug with a mock ninja move.

"Wow, I need to get you back to the MMA gym with me," Cyn critiqued the gesture. "That move wouldn't have stopped a three-year-old."

Lawrence had moved to sit on the top of the booth between Ros and Vera. Ros leaned against his leg, her hand gliding along it as she and Vera spoke. Cyn's gaze kept flicking over to a blond sub wearing leathers. He was playing checkers with another man. It was a mellow night. Progeny could be as much social venue as a BDSM play space. Cyn was studying the sub's broad shoulders, and getting some wary but intrigued glances her way. That checkers game might wrap up soon.

However, when Skye requested everyone's attention, Cyn's eyes came back to her instantly. The women were better than competent in translating and using basic signing, but since Lawrence wasn't, she used her voice software to bring them up to speed.

Concern wreathed every face when she was done, which helped reinforce where her mind was going on it. But it was Ros who cinched it. Her boss had been watching Skye's expressions. Rather than tossing out ideas and encouraging the others to do the same, the leader of their group had one question for her.

"What do you want to do?"

Skye met her gaze. "I'm going to go see him," she signed. "Maryshka's right. He's in trouble."

CHAPTER THREE

*S*kye pulled up to the garage and let her Mustang idle. Though Maryshka had described the destruction, seeing the burned-out bays, the broken asphalt and taped-up windows gave her a hollow feeling in her chest. Having the debris cleared away only made it seem more desolate.

A woman had been killed on this broken pavement. Tiger and Maryshka, or any of his crew, could easily have been additional casualties. She'd thought of it, certainly she had, but thinking it and seeing it...it was different.

She also expected the insurance company was finished with their appraisal. It was well past time to have contractors working on repairs or renovation. Instead, the abandoned feel of the place was uncomfortably like the gas station across the street, the one that had boarded up after Katrina.

Whenever she'd brought her car here for servicing, there'd been a welcoming energy. As it bumped over the curb into the lot, her Mustang would give an extra little purr, as if it was in for a spa day.

Some of that energy came from Tiger, his pride of ownership. King of his domain. She never had to wait long before he emerged to greet her personally. Sometimes wiping his hands on a rag, his brow cocked and firm mouth in a half smile. His frank personality possessed that confidence which assured his customers their vehicle would get what it needed for optimum performance.

While he kept things friendly and professional with Skye, the vibration between them since they'd connected as Mistress and sub was a permanent baseline. There was inevitably a moment when their hands would brush, or a glance would be exchanged, triggering that level of awareness between them. Intimacy. His eyes would linger on her, with potential. So much pleasurable potential she could bank and carry it until their next session.

He wasn't coming out of the building now, though. The whole place had wrongness gripping it, like a spell designed to steal something from a man when he wasn't paying attention, and then it was too late.

She cut the engine and got out, laying her hand briefly on the side mirror, as if touching her car's hand. *I know, baby*, she thought. *Let's see what's going on with our favorite mechanic.*

As she moved around the building, following Maryshka's direction, she saw the debris pile, and was surprised he hadn't arranged to have it picked up. She found his service truck, confirmation that he was here, since Maryshka said he used it to go to and from work.

The vehicle was normally parked out front. The striking purple, silver and teal tiger logo on the door, encircled by the Roseland Garage name in white lettering on a black field, served as a business advertisement. He also kept it clean. Today, multiple bug collisions were evident in the grill and on the windshield. She drew a line through a thick layer of road dust on the truck's black side panel.

The employee entrance was propped open with a cinder block. Except for the day he'd locked them out, Maryshka had said she could expect that, because he liked air flow. He was sparing with the A/C because of how much of it escaped through the open bay doors on a workday. He was used to working in hot and humid conditions.

The metal door creaked as she opened the door wide enough to step past the cinder block into a narrow hallway. To the left, a few feet away, a door proclaimed in stern red letters, *Employees Only, Danger*. That would be the garage access. She went the opposite direction, toward the back office that prior to this would have given him the necessary quiet to make client phone calls and deal with paperwork.

Paperwork he always put off as long as he could. From their aftercare conversations, she knew he'd much prefer to have his hands in an engine than on a stack of invoices. One of these days, he intended to hire an office person. When he wasn't so busy, that is.

That comment and her arched brow had made him laugh at himself. Small problems to a man who enjoyed his work.

She detected the faint drone of a TV and the smell of cigarettes. She trailed her hand along cheap paneling and noted a few framed photographs. A younger version of himself, holding up a set of keys, suggesting it had been the day he'd opened the garage. He had his other hand hooked in a jeans pocket, a defiance to the stance. *Try to knock me down*, it said. Yet in his eyes she detected a flicker, a candle expecting to be blown out.

He'd grown up a lot since then. That kind of defiance often came from an underlying insecurity, and she'd never seen that in him.

She stopped at the next photo. Maryshka leaned against his shoulder as he stood with his arms crossed, the rest of his crew grouped around him with various badass looks. In front of them was a motorcycle they'd customized for a community charity auction coordinated by the New Orleans PD. Thomas Rose Associates had donated a seven-night suite at the Hotel Monteleone in the French Quarter.

She'd been thinking a lot about him these past few days, and as she'd been thinking, she'd looked beyond the confident smile she saw in this photo, the maturity, to focus on the reserve that was always there, a door he'd never opened. Whether or not he chose to do so for her, consciously or subconsciously, would determine if she could do anything useful here.

"Who are you?" she mouthed as she studied the picture.

As she continued down the hallway, the cigarette smell grew stronger.

The office door was halfway open. He sat at a scarred metal desk, hand with the lit cigarette propped against his temple, long ash precariously close to the hair over his brow. He kept his hair short, but there was a thickness to it that revealed itself in subtle ways, a strokable wave in the back where the hair narrowed to a point at his nape. She'd often let her fingers play in the strands and follow that wave. He used a shampoo that smelled of bergamot, pomegranate and cucumber, a mix that was masculine and pleasant at once, though she was sure here the cigarette and garage scents would take the upper hand.

His long legs were clad in denim, one foot braced on the desk, the other on the floor as he sat at a slight angle in the chair. He hadn't shaved in a few days. He often maintained a clipped beard, but when he came to the club, with or without facial hair, he was well-groomed. He looked clean at least. Though his jeans were faded and ripped, and the black T-shirt he wore had holes, it wasn't a bad look for him.

From the tilt of his head, he seemed to be staring at the TV screen. It displayed a sitcom she was pretty sure he could care less about, but he was trained on it like the fate of the world depended on his understanding the plot.

Or was he? A stillness to him suggested otherwise.

As did the gun on the desk, resting inches from his unoccupied hand.

She saw that at the exact moment he grasped it, his foot coming down. The chair turned on its swivel and he was on his feet facing her, gun leveled.

The familiarity to the movement told her such vigilance wasn't new to him. The cold, still look in his eyes was that of a man standing alone on a wall, ready to defend it. What was behind that look said he knew it was a crumbling wall in a fallow field, but it was still his to defend, damn it.

As he'd risen, she'd also registered a slight hitch, a course correction as he found his balance. It didn't make the movement any less intimidating, not with those frigid blue eyes leveled on her and his jaw set like granite. But it gave her more information.

As did his reaction when he recognized her. Instantly, the gun muzzle was pointed upward. He swore and put it back down on the desk. Then stared at her. She waited him out. Waited to see what he would do next.

So she would know the path to take.

Silence was a coffin around him. When Tiger had taken a shower this morning, he'd wanted to hear the rush of shower water, running over his arms and chest as he lifted his hands to rinse the shampoo out of his hair. He'd stared down at his feet, the water swirling over the small tiles. Movement in his peripheral vision made him jump. Just the shower curtain. Rippling from the brush of his elbow and the splash of water against the folds.

The thrumming of the drops against his skin was like sound. But it wasn't. Tiger had shut off the water and toweled off. Found jeans and a T-shirt. He needed to go to the garage. Why the fuck he did, he didn't know, but that was what he kept doing. Maybe today he'd finally box up the stuff in the office and officially close the place up. Take the insurance money, sell the place and start doing one-man repair jobs and custom bike work at his place.

Him losing it with Larry had told him that was his best option. His crew didn't deserve that shit.

He got into the truck, white-knuckled the wheel, head on a swivel until he reached the office. Him, the guy who'd been comfortable at the wheel of anything since he could reach the pedals. Fuck, he missed the sound of an engine. Vibration was a mockery he hated.

Once at the garage, he did some paperwork. Bills. He had the battered TV on in the corner so he could glance at it on occasion. Like it was keeping him company. He'd turned on subtitles. Some kind of family sitcom, some stupid shit, and now it was a teenager trying to get his mother's attention. Mom. Mom. Mom. Over and over.

Expecting her to hear him.

If he didn't get his hearing back, which was looking less likely every day, he'd never hear anyone say his name again.

Oh, for fuck's sake. He was almost forty. Yeah, when really bad stuff happened, the kid part of the brain that never fully packed up and left would resurface with this thumb-sucking crap. Didn't mean he couldn't handle it like an adult. But he was going to explode out of his skin.

Aubrey would never hear *her* mom say her name again. *That* was something to cry about. Him, a mechanic whose hearing had already been scarred by a million engines, now relegated to full silence? That barely rated an eye roll. He'd been to racetracks and motorcycle rallies where no one could hear anything, and they were tickled as hell by it. If his balance wasn't total shit right now, he'd get on his bike and go to one.

That was the stuff that sucker-punched him. When he was trying to find normal, and the stuff that had been the easiest wasn't anymore.

No port in the storm.

The doc wanted him to go to a learning-to-be-deaf class. Said that would help him "cope" better. Yeah, if he set aside his general state of being pissed off and tried to do what they said, maybe. At the moment, he wasn't in the mood to do more than sit here.

He looked at the stack of unopened mail and the dark answering machine. Ten blinking lights before he'd turned it off. No need to answer. Anyone driving by could see they weren't open. He still should have had Chuck listen to them and write the messages down. He had a lot of loyal customers who didn't deserve him ignoring them. They'd helped make this into a successful business.

Until with one day, one act, it wasn't anymore. After some of the shit they'd said in the papers, who would risk coming back here? *No innocent bystanders killed.* When he'd read that, he'd almost driven right to the news station to squeeze that reporter's neck until his eyes popped and he shit his khakis. Nicole deserved better.

A vibration through the desk jerked his attention back to the present. Someone had come in through the side door. The doc had said that would happen, too. Things Tiger thought he used his hearing alone to identify, he also mapped through other senses, so he figured them out quicker than he'd expected. *Your other senses know the same things your ears do. They've just never had to play first string.*

No one was supposed to be here. Last week he'd chased off some punks who'd come to scavenge. But the thought of thieves wasn't what compelled him to take out his gun and put it on the desk. This might be the main reason he kept coming here, why he'd told his crew to stay away until he called them back. If he ever did.

Come on, fuckers, he thought. *Come back to get me. Be something I can kill. For Nicole and Aubrey.*

If they came down the hallway, he'd feel the change in air currents before they got there. A different vibration would say they'd gone into the closed garage bays. If that happened, he'd track them there. For now, he adjusted his position in the chair to align his peripheral vision with the doorway, even as he rested his head on his hand as if he were watching the TV. Letting the ash of his cigarette accumulate.

When the person stepped in, he was up, turning to level the gun. Just as fast, he pulled it up.

Fucking hell.

Skye wasn't the last person he'd expected to see, but it was pretty damn close, a toss-up between her and Santa Claus. And the squeezing panic he felt at her arrival was way worse than if it had been someone wanting to kill him.

He thought he'd lost the ability to panic years ago, thanks to over-exposure to far scarier reasons for it. A physical handicap apparently activated a part of his brain that had been left out of that lesson.

Skye startled at being in the crosshairs of the weapon, but when he immediately lifted it, she recovered nicely, as if walking into a room where someone was ready to shoot her was the norm. She held up two coffees and offered him one.

He had a pot of two-day old sludge in the corner, so hers looked far more appealing. As he put the gun in his top drawer and took the coffee, she slid into the chair across from him. When he took a sip, he welcomed the still-hot and much fresher medium roast.

She looked good, her pink-frosted lips wet from the coffee. Her trendy hairstyle had a streak of color to it—lavender today. The clothes she was wearing were the classy but fluid style that drew a man's gaze to her curves.

Her gaze was thoughtful. He expected his looked like a cornered animal, so he tried to settle down and sound normal. Like he could fucking hear whether he sounded normal or not.

"Your car have a problem?" he asked. "I'm not open, but I can send you over to Murray's. Red's working there and he's my best guy for a Mustang."

Mouth moving, silence coming out. It felt that way, a cavern inside him. He couldn't tell from her expression if she noted any differences. He also had another problem. She used those audio voices on her phone to respond, and he wasn't going to be able to hear that.

She rose. As she circled around the desk to him, she brought the guest chair with her. She sat down next to him, shoulder to shoulder, putting the phone flat on the desk between them. Brushing a hand over his shoulder, she gave him an absent smile. The contact felt good, but he still flinched, as if he was wrapped in barbed wire and her touch dug the sharp points into his flesh. She didn't react to that, leaning forward to type the message.

"No problem with the car. I came to see you." She straightened, pointedly waiting for him to read the screen.

She knew. Damn it. Maryshka. The girl was worried about him, and unlike the men he worked with, that worry would fly the coop of what he'd told her he wanted her to share. When his expression hardened, Skye typed again.

"Don't be a dick. She's having a rough time, too."

He blinked. Sat back. He was tired. He didn't want to deal with this shit. Thankfully, rather than push it further, Skye settled deeper into her chair and started watching the TV. Sipped her coffee. Nudged his toward him again.

So screw it, he drank his coffee and sat with her, not saying anything, and she seemed okay with that. It should have helped him relax, but he was wired like a bomb about to go off, a state he didn't want anyone else around.

No matter how he seemed outwardly, a Mistress like Skye would pick up what was going on beneath the surface. At length, she rose to shut off the TV, because he'd left the remote on top of it.

When she returned, she moved between him and the desk. Sliding her hips up onto it, she nudged his one foot off the edge so it came down to the floor. Before he could gauge her intent, she'd adjusted so the sole of her shoe was braced against his chair seat between his spread knees, her other propped against his thigh as she typed into the phone. She took her time, considering her word choices. Just like in session, when she deliberately gave him a few moments to toggle into the more serene state subbing gave him.

The fucked-up part of his head wasn't going for it. But the pull on it was there. She was wearing black heels, sleek and pretty, one of which was digging into his leg.

They weren't in a club. He needed to shut this down. He wasn't a sub outside club walls, and it surprised him that Skye of all people would push that idea. Up until now, she'd seemed to have an ironclad respect for his boundaries.

She extended the phone to him. When he reached out, she didn't relinquish it. Just let him close his hand over her cool, slim fingers as she held it up for him to read.

His fingers tightened over hers as he read the message.

Two choices.

Get on your knees.

Fuck me on your desk.

Watch TV until your brain melts.

Shit. "That's actually three choices," he said, for lack of anything else to say.

She lifted a brow, conveying that one of them really wasn't a choice at all. It was up to him to guess which one.

Skye had told the other women she'd handle this visit. Over the past couple of days, she'd framed it in her mind like an ambassador's job, checking on a friend to all of the TRA women.

He worked on their vehicles—the executive team and other staff members used his place. He always gave them fair prices and good work. Skye wouldn't trust her Mustang to anyone else. He'd also bought a modest marketing package from TRA—which had included the development of that tiger logo—when Ros showed him how they could grow his business. Though she'd been willing to do it as a barter situation, Tiger had insisted on paying like any other client.

Then there were the even more significant indicators, like how he'd helped Neil and Abby, and his protectiveness of Maryshka when he introduced her to Progeny.

All those things had only increased Skye's overall impression of him. He was a good man with a noble character. A strong personality.

In the club, they brought their personalities together to give one another what they wanted. Even needed. The levels of need they didn't touch were because that wasn't their relationship.

The relationship was about to change.

His alertness when she came in, the gun, said whatever had caused his sister-in-law to be killed here wasn't necessarily finished. That should make her take a big step back, but his tense body language, the dead look in his eyes, reached out and spoke to her. She could hear mortar being scraped against bricks, him building a wall against her, against everyone. Isolating himself.

Other things reinforced that impression. The overflowing tray of cigarette butts. A stack of singed pictures dropped haphazardly onto the seat of a second guest chair. They'd probably been salvaged from the walls of the burned-out bays. One was a business license in a wooden frame, the yellowed paper burned against the glass.

The stack of mail on the corner of his desk was topped by an obituary printout, pulled partially from an envelope. A handwritten note clipped to it said *Memorial at clubhouse* plus a date and time. Those last two had been circled in red, with an insistent arrow pointing to them. Below were two sentences in a more tremulous script.

Please come. For Aubrey.

So now, her own message delivered and waiting on an answer, she leaned forward from the desk and laid her hand on his face, the unshaven jaw. The familiar gesture snapped his gaze up to hers.

Her sessions were conducted primarily with nonverbal cues, and this was one her chosen partners learned quickly. A full palm to the cheek and jaw said *bring your gaze to mine and hold*. Through that lock, she commanded his total attention. If he needed a focus to slow everything down and put all that mattered into one place, she was that point. Nothing else required.

But he was hell and gone from that focus. Behind that burning gaze was a nature that belonged in a place tinged with fire, blood and lingering violence.

It was a little late to remember Maryshka's warning.

He rose. Big man, big shoulders, raw, urgent gaze. He put his hands on her upper arms, moving them up to her throat to cup the sides, his thumbs stroking over pulsing arteries. His hands smelled faintly of oil—they always did, though he soaked them before coming to the club, so they weren't so rough on tender female skin. She didn't mind the calluses, though. She read his language through his touch.

He'd stopped, his restlessness pushing against her like a storm wind. He'd made his choice, but he was waiting.

She formed one word with her lips. A permission, a command. One that freed a tiger.

Take.

His hands moved back to her shoulders, his fingers curling in the fabric of her blouse. Tight, twisting, sliding her off the desk, bringing her up on her toes, her hand falling against his chest for balance. He was as rock solid as an engine block, his heart pumping.

The seams at the shoulder ripped. His gaze flicked to the exposed skin, the satin strap of her bra. There was a marked line a strong man could walk, where he kept his touch gentle, yet left no doubt in a woman's mind what lethal things he could do with it.

She reached toward his face, testing, and he gripped her wrist, preventing the contact. Interesting, introducing a new note between them.

He leaned down, eyes intent. He usually used a mint-flavored toothpaste and strong soap to reduce the cigarette smell. Here it was sharp, abrasive. Cigarettes and motor oil, sweat and heat. They charged the erotic tension, electrifying the sexual need. He pulled her up to him by that tight hold on her sleeve, and mouths met.

They'd never kissed in session. Maybe he'd kissed her cheek at the end of an evening, a brush of lips as they took fond leave of one another. But they'd never *kissed*.

Her lips parted and oh... *Oh*. There was a swirling sensation in her head and stomach, a sudden hyperawareness of his grip and the press of his body against hers. She was back on the desk because he'd put her there, his hands at her waist. She wrapped her legs around him, keeping him close, though he didn't seem to be planning to go anywhere.

Take gave him leave to do what he wanted. She might suspect what direction he'd go with that, but the environment introduced less predictable variables.

She was aware of his hands and mouth, the concentrated heat and resilience of his body. That awareness plunged into a wave of answering response, her hands clutching his hips, her body arched against his as she moved her lips, tasting and responding to his hunger.

He'd pulled her blouse free of her slacks, and had his palms on her bare waist, long fingers framing her rib cage, with enough pressure to take up the space between the bones. His cock was stiff against his jeans and the thin layer of her slacks, the gush of damp heat beneath. He shifted from her mouth to her jaw, tipping back her head with an insistent nudge.

She quivered as he closed his mouth on her throat, laved her pulse, the sensitive pocket formed by her collar bones. His tongue followed her sternum to her cleavage. Sensation radiated out, tingling through her breasts, tightening her nipples. He went back to her carotid, up under her ear, nipping her lobe before he bit the side of her throat. His hands constricted on her ribs, her waist.

Abruptly, he went still, as if he'd turned to stone. A hard shudder went through him. Her breath was rising and falling quickly as she clutched him to her, but she went just as motionless. As aroused as she was, that stimulation was always about what was going on with the man under her control. Not just where her commands were taking him, but his own mind and heart.

Tiger's had just taken him someplace that told him he couldn't do this right now. *Damn it all.* If she shifted her touch to his ass and increased her grip, he'd interpret it as an order, that she wanted him to keep going. But with his head in the wrong place, that would make things worse.

Though it was more difficult than she'd anticipated to rein her own desires back—the man could kiss like a sex demon—she slid her hands under his T-shirt and found the wide expanse of his back. She stroked the contours down to his waist and played her fingertips along the inside of the waistband of his jeans, but kept it easy, taking them away from the intensity of the past few moments.

He had lifted his head and was staring at her as he sorted things out. A rueful look mixed with too much frustration crossed his face. His tone was light, forced. "Hope you don't think I'm not appreciative, Mistress. The stupidest fucking word for being offered the gates of heaven and asking for a rain check."

She reached down and stroked a hand over his erection, still pressing against his fly. She mouthed the word. "Noted."

That tight smile again. Tiger gave her a squeeze, then dropped heavily back into the office chair. She didn't want him that far away, so she leaned forward from the desk and tugged on the front of his T-shirt. He obligingly rolled the chair closer. She touched his face, then made a flat palmed motion horizontally in front of her, a wave to it before she let the move drift away to her left. Slow and easy worked for her.

Though his mouth had gone to a flat line, it eased a little. He understood. She handed him his coffee again.

When he leaned back in the chair, close enough his leg stretched out under the desk, she intended to brace her foot on his thigh again.

This time she decided to take off her shoe first. When the pump loosened from her heel, he closed his hand over it before it could freefall to the floor. After he carefully placed the shoe there, he did the same for the other one, then held that foot in his lap. He caressed her arch as she bent her knee and tucked the other foot under her leg. She picked up her own coffee.

He was back to staring at the desk. His mood unfortunately seemed to settle back into the roiling darkness inside him. He released her foot to rub a hand over his rough jaw. "Why did you come here, Skye?"

She held up her screen. "Because you need a friend. One you won't scare off just because you bark at her."

His broody expression didn't change, not until she typed another question. Then it turned to irritated confusion.

"How do I feel about body painting? You're thinking of having the Mustang repainted? That's the original factory color and it's in pristine shape. Why—"

She raised a hand, pointed at his chest and made a brush motion in front of it.

"Oh. *Body* painting." His brow lifted. "Am I the canvas or the painter?"

She typed again. "Charity event at Dale and Athena Rousseau's. We have a dozen or so artists. We're short one submissive volunteer. Open bar, good eats."

A hundred things passed through his dark blue eyes before he turned them away. He took a sip of coffee. "There's a lot happening with the garage. I need to pass."

While her intent wasn't to goad him, she damn well wasn't going to avoid what needed to be said. She tapped the desk to bring his attention back to her. She swept her gaze pointedly over the full ashtray, the dark TV he'd been staring vacantly at when she arrived.

His eyes flashed and mouth tightened.

She'd realized he was at a breaking point. Unfortunately, she'd miscalculated how close to it he was.

When he erupted from the chair, he took her from the desk to the wall in the time she'd drawn a startled breath. If he hadn't pulled his momentum, the impact would have jarred her to the bones. He held her pinned there with zero effort and a dark expression twisted with frustration and anger.

Cyn might be right about her needing more self-defense lessons.

"Out in the real world, I'm not a pet," he said. "If I'm barking, it's because I'm fucking intending to bite and it's a warning. You shouldn't have come here."

He released her as fast as he'd seized her. Then he pivoted, lifted his foot and shoved the desk. As it slammed into the far wall, his coffee wobbled but didn't topple. He took care of that, smacking it away so the liquid splattered the paneling, the cup bouncing off the TV screen.

She was by the door. She could bolt. He probably wanted her to do that. So she didn't. The truth might have been spoken lightly, but it wasn't a light truth. Like any fierce animal in pain, he needed someone who wouldn't be scared away. One who understood more about him and who he was than most.

Whatever he did next would validate that knowledge, or she would have to leave. Once her knees weren't quivering.

For now, she stood where she was, waiting. Hoping he'd stay turned away long enough the pulse in her throat would settle to match the stony look she'd locked into place.

"Fuck." He glanced at her. He still looked and sounded mean, but the words weren't. "You okay?"

Before she could answer, his gaze fell to the grip she had on her phone. Her hand was quivering, no matter that she tried to stop it.

His expression changed, became desolate. When he closed the distance between them again, she couldn't stop the instinctive flinch. He halted in front of her, but kept his hands to himself. "Mistress. Skye. I'm sorry. Shit. Shit, *shit*."

The agony in the words, as well as what he said next, proved her faith in him. "That guy, that's not who I am anymore. But it was at one time, and all this shit is dredged up right now, past and present, a future I don't know what to do with."

He drew a deep breath, and a hoarseness entered his voice. "I can't hear myself. Or anything else, and it's fucking me up so bad. You should just go. Really."

She took her own deep breath. Instead of listening to him, she pointed at herself, then her ears, then rested her hand on his chest, her gaze holding his.

I can hear you, that gesture said.

His anger drained away. When he spoke, he sounded tired. "Can you...is my voice too loud?"

She shook her head, pointed down.

"A little too soft?" A painful half chuckle. "My crew would say that's a first. If they were here."

She typed, held up her phone. Her hand had fortunately stopped shaking. "They should be," she told him. "You need your family right now."

His jaw flexed. "I'm pissed. Resentful like a fucking teenager. I went off on one of them last week for no damn good reason. Well..." He shook his head again. "Not for anything they did, not really. I'd visited the doc that day and there was no change. I could tell she thought there'd be some by now, if...I was going to get it back. She doubled down on telling me I should start looking at some of this stuff they offer deaf people, classes and shit. Take advantage of those resources... In case I end up needing them long term."

He grimaced. "She was quick to point out that stuff would be good even for the short term, but all I heard... It was the first time she really said the word as a permanent possibility, you know. Deaf. The only word I'm glad *not* to hear come out of my fucking mouth."

She closed her hand over the fist clenched at his side. He didn't seem to notice, the fingers knotted tight. "I wanted to burn all the info she gave me in a trash barrel, but I put it in my desk. Locked it away. I need to look at it, but every day I say...not today. Hell, I'm pathetic and I know it. That's why I don't want them around me, Skye. Or you. I want to smash something into pieces, and as I said, I've been that guy. I don't want to hurt anyone because I'm hurting. No one deserves that shit from me."

She bypassed that and focused on the first part. "Taking those steps, reaching out for those resources, resisting the lure of isolation, is an act of will," she typed. "You have a strong will."

He raised his attention from the phone to her face. "So do you. Is that how you did it?"

They'd never gone into that territory before, but given his current condition, she didn't take it as an inappropriate question. She chose a measured response. "Somewhat. A story for another time. When you're behaving like you've earned it. If you still want to know then."

The fingers slowly loosened, that hand going to her hip. Though he didn't close the distance between them, the look in his eyes seemed to move him closer. "You've raised my curiosity about a lot of things about you today."

Yeah, he wasn't alone in that. That kiss had opened some unexpected territory between them. They could go back down the road they'd been on only a few moments ago, but she knew the timing was regretfully wrong for it. Proving it, he sighed and changed topics.

"You going to make me go to this charity thing?"

Though she thought he'd intended to deliver the question with a teasing note, she picked up on the edge. One thing Tiger never did was play man-child with her. Instead of smiling, she gave him a Domme look. She lifted a finger, then put her head down to type.

The words were ready to be called, because she'd mostly learned to type at the same speed as she thought. Yet with the hearing world, she could use the audio to "talk" as she typed. In this instance, Tiger had to wait until she was finished. Unless she positioned herself where he could see the screen as she typed. Given the mood of the moment, she chose not to do that.

Tiger found a way to occupy himself. He braced himself against the wall by her, his hand still resting on her hip. She glanced sideways at him as he put his nose close to her hair and inhaled. The gesture sent a tingle through her ear, the side of her throat and across the top of her breast.

Though he drew back slightly to see if she would ping him for it, she decided against it. Damn it, she'd deleted a line.

She'd just punish him for that later.

She turned the phone around so he could read it. "I never make you do anything, Tiger. There are a lot of destructive paths in dealing with this. Wallowing is one. Just giving up and being carried along is another, so you don't have to actively choose or take responsibility for your path. That's not you. That strong will I mentioned shows in your active submission, your choice to submit to your Mistress's desires and commands.

"There's an expiration date on wallowing, and after you've passed it, you're just stinking up the world with self-pity. As a friend, I can only do so much about that. But the other path, the giving up and being carried along, that comes into my territory."

She saw pensiveness, a little irritation, and flashes of anger as he read. When he hardened against his jeans, she knew he'd reached her last paragraph.

"If the way you submit isn't true to yourself, I will always call you on it. If you fail to meet your own expectations, I will be even tougher on you than if you fail to meet mine. You don't have to ask me why— you know the answer to that in your gut."

As he digested that, she waited him out. A strong, alpha male who sought sexual submission learned to take a step back and reflect. He'd brought a good measure of that temperance with him when they'd started doing sessions together. He'd identified his hard limits without waffling and been confident in their initial negotiations, displaying none of the warning signs of being vague and uncertain, or dismissing too much of his own needs to please her.

She could see him struggling, not wanting to say what he ended up saying. As she'd said, resisting isolation, particularly at this stage of his hearing loss, required a tremendous act of will. Which was why the prodding and care of friends helped. "So any special requirements for this charity thing?" he said.

She held up the phone, flaring her nostrils for emphasis. "You'll have to shave and brush your teeth. Fortunately, you seem to have remembered what a shower is."

His expression eased, enough to put a familiar light in his eyes, a reassuring hint of himself. "Just in case, want to help supervise that shower? Ow..."

He caught her hand as she pinched his nipple through his shirt with sharp nails. Though she kept them short for her computer work, she still knew how to use them. He didn't pull away, taking the pain as his due. When she stepped back, smoothing her hand over the front of his shirt, he gave her a look that struggled between arousal and total churning uncertainty.

She resisted the urge to prolong her visit. Instead, she showed him another note. "I have to get back to work."

"Oh. Yeah, sure." He glanced at the disrupted desk, the spattered wall. "Uh...thanks for the coffee."

That made her smile. He gave her a wry one in return and escorted her to the propped open side door. Once there, she paused to type another message.

He squinted against the sunlight as he crossed his arms over his chest and waited her out. She showed him the screen.

"I'll text you the event details. By the way, when you're fixing an engine, do you ignore the tools that will help you get it running right again?"

His brow furrowed. "Not usually, no."

She nodded. Typed the follow up. "You should get that stuff out of the drawer and read through it."

He eyed her. "Should I consider that a command?"

This time, he wasn't looking for her to take his choices away. He was challenging her. So leaning in, Skye curled her fingers over his crossed forearms and tapped his chest.

You bet your fine ass, she mouthed.

Then she made herself get in her car and drive away.

CHAPTER FOUR

$\mathcal{T}$he first time Skye had visited the vast estate that Athena Rousseau called home, it had been for a barbecue and pool party. Though TRA had a business relationship with Athena, who had operated a global manufacturing corporation with her late husband, it was the connection to her current husband that had resulted in that invitation.

Dale Rousseau, a retired Navy SEAL, had once been Lawrence's team leader. He was also a Dom. When Ros and Lawrence became a couple, Ros and the rest of her executive team received invites to the intimate get-together.

Dale and Athena preferred the smaller venue of Club Release, but Dale was an accomplished rope rigger and had been a practicing Dom most of his adult life. He was routinely recruited for demos and workshops in club settings, including Progeny.

At the barbecue, Dale had been relaxed enough to wear shorts and reveal he was a below-knee amputee. In his normal attire of jeans, wearing his prosthetic, it was often missed.

"Don't let him fool you," Lawrence had noted dryly. "He can deliver a one-legged ass kicking, no problem at all."

Athena had served as her late husband's Mistress during their years together, with "served" being the operative word. She'd recognized her submissive side long before he passed, and providing Roy a Mistress had been part of her loving service to him. Then her path

46

crossed Dale's. She'd eventually embraced him as Master *and* husband.

Yet when it came to running a business or organizing a charity event, Athena donned a general's hat and made it all come together with true Southern steel magnolia charm.

The weather had cooperated, so the artist stations were spread throughout her gardens. Plan B had been to use her pool house, pavilion tents, and the solarium. Now those would remain social and refreshment areas for the guests. Tables under the pavilion tents were being loaded up with heavy hors d'oeuvres, while the pool area had the open bar.

The pool was populated by floating tea lights...and merpeople. Skye had paused to watch them doing sinuous dances around one another. Whatever adhesive and movie magic was making them look like actual mermaids and mermen was impressive, as was their ability to swim like one might imagine a merperson swimming. A chance to swim in the pool with them was one of tonight's perks.

Skye wouldn't mind swimming with the mermaids.

She stopped by the solarium to check the projection equipment for the big screen set up there. It would be showing a two-hour montage of sensual images on a loop, the score for it composed by Imagine Dragons. The movie had been provided by well-known erotic film producer Tyler Winterman. It was an exclusive viewing, not scheduled for public release until next year.

She moved on to the gardens. The guests who would be attending had paid ten thousand dollars a ticket to see acclaimed artists create masterpieces in front of them. Not on canvas, but on human flesh. Which was why dungeon masters from Club More and Progeny had been recruited to be here as well. They'd safeguard the fifteen volunteers, some submissives, some models from local art schools, who'd be positioned on the platforms. Plus the merpeople.

Skye trusted the DMs, but she'd keep Tiger in sight as much as she could. Her concerns for him weren't about some enthusiastic art patron trying to grope him before a DM could intervene.

Currently a small army was in the gardens. One battalion handled the setup for the stations, which included lighting for the raised platforms where the artists would work, and side tables stocked with their preferred materials. A catering brigade arranged the viewing chairs and cloth-covered high-tops as a resting place for drink glasses and hors d'oeuvres plates.

Another type of artist would be active in the back gardens. Three junk cars had been positioned among a grove of crepe myrtles and azaleas. Instead of working on flesh, these creators would work on metal. The results would be transported to the lobbies of major corporate centers in the city, each having contributed sizeable donations for the three benefitting charities.

That had been thanks to TRA's marketing help, targeted toward big donors like those. Even the giveaways and swag bag contents each attendee would carry home, valued at five hundred dollars, were mostly donated items.

Lights were strung along garden pathways, with signage to guide guests from station to station. In the center of the garden was a rotunda with a white-painted gazebo, delicate wood molding edging its red-shingled crown. As the day had moved from late afternoon toward twilight, musicians in black dresses, or slacks and short-sleeved dress shirts, had arrived and started practicing. The strings and wood-winds added to the dreamlike ambiance, as did the setting sun and evening breeze off the waterway and marsh that flanked Athena's property.

Skye wished she'd told Tiger to come earlier. Yes, she was busy, in charge of pretty much all the tech needed for tonight's event, but she would have liked to see him pitching in, helping, as she knew he would. Then she could have known he was here already, where she could perhaps find a few moments to draw him away and...

Act like an idiot over a male she'd never acted like an idiot over before.

The admonishment didn't stop her from checking the time. He'd texted her his ETA when he'd headed this way, and it just so happened she needed to get some additional things out of her car. Might as well be there when he arrived, if it worked out that way.

As she passed the pavilions again, she saw the artists meeting with Athena. They'd draw lots to see who'd be their canvas, and let the muse inspire them. An injection of unpredictability into the well-planned evening.

While not all of them did body painting or tattoo art as their main medium, they were all accomplished in crafting on human skin. They would start at eight and have until midnight to finish.

Many of them looked like they'd be at home on the set of a car detailing or tattoo reality show, with body art of their own, pierced brows and spiked hair. They wore the clothes they enjoyed creating in, mostly jeans and T-shirts.

She'd been the one who'd suggested to Athena the idea of drawing straws for the "canvases." She found herself wishing she hadn't. One woman had long black dyed hair and gothic eye liner that enhanced eyes the color of frosted sea glass. Her lithe body screamed sex, in snug jeans and a crop top that showed her navel ring.

She'd never objected to Tiger being with another Mistress, or having someone else handle him intimately. When their session was over, Skye had no claim on him. But that kiss...she kept thinking about that kiss.

The parking area was a mowed field Athena used to accommodate guests for her larger events. She'd hired valet service for those who didn't care for the walk, but Skye knew Tiger wouldn't use valet parking.

As she approached her car, she looked for him. And remembered the first time she'd been out front at Club Progeny when he'd arrived.

It had been worth a long look, a hot guy in denim and leather, pulling in on a mean-looking motorcycle. Watching him take off the helmet, rumple his short hair. Remove his gloves, slap them on his thigh before tucking them away.

She'd been sitting with Vera under Progeny's covered pergola, a break area for those escaping the heat and noise inside the club. While Vera was chatting with a couple of club members, Skye had been people-watching. Tiger's arrival had stayed in her memory, ready to be called to mind for the pure pleasure of it, him getting off that bike, muscles flexing, eyes reflecting the serious anticipation of finding a Mistress he could serve for the evening.

Once they started doing more sessions together, she knew the approximate time he came to the club. Which meant she developed a habit of conveniently being out there. It contributed to that simmering anticipation for what the scene would bring.

While no one else seemed to lie in wait for him, anyone with an eye for sexy man candy took a beat to appreciate it.

Where she distinguished herself was in the lack of subtlety. If he saw her, she made a point of letting him see her look. Thoroughly. Her reward was his slow grin, the heat in his eyes, which stoked her own further.

He'd also give her a slight nod of acknowledgement before he strode toward the entrance, where he was inevitably intercepted and accompanied by at least one or two fluttery female subs.

"It just kills them that he's not a Dom," Abby had said once, when they were in the parking lot at the same time. She'd given Skye a nudge and a smile. "Like a straight woman feels about a drop-dead gorgeous gay man. All of that alpha male feast, with not even a bite for me."

"Oh, he'd bite them if they asked," Skye had responded, using her Betty White voice, a choice that had Abby chuckling. "He appreciates women, Domme or sub, and will flirt enough with either to drive those fantasies."

But he was careful with the subs. Caring. He understood how they enjoyed touch, that sensual teasing, but also how to restrain it so he wasn't misleading them. Again, like a Dom. Picking up on what they needed.

"I've never seen him switch, though," Abby said thoughtfully. "Never seen him even try to play the Dom."

Neither had Skye. He knew what he wanted, what he was, and was clear about it. As a veteran member, he'd been recruited to help conduct the Sub 101 orientation classes. He also routinely mentored others, like Maryshka.

As she rolled through those pleasant thoughts, Skye had been scanning the parking lot, and now she located him. He hadn't come on his bike, but in a black antique Chevy pickup whose patina had a sheen in the early evening light.

He'd put himself at the back corner of the lot, and seemed to be staring at the dashboard. She could almost feel the struggle going through his mind. Would he get out? Or start the truck up and leave?

When he'd agreed to come, she'd known he'd have a lot of *what the hell was I thinking* moments between then and now. She suspected this might be the first time since the injury he'd attended a social event. But she'd never known Tiger to break a session appointment, never had him back out on anything he'd committed to doing. If he did tonight, it would tell her more about his state of mind.

Should she help him bypass that choice by starting across the parking lot, letting him see her, making it harder to choose that route? Or go back to the hundred things she had to do while he made up his mind?

In theory, he was here as one of the handful of subs she'd recruited with Athena for the event. But in her mind, because of his circum-stances, he was here as *her* sub. They might not be in session, but she knew the signs when a sub needed a Domme's guidance and that sense of her control. Her ownership, to help remind him of the structure of it and what it provided him.

Five more minutes. She'd let him sort through it. Then she'd act.

Tiger lifted his gaze to the windshield, the marsh view beyond it. He told himself he'd parked toward the back of the lot to protect the truck from being dinged. According to Maryshka, if it ever got a scratch, they might have to rush him to the hospital before his brain exploded.

She was probably right, but the quiet corner also let him think. Settle. On the way here, an ambulance had blasted past him. He'd been on a four-lane, and traffic had been light and spread out, so he wasn't in its way. However, he didn't notice its approach until the lights flashed in his mirrors. It had rattled him. Another thing to add to the list of things he had to stay conscious of in a different way.

He should just leave. Text her and apologize. She'd said they were one short, but he could text another sub, like Sy, so he didn't leave her in a lurch. Sy was always up for a last-minute change in plans. Hell, he routinely did sessions with Cyn, so he could handle the unexpected.

But Tiger couldn't just invite a replacement without checking with her first. And he was just too chickenshit to tell her to her face he was bailing.

Which meant he wasn't going to back out.

He'd thought a lot about her visit to the garage. Especially that kiss. And of course the invitation to have sex on his desk. She'd seemed committed to following through, but she'd smoothly changed course when he was too fucked up for the timing. But the very fact the offer had been on the table had been unsettling.

They'd done a lot of things in Progeny's private rooms. But not sex. Not him sliding his cock into her wet pussy, feeling her hands grip him, hold on as he thrust, took them both on that ride.

Having a hard-on was a good distraction from what he manfully refused to call terror when he contemplated getting out of his truck. However, he suspected it was better to turn his mind to other things to calm down.

He'd thought a lot about her approach. Not too solicitous, the "Let me help you, oh I'm so sorry you're going through this" stuff he would have hated, even if he hadn't been in a mood to hate everything anyway. She just took over, laid out his choices like she did in a session.

Get on your knees.

Fuck me on your desk.

Watch TV until your brain melts.

She'd even made it clear about him being here tonight. The choices were his, his will driving things, meeting her halfway.

That squeezing panic he'd felt when he'd first seen her in his office had evaporated when she'd blatantly reminded him he had a dick that worked. The savagery that had surged through him had worked too well. He'd nearly lost it with her. Which meant he owed her. So here he was.

He hadn't hated that kiss. Truth, it was an even bigger reason for why he was here, instead of guilt over his animal behavior. It had been a great kiss, one that had made him feel more like himself. At least for a few minutes.

He was shakier about this than he'd anticipated. He should have asked her to meet him in the parking lot.

Christ. He hadn't come here to be a clingy loser, desperate to stick close to someone who could handle communication and cover for what he couldn't hear. He had to do what she'd said. Kick his own will into gear and be the big-dick-swinging tough guy she expected him to be. Ready to serve his Mistress in whatever way she needed. If he faced something he didn't know how to handle, well, he'd figure it out. Like when something was wrong with an engine. There was always a solution. You just had to settle down, look for it, feel for it, listen...

"Goddamn fucking hell." Cursing when he couldn't hear himself curse took the joy out of it, but he did it anyway. Seizing the handles of his duffel, he shoved himself out of the truck. If it had been his work truck, he would have slammed the door hard enough to flip the damn thing.

But Maryshka was right about his 1955 Chevy short bed pickup. Figuring that the patrons tonight would be driving their high dollar rides, he'd decided his boy deserved to show off a little. The Chevy could hold its own among a crowd of pricey sportscars. In the past, having his truck at something like this had been a draw for amateur gearheads, those who might think of his garage for their more complex upgrades or repair needs.

Fuck knew how he'd handle those conversations tonight, so it was probably good he'd parked toward the back. He closed the door in a measured way. Dipped down to brush a little gravel dust off a white wall tire.

Then he headed across the parking area.

~

Skye let out a breath. When he'd left the truck, he looked like he wanted to kill something, but she saw him take a moment, pamper his vehicle. Maryshka teased him about taking it out to dinner on its birthday and anniversary.

When he saw her, his shoulders and expression eased some. Giving her a half smile, he moved in her direction.

Someone else was approaching him. Bethany was another sub, here tonight not to be a canvas, but additional waitstaff. She was one of those Tiger had mentored until she got her bearings. After the evening's sessions were over, Bethany sometimes gravitated to him to have a drink and talk sub-shop.

She was calling out to him. Since she likely hadn't seen him since the garage incident, Skye expected Bethany would greet him with an exuberant, caring hug, a gesture that fit her loving personality.

The problem was he didn't see her yet. Skye pointed, and Tiger glanced over his shoulder when Bethany was about five feet away. Not optimal, since she flung herself at him for that hug, but better than if she'd completely taken him by surprise.

He was still stiff as a board when she wrapped her arms around him. He put the duffel down while still in her embrace, holding her with one arm and easing her back while recovering his smile. He offered a nod or two as she chattered at him, as if he could understand her. He was going to try and fake it.

She'd been there. There was a time and place for it, but this wasn't it. This kind of situation, it just made things worse. Skye had reached them, and laid a hand on Bethany's arm, drawing her attention as she typed into her phone. Her brisk but reassuring Helen Mirren voice seemed the most appropriate choice.

"Tiger can't hear you, Bethany." She angled it so Tiger could read it, was part of the conversation. "His hearing was damaged in the incident at his garage. Just use your phone like I'm doing to communicate with him."

"Oh. *Oh*. Tiger, I'm so sorry." Bethany looked up at Tiger, realized he probably still didn't understand her, though Skye expected her expression gave him the gist of it. He'd clasped Skye's wrist as he read the phone. His grip tightened with a note of challenge, reflected in the flash of his gaze. He wasn't pleased she'd told Bethany.

Bethany dipped her head to her phone, typed fast and showed it to Tiger, even as she spoke the same words to him. "I'm glad to see you. Glad you're doing this tonight."

"I appreciate that." Tiger's expression looked as wooden as his response. Skye wasn't sure Bethany noticed, since she was flustered.

Her next words were directed toward Skye. While it was unusual for Skye to be viewed as the easier choice for "normal" communication, she knew most people made that choice subconsciously. Otherwise known as that state between being actively aware you were doing it, and not admitting it to yourself.

"All right. Well...it's good to see you both. I'll remember that, about the phone. I'd better get over to the rendezvous point and see where Athena wants me."

Someone unused to being around a deaf or mute person had to be given the time to process. It didn't change the fact a retreat like Bethany's could make a deaf person feel more isolated in his own head.

But that only meant he had to keep trying to communicate. No way around it; a lot of the work was on the side of the person with the "handicap." It might not seem fair, but he could be in the world or outside of it. Skye knew firsthand which decision was better in the long run. However, she also knew what it took to get there, which meant she was ready for his temper.

Tiger shook his head, indicating he wanted his say before she typed anything on her phone. "Telling someone about my hearing is up to me."

He hadn't let go of her wrist. Skye sent a pointed look that way and pantomimed a Psycho stabbing motion. *Move it or lose it.*

He blinked, but let go. She stuck with her frosty Helen voice. Though he was reading the words, not hearing them, the voice helped her project the tone in her expression, an important source of information for a deaf person. "The environment here tonight is no different from a club. Dom/sub protocols. Making everyone aware of any physical issues you have is important. Pride never trumps safety, does it?"

His jaw flexed. "You still took a choice away from me."

"You may be right about that," was her frank response, no apology. "But I was looking out for Bethany, too. She could have pulled one of her flying tackles, where she copped a piggyback ride." Squashing her D-cup breasts against his back and wrapping her generous thighs around his hips. Skye had seen her do it before. "You might have flung her off like a snake dropping from a tree before you realized it was her."

Though his expression remained dark, his lips twitched. Skye continued to type. "She'll spread the word, and people will know not to sneak up on you. You have enough to handle tonight."

His face shuttered. "Not much chance she'll be grabbing that piggyback ride now. Rabbits bolt slower than she did."

She put a hand on his chest and leaned into the contact, shifting to rest her shoulder where her hand had been. He could look down and see the screen as she typed. His breath was warm on her ear.

"You get used to it. You have to re-build relationships, and you'll lose some." She glanced up at him, noted the tightening of his lips, but continued, her fingers flying. "True friendships can weather it, be rebuilt. It just requires as much patience and caring on your side as it does willingness and commitment on theirs."

She changed from a serious mien to an arch look as she typed another short paragraph. "When she leaves tonight, get in her way. Offer her that piggyback ride. Cart her to her car, give her a hug and a smile. Ask her how her night went and tap her phone to encourage her to tell you. You have to provide guidance."

She swept her gaze over him. "You might get up close and personal with those D-cup breasts of hers. Some women are big into pity sex for the handicapped."

The blunt words startled him enough he took an extra beat to read them. His gaze narrowed. "We don't have that kind of relationship. I wouldn't ever use her that way."

Skye knew that wasn't necessarily true. He had no idea what he might do if he was starved for touch, contact, connection. Some form of communication that broke the wall of silence.

She'd intended to shake him up, but their conversation had touched a nerve, opening an unexpected narrow window into her own past. A past she'd healed, resolved and goddamned dealt with.

Glancing down at her phone, she offered a *sorry* meme, a flower with the word printed below it. Then typed, "I know. I was trying to get you out of your own head. I took it a little too far."

She didn't like to think of how easy it would be for him to seek that comfort sex, if he saw Bethany at the end of the night. She knew the answer to that, didn't she? She could always take him home herself.

He touched her shoulder. Her apology had been accepted. "I know you're trying to help," he said. "You are. I just don't have a road map for this."

"And you're a control freak," she responded on screen, giving him a half-smile. "You don't like not being at the wheel. But at least I know you don't have a problem with women drivers."

He made a face. He still looked surly, but thoughtful, too. He picked up the duffel. "As Bethany said, we're on a schedule. Lead on, Mistress. I'm here to serve."

CHAPTER FIVE

*a*n event coordinator would be meeting with the subs and models, giving them direction on what would be expected of them. Skye had met with her earlier to make her aware of Tiger's issue. The woman had assured Skye she'd typed out her notes and would go over them with Tiger, one-on-one.

So there was no reason for Skye to hover. While Tiger went to the changing tent, she returned to her assigned tasks.

As she made adjustments to the programming on her drones for video footage collection, her mind returned to another sub. Maryshka.

After seeing him at the garage, Skye had followed up with the girl, telling her that Tiger was going through a normal grieving process. She'd recommended that Maryshka keep reaching out to him, while she'd work on him from another angle. Maryshka had been so relieved by what she'd perceived as a "progress" report, she'd given Skye a spontaneous hug, followed by a blush and a stammered apology.

Female subs. They could be truly adorable.

When it was time for the artists to select their canvases, Skye circled back to the area where that would be happening.

Athena never overlooked the special touches. She'd obtained a handful of old paint brushes, and written the name of each "statue" along the wooden handles. She put them brush side up in a thick arrangement of colorful zinnias, set in an old tin can with artful smears of paint in the creased metal.

As the artists gathered around, the sun had fully set, the torch light darkening the hue of the flowers. Skye noted an artist who hadn't been there earlier. He was tall and lean, with a strikingly interesting Adrien Brody kind of face, straight slash cheekbones, mouth a firm line, and black fine brows, teased by a fall of thick dark hair short on his nape. He had no visible body art and wore dark jeans with a short-sleeved, wine-colored Henley shirt.

The male who accompanied him possessed a wide-shouldered, brawny build capable of knocking down anything that got in his way. Long, thick blond hair was tied back, and he wore a belted kilt with a snug fitting black T-shirt over his impressive chest and arms.

She knew the leaner male was the artist, not just because she'd done a quick skim of the program for tonight, but because he radiated the quality she'd noted in all of the artists. Their ability to see the world around them through a filter that translated the input to subject matter made them seem slightly out of kilter with the world, yet it was balanced by the kinship that became obvious when they were standing together.

The long-haired male slid a hand over the artist's shoulder, fingers finding skin under his short sleeve. The artist gave him a distracted half smile, but the bond between the two men was obvious. The artist gripped the male's T-shirt over his chest and gave it a rough tug before he brushed a kiss over his smiling mouth.

It was an indication of who held the top role, but the energy between them also hinted at an erotic history where who held the reins might be a fluid thing. Especially between two men who were both clearly Dominants.

Then a woman joined them, answering the question of who fulfilled their need for a submissive. Up until this moment, Skye would have said Abby was the most beautiful woman she'd ever seen. This woman was ethereal. Timeless. Like models in black and white still photographs taken decades ago, their names lost but their beauty impossible to forget once it was seen.

She moved between the men like a dryad in the company of the trees who held her soul. Her hand rested on the larger man's chest as she reached up to the artist's face to stroke an errant lock of dark hair back from his forehead. The brace of her hand on the blond's chest helped her with the reach.

She was talking, gesturing toward Athena, as if catching the artist up on what he might have missed. Like an assistant of sorts.

As he listened, the look in his eyes, in both men's body language, said this woman was theirs, at every conceivable level of possession. She glowed like treasure in the grip of that love and ownership.

The long-haired male clasped the woman's hand and said something that had her smiling. The two of them melted back into the gardens, her pressed close to his side, his hand at the small of her back.

As the tall, lean man moved closer to the group of artists, his gaze slid over to Skye. She was far enough away to escape notice, and she wasn't moving, standing in front of a bank of azaleas. However, he studied her with that artist's intensity, which amused her, though as an afterthought. She was caught by his gaze, his eyes vibrant and oddly still.

Holding that gaze was more difficult than expected. His expression shifted to one of casual courtesy, and he gave her a polite nod.

As she recalled more details from the program, she remembered why he'd stood out. He'd submitted a portrait for his bio rather than a photograph, and he was one of the biggest names here tonight. Evan Miller.

When he'd joined the other artists, she'd noticed they'd adjusted to give him a wider berth. Beyond the professional respect, she thought that was a good idea generally. Though he lacked his companion's brawn, there was an air about him that seemed equally daunting.

But as he approached the flower arrangement where Athena stood, that intensity altered to genuine warmth. He greeted her but didn't dally, plucking out a brush.

Skye had made a point of knowing where Tiger's was in the arrangement, so she knew that was the one he'd chosen. Confirming it, Athena's gaze lighted on Skye as she spoke to Evan. She gestured toward her, then shifted her attention to the next artist approaching the bouquet.

As he closed the distance between him and Skye, Evan held the brush in elegant fingers. Ones she imagined brought artistry to whatever medium he chose, as well as pleasure to the man and woman he called his own.

She'd been around plenty of Masters she held in high esteem. As a Domme herself, she appreciated the many shapes and styles that dominance could take. This male's brand of it had the subtlety of flowing water, one of the most powerful forces in nature. There was something...electric about what vibrated from his skin. Like she was standing close to live power lines when he arrived in front of her.

He'd seemed to make an effort to tone down that energy when he'd approached Athena, and she suspected he did so now as well. Evan lifted the brush. "Is there anything you'd like to tell me about my canvas?"

"Yes." She chose to use the Southern female voice when she typed her audio response. "He's deaf. It was recent, so he speaks just fine. He's not yet anticipating a lot of the things he can't hear, though, and his balance may give him some trouble."

She gave Evan further information on Tiger's other issues. The relative endurance of his knees and back, both impacted by a life of working on vehicles. She appreciated that Evan listened carefully, the way a good Dom did.

"What's the name of your giant?" she concluded. "The one masquerading as a human?"

"Niall." Humor touched Evan's gray eyes. "He'll be so disappointed his disguise isn't working."

He'd shown an interested flicker when she used the voice app, but that was all. None of the tension many people exhibited at first, unsure if they were going to be able to properly communicate with her, and finding it too late to cut and run.

"And the insanely beautiful woman?"

"Alanna." His gaze sharpened. "Why is this relevant?"

"Are they your family?"

"Yes. But you're not answering my question."

Oh yeah, Dom with a capital D. But so was she. "I am, in fact," she said, just as cool. "I wanted to understand how you felt about them. I don't know if you're monogamous with them or not, and that's not my business. But Tiger is straight. While he has no problem with the intimacies required for painting his body, he *will* get riled if he believes a man is touching him with sexual intent."

"I understand." Evan considered. "Do you think it would head off any potential misunderstandings if Alanna was present to assist me? She can also watch for any stressors related to his lack of hearing."

Skye nodded, pleased at the consideration. "Anything else?" Evan asked.

"No," she typed. "I look forward to what you'll create with him. He's already a work of art."

Evan met her gaze. "He's here because he's yours. I'll take care of him, don't worry. Though I suspect you won't be that far away."

He could bet on it. Skye took a breath as he moved off, likely headed to his assigned platform in the garden to check that his supplies and lighting were laid out according to the specs each artist had provided before the event.

She glanced at the time, and strode toward the house. Though she was reassured by the conversation, they had a few minutes before she had to do other things. She wanted to take Tiger to Evan personally, make sure he was in a good headspace, before she left them to it.

Tiger had emerged from the changing tent. She'd called female subs adorable. Looking at him, the word *adorable* didn't even cross her mind. He'd enhance the audience's anticipation and set Evan's artistic imaginings free like a flock of starlings.

He'd chosen the dark, clingy shorts he often wore for club scenes. Easy to remove, formfitting so she got a nice eyeful of his package and his ass, but keeping all of it contained until she wanted it not to be.

She'd told Evan he was a work of art, and he was. The motorcycle boots to protect his feet and get him where he needed to go added a gritty Tom Finland touch to the look.

Her gaze covered his wide shoulders, formidable biceps and flat stomach. He didn't have the sculpted six pack, just the muscle and fit shape of a man who worked hard in excessive heat. He wasn't a heavy eater. At catered club events he opted for a modest amount of food followed by an after-meal cigarette outside.

He'd shaved his face fully tonight, leaving it smooth. The tattoo that covered his upper arm with the jungle scene was a blur of shifting color in the torchlight, but she noted the jagged scar across the top of the elephant's head. It cut through the adjacent lion and a crimson tropical bloom camouflaging the big cat. Probably where debris had hit him during the explosion.

She put that disturbing thought away. Alanna was with him, and typing things on a tablet for him to read. Whatever it said, it was making him smile, putting him more at ease, as were her vivid expressions and hand gestures.

Evan must have sent her a text heads up to get her involved right away, just as he'd discussed with Skye. Skye should appreciate his consideration, instead of having an urge to chop off the dainty fingers Tiger was currently clasping to keep the tablet still as he read.

Like he'd done with Skye and her phone.

Don't be an idiot.

She saw no flirtation in Alanna's manner, only friendly reassurance. Skye suspected she was giving Tiger specific information about Evan, tidbits that would set Tiger further at ease, help him relax the erratic vigilance that was an obvious weight on his shoulders.

She was doing such a good job of it, Skye objectively considered backing off before she was seen. Let the girl take him to Evan, get him started without her involvement. It would reinforce her confidence— Tiger's confidence—that he had this under control.

Then he glanced up and saw her. The genuine pleasure, the sweep of his gaze over her, reinforced by his attentive body language, pleased her. Though there was a lava flow of tension beneath the surface, nothing suggested the excessive relief that came from dependence on her presence, a reaction she would have had to resist enabling.

He was handling himself. He wanted to be near her *for* her.

Alanna offered Skye a warm smile and respectful nod, a core deep submissive acknowledging a Dominant. "I'll see if my lord needs anything, and meet you both there."

Even in a club, courtly ways and the use of 'my lord,' could sometimes seem jarring. But it sounded as natural on Alanna's lips as *Master,* and obviously meant the same to her.

Tiger said "Thank you," for both of them, so Skye didn't have to type it. Her sub, reading her needs as well as Alanna likely did Evan's, if she was this on the ball with total strangers.

As Alanna moved away, Skye appreciated that Tiger didn't take his gaze away from Skye. Any man with a pulse would have stolen a quick glance at the perfect heart-shaped backside, trim waist and flowing, flame-colored hair. Alanna moved with the sensual grace of an exotic courtesan, trained in the arts of pleasure since puberty.

Flattening her palm on Tiger's chest to feel the thud of his heart, Skye brushed her knuckles over his smooth jaw and raised a questioning brow.

"The info you sent said they might want to do some face painting," he explained. "So I figured a smooth shave would be helpful. The chest and other places, he'll just have to work with as is. Being as hairless as a ten-year-old isn't my thing."

He did keep the hair around his cock groomed, but she liked his body hair and expressed it now by threading her fingers through what was on his chest, a petting that lingered.

He stood still, head dipped down to watch her hand. While many men were eager for the more blatant sexual overtures in a woman's touch, pressuring her toward areas further south, a submissive could be different. By letting her please herself, he was introduced to the erotic potential of other zones. Especially if her pleasure increased his own.

With Tiger, it exponentially increased it. She didn't want to devote energy to "talking" right now, except with her hands and expression. She stroked him some more, then she leaned in, the pressure of her fingers telling him to remain still. She put her mouth on his throat, set her teeth and lips there, and bit him, even as she also sucked hard on his flesh, tasting him with tongue and lips.

He shuddered, hands closing at his sides as he obeyed her directive not to make contact. She had no such restraint, reaching around to grip his ass through the clingy fabric, enjoying the muscular buttocks that flexed under her touch, almost dislodging her hold. The man was in fine, powerful shape.

Beyond the demands of his job, he used homegrown methods to keep himself that way. Tires he dragged with chains, lifting and lowering an old engine block. Chin-ups on a bar mounted in the barn on his property. Elevated sit-ups, on a plank raised by cinder blocks on one side.

She'd never been to his home, but as part of their initial interview together, she'd wanted to know what he did to stay in shape. Those measures, plus long hot days working in garages or riding motorcycles, gave him the energy and strength to serve several Mistresses in one night and exorcise his demons.

She and every woman who'd enjoyed his body needed to send those demons flowers and chocolate, to thank them.

She expected he'd returned to those workouts as soon as he was medically cleared to resume them—probably even before then. Pushing himself to sweat-coated exhaustion would help with the suffocating feeling of a silence he couldn't break.

She pressed up against him, sliding one hand around the front to cup his testicles. She administered a firm squeeze there before stroking his cock, giving it a proprietary pull. Already semi-erect from standing mostly naked before her regard, he went full mast under her touch. She looked up at him to see if he'd received the message her touch conveyed. He had.

"I got it, Mistress," he said. "Yours."

When they continued toward their destination, they discussed what he would be doing. As she'd expected, he wasn't entirely comfortable with his artist being a male, but she reminded him. "You're a canvas only. His touch will be intimate, but only for the art. It's all right if you do get aroused, though. That's expected."

Expected, hoped for, anticipated...

His wry look said he picked up on what likely represented not just her own wishes, but those of the patrons who would be watching.

"What do you know about him?" Tiger asked.

She'd shown him the program that indicated Evan was indeed one of the most prominent names here tonight, an artist who was accomplished in so many mediums—photography, canvas, metal, clay, et cetera—he was reviewed as "one of the most diverse artists of our age." So she knew Tiger wasn't asking about his professional credentials.

She typed, "He's a Dominant, part of a committed threesome. You've met Alanna. The other is a big Scotsman. He's also a Dominant, though I think he switches for Evan. They share Alanna. Who is so beautiful she makes me consider changing my sub gender preference."

"If you want to test that out, I'm happy to watch."

She rolled her eyes at him, fingers busy again on her phone. "Dale spoke to every artist before they were invited, to be sure they under-stand consent and respect. If anyone forgets, the DMs are here, and they know your safeword. If you forget it, you have your fall back."

"'Get your hands off me, motherfucker, before I feed you your dick?'"

She grinned, typed. "That's the one. What did the coordinator tell you to do?"

"I have a list of poses. I stand on the platform and every fifteen minutes, I shift into another position, to challenge the artist and keep it interesting for the audience. I don't speak or move except for that. When the artist is done...I wait for you to tell me I'm done."

He looked at her. "The others were told the artist would let them know when they were done."

"Yes. They're not here tonight with a Domme. You are. Do you understand?"

He held her gaze. "Yes, Mistress. I do."

She stopped to type the next part, because she wanted to empha-size its importance. He touched her back, a gesture that told her he liked it when she adjusted so she was leaning against him and he could gaze at the screen as she typed.

"Follow the artist's direction. For all intents, you *are* a statue. Still. Peaceful. Watching the world, nothing else required. Allow the guests to gaze upon you, appreciate your beauty, your stillness. Your submis-sion to the process and what you've been told to do."

He touched her face, drawing it up to his. He wanted to see her expression, something most deaf people needed, but she suspected he had other reasons. "That's your command, Mistress?"

"It is." She decided to tack on some additional thoughts, to play with his imagination. *Tap, tap, tap.* "If we were doing this entirely my way, I would use a cock teaser on you, watch you fight the orgasm as you were commanded to stay still. I'd turn it on at random times, never enough to let you come, but to keep you hard, aching. Twitching."

He would show a fierce concentration during such times, on the cusp of a plea that would never pass his lips, but the need he showed was something she savored.

Thinking of it, she let her lips curve before she typed some more. "Your impressive cock will give all the women here fantasies to take home with them. Maybe we'll have our own private art session later. I like painting."

An intrigued light kindled in his gaze. However, it was time to get where they were going. Shifting to his side, she gripped his elbow, letting him escort her the rest of the way to Evan.

As they approached, he lifted his head. The sharp gray eyes brushed over Skye to Tiger and held, an artist considering the possibilities.

She turned to Tiger. She studied him a long moment, while Evan waited quietly for her evaluation. She nodded. Tiger was good. That tension was still there, but she'd planted the right seeds. She touched his arm, but then made herself turn away and leave them without looking back.

She was a nurturing person, but not to excess. If a sub wanted a mother, he had the wrong Mistress. Anyone under her care received what he needed and deserved, delivered in a no-nonsense way with the right hint of kindness, proof that she cared without going overboard with it. It was her responsibility as a Domme, making sure she left him in as good or better shape than before a session started.

Which was why it bemused her, that she was struggling with a feeling akin to a parent dropping their child at school for the first time. Registering the absurdity of it, she quashed the feeling and went about her business.

Fortunately, since it was getting close to time for the paid guests to arrive, the pace to finish every detail and issue last minute instructions accelerated. Everyone, including herself, got pretty busy. By the time the first car pulled in—a black Lamborghini—Skye had done all of her last checks.

She'd also changed clothes, into a sexier, artsier version of her client-meeting work wear. Black slacks and a sheer blouse printed with the melded rose and grey hues of a Monet painting, a black lace bra beneath. She wore a ceramic rose pendant flanked by crystal stones, and matching earrings that offered a muted glitter as she moved.

While riding herd on the audiovisuals, she made time to greet those patrons who were existing or potential clients for TRA. Though Ros didn't expect her to handle the schmoozing to the extent she herself did at such functions, she would bitch at Skye if she didn't at least say a polite hello.

Beyond that, she kept herself removed from the flow, and not just because of the tech side of her job. She wasn't going to let anything distract her from keeping an eye on Tiger. Or deny herself the pleasure.

She made sure her route took her within view of him every twenty minutes. The pose change wasn't just to increase the challenge to the artist, but also to keep the subject from feeling any muscle strain. His current position was what Skye thought of as the Olympic discus throw, one leg slightly bent, upper body canted, one arm lower, torso twisted, head tipped to look toward the sky.

She thought of her hint about the cock teaser and ways she could employ it. Keeping him in this exact pose, she'd watch his thighs tremble, that toy vibrating under the head of his cock, making him spurt pre-cum. His smoke-roughened voice would get even more hoarse as he uttered one word, like a blessing and a curse.

Mistress...

No personal pictures were allowed, but the two professional photographers Athena had hired were circling. A husband and wife team, their photos would be compiled into a commemorative book for the attendees, including short interviews with the artists about why they'd chosen to decorate their living canvases as they had.

Athena had wanted a male and female perspective in the pictures, and Skye agreed with the decision. She'd volunteered to do the layout for the book after the event, and looked forward to seeing what they'd give her to work with.

Each time she checked on Tiger, she forced herself to gauge his state of mind with a quick glance. Like the patrons gathered around or seated on chairs, raptly viewing the scene, it would be too easy to be drawn into what Evan was doing. His hands moving over Tiger's body, sculpting whatever he was placing there. She did note the tools changed—sometimes a brush or flat stick, sometimes his fingers.

Even with Tiger on the platform, his eyes sometimes on the horizon so she was below his line of sight, she knew when he'd caught a glimpse of her. His nostrils would flare, his lips press together. That, and the minute easing of his shoulders, told her he was aware of her presence. And that he was okay.

Evan had kept his word, though that humming energy around him said he was aware his subject was a living, breathing submissive, ordered to stay motionless under his touch and command. Such a thing would always engage the deeper levels of a Dom's makeup, but he treated Tiger purely as a canvas. She saw no flags that would make Tiger uncomfortable, cross the set boundaries.

"Dinna fash yourself, Mistress," a deep voice came from her left. "When he's creating, Apollo himself could show up with a gallon jar of lube, ready to bend over and take Evan's pole to the hilt, and it wouldn't matter. He'd just get this impatient little wrinkle in his brow and brush that inconsiderate god out of the way of his art."

Niall gestured toward the platform where Tiger stood. His current pose had his back arched, his arms up and bent, biceps bunched as his overlapped fists rested just over his eyes. It was as if he were offering an homage to the sun on a horizon. Feet braced, thighs and ass tight. Under the shadow of his fists, his dark blue eyes were like the back sides of stars.

"But I'll also tell ye, he's fully aware of every shift of your man there, any tension in his head or body. He's having a care for him. Since you seem a good Mistress, I expect you've already noted most of that."

"Sounds like the voice of experience," she typed. She used Angelina Jolie's voice. The sensual purr seemed to fit the mood gripping the garden. And herself.

"Oh, aye and nay. We've been together long enough Evan knows how far he can abuse me before I have to knock his head into a wall. It's like the saying goes. Family longs for the consideration we'll give total strangers."

He sent her a grin, though, showing his deep fondness for the artist. His love. "Ye also have your backup team." He tilted his head toward a bench screened by trees, where Alanna sat. Her knees were drawn up, bare feet curved over the edge, but her eyes were fixed on Tiger. "If anything is amiss our Master doesnae catch because he's too far gone in his heid, she'll see it."

"I've never seen a woman so beautiful, and with such focus," Skye typed.

"It was what she was trained for. But what keeps it straight as an arrow is her desire to serve us. She's pure love and loyalty, and nae but a stump could miss it. The depths of that loyalty are beyond what even God imagined possible when He was creating her." Niall sent

Skye a faintly amused look. "And when you can surpass God's expectations, become more than what He created, well, that's quite something, aye?"

That piercing vividness in Evan's gaze seemed to exist in Niall's tawny gold eyes as well. "Evan says she's the living, breathing definition of what every artist tries to achieve. I dinna know exactly what he means, but it feels right."

Alanna's gaze shifted to Niall as if she'd heard him. Her eyes filled with joy as they rested on the Scot. Then she was looking at Tiger again.

Niall sighed. "Now I expect one of us will have to beat her, to keep her from being too full of herself."

"I just figured I'd beat *you*, for causing the problem."

Despite Niall speaking in a low voice, Evan had heard their conversation. Though there was no prohibition on talking, Skye noted most patrons, like them, were keeping their voices down, to respect the artist's concentration. For the most part, the haunting music from the rotunda held the upper hand. It drifted through the garden like night-flying butterflies, mixing with frog song.

Evan hadn't looked away from his work as he spoke. Skye was trying not to look too closely at the details, because she wanted the full effect when it was done. However, she and Niall stood near enough to Evan, off to his left side, that she followed Evan's hand, moving over Tiger's back as he sculpted texture into a thick gold metallic paint.

"Ye can try, ye skinny *bod ceann*," Niall responded. He winked at Skye, translating in a quieter voice. "Dickhead."

Skye took a last quick look at her charge. It seemed Tiger had found his center, a floating calm, by following her direction. Adhering to the simple list of expectations. A slight tilt to his mouth suggested he'd once again noted her presence, and that pleased her.

Smiling, Skye moved onward. Multiple screens were scattered throughout the gardens. Cameras she'd placed near the artists fed into those screens, so patrons strolling from station to station could see what was happening at more remote ones.

She returned to the audiovisual pit she'd set up near the music rotunda. While she adjusted a picture resolution problem she'd noted on Screen 7, and a faint static issue on the speakers projecting the music into the south side of the gardens, Nakul showed her clips of the drone footage.

"It's coming in great," he said. He was an employee of the audiovisual supplier for the event, and had done the delivery and install for the evening's equipment rentals. Though Skye had the lead on coordinating all the audiovisuals, at her recommendation, Athena had retained him for the evening to support her. With this much tech in play, it was better to have one person at the controls and one person circling, identifying troubleshooting needs.

"I'm yours to command, miss," he'd told her at the beginning of the night. Her favorite words from any man. Though Nakul seemed oblivious to their significance, Athena had coughed to cover her laugh as she introduced them.

Nakul was an older man who didn't get easily rattled by tech glitches, which likely made him a popular choice for high-profile events like this.

The clip he was showing her now was from the back gardens, where one of the junk car artists was airbrushing a chariot pulled by golden white horses onto the metal. Their heads were tossed back in wild abandon, teeth bared. They ran against a sunlit sky, the rays shooting up around the broken-out windows. On the roof was the receding night, a moon among a shower of shooting stars.

Nakul nodded to the screen for the second drone. The female artist with the Goth look had painted her sub's upper torso a slick blue. Crimson maple leaves were painted over her breasts, the silver veins of the leaves running from her nipples. More leaves seemed to be falling down her torso, pooling together over her mound and hip bones. Her face was the same blue, eyes highlighted with white and silver paint.

Because a full body art job could take far more than four hours, the artists were doing partial coverings. Even so, what they had managed to do in just a couple of hours was impressive.

As the drone moved on, it hovered over a bearded artist wearing a utility kilt and a green silk turban. He'd painted a waterfall from the neck to the thighs of his canvas's body, the water curling and rushing over protrusions of rock inspired by the male's musculature and limbs.

Nakul flipped her to footage from the station that had been left cloaked by night, except for downward-facing ground lights that brought the audience safely along the foot path, and the lighting needed to make the neon paints she was using glow.

This artist looked like a large-breasted and wide-hipped priestess, in a flowing black smock she'd donned over a crinkled ankle-length skirt and tie-dyed cotton shirt. With the paints, she'd turned her model's face and shoulders into that of a sci-fi creature, possibly inspired by the ocean creatures who lived at depths where the only light came from the glow of their own bodies.

The model and artist had given permission for the patrons to get hands-on with the canvas. The audience dipped their fingers in the glowing color of their choice and added random swirls and streaks to the skin below the artist's creation. She came in behind them and enhanced those marks, connecting them into a larger design.

Skye approvingly noted the DM assigned to that area was staying close, to ensure no one took that too far. And that the female sub was doing okay with it.

"Everyone seems enchanted," Athena said at her elbow.

The hostess had donned a glittery gown that showed off her excellent legs and toned curves. A swimmer who used her pool for her workouts, Athena's forty-something physique would have been envied by a woman of any age. A Navy SEAL trident pendant graced her cleavage.

Earlier in the evening, when Athena leaned over to light a candle on one of the tables, the trident had dangled forward and turned, revealing the engraving on the back. Since Skye was helping her, shielding the candle from the breeze, she'd been close enough to see the words. *Property of Dale Rousseau.*

"You two are doing an excellent job," Athena told her. Nakul gave her a little salute before returning his attention to the controls and screens.

"Is everything acceptable to you, with respect to Tiger?" Athena asked. At Skye's nod, she smiled. "I'm glad Evan drew his name. I figured they'd do well together. If I don't get a chance to tell him myself, let Tiger know we all hope he opens his garage again soon. Dale says he and his people do outstanding work."

"Where is Dale tonight?" Skye typed, sticking with Angelina's voice.

"A demo in Baton Rouge. He hated to miss this, but he'll enjoy the book you and the photographers are putting together. Plus the drone footage DVD."

Athena glanced toward the screens. "Evan told you he and Niall won't show up on any of this, right? I assume they're wearing one of those devices bank robbers use that scrub them from photographic imagery." She chuckled. "Though I prefer to think they're vampires. They're certainly mesmerizing enough."

Skye liked the idea herself. Even though it was sort of unsettlingly accurate.

Athena continued, "I expect he has his temperamental eccentric artist reasons for not wanting to be included in any of the visuals, but I'm glad he had a solution that keeps you from being stuck with the work of editing him and Niall out. Are you still okay with getting the initial layout ready by next month?"

Work was busy, but Skye had already planned to spend her evenings with it, so she nodded. Then she typed, "Is everything else going well tonight?"

"Yes." A brief frown crossed Athena's face. "One of our visiting Doms misinterpreted the environment earlier in the evening. He decided to pat Alanna on the ass and wrap his hand in all that long hair."

"Where did Niall put the body?" Skye typed.

The laugh lines around Athena's green eyes crinkled. She sent Skye a conspiratorial wink that reminded her of the Mistress side Athena had once wielded so capably. "You can't tell when Evan is absorbed in his art, but he's just as protective toward both Alanna *and* Niall.

"Alanna handled it, though, very smoothly. I was nearby when it happened. He asked her who she belonged to. Before I could barely blink, she'd put his hand away from her and said, 'Not to you.'

"I think she must have pinched a pressure point, because he was rubbing his hand. She politely asked if she could get him something from the bar. To his credit, he did apologize to her. He came to me afterward to do the same."

Which was good, because if the Dom hadn't self-corrected, Athena would have been on it herself. Athena didn't suffer fools, or being taken advantage of. Skye pitied whoever tried, since beyond Athena's own formidable will, she had the forcible backup of a loving and protective Master.

One of the caterers was approaching to corral Athena for a question. She touched Skye's shoulder, a fond gesture. "I'll go see what that's about. Thank you again, both you and Nakul. I admit I was concerned about technology catastrophes. They're always the rule for events like this. You've stayed on top of it and made sure everything worked beautifully."

She met Skye's gaze. "I know you told me you weren't certain if you would stay the night, but remember, that blue and white guest house on the northwest side of the gardens is reserved for you. It's a peaceful and very private place."

Athena glanced toward the spot where they could see Tiger on his platform, albeit at a distance where the garden foliage obscured most details. Mischief wreathed Athena's gaze, another echo of the Mistress who recognized what pleasures Skye might have at her fingertips. "You should find everything there you need to remove the paint. Once you take ample time to enjoy your own private viewing."

She winked and moved toward the server.

CHAPTER SIX

hen Evan set aside his paints at eleven-forty-two, Skye turned things over to Nakul and told him to find her if he had a problem.

Though a sizeable crowd of patrons occupied the prime viewing area, Evan beckoned to bring her around the velvet rope barrier between his work and his audience.

When he offered her the stool he'd vacated, she slid onto it, but her attention was already on Tiger. She finally gave herself permission to take in every detail.

The metallic gold paint Evan had used was built up like scaled armor over Tiger's non-tattooed shoulder. It also covered that side of his chest, down to his abdomen. He'd had Tiger remove the shorts. From the abdomen down, Evan had thinned the covering, creating a gleaming second skin in a swirl of orange, black and ivory. A tiger's colors, covering Tiger's hips and pelvis, his upper thighs. His cock was coated in black.

"I waited on you to set the final touch." Evan extended a handful of gold jewelry. His gray eyes looked lit by lightning. "If his Mistress thinks her tiger needs it."

It was a spiral cock ring, the ends capped with gold balls. A triangle of chain mail was threaded on the base ring with a set of spaced beads that would keep the mail from bunching as the wearer moved. The mail would drape behind the cock and in front of the

74

balls, forming a tantalizing frame for his organ and a teasing curtain for what lay behind it.

She made the sign for *beautiful*, fairly easy to interpret, and pointed to Evan. *Yours?*

"I've used ones like it. This one is a gift for you." He dipped his head to Skye. "For loaning your sub to me. You can have him move however you like. The lower areas have dried. However, the scale paint is only surface set, so if you press your fingers into it, you'll get wet."

A flicker of a smile suggested that could offer its own pleasures. Evan turned away, circling around in front of the velvet rope to engage his audience and answer questions. It left her a semblance of privacy with her "artwork."

Tiger's current pose was a shallow lunge, head and upper torso turned as if he'd just finished a sword strike. He was staring toward the horizon, looking away from where she'd stood with Evan when he'd handed her the cock ring. He might not be aware of her presence.

She slid off the stool to sit on the edge of the platform. When she touched his ankle, wrapping her fingers over his calf, she tapped him once. In their sessions, depending on what they were doing, it meant hold his position, but turn his attention to her.

His chin moved down slowly. His gaze passed over the attentive audience, but quickly flicked down to find her, shut out his awareness of them.

She lifted the cock ring, her brow raised. She let him see she wanted to put it on him, was looking forward to handling him in front of the crowd. Showing them who had the right to touch him like this. And who didn't.

Whether or not he saw all that in her face, he gave her a slight nod. His dark blue eyes remained fixed upon her. But his cock, at semi-rest, began to harden and rise.

Evan had left a tube of lubricant sitting discreetly on the corner of the platform. She oiled up the coils, appreciating the way it made them gleam. As he'd indicated, the black paint over Tiger's cock wasn't affected by her sliding the spiral over his cockhead and working it down on the thickening member. She let her fingers play over him, noting the oil made the black glisten even more.

She made sure the ball capping the higher end of the coils pressed against that sensitive V-spot underneath the frenulum. She adjusted the triangle of chain mail, smoothing it over his testicles. She liked the way it looked, a gleaming backdrop to his erection.

She heard the female murmurs of appreciation for the size of his response as she checked the placement of the spirals, ensuring no flesh was being pinched. When she was done, she sat back and did what the audience was doing. Appreciated. With the sole privilege of being able to do it far more closely.

If she hadn't been cognizant of their duty to the patrons, she would have commanded him to turn and face her, ignore anyone else. But after the stroke of midnight, the event would be done, and she could indulge herself.

She caught Evan's eye so she could convey her deep pleasure at his efforts. He nodded, but directed her attention to a folded slip of paper on the edge of the dais. It was instructions on removing the paint; a simple application of water, using a gentle soap if needed.

As Evan moved back around the velvet rope, Niall and Alanna arrived to join him there. Tiger's attention remained on Skye, as if his eyes had been painted to forever look in her direction.

"Master, he's amazing," Alanna said quietly. "All he needs is a sword."

Niall's pointed glance said Tiger was already well equipped in that department. It had Skye hiding a smile. Catching Niall's amusement, Alanna colored. She chuckled, but sent Niall a censorious look. "The art was so beautiful, I wasn't even thinking of that."

"I'm no' so much of an art fan," he said.

"Truer words." Evan reached out to tug Niall's hair. When Niall fended him off, Evan grasped the front of the Scot's T-shirt and brought Niall close enough to nip sharply at his mouth. His other hand slid partway under the kilt, baring an expanse of muscular thigh.

Alanna's attention immediately shifted to the two men. Niall's tawny eyes went molten gold. "So it's like that, is it?" the Scot murmured. He tilted a considering glance toward Tiger.

Since Evan preferred men as much as women, Skye supposed it would have been arousing, having his hands on a body like Tiger's for the past several hours. Niall looked ready to handle that, with an edge of sexual violence that any Mistress would pay good money to watch. The Scot gripped Alanna's abundant hair, bringing her up to his mouth while Evan's hand closed over her hip. The artist erased the distance between them so he had his hands on both of them.

When he glanced toward Skye, his irises had become so silver she thought it had to be a trick of the light. "Enjoy," he said, and then he lifted a hand to the people still assembled. "Good night."

The music in the rotunda paused. Several musicians began striking silver triangles, the measured notes echoed by a trilling answer on the flutes, like a piercing bird call over mist-covered waters.

One, two, three...

Evan, Niall and Alanna slipped away on one of the garden paths. Skye was sure Evan was taking them somewhere he could sate himself.

Sounded like an excellent idea.

She rested her hand on Tiger's leg again. He hadn't moved. He'd remembered that he wasn't done until his Mistress said he was.

Her gaze coursed over his turgid cock, pulsing inside that golden spiral, and how the torchlight made the chainmail glitter. She wanted to run her hands under it, grip his testicles, play with the contrasts between velvety flesh and metal heated by it.

But she kept her hand on his knee and continued to gaze up at him. Still and motionless, as if they had both become statues.

When the clock finished, it meant he was all hers again.

She held up her phone. "You're done. You did well. Athena offered a guest house for the night. Stay with me."

He looked at the screen, and at her. Then her silent, golden-plated warrior gave her a nod.

~

The guest house had a wading pool and patio framed by a cottage garden, a lattice wall screening the area from the main house without blocking the view of the marsh and inlet. The water rippled silver in the moonlight.

There was also a hose with a hot water option coiled up near the wading pool, so Skye had Tiger stand on the patio near it, his feet braced and hands laced behind his head. She moved around him, looking at Evan's work from all angles. The orange, black and ivory bold strokes, part stripes and part swirls, covered his buttocks and the backs of his thighs.

He had a second tattoo in the center of his back, an infinity symbol made of razor wire. Crimson and black blood dripped from it. He'd told her he'd gotten it when he was a teenager, and it had the fading color and less sharp edges that confirmed it had been acquired as a rite of passage. Unlike the vibrant details of the one on his shoulder.

She trailed her fingers over the borders between tattooed, painted and unpainted flesh. Caressing his cock beneath the spiral ring, she dragged a nail across his slit, then closed the chain mail over his testicles, tightening her grip to provide some discomfort. Which she soothed when she let it go and put her fingers beneath it to stroke his ball sac.

She gazed at the metallic gold scales on the one side of his upper body, but she didn't disturb the hardened surface. Not yet.

"Stay here," she typed. "I'm going to change clothes. No talking or moving until I command it."

His expression was hungry and full of need. Needing her. She liked him on that edge, and showed it, trailing her fingertip over his navel, then his hip bone. Moving closer, she gazed up into his face. "Wait. You wait for me." She mouthed the words slowly, enunciating. Gestured to him, to herself.

"Always, Mistress."

Satisfied, she stepped back and went into the cottage. Though she hadn't been sure she'd stay overnight, she'd been prepared, and had retrieved her bag from her car, leaving it in the bedroom when they arrived at the cottage.

The bed was king-sized, plenty of room to share it with a big man. If she was feeling like sharing the space. A Mistress's prerogative.

Athena encouraged visitors to bring their swimsuits. With Tiger's presence in mind, Skye had given thought to her choice. As she put it on, her body tightened, anticipating his reaction. A white string bikini, which could be adjusted to cover as much or as little as she preferred. The thin silken top shaped her nipples.

She tied a mid-thigh wrap over the suit, hiding it from view. On the way back to Tiger, she stopped at the kitchen to see what options the pantry and refrigerator offered. She found ample snacks and beverages, including a Mexican sauce and salsa sampler with fresh chips. Athena thought of everything.

She was hungry for other things right now, but that salsa was going to come in handy. When she emerged from the cottage, she was approaching him from behind, though she made sure the lighting from the house cast her shadow, alerting him to her return. The slight shift of his shoulders told her he'd noticed. She trailed her hand over the infinity symbol on his back, then moved to his tattooed shoulder, pausing on that scar. He tensed when she touched it. Not from pain, but from memory, so she didn't linger.

She'd told him not to move, and he'd obeyed. He didn't turn his head toward her. But the muscles under her hand were vibrating with energy.

She took her time, sliding her body against his buttocks, her upper thigh teasing his. They'd walked to the cottage with him like this, naked. She'd tucked his shorts in the overnight bag he carried for her. When patrons reluctantly taking their leave saw them, they had devoured him with their gazes, lingering on his cock in those snug spirals, the glitter of the chain mail rippling over his balls. The graceful movements of his body, the flex of his buttocks. She'd laid her hand on his elbow, guiding him. Staying in between him and them. Telegraphing ownership.

Now they were alone. She didn't have to think of anyone else but him, and her own desires. Turning away from him, she untied and dropped the wrap and her phone on a nearby chair. She sauntered to the wading pool, pausing to dip her toe in, her arms lifting to her sides to balance herself on one foot. The concrete apron wasn't wide, so she wasn't surprised to find her outstretched hand clasped in his as her statue came to life, reaching out to steady her.

When he broke a rule, it was almost always for her benefit. To care for her.

The water's temperature was comfortable. She followed the steps into the pool, deep enough at this end to reach her breasts, and dropped below the surface, immersing herself. When she came back up, she pushed her hair back, feeling the water wash over her body. As she turned around, she gestured to her eyes, then pointed up. She wanted his eyes on the heavens.

To avoid temptation, until temptation commanded him to do otherwise.

She could see the effort it took him to obey, especially as she came back up the stairs. She came close enough to touch his chin, then pointed to his eyes. *You can look at me.* As his eyes lowered, she stepped back.

His breath sucked in. His gaze greedily followed the beads of water that rolled along her arms, the translucent fabric that showed the shape and color of her nipples, the folds of her sex, the hint of trimmed hair at her pussy.

She moved back another step. Her touch had told him he could look at her, but she hadn't yet given him permission to speak. His throat worked, his eyes sharpening. She pointedly looked behind her, so he knew she was aware of where the pool edge was.

Retrieving her phone from where she'd left it, she took a photo. She wanted to capture that hunger in his eyes, intensified by their proximity and lack of any distractions to dilute it. Then she took shots from different angles. God, that fine ass, his profile, the way he lasered in on her in his peripheral vision.

When she at last set the phone down on a patio table, she went back into the pool. Resting her back against the side, she sipped from the bottle of water she'd retrieved from the kitchen and just looked at him. Looked and looked.

She had him do a quarter turn. Show his flank side. The jut of his painted and bound cock, high over his thighs, the gold of the rings glittering. Then another turn to display his wide back, the tiger stripes and swirls over his ass and upper thighs again. He didn't like not being able to see her, the tension easing only when he turned her way again.

"I'm pleased with you. Proud of you." She did it in ASL, American Sign Language. He wouldn't understand, but she projected it in her expression, let him draw his own conclusions. There was no frustration to it right now. Everything was like flowing water that would carry them to understanding, at its own pace and time. It would catch up as needed.

She set the bottled water aside and came out again. Her skin might chill from the evening breeze off the marsh, but the look in his eyes created a furnace within her. His craving was building into a savage need. That was where she wanted him. Not thinking about his inability to hear, the damage to his garage, or the fate of his employees. And especially not his sister-in-law's death.

She wanted him wanting her so badly he couldn't think of anything but when she'd let him have her.

If she'd let him have her.

Her care of his state of mind was the only thing that could keep up with her unexpectedly strong need to be wanted that way. By him.

The black paint at the tip of his cock glistened. The spirals were biting into the swelling thickness of his length.

She retrieved her phone, dipped her head and typed. Came to him and lifted the screen to show him what she'd written. "I'm going to remove your armor. Will you trust me to do that?"

A slow nod, those dark blue eyes holding more desires than a lifetime could plumb. The thought made her tremble. She set the phone aside, leaving her words lingering in the air between them. The rest of their communication, the things she had to say to him, would be nonverbal.

She at last put her hand on the metallic scales covering his chest and arm. She pressed through the outer layer of texturized paint to the soft wet layer Evan had warned her was just beneath. Sliding her fingers through it, she spread the gold across the base of his throat and his collar bones, to his tattooed shoulder.

Though he was forbidden to touch her until she gave permission, she suspected he would have restrained himself anyway, not wanting to get paint on her suit. He was considerate that way, though she found herself mildly interested in what kind of pattern him pressing against her would leave on the fabric. She loved the feel of his body, the hard bone and muscle beneath the slickness of the gold.

She painted the bare side of his rib cage, remembering the model who had been used for finger painting earlier. Had it teased the patrons who'd never been in the role of a top, having the ability to draw upon a person who was holding still for their pleasure and exploration?

She could highly recommend it.

Picking up the hose, she noted the sprayer's different pressure options and started with the lowest setting. She rinsed her hand before removing the cock ring and chain mail carefully, setting them aside. She could feel his attention, how his head dipped above hers as she handled him. His thighs quivered, muscles flexing in reaction and self-restraint.

She began to rinse him, starting at the top and working her way down. As she rubbed the paint away with her hand, she removed Evan's creation to reveal the man beneath. Gold ran down over the stripes, flecked the black on his cock like gold dust against dark, glistening stone. Black and gold. The Sam Sparro song was in her head, with its note of sensual anticipation as she played with his nipples, flicking them with her short nails. His lips parted, eyes firing further.

She moved to hips, upper thighs. She checked to ensure the coils hadn't left his skin irritated, but she wanted him to verify it. Resting her hand on his upper thigh, she drew a pointed stroke with her thumb along his cock and lifted a questioning brow to him.

"No, Mistress. It didn't hurt." A tug of his lips. "Not in the wrong way."

Front, back, cock, balls, ass, thighs, another pass over the chest. Her hands were tingling, as was the rest of her, as she drew it out for both of them. When all the paint was gone, she moved in front of him again. Her lips curved and she picked up the cock ring once more, removing the chain mail so she was holding just the gold spiral with its beaded ends.

His breath caught on a partial oath as she lubed it up by putting it in her mouth, letting her saliva get it slick. Then she slid it back on him and closed her hand over it. Caressed, stroked, until he was twitching with the fight not to come.

His breath came out in a harsh rush. "Fuck...Mistress..."

She stopped. Waited until he regained control. She wasn't done yet, but she decided he'd earned a reward. She made an "one" gesture, and touched her slightly pursed lips.

One kiss.

Five fingers and a touch to her mouth, followed by an outward flowing gesture.

Five words.

She'd let him say five words.

He did the kiss first. Leaning down and in, he put his mouth to hers. At the contact, he shuddered, and she swayed into him, her hand going to his biceps.

He broke a rule, hands moving to her hips to hold her, but the respect of the touch honored her command, conveying consciousness of intent.

Yet the burning in his gaze gave her something far less planned. During the painting, Tiger had entered a subspace of sorts, immersed in the experience. He was fully present now, but the aftermath washed over them, so that when he spoke, she agreed with the five words he uttered.

"Words can't cover it, Mistress."

Because emotions flourished in silence.

She eased back to move behind him. Put a hand on his back, a hint of what was coming, before she raised the sprayer's pressure setting. Not to the highest one, but enough to have his back flexing at the sting, and then his body jerking as she parted his buttocks and let the spray tease the sensitive rim in short passes, circular patterns. He struggled to stay still, and when his lips were parted and fists clenched from the effort, his breath was a string of those harsh gasps. He was showing an impressive ability to control himself for her, even while obviously holding to the edge with bloody fingernails.

She shut the water off. He'd earned that kiss. And a lot more. But she was in a mood to draw that payoff way out. Let him prove to himself how much further he'd go for her.

She dropped a folded towel on the concrete and tugged at his arm, a signal to go to his knees. Once there, she guided him forward, onto his hands and knees. Pressing her toes against the back of his thigh, she commanded him to spread his knees, out to the edge of the cushion the towel provided. A touch to his chin brought his head up, eyes straight ahead. She stood before him, stroking his hair, well aware his mouth was inches from her pussy, close enough to have him salivating.

He didn't get that yet. When she moved, trailing her hand along his back, she enjoyed the tension in his buttocks, noting the access his spread legs gave her to his impressive testicles. The slight quiver in his thighs stilled as she retrieved the hose. Turning it up to full power, she tested it on her thigh. The results gave her a satisfying sting of anticipation.

She started between his shoulders and moved over his neck, down his back and sides, watching the jets hammer the rippling muscle. Then she moved over his hips, his taut ass, finally targeting the base of his testicles.

He jerked under the spray's sting, but his fingers dug into the concrete, holding. When a sub accepted the discomfort, the pain, the right things became even more arousing. Watching him work toward that goal, because he knew it would bring her pleasure, took her for the same ride.

She angled the spray to pummel his rim between his buttocks. As she did, she gripped his wet testicles in her other hand, exerting pressure to make him lift his gorgeous ass higher. He groaned at the increase in sensation, his cock so hard and tight it hung heavy under his abdomen. The spiral cock ring glittered with water droplets.

Silence wasn't a cage. It was a new universe to explore, and he wasn't alone there. Enjoying a sub she could take deeper into that knowledge than most incited a surge of raw pleasure she hadn't experienced before.

A Mistress could find Domspace, especially when a connection with a submissive brought moments every bit as satisfying as a physical orgasm, a transcendent state where everything seemed possible.

"Mistress." He was shuddering, his face working. He was almost past the point of control. When she'd released his testicles and turned the spray on them, she'd put a hand on the small of his back. She'd kept her touch on him whenever she was out of his line of sight, a reminder she was there.

After his utterance, she tapped it out against his shoulder. A five-count beat. One Mississippi, two Mississippi. Sometimes she'd let him know how high she was going to count by mouthing the number in his view. This time she didn't. She heard him strangle out a half chuckle, a desperate groan.

When she stopped at twelve, he was rigid with the effort to keep from coming. She set the sprayer aside and bade him stand before her. As his body quivered with barely leashed need, she checked his cock ornamentation to ensure he wasn't having any issues there. As he watched her with feverish eyes, she proceeded to dry him off. His erect cock brushed her upper thigh. When she had to move closer to reach his shoulders, she pushed his shaft down and straddled the head, trapping it between her thighs and the crotch of her swimsuit.

The ribbed feel of those rings against her clit was intriguing. Whereas the feel of her in her wet swimsuit against him evoked a near growl. A man wanting to throw her down, plow himself between her legs, but restraining that primal instinct under her command...it was a potent nectar to a Mistress. To her.

"I thought Cyn was the sadist," he muttered.

He'd risked breaking the order for silence. While he'd accurately gauged her mood and sense of humor, she still gave him an admonishing look, a reminder finger to her lips, though she tempered it with a wink.

Setting the towels aside, she crooked a finger at him to lead him inside. She had him stand in the kitchen as she retrieved the mat she'd discovered in the bedroom closet. She unrolled it on the kitchen floor and took the salsa sampler from the pantry. Gesturing to the mat, she indicated she wanted him on his back.

When he complied, she dropped to one knee, cupped his elbow and biceps of one arm, following those contours as she stretched the limb out to the side, palm facing upward.

Because of how his eyes burned upon her, she knew his imprisoned cock would welcome her touch and attention, even if it was only to dig those rings further into his flesh with her grip. She suspected she could compel him to come through that pain with nothing more than a command to do so. When he was broken open this thoroughly, the depth of his need to serve was limitless.

Steadying herself after that heady thought, she straightened. After she circled him, doing a leisurely perusal of his long, powerful body from all angles while she stood over him, she used one foot to nudge the inside of his right thigh, a command to spread himself wider for her. His cock twitched as he obeyed, and she let her gaze dwell there. Some gold paint flecks remained on the head, occasionally catching the light like sparks.

Kneeling by his side again, she picked up one of the salsas, a green tomatillo, and tipped the jar over his palm. She put a quarter-sized amount there, then, setting the container aside, she stretched out horizontally over his face. Bracing her palms on either side of the hand holding the salsa, she dipped down and tasted. Using her tongue, she spread the sauce out to his fingers, sucked his forefinger into her mouth, did it to the other digits as well.

Her thigh was pressing against his jaw, her breasts in the thin, wet bikini top against his forearm. She could feel his breath against her, knew he would be looking at everything he could see but not actively touch. A sidelong glance showed his stiff cock against his belly, wetting that narrow arrow of hair down toward his groin.

She shifted, straddling his chest, and dipped her fingers into another sauce, a red one, tasting it before she gave him the same opportunity, painting it on his lips, letting him nip at her fingertips as he sampled it. His gaze flickered and she raised a brow, giving him permission to offer a reaction.

"Not too spicy," he said roughly. "But the flavor's good. A lot of tomato. Glad you're not Cyn. She would have wanted the hot stuff, and put it in places I don't want to think about."

Her lips curved. Figging had always been a hard limit for him. *"A flamethrower shot up my ass isn't in my fantasy playlist, thanks."*

She moved to sample another salsa choice on his upper thigh, so close to his cock her temple brushed it. He muttered an oath as she closed her mouth over his shaft, used that pressure and her saliva to ease the cock ring off, one ring at a time bumping over the sensitive head.

As she sat back on her heels and set the toy aside, she gazed at his organ with pleasure. Not only did it remain just as erect; without the spirals to contain it, it thickened.

It wasn't just good salsa that could get a girl's saliva going.

She sampled the next salsa in the hollow of his throat. Gripping his jaw, she held his head tipped back, increasing the strain on his neck. Then she wrapped her fingers around his throat and dug her nails into it.

As expected, the hint of roughness arched him up to her, the muscles in his arms rippling. She shifted so one shin was over his thigh, pinning it down, her knee braced against his testicles as she lifted her head, licking the remains of the oil from her lips. His gaze followed the movement. He had unusual eyes, a darker blue than one usually saw in the spectrum of blue-eyed humans, and it was easy to get lost in them.

The first time she'd done so hadn't even been at the club. It had been at his garage.

She'd had a stressful day. Work-related, plus some personal shit. She'd brought the Mustang in for a repair and he'd been going over the service order with her. Since it was a formality, both of them knowing what the car needed, she'd taken a moment to enjoy the color of those eyes, the authority and competence they reflected.

"Mistress?"

He never called her Mistress at the garage. However, that day, he'd apparently said her name and she hadn't responded. With no one close to them, he'd spoken the one word, calling her back. Then he'd leaned in, spoken quietly.

"I'm yours to look at however long you want, if it helps improve your day. Looks like it's been a shitty one."

He was intuitive, often understanding so much. There was a give and take between Mistress and sub when it was done right, and he excelled at that closed circuitry.

A few days ago, she'd told him wallowing had its place in dealing with hearing loss. Coddling or rewarding too much, too soon, were the dangers for those who cared about him. But now she found herself overwhelmed with the desire to give him something for the effort it had taken him to come here, to not only leave his comfort zone, but then fucking excel at serving the Mistress who'd invited him.

As she considered what reward she might choose, she reached for the last salsa. The creamy white sauce had a touch of green from the cilantro lime seasoning. She covered his cockhead with it. Then she dipped her head and covered it with her mouth again.

There was a coolness to it, and she discovered her favorite of the sampler, forever bound to tasting it first on his rigid member. She sucked and swirled her tongue over him, absorbing the flavor, aware of the trembling of his strong thighs, the clench of the hands lying out to either side of him, the rise and fall of his chest.

He was really battling to hold onto that orgasm. She'd never made him work so hard for it. This session might become a new favorite memory, to go along with her new favorite salsa flavor. Sliding her hand up his chest, she tugged on the hair. When she ran her thumb over his nipple, flicked it with a nail, she earned a guttural oath. She moved to his navel, played there, then slid off his cock to nip at his testicles, teasing his frenulum with her tongue. An even harsher sound broke from his lips.

"Mistress...can't..."

She lifted her head, mouth upon him, and his fevered gaze dwelled upon her. As she gave him a slow, teasing lick, she also gave him a reprimanding look. A question demanding an answer.

"Not without your permission, Mistress. But fuck, you're making it hard."

Good. When she finally allowed him to come, she wanted him lightheaded and unable to walk for at least a half hour. She looked forward to that, where she could care for him without offending his male pride. Where he'd be disoriented enough that he wouldn't place such tending in unwise emotional territory.

He was on tenuous ground on a lot of things. She wouldn't make it more unstable, change the slope to roll him toward too much dependence on anyone other than himself. But it was curious, how much she wanted to cosset him, protect him, help him. She'd expected warning signs of over dependence from him; knowing her own inclinations might add to that danger was unexpected.

But identifying the flags was enough to manage it. That thought helped her choose what she wanted to give him as a reward for tonight's efforts.

She did one more deep suckle of his cock, going down on it as far as she could. Tiger had length *and* girth to him, and she had a small mouth, something a man could enjoy, that tight, slick space sucking on his organ. She came off it with a slow slide, then sat back on her heels. The position arched her back so he would see her stiff nipples jutting against the thin bikini top. The curve of one ass cheek was exposed by the fabric riding high on it.

She took a breath. She didn't want to fumble the phone. When she was done typing, she held it out so he could read it with an agitated gaze.

"If the choice was yours, how would you fuck your Mistress, Tiger? No thinking: first position that comes to mind."

That startled him. However, other than the brief hitch to digest the demand, understand what she was asking, he responded as if it had been right there, no need to think it through. He might have fantasized about plenty of positions at other times—just as she had—but in this mood, he knew exactly what he wanted.

"From behind, Mistress."

A succinct answer. When the male animal took over, choosing to toss his quarry face-first and ass-up over the nearest flat surface and drive into a wet cunt wasn't a surprise. Yet with Tiger, she had a feeling it would become more than that.

Even if it wasn't, it wouldn't be a disappointment. She wouldn't give him a gift that didn't please them both, because he wouldn't want that kind of gift. Her body was aching to have that big, impressive cock driving into her, feel all that strength dedicated to bringing them both to peak.

She stood, looking around to consider her options and the important variables. Like his height relative to hers.

She moved to the dining table, aware of his gaze upon her swinging, barely covered ass. The table was a sturdy rectangular butcher block with bench seating on either side. She moved the delicate blue vase and its arrangement of yellow flowers to the kitchen counter. Propped the long cushion from one of the benches in the narrow spot between the table and the wall, a provocative message about why the buffer would be needed.

She retrieved a condom from the bag she'd moved to the sofa. Returning to the table, she placed it there. As she eased herself to her elbows at the end, she tossed strands of hair out of her eyes to look over her shoulder at him. Reaching back, she ran her fingertips over one edge of the bikini bottoms. They were already hiked up from her movements, but the gesture was a command.

Come and get it.

~

Holy fuck. Of all the things he'd expected tonight, this hadn't been on his radar. A Mistress like Skye offering this...

Holy fuck.

Tiger remembered his thoughts about the last scene they'd had, before everything had changed. What she'd done outside and now on the kitchen floor, it had possessed that same different quality. A deeper connection somehow. And for sure way more demanding. His cock almost missed that damn coil, the restraint it had provided against his raging desire to spurt his seed.

The lead up and setting could have contributed to the "different" feeling. The painting, the environment. He'd certainly worn cock rings and had floggings as intense as the stinging water spray on his balls.

But no...all of this...it was more.

Tonight had been a serious-assed wakeup call. He'd been living like a zombie, hiding from the world. Everything here was the opposite of that. Especially how he was wanting her now.

His vigilance about his surroundings, heightened tenfold because of his inability to hear, had caused him some tension with Evan, but only at first. When Skye had walked away, Tiger had focused on her words, her last instructions. He'd let them guide him to that state a submissive could embrace. When he trusted his Domme.

He'd given her his trust without her even standing there.

He'd converted the touch of Evan's hands into a preparation for his Mistress, the art all for her, to please her. Reinforcing the thought had been easy, since she'd often passed by, letting him see her checking on him.

He'd had no doubt she would. He was fine, a grown man and sub who knew how to safeword. He could kick the shit out of most anyone who didn't respect that.

But he understood, maybe as well as she did, what a Domme required of herself. That expectation wasn't influenced by the sub's assertion. It was another part of what the relationship was. What he could count on.

Then she'd told him she wanted him to spend the night with her here, in a cottage where it was just the two of them. No distractions, no need to be vigilant, except in his attention to her demands. Which was good, because those demands just kept coming.

And what she'd just told him by bending over the table *was* a demand. Yeah, the kind a sub got when he'd been very, *very* good, but that didn't mean his Mistress would let him slack off. She expected him to impress her. He'd fuck his dick off to do that.

He rose. As he did, the world tilted and he swayed toward the fridge, his hand shooting out to brace himself. Her brow sharpened, and her muscles tightened as if she'd push herself up to come to him.

"Hell no, don't. It's just the damn ear stuff. My apologies. Just give me a second, Mistress. Please. Fucking hell."

He should blame it on most of his blood currently being below his waist, because he sure preferred that explanation. Regardless, he'd make a deal with the devil to walk a straight line to her and give her what she needed.

Fortunately, no brimstone was needed. The world steadied and he moved toward her. One step, two steps.

Since she'd brought the primal part of him to full life, he guessed she wouldn't be surprised if he ran at her like a rutting bull, aiming for a slick pink target. A savage part of him was totally on board with that.

But the memories a person wanted to keep weren't meant to be rushed. Seeing Skye Sumner bent over a kitchen table was at the top of the list of those kinds of memories.

Her luscious ass was mostly revealed by that white bikini made by the sex gods, the sides of her breasts exposed by the top. The feathers of white hair she'd tossed back from her brow had fallen forward again, partially curtaining one expressive dark eye. Her lips were moist and parted.

Shit, if she hadn't been waiting for him, and his cock wasn't a hundred percent that rutting bull, something in his heart and gut would have wanted to stay looking at her as long as the world turned.

But her elbows would get tired. She'd get a crick in her neck, looking back at him. He came forward, but before he touched her, he knelt, kissed the back of her knee. A reminder of his respect—in case he lost it a moment later and fucked her like a jackhammer.

Rising, he put his hands on her waist, let them glide down her hips, thumbs over the curve of her ass. *Goddamn.* He'd seen it in slacks, jeans, a snug skirt. Even when it hid under the more flowing clothes she often preferred, he could mark the twitch of the buttocks, call fondly to mind how they looked in tighter choices.

He slid his gaze over her bare shoulder, the way her chin brushed it as she watched him. Lingered on her lips and the bikini top fastener between her shoulder blades. He'd told her he wanted to take her from behind. But his fantasy wasn't to act like a top. It was to surprise her, give her what would be memorable for her, too.

He leaned down, hands back at her waist, and placed a kiss at her nape. When he'd first met her, her rock band hairstyle had caught his attention, the long silk on one side, short and spiky on the other. A mix of white-blond with an occasional streak of a different color. It fit her computer nerd persona pretty well.

A beautiful, sexy computer nerd.

He inhaled her scent, kissed a few inches below the nape, worked his way down her spine. Light feather kisses, soft and slow. Putting how much he cherished her offer, how much he valued it, in the contact. Everywhere he kissed and touched her, he wanted her to feel a burst of searing pleasure, like biting into a favorite food. She was definitely his top choice for a meal.

During sessions, he paid close attention to how she touched herself, as well as how she reacted when she did allow him to touch her. So he knew where she was most responsive, what kinds of contact built her toward that climactic concentration of energy.

He caressed her hips. He didn't want to take his hands from her, but he paused to rip open the package, roll the condom on. Then he had his mouth back on the valley of her spine, hands sliding to the outside of her breasts, fingers wrapping over them to caress her through the silky fabric. Christ, her nipples were swollen, needing the squeeze and flicking he gave them. Her hips jerked up, ass brushing his cock. Fucking heaven.

He untied one side of the bottoms, letting them slide down her other thigh to get them out of his way. He could have left them on and just pushed the crotch out of his path, but he didn't want anything rubbing against his dick that wasn't wholly her and her sweet pussy. The condom was bad enough, a necessary evil.

As he placed another kiss between her shoulder blades, he put his cock to her opening. As the significance hit him, he paused, his hands flexing.

He'd never been inside her.

"Thank you, Mistress," he muttered. If he had intended to drive into her the way his cock wanted, this was the moment he would ask her how long it had been, so he didn't enter too fast or hard. Aside from knowing she had a sweet car and the TRA Mistresses were her best friends, he didn't know much about her outside the club. If she was in a relationship, or casually banging a new guy every week.

Somehow, he doubted both possibilities. But the question had more significance to him than it had only a few days ago. He wasn't going to look too closely at that right now. His hands were full enough. Literally. She had beautiful breasts, enough to overflow his grip, and he had big hands.

He came into her easy, a gradual glide, where they felt every excruciating second of the entry, the friction between their two bodies.

As he pushed through that gateway, he rubbed his jaw against her back, put his mouth back on her nape. Her neck was one of her most sensitive areas, and he gave it attention as his lower body sank into pure bliss. She had a small, tight pussy, and he had to bite back a groan. His balls drew up, ready to go the second he released his mental chokehold on his cock.

Or she ordered it. As an experienced sub, the latter usually won the day for him. Tonight had been an hours-long foreplay session, but the training he'd had in holding back with multiple Mistresses, including this one, gave him the control to hold out now.

Though it was hard as fuck.

She was quivering too, her breath coming fast, eyes glazed as he gripped her hips, then went back to her breasts, using a hold on them to drive in deeper, still slow, still easy, but letting her know he was there, and going as far as that channel would let him.

She might be able to have a vaginal orgasm, but no way was he going to count on that, or go before she climaxed. Even when she commanded him to do that, she knew he disliked releasing before she did.

He squeezed her right braced hand. Then he slid his hand under it, capturing her fingers in between his. From there, he brought their linked hands in between the table and her body. A mute request that she place his hand on her cunt, with her own pressed on top of it.

She gave him that blessing, her hand tightening over his fingers as she brought him to her clit and labia. He slid over that slick, velvet flesh, treasuring the ripple that went through her. He had his chin close to her shoulder, so he saw her bite her lip. He closed the gap to do it himself, marking that lush bottom lip with his mouth.

He would have withdrawn, not wanting to compel the intimacy of a kiss, but she turned her head to let her mouth more fully fuse to his. He didn't have to be invited twice. Yet since he wanted to do a good job stroking her pussy, and that required focus, the kiss became hers. She devoured his mouth, tongue tangling with his. The vibration through her would have been a hum of noise, if she had a voice.

She was having trouble holding herself up on one arm. No surprise, since a hulking two-hundred-pound man was flush against her. He slid his other arm around her, forearm resting diagonally between her breasts, hand wrapped over her shoulder. She gripped his forearm, and he tightened that hold, showing her she didn't need the table. She had him.

Slow in, slow out. Torture devised in heaven and executed by the angels. Probably the kind that became fallen ones and offered temptation to mortals.

He didn't want to think about fallen angels, so he squashed that thought and focused only on her. The wobble of her breasts against his arm, the puffs of her breath against his jaw, the press of her ass. They all built the sweet rhythm between them.

As she pushed into his strokes, the impact became more forceful, but no faster. He knew what it was to bring a woman up slow enough she broke into a million gorgeous pieces when her climax took her. Like watching a summer rain shower from the back of his garage, the drops bouncing off the tires and scrap metal, sparkling in the air as the sun refused to completely disappear, the rain drops infused with its heat.

She made him think thoughts like that. Poetic shit. And then she climaxed, and as he'd told her, no words could cover it, how it made him feel. He missed hearing that gasping breath sound she made, but he could imagine it. She'd tucked her head down toward her shoulder, but he envisioned her lips stretching, the glazing of her beautiful eyes, and felt the rigid jerk of her body against his. As he held her tight and kept thrusting, her cunt milked him. Fucking agony and bliss.

His cock leaped at the chance to follow, and an erratic tap at his hand told him he had her permission. The table scraped the floor as his hips bucked, driving him forward and taking her even harder. He rode that churning wave, his pelvis against her ass, the two of them rolling and rippling together as he jetted into that condom, inside the wet, dark pleasure of her cunt.

The opposite end of the table beat against that bench cushion with every thrust, protecting the wall from annihilation. It gave him a visceral satisfaction to see it. As did the bite of her nails into the table surface, and the way she lifted to meet those thrusts, urging him to increase their impact.

When at last he finished, still holding tight to her, it took a while for his vision to clear. But when it did, he noted she'd lifted her head enough that he could see her face, and it looked like her world had been rocked in the right way.

Which all in all was a damn nice balm to the helplessness he'd been battling for the past month. Whether she'd planned it or not didn't matter. Skye was never coy about that shit. She never denied doing things to help her sub, or when those things had a personal benefit to her. What improved him made him a better sub for her.

He liked that forthrightness. It was something he had himself. Maybe he'd lost his grip on it, but tonight he'd found it again. Through the grip he had on her.

He increased the hold of the arm he had wrapped across her, waist to shoulder, and held her close when she leaned into his support. Her cheek lay against his knuckles as he rested his head on top of hers. He didn't ever want to pull out, but now that the desire was ebbing in that pleasurable, post-good-fuck way, she was going to get uncomfortable. Still being mashed into a wooden table by a big guy, after all.

Slowly, he withdrew. He dumped the condom in the nearby trash, then dropped to a knee. He caressed her back, her hip, as he put his mouth to her cunt. He cleaned away her climax, licking her essence off her quivering thighs. When he picked up the bikini bottoms, she shook her head as she straightened and turned. She brushed her fingers over his head, a sweet thanks.

Unhooking the back of the bikini top, she let it fall, standing before him as naked as he was to her. She was swaying, a half-smile on her face.

Hoping his head didn't go wobbly and screw this up, he rose and slid his arms behind her back and knees to pick her up. It surprised but didn't displease her. She settled her arms around his neck as he took them back outside to the pool. When he set her down at the steps, he clasped her hand, inviting her into the pool with him.

They circled one another, arms floating through the water. He sank down, letting his legs bend. Watching her drift before him recalled the mermaids they'd seen earlier, swimming in sensual dances. Her hair floated over her brow as she dove under and found him, hands sliding along his thighs, ass and back before she surfaced in front of him.

He couldn't hear anything. She couldn't speak. And yet there was no lack of communication. When she settled on the steps, he slid onto the one behind her, letting her rest against him as he stretched his arms out to either side. She tugged them off the pool's edge, linking them loosely over her waist and bent thighs. Worked for him.

He was glad he hadn't seen the mermaids skim out of their costumes and morph back into land creatures. It was nice to have the memory of them only being mermaids.

Just like sitting inside this memory. Him and Skye, not needing any words, the night stretching before them with no reason to think about anything but each other and this.

Not until tomorrow.

CHAPTER SEVEN

"*Words can't cover it, Mistress.*"

It made Skye shiver, thinking of him, his touch. And she'd been doing that a lot.

Even here at work, with multiple windows open on her three screens, a conference call in thirty minutes, plus layouts to finalize before lunch to show Cyn. Their senior account manager was meeting with RNS Travel mid-afternoon to show them the campaign TRA had developed for them.

And yet... Skye paused, her fingers hovering over the board, her eyes on the screens but not seeing them.

She'd given him that fantasy on the table, and he'd executed it, but not like a Dominant. She dwelled on the memory of featherlike kisses along her spine, her nape, conveying his care for her, as he slowly eased in. Then there was how he'd wanted her to grip his hand, bring it to her clit, still directing him, to help bring her to climax. To make sure she received satisfaction before he did.

He'd aroused her so deeply and thoroughly, bringing submissive need and alpha drive together in a pleasurable, indescribably perfect mix.

Focus, she admonished herself. She updated the marketing project details and checked her team's work. She had three people under her supervision to bring the tech and graphic aspects of Cyn and Ros's marketing concepts to life. And to execute the analytics to evaluate their performance once they went live.

When she'd joined the boutique firm, it had been small enough she'd handled all that herself. But that had changed. It had been new to her, being a manager, but Ros had taught her how not to overload herself by micromanaging. Investing the time to expand her people's skill base, communicating her expectations to them clearly, led to her trusting their work and not shouldering so much herself.

Still, she loved the creation phase, both for programming and graphic design, so she would always keep her toe in by occasionally taking beginning to end responsibility for certain projects. As the head of her department, she also reviewed final outputs before release to Ros and Cyn, and ultimately the client. The internal customer was as important as the external ones.

Primarily because Cyn would delight in giving her crap if a mistake was made. The five-woman executive team enjoyed what Abby called a "cutthroat but supportive" competitive environment. *"What else would you expect from a group of Type A overachievers?"*

Skye found one minor glitch, fixed it, then sent a heads up to Paula so she'd be aware of the quality check, to improve that on the next round.

As she did that, Skye was attuned to the hum of activity in the three-story building, a historic mansion in New Orleans' Garden District. Because her office was closest to the wide staircase, she had good reception for the chatter that floated up from the lower two floors.

She smiled a little, hearing Bastion's laughter. Though their tall and broad-shouldered office manager had his desk in the first-floor foyer, his baritone carried.

It was a good environment, but the high expectations extended to all, to succeed for their clients. They came first. When the general number was called during office hours, Bastion picked it up. No voice-mail gateway for TRA.

Though not formally educated in marketing or office administration, his aptitude for it had resulted in him moving from reception to administration within months of being hired. More than once Ros had offered him an entry level account manager job in Cyn's department, but he preferred to run the office. Since he did it so well, Skye thought Ros was relieved that he felt that way. Filling his size thirteen shoes would have been a challenge.

Skye had a "Bastion" voice in her library. The first time she'd used it, Cyn had shot Ros an arch look. "She can do that with all of us, you know. She'll convince the bank she's you and siphon money into an offshore account."

Ros had shrugged. "As far as I'm concerned, she can take whatever she thinks she's worth. For her skillset, I'm probably not paying her enough."

Money wasn't why Skye worked for Thomas Rose Associates, though she was more than fairly compensated. When she was a freelance contractor, Ros had seen the work she'd done for a competitor and emailed her. The more they'd corresponded, the more Skye had liked the sound of TRA. When Ros talked about her business partners and long-time friends, CFO Abigail Rose and Veracity Morgan, and their plans for expanding the business, Skye had felt something unexpected.

The desire to be part of a group. A team.

From the time she'd graduated, she'd worked for herself, having accumulated enough contract work in college to pay for the tuition and gather a client list, most of whom didn't realize she was mute.

Early on, she'd been excited about working for a company. But after several failed interviews, she changed her mind. Time and again, the hiring manager shifted from her impressive abilities to the one thing that didn't impact her work. After the inevitable canned gushing over her accomplishments, how she'd overcome her "adversity"—as if the inability to speak impaired her brain or tech skills—she'd get the inevitable response: *We've hired someone who is a better fit for our needs.*

She'd gotten over herself a long time ago, putting hurt feelings away. People weren't automatically assholes just because they thought her muteness was too much of an inconvenience or a hindrance to their business. She knew ways to help them get past that and see her, not what made her different. Prove that it didn't impact her work or who she was. And yet...interacting with the world with one sense tied behind her back could be draining. Exhausting.

While she wished to belong somewhere it really wouldn't matter that her voice didn't work like anyone else's, wishing for what wasn't realistic added to the exhaustion. She'd embraced the freelancing.

When companies succeeded because of her efforts, she accepted their thanks, but passed on the awards banquets, or the invitation to lunch from intrigued male contacts. She celebrated her successes with a night of gaming and a trio of cupcakes from a nearby bakery. While riding the sugar high, she'd build cities or kick the asses of bosses with her online raid team.

However, when Ros offered a group interview with her team, Skye took it, even while telling herself she was setting herself up for another punch in the face. It was a video call, but she blocked the picture and used her "normal" voice for the audio, the Southern female she'd compiled from several favorite accents and voice types. The modulator she'd designed, with settings to project specific emotional states, had a patent pending. It could pass as a "real" voice.

They didn't block their video, so she could see Ros, Vera and Abby in their sunny board room, lit up by a bank of windows, a network of oak trees outside it. She knew they were in New Orleans' Garden District, just a hop across the river from her current Algiers neighborhood. Another plus she refused to call a good omen.

She'd expected the women to be well put together. Effective marketing people knew their appearance was part of the package they were selling. They enhanced what looks they had with the right tools. Fashionable dress, a good hair and nail salon, expertly applied makeup. With the addition of an infallibly professional and warm demeanor, they built client confidence.

The TRA women had all of that. But they had the *more* factor, too, a genuine quality, too strong to be doubted.

Rosalinda Thomas and Abigail Rose had founded the company. Ros was CEO, and there were no chinks in her armor. She had a sharp, New York City native expression, her multi-faceted blue eyes holding a vast pool of business savvy and intuitive judgment. When Skye spoke to Ros, or any of the other women, she was paying attention. Close attention.

Rosalinda was attractive, not beautiful, the physical appeal integrated with an intense charisma that conveyed confidence. If she told a client it would happen, the client would have no reason to doubt it.

She also had some humanizing tells. She liked to flip and tap a pen end to end on the table as she talked or processed. She was in close nonverbal communication with the other women, a lot of eye contact, slight shifts of the body or minute facial expressions. The other two women had faith in their CEO's leadership. And, important to Skye's assessment of working for TRA, they respected her.

When Ros rose during the meeting to replenish her coffee, her four-inch stilettos drew Skye's attention. The upper was a deep blue that matched the blouse under her tailored short black jacket. The shoes were tipped in silver at the toe. From the back, that embellishment spread out into a serpentine scroll along the sides. Her fitted skirt displayed excellent legs and a toned body. The unexpected shoe choice said Ros was vain in an indulgent, harmless way. She enjoyed being who she was, with no apologies.

Abigail was astonishingly beautiful. Sunrise gold-red hair and cat-shaped hazel eyes, coupled with a figure and complexion that celebrities would sell their soul to get. She inspired a heart-tightening poignancy Skye couldn't quite interpret, as if something about her was fragile. However, her quiet competence and command of numbers made it clear why she was TRA's CFO and co-founder of the successful boutique firm. When she engaged with Skye, she had the same natural listening skills that Ros did.

Abby's southern roots softened Ros's edges in a New Orleans setting. She moved in seamlessly on certain points that Ros would have stated more brusquely, but in the way of all good partnerships, they complemented one another's strengths. As Ros passed behind Abby's chair, Skye noted she dropped her hand on the back of it. The incidental brush of Abby's shoulder spoke of the connection they had. Family, even if not by blood.

Vera had an openness to her that could easily disarm, making a person reveal far more than they'd intended about themselves. Not a bad trait for the HR and legal arm of the business. Intelligence gleamed in translucent gray eyes. Her long black hair had been pulled back and held with combs, revealing the shaved sides beneath and the rings along the shells of her ears. Her wet, burgundy lips pursed with interest at Skye's responses, one dark brow often arching before she'd punctuate the curiosity with a pleased smile at Skye's answer.

The scoop neck of her gray silk shirt revealed a silver pentagram. The shirt was belted over cream-colored slacks. The less common religious icon said TRA respected the individuality of their staff. If she had any doubt of that, Bastion, their office manager, completely eradicated it.

The office admin had the physique of an NFL quarterback and a runway model's fashion sense. His dark locs went to his waist and were tied back with a braided cord. The twists of silver and purple picked up the colors of his short-sleeved dress shirt and black slacks. The buckle on his belt was a Chinese dragon's head, its serpentine body winding through the first belt loop on one side.

She'd seen that when he rose to refill his tea. He gestured to Vera, apparently a fellow tea drinker, and she nodded, passing her mug to him via Abby. The mug was gray, with the purple, silver and black TRA rose and fleur-de-lis logo. When Bastion returned it to her with her preferred blend, Vera gave him a thumbs up and a sign of shivery bliss when she took a sip.

All those details formed potential stories and positive impressions in Skye's mind. Ros and Abby had samples of her marketing, graphic design, web and social platform capabilities, but it was clear the call was about establishing rapport.

They treated her with respect, as if she was already worthy of being accepted in their circle. They asked all the right questions, open to learning what they didn't know, willing to respect her skills and integrate them into their business goals.

When Ros exchanged a significant glance with the others, receiving slight nods, Skye assumed the call was being brought to an end. Instead, Ros showed her that the decision had been made on their side.

"Look, the salary we can offer is good, but you can earn more doing what you're doing. Probably already are. But since you agreed to this interview, I'm guessing there are other things you value that we can provide."

The shrewd blue eyes gazed into the camera. "I'm currently looking at a senior account manager I feel will be a good fit with us. If she comes on board, that and the person in the position I'm offering you will be the five-spoke wheel that will take TRA where Abby and I see it going. This executive team won't be about making sure you're at work on time or counting your sick days. We'll be working damn hard to take this company to the next level. As long as you're contributing to that, we'd see you as a partner."

Those feelings inside her increased. She was good on her own, strong on her own, and yes, making more than the sizeable salary Ros was putting on the table. But she liked these people. Their drive, their professionalism, and the way they bounced off each other, the bonds they displayed. She felt an inexplicable kinship with them, and they hadn't even met face to face.

She wasn't a coward. But Skye took one more second to enjoy the possibilities, then steeled herself. "I'd like a couple of days to consider the offer," she typed, the voice projecting the appropriate level of interest. "But I'd like to give you time to do the same. I haven't disclosed one issue you might feel isn't the best fit for your business."

She hated the term, but it worked.

Ros's brow rose. True to the qualities Skye already appreciated about her, the CEO didn't rush to assure her without knowing what "it" was. "All right. Lay it on us."

She ripped off the band-aid in a calm voice. "I'm speaking to you with a voice app. I routinely use it to communicate with clients. I'm mute. I'm not deaf, but I can't speak, due to a childhood accident."

Ros blinked once, then glanced at Vera, Abby and Bastion. Skye quelled the childish urge to disconnect the call. She steeled herself for the rejection, already prepping herself to contain pointless anger and frustration. Keeping the software on the "pleasant" setting was useful for that. An additional advantage to electronic voices; she could cover the stronger ones she might be feeling.

Though not so much if she typed "Fuck off." She wouldn't do that here. Instead, she composed agonizingly polite responses in her head during the handful of seconds before Ros spoke again.

When she did, Skye found herself, well...speechless.

"I knew that before our first contact, Ms. Sumner. We didn't consider it a factor in our decision."

Not "we were so amazed by your ability to 'overcome,'" the inspiration porn and praise that made her cringe. Nor the careful retreat she'd feared. Simply, "we didn't consider it a factor."

Her fingers trembled over her keyboard. Though she told herself she was getting overly emotional, making her prone to exaggeration, she felt like a door had been unlocked and she'd been invited in. Welcomed.

"I'm looking for a specific fit with this team and company," Ros continued. "So when I saw the work you'd done for several other firms, I did my research. I thought it odd no company tried to grab you up right after college. Or even during. So I had Bastion follow up with a couple of the firms that turned you down."

Bastion raised his cup of tea toward the camera. "The best spy network there is—admin and executive assistants."

Skye wasn't sure how to respond, until Ros bared her teeth in a feral smile. "If you honor us by joining the team, I'll send those companies a fruit basket, thanking them for their short-sightedness."

Abby took over, her expression sobering. "We won't put you on the spot, but if that was your reason for being audio-only, would you like to go to video now?"

Fortunately, she'd chosen to wear business attire. She'd done so because it put her in the proper frame of mind for the interview, but now she wondered if she'd subconsciously known—hoped—they might reach this point.

After a brief hesitation she typed into the keyboard. "Certainly."

She still might not accept the job, and even if she did, she might not end up being the "best fit" there—though this time, for reasons of her own. But she connected the video. Ros's smile broadened, as the others looked amused.

"I win the bet," the CEO declared. "Vera said you'd be wearing pajamas, but I knew you'd be dressed for work, no matter where it happens."

Skye glanced down at her blouse and slacks, her tastefully chosen jewelry. "These *are* my pajamas," she said, deadpan, which set them all to laughing and had her offering a genuine smile of her own.

"If there are no other questions..." Ros looked at each of them, then to Skye. Skye shook her head. "We'll give you the time to consider our offer. But we would like you to be a part of Thomas Rose Associates, Ms. Sumner. And if you decide against it, I hope you'll share with me those reasons so I can have the opportunity to resolve them."

If that scenario came to pass, Skye had no doubt Rosalinda Thomas would address every issue she had.

"If you don't have plans," Ros continued, "you're welcome to join us for dinner. No talk of the job, unless you have questions. I expect you'd like to see what chemistry we have. As well as what other common interests we might share." The blue eyes gleamed.

"I'd love to join you for dinner," Skye responded. "And please call me Skye."

~

Back then, Skye hadn't known what Ros meant by "common interests." But Ros's selection process for her executive team had included an intuition for who each of them was in their personal lives.

Several months after accepting the job, she'd joined the women at Club Progeny, at Ros's invitation. A CEO who hadn't considered her muteness "a factor," had also seen the Domme in Skye, opening up another path for her, this time in relationships. That path was one she'd never considered, but only because she hadn't been part of the Dom/sub world before. As soon as she was, her definition of where she could find a home expanded once again.

"You made a mistake."

Skye came back to the present to see Ros, her friend, her boss, the captain of their ship, standing in her doorway.

When Skye made the sign for "Pardon?" Ros held up the folder for the RNF account. "You printed the social media platform screenshots for Victoria's Vintage instead of theirs. While I'm sure there is some kind of connection between shabby chic and travel services, you'll have to clarify that."

Skye was already opening the right files, fingers skimming over her screens, swiping the images over to the proper page in the presentation file. She reloaded it, then printed one for Ros to have in hand. "Sorry about that," she signed. "Needed more caffeine this morning."

"Hmm." Ros leaned in the doorway. "You never make mistakes."

"Everyone makes mistakes."

"Yes. But we never see yours, because you catch them first."

"An off day."

Ros glanced at the new print out, her tone casual. "The art show went well the other weekend. I understand Tiger and his artist received some of the biggest tip donations."

"He was beautiful. He deserved them."

"Athena said his responsiveness to you added to that considerably.

It's rare to see that level of synergy between a Mistress and sub who aren't in a committed relationship. But you have done scenes for a while. And the dynamic has changed since Abby has mostly stepped out of the picture."

Skye frowned. Signed. "Tiger and Abby were never in that kind of relationship."

"No. But they were close. Close enough that he probably had some regrets after it was clear the opportunity for more with her was gone. No matter that he didn't see himself as looking for that at the time."

Skye triggered her frosty Helen Mirren voice. "Are you making a point or just trying to annoy me?"

Ros lifted a brow. "I'm seeing if it *can* annoy you, and what that might tell me. You're being awfully tight-lipped about him. Cyn told me to use the Abby angle to get you to spill."

Skye's fingers flew. "Sounds like something the Queen Bitch Sadist in Charge of Annoying the Shit Out of Everyone would say."

"She'd have that as her job title if it would fit on a business card." Ros gave Skye a faint smile. "I'm not trying to piss you off. Just tease you a little, because we like seeing what's going on between you two. Whatever it is, it looks right, feels right."

She lifted the printouts, her expression becoming more serious. "As for this, I'm making an educated guess it's because your mind might be on him. What he's going through is tough. We all care about him, and you."

A reminder that Skye had no need to be defensive. She paused, then signed again. "Our relationship is becoming something different. I don't know what yet."

"But you want to pursue it. Exclusively?"

The word gave her a jolt, not because she hadn't thought it, but because someone else was pointing it out. Did thinking about him as much as she was doing—his touch, words, and sheer presence hovering in her subconscious and higher levels—a few lower ones, too —mean that? She didn't know.

As she struggled with the answer, Ros's eyes reflected a shrewd-ness. "Are you okay?"

Communicating complicated emotions to her friends in ASL went a little beyond their grasp of signing. The only signing practice they got was with her, after all. So she went with the voice software.

"I had a few relationships as a teenager, and in college. Not much since then. I met you, you introduced me to being a Domme, and that's where I decided to let it stay. It was fun, pleasurable. Easier for where I was in my life."

Easier than being with men who liked having an armpiece who never interrupted them. Or those who thought her inability to talk meant she needed to be saved. A novelty that always wore off.

She'd thought about seeking a relationship with someone who had been born deaf or had been so for most of his life, but socially those men gravitated toward others in the deaf community. A community comprised mostly of those who shared a lifetime experience with hearing loss, including children of deaf parents.

"I don't fit a lot of places," she signed, thinking of all that.

"You fit here."

Yes, she did. Looking toward her window, Skye watched a group of tourists pause in front of the mansion's wrought iron gate as their guide likely talked about the Greek Revival and Italianate architecture of the three-story structure. It had been designed by Henry Howard, the same architect responsible for a plethora of other New Orleans historic homes.

Tiger's deafness was a tragedy, a loss for him. But she'd never had a scene that worked as well as it had in the cottage at Athena's. She didn't know if it was because of that, or the circumstances had lowered her guard with him, allowing her to want and ask for more.

Ros sat down in her guest chair. Her expression said she was ready to listen. While she was right, that Skye tended to stay pretty quiet about certain things, she found herself opening up on this. She continued to type, the voice now her Southern female one.

"I feel things for him. I'm learning things about him I didn't know, and it's turning my attention to things I didn't realize I still wanted... this much. He kissed me. I let him kiss me, and it was..."

As she paused, seeking the right word, a slow smile crept over Ros's face. "Spectacular?"

Skye grinned. "The man can kiss, yes," she typed. "And you know what kind of sub he is. If he knows you like something, he's ready to offer it and get even better at doing so." She sobered. "He's also got a lot going on in his life. Not just the hearing loss, but the death of his sister-in-law. I hurt for him."

"Are you worried if you help him, that bond will deepen further than you're ready for, or it will go that way for the wrong reasons?"

When Skye nodded, Ros chuckled. "I think that's why they call it falling in love instead of strolling into it."

Absurd terror spiked in her lower abdomen. To cover it, Skye fired one of her foam stress balls at Ros. Her boss caught it, squishing it a few times, her burgundy nails overlapping on the stress toy. Her countenance had become thoughtful. "That first night I took you to a club and you watched me scene, do you remember it?"

"Of course," Skye signed.

"That same night, you joined Abby to tag team Sy. You had such a grasp on it from the beginning. You handle things like a boat that can't be rocked, Skye. If storm clouds gather, you blow them away and create sun and smooth seas."

Because she didn't let her feelings take over. With Tiger having so many uncertainties in his life, she'd been focusing on being there for him. If she let her emotions become part of the equation, she might steer the boat into stormy seas she couldn't calm. She could capsize, right into his arms.

Per her earlier thoughts, she definitely wasn't the damsel-in-distress type. But his arms supported and steadied. They didn't hold her back. She liked the way she felt in them, with his attention on her.

She thought again of his touch, his kiss. How he'd spoken those five words, *words can't cover it, Mistress*, so close to her mouth, his eyes locked with hers.

Ros leaned over and ran a light finger over Skye's forearm, resting on the desk. She had gooseflesh. Skye gave Ros a half smile, a shrug. Then repeated it on her phone. "The man can kiss."

Ros chuckled and rose. "I better get back to things. It looks like you have plenty of company in your own head." At the threshold, she looked back. "I assume you know if you or Tiger require any kind of support from us, you have it."

Skye signed a thank you. A glint appeared in the blue eyes, Ros's lips curving. "Though I like seeing your face, most of what you do for us can be done remotely. You work an insane number of hours. Even more than me." Ros winked. "Take whatever time you need with him. And in case I'm not being clear, yes, hot sex with a submissive male is an acceptable reason for adjusting your schedule and taking off early for the weekend. Though I likely wouldn't post that on the shared company calendar."

Skye pulled out the big guns. Literally, a big gun that fired six foam balls on automatic repeater. She usually used it on Cyn, with a paint ball gun backup if Cyn didn't take the hint.

Ros retreated, laughing.

Skye put the toy gun away. As she did, another pleasant memory crossed her mind. Before Tiger had taken his leave of her the morning after, he'd walked her to her car. They'd been holding hands and she hadn't let go. He'd brushed a kiss over her mouth, with her responding in kind, sliding her hands into the back pockets of his jeans to get one more squeeze of that irresistible ass.

Lust. Just lust, and enjoyment. But she thought of his gaze upon her, the hunger and yearning. How she'd felt an ache in her heart, like a teenager having to say goodbye to her crush for the unimaginable length of a class period they didn't share. Crazy.

Ten minutes later, she packed up for the day and headed out the side door.

Ros's office had a window view to the back parking lot. Though it was canopied by ancient live oaks, she could see her IT/Communications manager emerge, put her laptop bag in the Mustang and depart.

The CEO's serious eyes filled with an approving warmth. She hoped for the best for their friend who had struggled with loneliness for too long. Ros's glance went to the picture on her desk of herself and Lawrence. It was from a barbecue and pool party they'd attended at Dale and Athena's. Lawrence was in the water, Ros sitting on the pool edge, his capable hand wrapped around her calf as she rested hers on his shoulder, the two of them oblivious to everyone else.

She'd learned later that several people had captured the image on their phones, but no surprise, Skye had taken the best shot. This one.

She and Lawrence hadn't done the marriage thing, because so far it wasn't something that called to Ros. To her, the Mistress and submissive bond held all of that and more. That picture reflected everything a wedding picture was supposed to do. It said what lay between them was forever.

People were different. Abby and Neil had chosen the traditional marriage path, but with Abby's schizophrenia and Neil being an active SEAL, they had so much non-traditional in their lives, so much unpredictability, Ros understood the desire to inject that solid bond into the life they were now sharing.

Vera, Cyn and Abby saw what she was seeing. Skye had started down a road with Tiger that might move from a moment to a journey. What that would look like would be up to them.

While Ros was glad Skye was showing signs of being willing to take that ride with him, the worries Skye had were sound ones. Tiger had experienced major upheaval. How he would adapt to that would determine if he was ready to enter into a healthy, lasting relationship.

Those were concerns Skye and Tiger would manage. Of greater import to Ros and the rest of the team were his family ties.

Because they did care deeply about Tiger, Ros had tapped friends in law enforcement for more information when the attack on his garage happened. The Fallen Angels were bad news. Not the kind of group a man got to leave. Particularly if he was born into it, and his brother was the current President.

Tiger seemed to have managed the distancing—until his sister-in-law was killed in his parking lot. There was no telling what else that world might inflict on Tiger. Or how that could impact Skye.

While that worried Ros, in fairness, when she and Lawrence had met, a gang had been trying to kill *her*. And it had all worked out.

Rosalinda indulged herself in a light trail of fingertips along Lawrence's shoulder in the picture. For the right man, the right submissive, any risk was worth it.

He worked as a coach at the local community center. She might just drop in on him at lunch time.

Sometimes even a few hours without him was too long.

CHAPTER EIGHT

*S*kye paused at the garage bay entrance, the undamaged one furthest from the destroyed front office. It was a good thing she'd come well ahead of Maryshka's planned arrival, because if her boss knew she'd seen him like this, the poor girl might be buried in that debris pile beside the shop.

Tiger was singing. Off tune, but what he lacked in skill was balanced by volume. The lyrics to The Contours, "Do You Love Me," echoed off the walls and bounced out into the parking area.

"Noooow that I can dance..."

He was mopping the bay floor as he rocked forward and back, did a two-step, then a box step. He used the mop as dance partner, microphone and anchor point. It was a delightful surprise, finding Tiger wasn't afraid to dance.

Watch me now...

Work it, work it out baby...

He wasn't sunk into a broody miasma in his office, closeted with his gun and cigarettes. The business license had been put back on the wall, near a current year calendar that featured antique cars and 1940s style pinup models.

Maybe the art event had helped kickstart this renewed interest in the condition of his garage and its re-opening.

He had a natural rhythm, intriguing her with the rocking movement, the turn and stretch of his upper body, the flex of his backside under denim, the shift of thighs and footwork.

She'd fallen into the habit of exercising her sexual desires only at the club. Work kept her busy. That, coupled to her heretofore lack of interest in cultivating a romantic relationship, had made exploring her desires in the outside world unnecessary.

But there was necessary, and there was indulgence. She had no problem with indulgence, if the opportunity presented itself and offered something worth her attention.

Tiger was checking all those boxes in bold ink.

She'd noted his balance issues at Athena's. He'd had some troubles with poses he was supposed to do for Evan, but the artist had smoothly guided him into more stable modifications before Skye felt the need to step in.

When Tiger wasn't self-conscious about it, that issue improved, no surprise. If he had a misstep or two during his dancing, he made the course correction with barely a falter.

One thing wasn't going as smoothly. Though at first his dancing and singing had her smiling, that smile died away as she saw that enthusiasm reveal itself for what it was—a mounting frustration with the silence in his head.

"Do you love me?" he snarled, Motown suddenly delivered with the force of Steven Tyler screeching "Walk this Way." The words slammed against the bay walls and bounced back as Tiger's dance steps became a warrior stomping, front step, back step. Then he jerked to a halt, lifting and slamming the mop down like he wanted to spear the concrete.

"Goddamn it. Can't hear it. Can't hear it." He shook his head, a snap. "Shut the fuck up. Quit it."

He resumed pushing the mop, only this time it was with grim determination, and no music. No dancing.

That wouldn't do. She went to a work bench where a mounted set of speakers and a dangling connector rested on an upper shelf fortunately within her reach. Since the speakers weren't scorched, she assumed they still worked.

His head came up, turning toward her as she caught his attention. She tossed him a look over her shoulder, did a little spin, and lifted a palm, a quelling movement before he felt the need to say anything about his dancing and singing, or what had come after.

She plugged her phone into the speakers, then found the song she wanted. When she pressed play, she confirmed the speakers worked, just as well as she needed them to.

Turning around, she found him leaning on the mop, watching her with a mixed expression. He seemed cautiously glad to see her, though still gripped by the strength of the emotions he'd expressed before he saw her. And those were integrated with some discomfiture that she might have seen his outburst.

When she beckoned, he set the mop aside, crossing the room to join her at the speakers. He was a pleasure to watch walking, even with the conflicted expression. She touched his face, the light caress evoking a faint smile from him. He wanted to kiss her, badly enough she could feel the desire for it on her own lips. She suspected his decision not to try it had more to do with what was churning in his head than seeking her permission.

She adjusted the bass on the speakers, then took his large hand and placed it over one of them. Her toe was already tapping, hips swaying from the heavy beat of "Shut Up and Dance" by Walk the Moon. She'd propped her phone on the shelf so he could see the upper screen was displaying the lyrics, the lower flashing with the beat.

His lips tugged. Some of what she'd first glimpsed when he was dancing returned. When she arched an expectant brow and glanced at the open floor, he gave her an actual smile. He took her hand and drew her into that space, guiding her into a turn under his arm, a curl back against his chest and then out again.

She showed she could keep up with him on the twists and twirls. If he had balance issues, he was able to correct them using her grip and the press of her body. In return, he supported her when she moved out and back, their hands on each other as he brought her to him again.

He knew the song well enough that he stayed with the beat when they turned away from the phone. They crossed the non-wet part of the floor together, face-to-face, releasing one set of hands to walk side by side, then returning to both clasped together before he spun her again. His hard waist passed under her touch, his on her hip. He was voicing pieces of the words, a quiet current under the waves of lyrics.

This woman is my destiny...

Her stomach did a flip. She answered him with a half-smile and mouthed the answering line. "Shut up and dance with me."

His wicked grin as he picked up the words, the thump of the music, the movements of his body, the mood and potential, prompted her to change the choreography.

She put a hand on his chest, taking him to the wall, making sure he felt the impact of her intent. She bade him stay and retrieved the mop. The dramatic twirl she did with it gave that grin a matching twinkle in his eyes. A more serious heat took over as she threaded the handle behind him, under his arms. He followed her cue to lift his hands and grip it. She tapped the wall, pointed to him.

Stay against the wall as if I chained you there.

That last part was what she wanted to say to him, but he understood the self-restraint part, so she left it at that.

"I wish I'd kissed you when you got here," he said.

Her fingertips drifted over the impressively bunched biceps. A submissive male, one with arms like this and a burning gaze like that, who understood her language, what she was feeling, was suddenly better than a pot of gold at the end of a rainbow. She was ready to slide right into the riches he had to offer.

Rising on her toes, she kissed the hell out of him, devouring the mouth that had belted out those lyrics. If she had known he could kiss like this, she wouldn't have denied herself during all those sessions.

But would a kiss then have had the same power? Had the current circumstances given it a quality that maybe hadn't existed before? A kiss was connected to feelings, after all, which, when growing and changing, could increase its potency.

Regardless, that potency was undeniable. He made a sound against her mouth, a growling vibration she felt in the sweep of his tongue, the caressing pressure of his lips. He wanted more, even as he stayed in the position she'd dictated. She'd sate herself first. He'd expect nothing less.

While he exercised that self-discipline, she'd perversely test the limits of it. She pushed up his T-shirt and spread her hands over him, enjoying the tough body of a man who pushed himself.

"He's crazy strong," Maryshka had told her. "Once, we found these kittens in an old drainpipe. There was a really heavy grate over it that had been concreted into place. Tiger busted it free with a hammer, then lifted it straight out. Red said when he tried to lift it on his own, he couldn't do it. Tiger tossed it aside like it was nothing."

It had stuck with Skye, the idea of those strong hands pulling the grate loose and tossing it aside one moment, then cradling a frightened kitten in the next. Pure gold for a woman's heart, those kinds of images. Enough to make her laugh at herself.

She still thought about it.

She put her mouth on his chest, over a nipple, scraping with teeth. She licked over the tattoo, nipping at the animals, tracing the curved blooms of the tropical flowers. A gentle touch of her tongue to the fresh scar over the elephant. Her hands skated down to his waistband, slipped the button of his jeans. A slow slide beneath heated fabric let her find him, stretch him out, stroke.

She heard his oath of reaction. She would use their surroundings even further, give him even more reason to get this place cleaned up, see beyond what had happened here and bring it back to what it had been. With a few new memories to inspire that effort.

The beat of the music was heavy and fast in her blood. It had switched to Elle King's raspy and edgy "Where the Devil Don't Go." Perfect. Taking a handful of his T-shirt, she drew him away from the wall and directed him to drop the mop. She didn't let him go, though, continuing their walk together until she reached the creeper, the wheeled thing that mechanics used to work under cars.

This one had open slots on the sides for handholds, a very useful idea. She used her foot to pull it away from the work bench. Once it was out on the open floor, she tapped his chest, tugging on the shirt, and pointed to the device.

She wanted the shirt off and him lying on the creeper.

His gaze upon her, he reached for a switch on the wall. It took the garage door back down. As it trundled into place, ensuring their privacy, he removed the shirt. Her gaze covered the terrain he exposed, the furred chest and hard stomach, the broad shoulders. She inhaled the heated scent of him, faint sweat and male skin.

He handed the shirt to her before he lowered himself. The creeper supported his head and torso to just past his backside. He braced his feet on the concrete, knees bent. Ready to push off, if there'd been a car waiting.

Glancing at the pegboard shelf below the speakers, she relocated the bag of foot-long zip ties she'd noted when she'd plugged in her phone. With a satisfied smile, she retrieved a handful and dropped to her heels next to him.

As those blue eyes remained on her, containing the welcome heat of a fire on a winter day, she put his hand over one of the creeper's open side slots. She zip-tied his wrist to it, leaving enough space for circulation. With some effort, he could also pull his hand free. Honoring his limits of no hard restraints.

She stepped over him, doing the same to the other wrist before she trailed her fingers over his chest. Enjoyed the rise and fall of it, the curls of hair, the skin damp from today's heat and his exertions. Including dancing.

She liked how he looked at her when she tied him up. *Let me please you,* his gaze said. His muscles stayed taut when he was restrained, always ready to throw himself against the bonds to break free. It told her even a light restraint was a personal test for his ability to submit to that kind of control. When she wanted him to relax in his restraints, she had to order him to do it.

Right now, she liked the look of those tight muscles.

She stood between his bent legs, the large, braced feet. Today she was wearing a skirt whose black folds were embroidered with feather quills on a shimmering black crinkle voile. She slid her hands beneath it in the back, denying him a view as she brought her panties down. She used the support of his bent knee to step out of them. When she dropped them on his chest, she put her two-inch block heel on his turgid length, applying pressure as a muscle flexed in his jaw.

"Come down here, Mistress," he rumbled. "I'll make you feel good. Rub your pussy on my face, on all of me. Mark me as yours."

Fire rippled through her. He'd talked dirty to her before, but there were deeper things happening here, like that kiss. Requiring a different track.

She unbuttoned her shirt, a pale gold sleeveless cotton blouse with a Mandarin collar and embroidery along the button edge. Parting the fabric, she revealed the matching lace beneath, holding the weight of her breasts. As he watched, she trailed her fingers between them, toying with the mermaid pendant she wore as a necklace. Her earrings were ceramic gold and black ocean waves, teasing her neck.

Dominance and submission were all about the nuances. That was where the poetry was, the adventure, the unfolding of the story.

A female sub might stand over her Master, between his knees, undressing as Skye was doing, for the pleasure of his gaze and to obey his command. A Mistress stood over a bound male, giving him the privilege of watching her undress, a gift subject to her desires, to how well he conveyed his gratitude.

In Tiger's gaze was the watchful appetite of a wolf and the reverence of a temple guard, worshipping the goddess he protected. A powerful mix. One she wanted to reward, not just as a Mistress, but as a woman whose loins had tightened and whose heart had pounded from passion to pain to joy and laughter, to utter need. All while she watched him dance with a warrior's power, shout his defiance through the words of a song. She'd let his darkness rise and then fall again under her touch, at her invitation, so he didn't have to dance alone.

Shut up and dance.

This woman is my destiny.

She'd never thought about being a man's destiny. She'd had too much going on in her life to prioritize something like that. She suspected it had been the same for Tiger. But just like those D/s nuances, life had its own poetry, its own story to direct. It seemed to know when it was time for a plot change. To fork off in the direction it was intended to go.

She shrugged out of the shirt, let it flutter to the floor and stood in bra and skirt, the heels she'd worn. She reached into the bra, withdrawing a condom. She dropped that on his abdomen, on top of the panties, enjoying the quiver of response that went through him. When she unfastened the bra and let it slide down her arms, his gaze stayed on her eyes, giving her heart a flutter. Slowly, she nodded. He had her permission to look.

His gaze lowered. When he wet his lips, her nipples tightened, sending another jolt through her lower belly. She cupped her breasts and gave them an easy stroke, showing her appreciation for the body she'd been given, the delight it brought her, that she could share if and when she chose.

Sliding the skirt off her hips, she stepped out of it. She retrieved the panties in a deep bend, her feet spread and upper body braced over him. His gaze followed the movement of her breasts, the teasing rock of the mermaid pendant between them, then the adjustment of her hips as she straightened and moved away. She draped all the clothes over a shop stool, her jewelry on top, and then turned toward him, fully naked except for the shoes.

She'd made the gesture that said he could keep looking, and he did. Thoroughly, appreciating what she was offering him. He lingered at the curve of waist, the thighs, gaze sliding down to her shoes, then coming all the way back up. When he finally reached her eyes, his own reflected strong emotion and physical desire.

"Thank you, Mistress." He couldn't hear himself, but the low rumble of his voice said he knew what tone she liked to hear from him. And what words. "I want to touch you."

She lifted a shoulder, a noncommittal response. She wasn't ready to give him that. Right now she wanted to ride. Dropping to her heels next to him, she opened his jeans, reaching in to grip and bring him out of navy blue boxer briefs. And stroked.

She liked his cock. As she unrolled the condom down his length, she took her time with it, caressing and squeezing. His arms flexed against his bonds. She straddled him, braced herself on his chest. Locking her gaze with his, she lowered herself down.

They'd taken their time at Athena's, discovered, explored. In the heat of his garage, she just wanted to take, to bring him to orgasm, to use him. To show him she was using him because she was aroused, because he'd shown her how much pleasure he could bring her. Because he was a hundred percent capable of satisfying her.

She'd seen how it built his confidence, knowing that his sexual self, his appeal to her, wasn't impacted by his hearing or what had happened. Some portion of his life hadn't changed.

Though the irony was that it had. It had opened up things between them, making their sexual chemistry more intense. Better.

Well, that worked, too.

"I'm here for you to fuck, whenever, however you want, Mistress." His voice was rough as their surroundings.

You're damn right you are. She could say things like that in her head, just for herself. Fortunately her inability to speak kept her from blurting out things she'd regret later. Usually she thought that was the right thing, a saving grace from making sexually-driven emotional faux pas.

But she found herself wishing he could have heard that thought. She would have liked to see if it elicited an answering flare of possessiveness in his eyes.

A good way to set herself up for disappointment. Instead, she'd focus on what would definitely *not* be disappointing. On top of finding out she liked kissing him, she'd discovered she liked fucking him.

She *loved* fucking him.

As she squeezed down on him, she threaded her hand through the longer hair on the right side of her head, released it so the wisps brushed her shoulder. She dropped her other hand to shape her breast, play with the nipple. She was devoured by his eyes, immersed in the energy coming off his taut muscles and in the lift of his hips to drive into her, meeting her downward motion.

He had his feet braced to help her with the impact, the depth of their coming together. He followed every movement of her hands upon herself, telling her with the set of his mouth, the fire in his eyes, he wanted his hands on her, to be the one to give her that pleasure.

When the rippling pleasure of a climax came closer to taking her, his tension against his bonds broke the tie on his right hand. He replaced its hold with a death grip on the creeper, showing her it wasn't the zip tie that held him. It was her command.

She liked that, too. Some things could just make a girl's heart beat faster, no matter how civilized she considered herself. Even with that climax so close, she managed to convey it, her feverish gaze sliding to his other wrist.

Reading her wish, he snapped it free, sending another wave of ecstasy through her. Now that hand gripped the creeper as well, no restraint on it but her will.

He knew to lower his gaze, because she didn't permit him to look at her when she climaxed, but the reluctance in his expression, the longing to do so, was so evident, she almost gave in to it. But not today.

She dropped her head back as the climax grabbed her. She rode him hard through it, and then, when it finally started to ebb, she tapped the base of his throat, telling him he could lift his gaze, and mouthed the order. *Come.*

He let go with a groan. It was a good thing he'd locked the brake on the creeper, because it still scraped a foot or two across the floor from his feet pushing against the concrete. She braced her hands on his chest and the side of his throat, the best holds to ride this bronc. She dug her fingers into his flesh like spurs, urging him to buck harder, deeper.

The aftershocks washed through her, an endless pleasure. Only when the climax had passed through him and his dazed eyes cleared did she stop that sensual rocking. When she gave him a thoroughly satisfied, approving look, he chuckled. After he caught his breath.

"I'm on the verge of making an incredibly cheesy comment about personally handling your oil change and service today. I'd say sorry for it, but it's your own fault. You scrambled my brain and shot it back to puberty."

She gave his chest hair a harder yank, but she was smiling. His cock twitched inside her, sending a little twinge through her lower vitals. Reluctantly, she slid free of it. Though normally he would do it, she brushed his hands away and removed the condom herself, setting it aside before tucking him back into his underwear. She also zipped and buttoned the jeans herself, cupping him through them with a more proprietary touch than her norm.

When he sat up, she stayed on his lap. He put his hands on her upper arms, his attention sliding to the breasts brushing his chest. With a notable effort, he shifted his gaze away. Toward her clothes. "Can I return the favor? I'd like to."

At her nod, he helped her up. She tucked the jewelry in her bag and set it aside to don them later. Bemused, she noted Tiger used his fingertips to pick up the panties and held them that way as she stepped into them. When he brought them up to her hips, he smoothed his touch over the band and her sensitive flesh before he retrieved the bra. He threaded the straps over her arms and deftly hooked it when she presented her back to him. Wherever he touched her, her skin practically sighed with pleasure, wanting more.

Picking up the blouse in the same careful manner as the panties, he held it out for her. After she slid it onto her shoulders, he gave her an appreciative look. "Fuck, you in an open shirt over your lacy stuff... you'd fit right in on my pinup calendar." When she tilted her head to look up at him, he ran his knuckles over her cheek. "But if you're determined to button it, you better handle that. All the calluses and burrs on my hands make a mess of soft and silky stuff."

As she performed the task and put on her skirt, he glanced toward the wall, drawing her attention to the calendar he'd mentioned. A woman with a 1940s hairdo and painted lips sent the viewer a teasing look as she bent low beneath the raised hood of a red vintage Chevy pickup. She wore lined stockings and teetering red pumps.

"I've always had a fantasy of putting on a woman's stockings, but a mechanic's hands would shred those."

She disconnected her phone from the speakers and typed a response. "You would look fabulous in fishnets."

"Put them on *her*." He shot her a look. "You know, when Maryshka acts like a smartass, I threaten to spank her."

Skye arched a "Do you feel lucky?" brow and he chuckled, holding up both hands and taking a step back.

"Have you had any lunch? I made some stew last night that turned out pretty good. I have enough to share. Plus biscuits."

He cooked. That was enough to pique her interest. Plus she was hungry. She hadn't stopped for lunch after she left the office. When she accompanied him to the rear office, she noted the less scorched pictures dumped in his guest chair had been put up on the walls. Insurance paperwork was organized on the coffee table in front of the worn leather couch. He also had a new answering machine, one with a transcript display screen.

He noted her glance. "Yeah, I've been going through the stuff the doc gave me. The answering machine seemed like a pretty good idea. You know, until something changes."

Though the last statement sounded hollow, it didn't detract from the positive signs of him moving forward. As long as he was taking advantage of resources to help him in his current condition, there was no reason he had to accept his hearing loss would be permanent.

For one thing, there was no way to know if that was true. He'd likely searched the Internet and stumbled on the rare stories of deaf people getting their hearing back after a much longer time than would have been expected. More realistically, there were plenty of partial hearing return stories, too, usually a few months after someone had lost it from a trauma like he'd experienced.

Far more concerning to her was the memorial notice. The mail beneath it was absent, but it remained on the corner of his desk, the obit still pulled partially from the envelope with the sticky note on top. Like an explosive he was pointedly leaving untouched.

Retrieving a container of stew from a cooler bag he'd left in his chair, he took her across the hall to a tiny break room that had probably once been a supply closet. It had room for a counter, microwave and fridge, one table and two chairs. When he propped open a back exit door, it drew air into the stuffy space. She saw a patio beyond the exit, with some seating made from cinder blocks and planks, plus a table made of wood and a stack of tires.

While the stew heated in the microwave, he plucked two fast food packs of plastic utensils out of a large tomato sauce can overflowing with them on the laminate counter.

He hadn't asked her why she was here. But after their time at Dale and Athena's, perhaps there didn't have to be a reason, other than wanting to see one another.

Like a couple in a relationship.

Was that as much of a startling thought for him as it was for her? Or was he following the unspoken rules of relationship growth? In those first tentative stages, a man didn't ask "why are you here?" because that suggested the woman had to have a specific reason for visiting, and he didn't want to make her feel like she had to have that.

Oh hell. She'd rather cut her throat than navigate the insipid mind games of relationships.

She didn't have to. She could conduct this relationship outside Progeny with the same structure, purpose and clear communication she did within it. Stay away from the nebulous crazy-town area.

He invited her to sit at the break table and put the container of stew between them with two spoons. The small fridge had beer, bottled water and a six pack of grape soda.

"Red's favorite," he told her. "Has enough sugar in it to give you instant cavities."

She chose the water. As they settled at the table, she put her phone between them. She inhaled the stew's fragrant aroma and typed two words, then signed them, turning her hand over in the palm of the other hand, then back again.

"You cook?"

He studied the gesture, the typed words. "I do."

"Self-taught?"

"Mostly. Self-preservation." What flitted through his expression suggested she leave it there, unless he volunteered to say more. He obviously didn't.

He waited for her to take the first bite. It was things like that which made an impression on her. Certain submissives saw even the smallest gesture of deference as a way to serve. To show care. Dominants often had the same mentality. Though it came from a different angle, the motives were similar.

She chewed, swallowed. It was good. Really good. Flavorful, rich in taste.

As they ate, she asked him about the garage clean up, where they were at in paying the claim for the damage, how soon he could get things up and running. How the deaf resource classes were going. Not to be nosy, not exactly. She was noting what things brought frustrations to the surface.

He was making good steps, like reading the material the doctor had given him. But he was still stalled on attending the Total Communication class, which as described would help him use multiple ways to communicate. The class would also offer the chance to connect with others going through what he was. They could offer him insights into what he was experiencing, especially for the parts of the path they might have already walked ahead of him.

She gave that some thought as she nudged the bowl toward him, telling him the rest was his. Then she made her decision. Typed. Held up the screen.

"Are you going to the memorial service?"

Instant face shuttering. "What?"

She didn't repeat herself. It was right there for him to read, after all. She typed a follow up question. "Who's Aubrey?"

Putting down his spoon, he scowled. When he was pissed, he really did look intimidating. That didn't concern her as much as what it represented—how quickly he would raise a wall between them. "Reading someone's mail is rude."

The obit and note were on his desk, in plain sight. Not talking like everyone else could had taught her not to waste time or energy on what wasn't necessary, what didn't need to be pointed out or repeated. A prolonged silence, an attentiveness, often brought her what she wanted. As a Mistress and in business. In most interactions, really. It didn't work on Ros and Vera, because they both knew the tactic. They used it themselves.

She had no idea if it would work on Tiger. Her intent wasn't to manipulate him. It was to help. She hoped whatever was going through his head would land on that truth. After several moments, he sighed, propping his elbows on the table. "She's my niece. Nicole's daughter. She's six, she calls the elephant in my tattoo Hermione, and likes to pet it. She was there...that day."

He stood up abruptly. "I should get back to work. I've got an adjuster coming for a follow up on the lift and electrical work needed in the damaged bays. Maryshka's going to come translate for me, be the go-between."

She knew that; she was still an hour ahead of the appointment time Maryshka had told her about. It had gone into her spontaneous calculation of whether they had time to do what they'd done in his garage.

However, with a short nod, Skye rose. As he accompanied her back out into the hallway, thoughts rippled through her head. Earlier, she'd told herself not to take steps that could manufacture a false sense of intimacy, put their relationship down a path neither had intended for it to go.

Whether foolish or not, she was re-evaluating. And about to take a big damn step over that line.

She stopped at his restroom, indicating with gestures he could go back to the garage while she used it. Watching the tense set of his shoulders as he strode up the hall, her heart tightened.

Everyone went through hard things. Reaching out, asking for help, being willing to share what he was going through, was the best route toward independence, even if it had a different look than before. For a man who'd handled things for himself most of his adult life, it was difficult to recognize asking for help as a form of self-sufficiency.

When he disappeared into the garage, she returned to his office and picked up the memorial notice and obit. She wrote on the back of the sticky note, reattached it to the obit with a piece of tape from the dispenser on his desk. After she dropped the paper in his chair, she also dumped his ashtray contents in the covered metal kitchen can.

Using the scratch pad on his desk, she wrote him another note and left that in the tray.

In the garage, he was putting away the mop and rummaging in one of his toolboxes. Skye considered lingering, in case Maryshka got hung up at work and Tiger needed help with the adjuster. However, figuring out how to communicate with a stranger on his home turf was an easier testing ground than most. Compared to standing at a store checkout, a line of impatient people behind him.

Learning to anticipate and plan how to communicate effectively, regardless of the situation, was a lifelong challenge with a hearing or speech problem. She'd do him no favors by giving in to the softness of her heart and doing what it wanted her to do, seeing him alone in his garage, struggling with so much.

He was a grown man, not a goddamn puppy.

He'd reopened the garage bay, so when she started up her Mustang, the vibration and puff of heated air from the car alerted him. He turned, surprise crossing his face. Concern creased it, but she pressed two fingers to her lips, turned the kiss toward him. Just like at the end of one of their sessions. Then she pulled out of the lot.

Tiger stared after her. Shit. She didn't look pissed, not exactly, but her departure without a more personal good-bye twisted the knife of regret. He'd been bullshitting her about needing to get stuff done before the adjuster arrived. He'd done all that last night when he couldn't sleep. The mopping had been busy work. He'd felt too restless to sit in the office and deal with paperwork.

He hadn't meant to snap at her, but his business had always been *his* business. Yeah, he was grateful for her advice on the hearing stuff. Much as he hated feeling like a kid on his first day at the Y learning to swim, he'd faced the truth, that he'd have to swallow that feeling and learn what he needed to learn. But the memorial service...that was entirely different.

He returned to his office. When he saw the obit and attached note in his chair, he frowned, then picked it up. Skye wrote in broad, clear print, nothing feminine and swirly about it. For a woman who knew the value of clear communication, the style made sense.

I'll be your plus-one for this. Pick me up at TRA at noon on Friday. She'd signed it, *Your friend.*

He bit back a curse. He didn't need to be fucking handled. He wasn't going to let himself use her that way. He wasn't that kind of man or submissive. He served Mistresses at the club; they didn't serve him, and that went for outside the club, too. He handled his own life.

But his gaze fell on the obituary, the close-up of Nicole's smiling face. The photo had been taken at her wedding reception. She looked like a woman who believed in happily-ever-afters. At least she had then.

He flicked the note with meditative fingers. Skye had underlined that word *friend*, turning his mind to their earlier conversation about that. And what he'd told her. Thanking her for not being scared of his bark.

He turned the note over, looked at the old fashioned, feminine script. Written by Nicole's mother, Rose.

Please come. For Aubrey.

Yeah. And maybe for himself, as bad an idea as it probably was. Having someone with him who understood things the way Skye seemed to couldn't hurt. It might keep him from doing something he would regret.

Like kill his fucking brother.

When he sat down and reached for his cigarettes, his attention was caught by the note in his ashtray. His lips twitched.

Stop stress smoking yourself into premature lung cancer. Or I'll ignore your hard limits and shove a lit one up your ass.

Sometimes, she really did channel Cyn.

CHAPTER NINE

"Ms. Sumner." Cyn leaned in Skye's doorway and crossed her arms. "A fine-looking man with a tight ass is at the front desk for you. Can I have him if you don't want him?"

Vera appeared at her shoulder. "Inappropriate workplace conversation," she noted. "Exactly what I expect from you, ninety-nine percent of the time."

"What happens on the top floor, stays on the top floor," Cyn responded. "But since I aspire for a hundred and ten percent inappropriate behavior, I'll work on that."

"My joy runneth over. I'll double my Xanax prescription."

Skye finished the last check on the analytics for Monday's staff meeting and shot it to Abby for review. Then she closed down her screens and rose, shouldering her purse.

Yesterday, in the morning executive team meeting, she'd told Ros and the others she was attending the event with Tiger. Though there'd been significant exchanged looks, she hadn't been teased. Probably because of the nature of what she was attending and why she was going.

To support a friend.

The first one to speak had been Abby. She'd met Skye's gaze and said, "Is there anything the rest of us can do?"

It had given Skye pause, a little heart bump. Abby asking the question was an official acknowledgment that Skye had taken the lead on the male submissive they considered one of theirs.

She'd told them she'd keep them in the loop, but nothing was needed at this time. However, there'd been more than a ripple of concern when Ros asked about sending a bouquet and learned the event was being held at the Fallen Angels' clubhouse compound.

"Tiger wouldn't take me anywhere I'd be in danger," she'd signed firmly. "You all know that."

Familiar with his protective instincts, they'd grudgingly accepted it as truth. Ros still made her promise she'd text throughout the day.

Now Skye arched a brow at Cyn and used her disapproving Vera voice, which made Vera chuckle. "No, you can't have him. You sound like Bastion."

"Who do you think I was quoting?" Cyn shot a half-smile at Vera. "Don't have an aneurysm, HR nazi. He said it before Tiger crossed the threshold. Under his breath. To me, because we were at his desk. No corruptible innocents, aka staff, heard us."

Vera shook her head, then swept her gaze over Skye. "You look good," she said.

Skye wondered if she appeared to need the reassurance. She was about to meet Tiger's blood family, and that relationship seemed rocky. She'd gone for a more conservative look for her, a black tailored skirt with a V-shaped border of lavender embroidery at the front waistline. It matched the simple blouse, the neckline offering a discreet glimpse of lavender lace beneath.

For jewelry, she'd chosen a thumbnail sized silver cross necklace, left to her by a grandmother who'd died before she was old enough to remember her. She'd paired it with small hoop earrings and amethyst-studded ear cuffs. Three-inch black pumps with narrow heels were the finishing touch.

She wanted to appear calm and in control, in case he needed that steadiness. Usually burying her own nerves was easy, thanks to long practice. Yet even after all these years, entering an unfamiliar social environment could cause a few twinges of anxiety about her communication challenges. Especially if she was anticipating conflict.

Since he was far newer to having that experience, she expected Tiger had thrown up at least once this morning. Or handled his nerves the way a tough biker guy did. Smoking a pack of cigarettes and snarling at anyone unwise enough to cross his path. Squirrels, ants. Dust motes.

Pressing her lips against a smile, she took the carpeted winding staircase down to the foyer. She hadn't really thought of what he'd be wearing, so absurdly, she expected to see him in much the same outfit he'd worn at the garage. Jeans, T-shirt. Maybe just a little cleaner and less worn.

He was wearing a *suit*.

The blue dress shirt picked up the color of his eyes, and a pewter Harley pin held a tie with thin stripes of an alternating dark and lighter blue against it. The suit jacket and slacks were a dark gray, the cowboy boots under the slacks a polished black alligator skin.

Now she understood the gleam in Cyn's eye and the sexual interest Bastion had expressed, since Bastion enjoyed both genders. To the point he didn't shy away from taking on two subs in the same session.

I'm greedy. If I see two tasty things on the buffet, I'm having them both, before someone else snatches them away.

What she was looking at was more than enough for her. Tiger was exceptional suit porn material.

She was pleased to see he was having an actual conversation with Bastion. Though he had the manners to come in for her, she expected he would have been tempted to appear occupied by the front window view while waiting, self-isolating, making conversation unnecessary. Which was what you did when you couldn't hear what people were saying to you or understand it.

But Bastion had his computer screen turned around toward Tiger and was typing his side of the conversation. As she came down the steps, she heard Tiger's responses and realized they were talking about motorcycles. Bastion had been considering getting one. As Tiger responded to his interest, his deep voice echoed through the open foyer. He laughed as Bastion pulled up a mean muscle bike photo.

"Yeah, man, she is a beauty. But that's a quarter million dollar bike you're looking at. Definitely not what you buy if you're just starting to ride."

Bastion chuckled. "Oh, honey, I'll just tell Ros I need a bigger raise for my next inevitably exceptional review."

He was speaking the words as he typed them, making it easier to convey emotional cues. Tiger was already learning to keep his attention on a person's face, and he did so now, shifting it between Bastion's expressions and the screen.

The day after she'd visited him at the garage, he'd texted her that he'd finally attended a Total Communication class. His intelligence and will had won out over emotions. She was proud of him.

She knew he had a lot of hard days ahead, though. She'd been mute since she was four years old. So while she hadn't experienced the hurdles an adult losing their hearing or ability to speak would, she understood that the lifetime of challenges never truly ended. When she'd eventually started volunteering for the community center special needs programs for the newly deaf, her understanding had been both confirmed and expanded by their experiences.

A person progressed, thought they were doing great, and then they'd hit a trip wire, something they hadn't expected. For a toddler, falling down and getting back up was part of the process, no frustration. For an adult, it could be far more traumatic.

Plus, a toddler was working toward "normal." For the newly deaf, the real kick in the face was when they realized they'd thought, whether overtly or more subconsciously, that they'd eventually find the "normal" they'd been before they lost their hearing.

Maybe Tiger wouldn't have to face that one. But if he did, she knew he'd get through it.

She'd make sure of it.

He straightened from the computer and saw her. As his gaze slid over her appreciatively, she returned the favor. The suit had an excellent fit. Which meant having it altered for those broad shoulders, the tapering to his hips, and the right amount of cuff showing beneath the jacket sleeves. Since she expected that tailoring hadn't happened in the past several days since he'd made the decision to attend this event, she wondered when he'd bought the suit and why.

Bastion offered a dramatic eye roll and fanning gesture behind his back. But when her gaze came back to Tiger, her spurt of amusement became something else.

His respectful nod was akin to the swoon-worthy tip of a cowboy's hat. His expression confirmed the Mistress and sub undercurrent between them outside the club was starting to compete with whatever force pushed water over Niagara Falls.

Before she'd written "friend" at the end of the note in his office, she'd found herself pausing. The word had been appropriate, conveying that she was offering to go with him to be supportive. But it wasn't what she'd wanted to write, and that was what had given her pause.

She'd wanted to write "your Mistress." Especially after taking him so decisively on the concrete floor of his garage.

Maintain status quo, she reminded herself. Same structure and rules as the club. It was the safest track, for both of them.

She reached the bottom of the stairs. Made the gesture of "you look nice." It was a brush of the hand near the face, then pointing to him. Her added smile helped translate, but some gestures didn't need much interpretation.

Tiger actually blushed, sending her heart in a slow flipflop. While he cleared his throat, she sensed Bastion's fascinated amusement. Tiger pointedly ignored him.

"You look better," he said. "I'm glad I clean up good enough to be a decent-looking escort."

Though he seemed okay, she heard the tension in his voice, picked it up in his movement toward her. A lot of stuff was boiling under the surface. While she expected some of it was the hearing issue, the rest of it, the bigger part, was family. Loss. Things he would be facing today.

She was glad she was going with him. As his friend *and* his Mistress. Before it was over, she sensed he would need both.

She glanced at Bastion. The office manager, as prescient as always, answered her unspoken question. "I'll call Stokes before day end and see if they need anything else. If Paula can't handle it, you know she'll text you."

He typed it as he spoke, still including Tiger in the conversation, a consideration she could have kissed him for. Yes, Bastion had every reason to be confident about his annual review.

Tiger's brow creased. "If you have important stuff to handle, I don't want to take you away from your job. I can do this on my—"

She stepped up to him, adjusted his tie just for the pleasure of spreading a hand over his chest and feeling that familiar firmness under the unfamiliar clothing. And to tighten it, a subtle threat of choking. When his faintly amused eyes met hers, she mouthed the words.

Shut. Up.

"Yes, ma'am," he murmured. "You really do look good. Good enough to eat, by the way. How do you say that in sign language?"

She gave him a narrow "behave" look, which made his smile deepen. Tossing Bastion a farewell look, she headed for the door. Tiger beat her there, opening it for her, and brushing his hand against the small of her back. She decided not to treat it as an overstep, mainly because she liked it.

He paused before following her, though, looking back toward the second floor staircase landing. Ros had appeared there. Tiger met her boss's gaze and gave her a nod. Ros answered it with the same, her expression serious, then shifted her attention to Skye. She lifted her hand in farewell, and headed back up toward the third level.

As he pulled the door closed behind them, Skye was already typing. "What was that about?"

"Your boss gave me a talking to when I arrived. Wanted to be sure you'd be safe today." Tiger took her hand, squeezed it. "And you will be. This is at the clubhouse, but it's a family thing. Nothing bad is going to go down today, and the property is secure. Nobody strikes the Fallen Angels on their home turf."

Ros must have told Bastion to let her know first when Tiger arrived. While Skye thought about being offended by it, Tiger must have read that from her. "Hey, it didn't bother me. Just the opposite. Having a family who cares about you, who has your back, no matter what? There's nothing wrong with that." His expression became hard, more brittle. "Where we're going today is the opposite of that."

Cyn rejoined Bastion after Skye and Tiger closed the door. She shifted to see them through one of the tall front windows. As Skye and Tiger walked toward the gate, Tiger's hand hovered at Skye's elbow, saying he'd noted the uneven pavement of the walkway. Like most of the sidewalks in historic New Orleans, it had become that way due to the roots of the old oaks that flanked them.

With a tilt of his head, Bastion drew Cyn's attention to the office area through the archway to his right. Several staff members were at the windows, enjoying the look of Tiger at their IT/Communication manager's side.

"The women have been ogling him since he crossed the threshold," Bastion said under his breath. "Disgraceful."

"Tell Vera she needs to do a blast," Cyn responded. "Only upper management has ogling privileges."

Tiger held the passenger door for Skye, giving her a hand up onto the running board. He had brought his work truck, with Roseland Garage printed on the side. The black truck gleamed from an obviously recent wash and polish. The graffiti-style tiger logo was vividly eye catching. Even at this distance, the cat's gaze pierced the viewer.

"Nice work," Bastion said. "She put extra effort into it."

"Yes, she did." As Skye settled into the passenger seat, Cyn moved to the window to get a closer view. She saw Tiger slide into the driver's side, say something to her. Skye made a gesture.

You're welcome.

Bastion came to her side, arms crossed over his broad chest. His locs brushed the firm set of his ass in dark slacks. Cyn knew a lot of subs who'd gotten their own ass beaten for not being able to keep their eyes off of that toned perfection. And welcomed the punishment.

"Looking at that logo," he said thoughtfully, "you could say she put her brand on him a long time ago. Even if she didn't realize it then."

Cyn shot him a look. "Seriously? Save that BS for Hallmark movies."

"Such a cynic. Are you sure that's not what your mother meant to call you? Cynic instead of Cynbad?"

"Bite me, bitch."

Bastion bared his teeth, his dark eyes sparkling. "Anytime, mean girl."

"Children."

Ros had returned and was standing on the bottom step. As Bastion gave Cyn a wink, moving to his desk to pick up an incoming call, Cyn went to Ros. "You worried about this?" Cyn nodded toward the front, where the truck was pulling away.

Ros's lips pursed. "Just like you and Abby, Skye's childhood taught her extreme self-reliance. If things don't work out, it won't be the first time she's suffered a broken heart. But if it happens, we'll be there with the first aid kit."

She headed for the first-floor office area, but gripped Cyn's shoulder briefly as she passed. While Cyn didn't much care for touchy-feely gestures, Ros's touch always held a firm reassurance, which was welcome now.

Cyn agreed with her sentiment. None of them liked to see the others suffer emotional blows, but each of them was resilient enough to get through it. Which meant the concern Cyn detected in their boss wasn't about that. Skye getting in deeper with a man who had zero degrees of separation from a criminal organization, one that had caused a murder in his own parking lot? That was far more likely to be keeping their boss up at night.

She wasn't alone in that.

~

The Fallen Angels clubhouse was a well-patrolled compound, and Tiger noted those security measures had only increased since he'd last been here. At the main gate, a pair of watchful prospects he didn't know stopped every vehicle to give it the once-over and confirm the identity of the drivers and passengers. It suggested shit was still going down, even weeks after Nicole's death. Retaliation, realignments, power bids, all sorts of back-and-forth bullshit.

But as Nicole herself had said, it was never-ending. The security today might not even be related. It might be the norm.

When Tiger pulled up in his truck, he told them who he was. It still required a call to the clubhouse. As he waited, he was silent and tense. Skye's hand moved to his thigh, rested there. He almost hoped Colt would tell them not to let him through. He could take her to a nice dinner somewhere and say fuck this.

Instead, the prospect got off the phone and gave him an unsmiling nod. Eyes curious but not unfriendly, so Colt had only confirmed Tiger was his brother and safe to let in. Not, "He's a backstabbing piece of shit coward and traitor to the club," his words last time they'd had a conversation of any significance.

Skye had switched the phone to its record setting and let him hold it. So when the prospect told him to head up to the farmhouse and the parking for vehicles was on the left, he'd glanced at the screen to understand what he'd said, then given the kid a nod and eased forward.

The prospects had barely given Skye a look except to note she was hot. In this world, old ladies and sweet butts, otherwise known as wives and biker groupies, could often fight like hellions, but they were almost never viewed as the same threat as the men.

An assumption Colt should really fix. Otherwise, during some raucous clubhouse party one night a woman with great tits and a hidden AR-15 might take out half the club.

He'd told Ros that Skye would be safe today, and he knew she would be. He still wasn't sure if he felt good about her being anywhere near this world.

"Do any of them know you can't hear?" Skye had taken the phone back to type the question and show it to him.

He shook his head. "My brother and I haven't spoken directly since my father's funeral a couple years ago."

"Not even right after Nicole was killed? So Colt could find out what happened from someone who was there?"

"No." Which had told Tiger his brother knew who had done it. Because of that, those who killed Nicole would be taken care of by the MC. The police knew that, too. Another reason they wouldn't expend much effort on finding the perpetrators.

It just perversely rankled, that Nicole's life didn't count for much outside the MC world. Guilt by association.

As Colt's brother, Tiger had that as well. Some brass newer to the district had put a tail on him for a week after he got out of the hospital. However, Del Hernandez, a cop whose Indian Scout was regularly tended at Tiger's place, made that go away. Having to have someone vouch for his character chafed, but he'd been used to that most of his life.

And in that dark part of his heart he had to keep under wraps, he was glad Colt would kill those who'd hurt Nicole. If they'd hurt Aubrey, Tiger knew the harrowing truth; he would have gone back to the Fallen Angels and stood shoulder to shoulder with Colt to cut apart the bastards piece by piece. It wouldn't have mattered to him then, his bone-deep knowledge that the blood-taking never ended in the outlaw MC world.

He'd worked hard to distance himself from that world, but being born into it, the farthest he could get was only a step over the line. The police keeping an eye on him made total sense. They knew that truth as well as he did.

A year after he'd left it behind, an FBI guy had shown up on his doorstep, trying to get him back into it to work as an informant. Tiger had told him to get the fuck off his property and never come back.

He remembered the guy had left his card and given him a knowing look. "Better to go back for the right reasons than for the wrong ones. Being part of a crime family is the hardest habit to break. Makes meth and heroin look like Skittles, man."

When Maryshka had written down the answering machine messages from his old machine, Del had been one of them. *When you're back open, let us all know. My Scout misses you. Don't forget who you are, man.*

Del knew, too.

Coming back to the present, Tiger pulled into the parking area. A forest of bikes was off to the right, polished chrome marked with black ribbons. They'd do a ride to the cemetery after, an honor guard to lay flowers on her grave. If he'd brought his bike, he might have joined them, despite any dagger looks. A piece of his heart would always continue to beat here. The very proximity of the missing piece made the rest pound harder.

It sucked rocks when you had to treat your family like a cancer, cut them out to save what was left of your life. It never went away; it was just forced into remission by goddamn stubborn determination. Fortunately, the memories stayed so present in his cells he never forgot what being poisoned by it had felt like.

A hand rested on his, white-knuckled on the wheel. He turned his gaze to Skye. She probably saw the desperation. He wasn't going to rabbit, but this was the other reason he wasn't sure about her being here. He'd already shown her some of his shittier sides. They would pale in comparison to the monster that could come out when he was dealing with family.

"Whatever happens in there, I'm sorry if any of it spills onto you," he told her. "Just promise you'll let me drive you home, even if I piss you off or do something stupid. I don't want you asking anyone else for a ride. Or walking alone the half mile to the gate." Since they sure as hell weren't going to let Uber in.

She signed something that felt reassuring, especially combined with her calm expression. She also typed it out on her phone. *It'll be okay.*

The universal mantra that surprisingly often worked, even when things were definitely not okay. He'd take it. "Wait there."

He came around to open her door and help her out. As he closed the door, she put her hand on the logo she'd helped design, gave him a smile as she patted the tiger on the head.

He sent her a look. "Did you do that to him instead of me because I'm too tall? Or because you didn't want to embarrass me in front of the other kids?"

Her smile deepened and she stepped onto the running board, using his hand at her waist and hers on his shoulder to balance herself before she patted the top of his head, then stroked her fingers through his hair. She liked to trail them through that wave in the back that narrowed down to a point at his nape. He would have shaved it as close as a basic training recruit to get rid of it, but all the Dommes seemed to like it. Particularly her.

Leaning in, she pressed a kiss to his mouth. When she drew back, she gave him a pure Mistress look and formed three words with her pretty mouth. Reassurance and command.

You've got this.

~

The clubhouse was a big barn with a lot of modern conveniences. A well-stocked kitchen, sleeping quarters for single club members, a vast central partying area with flat screens, a pool table and a bar. Further in was the arsenal, plus the meeting room for Colt and his ranking members. An attached garage provided a big, well-equipped area for maintenance and tinkering with bikes or other vehicles.

Today that central area had been cleaned up and decorated with flowers. The less appropriate details, like neon beer signs and naked pinups, had been removed or hidden behind drapes. Chairs had been wiped down and garlanded with flowers, the tables set with candles and wreaths, circling photos of Nicole.

It looked nice. The old ladies and sweet butts had done a good job. No matter Nicole's problems with Colt, their affection for her was obvious in the care they'd taken.

As Tiger's gaze passed over those women, seeing the pain in their eyes, the grief that this event had resurrected weeks after the loss, he ached. It should be Nicole here, dressed in black, mourning a fallen member, not a woman.

She would have worn something a little inappropriate, like a short black dress, too tight, high on the thighs. She'd have put it with stiletto heels, probably a pair with a bit of sparkle on them. But her expression would have reflected somber grief as she watched Aubrey play with the other kids, and talked in low tones with the women, helping to set food out and check that everyone had what they needed.

He stopped at an open ice chest near the bar and took a beer. As he gestured to Skye, asking her preference, she pointed to a wine cooler. He twisted it open, putting a cocktail napkin with it for the condensation, and handed it to her.

Colt stood in a knot of members across the room. Like Tiger, he was wearing a suit. They'd change into their cuts when they did the honor ride. He was talking to people obviously offering their condolences.

She's dead because of you, you shithead.

Before he'd come here, Tiger had known what was simmering in his own gut, but he wasn't prepared for it to go to full boil so fast, mixed with old stuff that never got old enough to be forgotten. When the people moved on toward the ample hors d'oeuvres lined up on the bar, Colt looked his way. As their eyes met, Tiger managed a neutral nod, but that was all the bitterness in him could manage.

He turned away before he could register Colt's response, instead guiding Skye toward a corner. Avoiding conversation with other members was easy enough, since most acted like they'd rather eat glass than talk to him. The unfriendly looks were accompanied by muttered words.

Joke's on you, fuckers. I can't hear you.

When Skye's concerned gaze turned to him, it reminded him she could. With a squeeze of her arm, he told her it was okay. No reaction needed. He welcomed the shunning over anyone being friendly to him. Even beyond the can't-hear-shit thing, he was too vulnerable here, too wound up. His chest was so tight he might have a fucking heart attack if he drew too deep a breath.

Goddamn it. He forced himself to take that breath. In four beats, out four beats. A Mistress had taught him that. Abby. Skye used the tactic, too. To help him hold out when they had him riding an edge, whether pain or pleasure, or if he tapped into that dark side of himself and his head tried to take him to a bad place in scene.

He was here for one reason. Thank fuck, that reason had presented herself. Skye touching his forearm gave him the heads up. He saw Aubrey bolting in his direction, evading the hands of the older woman with her.

As Tiger dropped to his heels, Aubrey locked her arms around his neck as if she'd been thrown from a shipwreck into a heaving sea, and had finally found the one piece of wreckage that could keep her afloat. He held her as she clung. Her mouth was moving, but her shaking said she was crying, so he figured what she was saying didn't matter as much as him holding her and letting her talk.

That was pretty much what most women needed when they were upset, so he now had an advantage most men didn't. He could respond to the nonverbal cues for comfort and affection while not doing that annoying thing Maryshka told him so many men did. Trying to fix instead of listen.

"She can usually fix it well enough her own damn self. She's just looking for the emotional support fuel to do it."

The grim humor didn't overcome the heart piercing agony of his niece's grief. He did want to fix the problem. Everything in him ached and raged at her pain. For the millionth time, he wished he could have anticipated better, gotten Nicole out of harm's way. He wished he'd been their target, the estranged brother who didn't matter, whose death didn't signify.

Colt might even have had some kind of memorial observance like this if it had been Tiger dead in that parking lot. The rituals would always be observed, a space for regret, reflection, and then closure, as the living moved to the next chapter of their fucked-up lives.

At least his doubts about whether he should have come or not melted away with Aubrey in his arms. This really was why he was here.

Aubrey pulled back and framed his face with small hands. "I love you, Uncle Tiger," she said, so earnestly he had no problem reading her lips.

"I love you, too," he told her, wiping away her tears with his beer napkin. He'd left the bottle on the nearest table at her approach. "I'm really sorry about your mom."

The tight-lipped older woman had caught up with Aubrey. Rose, Nicole's mother. The one who'd written the note and sent him the obit.

From the way she was hovering, Tiger expected Aubrey had been staying with her and Bill in Florida until things settled down. He hoped Colt had sense enough to let that become a permanent relocation.

Skye's hand was on his shoulder, drawing his attention to her screen. She'd turned on the mic, so Aubrey's words swirled across it. "Grandma and Grandpa took me to Disney, to the Animal Kingdom, and I saw tigers, like you. And an elephant, like Hermione." She traced her fingers over the suit coat where the ink was. Her nose wrinkled a little, a smile in her wet eyes. He glanced at Skye's screen.

"You smell like aftershave. It's nice, but weird. Different from how you usually smell."

She didn't ask about coming to the garage. Even the indirect reference to it had her shifting nervously, glancing up at her grandmother.

He doubted his place would ever ring with her laughter again. He wouldn't see her standing next to Maryshka, learning how to handle a wrench or repair an engine. He regretted that, but he got it. He considered it a precious miracle she didn't associate him with the trauma of her mother's death. More words appeared on Skye's screen.

"Maybe you can come down to Florida sometime and go to Animal Kingdom with me. Grandpa says if I live there, they'll get a pass. I can go every day if I want."

"Yeah," he said. "That would be cool." His throat was thick, probably making his voice hoarse. He swallowed and looked up. "If it's okay with your Grandma Rose."

Her look was all sorrow, her shoulders stooped with it. When she spoke, the mic didn't pick it up, probably because she was soft-spoken and standing behind Aubrey. White noise in the clubhouse had swallowed the words. But Skye typed fast. When she held it up so he could see, the thickness in his throat increased.

You will always be welcome in our home.

He rose to his feet, keeping his hand on Aubrey's shoulder. Rose had watched the exchange. Slowly, she touched her ear, a question.

"They say it might come back," he said. "I don't know."

Rose gripped his hand with one covered by cool paper-thin skin, her fingers slightly trembling. Her behavior toward him said how much Nicole had shared with her mother about his role—or lack thereof—with the club. Plus the efforts he'd made to sever that cord entirely, with no other survivable option.

But Nicole hadn't survived it.

He supposed his stiff body language, the obvious desire not to be here, how he wasn't standing with Colt, reinforced that estrangement. If seeing him in that state helped reassure Rose he was her ally and Aubrey's, he was glad for it. He could handle feeling like a dirty bomb had been detonated inside him, stabbing his heart and gut with nails.

Skye had the phone's mic positioned close to Aubrey again. She wanted him to come look at the cupcakes on the buffet. With a nod to Rose, he followed her there.

Seeing the familiar foods was like seeing the bikes. Evidence of a world and family he'd once had. Sondra's Better-than-BJ fried chicken. It even had a card with that written on it. When Aubrey asked who BJ was, Breaker answered, his gruff voice picked up on Skye's discreetly held phone.

"BJ stands for Bobby Joe. Better than Bobby Joe fried chicken. Just a saying, kid."

Breaker met Tiger's gaze with a pained grin, an expression that quickly shuttered when he realized who he was tossing that look toward.

Tiger shifted his attention back to the bar. The pound cake garnished with fresh strawberries would have come from Rex's old lady, Maggie. She had a green thumb deeper than the hills of Ireland.

Family was family, whether the Cleavers or the Sopranos. Even a serial killer probably went home for funerals and weddings. Stood at a buffet deciding whether he'd have his aunt's apple pie or his mom's peach cobbler, then decided to overstuff himself so as not to offend either.

He needed to get the fuck out of his head. He'd started the day with a low-level throbbing headache, and the extra-strength OTCs he'd popped with the beer didn't seem to be keeping it down. The doc had warned him to watch out for the ones that escalated, but not much he could do about it for this.

Aubrey hadn't taken a cupcake, so he asked her if she wanted one. "I just wanted you to see them. Momma made good cupcakes, too." Sadness filled her eyes before she seemed to push it away and made a brave face. "You should have one. You look thin."

The imitation of Nicole's motherly side startled him. Rose met his gaze, unspoken pain in hers. Though the last thing his throbbing temples wanted was an injection of sugar, he had Aubrey pick him out just the right cupcake.

When he had it cradled in a napkin in his hand, Rose was approached by other well-wishers, so she drew Audrey into their midst. Tiger watched them offer their comfort to Nicole's mother and daughter. Saw Aubrey nod, respond, but her gaze was staring through them.

She didn't need to be here. But he couldn't do anything about that, either.

Skye was still at his side, her light fragrance in his nose, the incidental brush of her body against his side. He'd put his hand on her lower back a few times, letting her know he wasn't wandering away, either. Just because his head was fucked about all this didn't mean he'd abandon his responsibility to watch out for her.

She'd insisted on coming, not taking no for an answer, being his friend, a Mistress looking out for her sub. No matter that that was a weird dynamic outside the club, he felt it from her. He didn't need it, but having a person in his corner here didn't feel wrong or bad.

But he'd picked up her thread of tension. She was more than competent at navigating the unknown; God knew she'd proven that, was opening his eyes to it in ways he hadn't recognized so deeply in her before all this had happened. However, just because she could handle things didn't mean he shouldn't step up, be right beside her to help with a new environment filled with strangers.

No one liked having to fight dragons alone, especially when plenty of times one had no choice in the matter.

Tiger guided them to a high-top table and peeled back the wrapper on the cupcake. When he offered to split it, Skye took a bite as he held it, her own hand coming up to clasp his wrist. A look of pleasure crossed her face.

"When I was a kid," he told her, "the old ladies used to rent a VFW building to do a Sunday brunch for veterans and anybody who needed a meal. $5 a plate for those who could afford it, and you could donate more to cover other people's food."

His dad and the older ranking members had known the benefit of promoting the folksy, romantic rebel outlaw view of biker gangs. Riding in parades, having picnics in the park, attending big motorcycle rallies. Places where people could gawk at the rough-looking folk, acting like any other family.

It was said 99% of bikers were law-abiding MC enthusiasts, not criminals. Outlaw clubs like the Fallen Angels took pride in calling themselves the 1%. One-percenters.

Yet a kid OD'ing from the drugs they helped distribute, dying in his bedroom in his own shit and vomit, found by his mom? That was the kind of image they sure as fuck didn't promote. Taking out rival gang members and dumping the bodies, buying and selling illegal goods and guns to suppliers whose other business interests included human trafficking, arms dealing to FBI watchlist terrorist groups, and deeper, more crazy shit...

His dad had led them further down that path than the previous President. He'd said they weren't directly involved with those groups, just doing "other" business with them. They weren't responsible for end results. Colt hadn't changed tracks since his death. Nicole was proof of it.

The folksy family stuff wasn't fake, those good memories still capable of pulling at Tiger. *The Godfather* wouldn't have been much of a movie if it had only been about killing and crime, unlikable shitheads doing awful things. It was the family stuff in the middle of all that which kept a grip on the heart and memory of those born into it, and made normal folk believe they were all just the same.

They were. And they weren't.

Skye's hand was on his wrist. He pulled out of his head and pointed to her portion of the cupcake. She'd eaten half of it. "Good, right? If you'd brought a giant purse, we could have dumped a half dozen into it. We'd just have to keep the frosting from making a mess."

In answer, she pulled the frosting off his untouched half in one layer. It was brittle on top and creamy beneath, reminding him of the scaled paint Evan had put on his body. That Skye had spread over his flesh.

She broke the frosting into pieces, putting one in her mouth before she offered him some. When he parted his lips obligingly, he enjoyed a subtle lick of her fingers. Her eyes had reflected an ongoing concern for him, but his tease brought gentle laughter to their dark depths. Her mouth even softened in that interested way when she was a little aroused by him. He wouldn't mind getting the hell out of here and making her a lot aroused.

She held up the naked cupcake and pantomimed wrapping it up and putting it in an invisible purse. But now he wanted them *with* frosting, so he could lick it off her lips and other parts.

Her gaze sharpened, hand falling back to his arm at the same moment a much harder set of fingers bit into his other one.

Dampening his hypervigilance took deliberate effort, especially when he couldn't hear anything coming at him. He thought he'd managed it, but an aggressive touch triggered an unavoidable reaction. He locked onto the offender's wrist and twisted, wrenching free of the grip. When he recognized his brother, he stopped short of breaking anything. Or following it up with a face punch. When Tiger released him, in the same shift he stepped into Skye, forcing her back a step and putting himself in between her and Colt.

A good choice. Because as he faced his brother, the anger in Colt's face, the electric tautness of his powerful body, reminded Tiger how dangerous Colt could be. Like anyone who lived in this world.

He'd been an idiot. Ros had been right to be concerned. Hell, Rose's body language had telegraphed it. If she had to bring Aubrey, couldn't stay in Disney World and say fuck this memorial event, she'd wanted to have an ally present as dangerous as Aubrey's own father.

There was no "safe" here.

Tiger made a gesture at his side he intended Skye to see, an unspoken command to stay where she was. He didn't order Mistresses around as a general rule, but he'd turn into a goddamn Dom himself if needed to keep her safe.

Fortunately, once he got that squared and focused on his brother, he saw in Colt's face what he'd seen in Rose's. A different version, but the same roots. Pain and anger, grief and sleepless nights, a man's ragged-ass soul torn down the middle, the poison of his life eating it up.

Tiger had his mother's facial structure, such that he sometimes saw her ghost in his reflection. His brother's face looked more like their father. Squarish features, good looking in a brutally charismatic way. His hair, shoulder-length, framed a bearded face. His eyes had the fixed look possessed by everyone who'd seen too much bad shit. Tiger had gotten far enough away to bury it in a shallow grave, but it could excavate itself pretty damn fast, so he and his brother probably had matching expressions at the moment. Both men had inherited their father's size and breadth, which meant the people closest to them had quieted, infusing the air around them with heated tension.

His brother stabbed his chest with an angry finger. Tiger caught Nicole's name on Colt's lips, the word "never." Plus enough conjugations of the word "fuck" to spray him with saliva.

The gist was obvious. Why the fuck was Tiger here, the man who should have stopped it, should have protected Colt's wife from dying, his daughter from losing her mother? What kind of fucking pussy let her get shot and bleed out in the fucking parking lot?

He'd accept all that as his due, but at the escalation of heat, his own barely banked rage flared high. He wasn't going to let his brother off the hook. "MCs don't come after families like this," Tiger interrupted him. "Who did you get involved with?"

Colt's expression hardened. "Not your business. Is it?"

Tiger got the first three words, enough to curl a lip and fire back. "It is when your wife dies in my arms."

Skye thrust herself between them. Before he could grab for her, she'd shoved Colt back, startling both men. She thrust her phone at him. Whatever came out of the voice app had Colt staring at her. Then his gaze shifted to Tiger. Confusion and shock were there, but they didn't dilute the anger.

She'd told him. Maybe Colt would be smart and walk away. Tiger wasn't counting on it. What was worse, he almost didn't want him to. Fuck four-count breathing. He wouldn't mind crunching his brother's face into pieces on the edge of that bar.

Vampires didn't crave blood the way he did right fucking now.

~

"If she hadn't fucking been there, if you hadn't been sniffing around her, if—"

The implication pissed Skye off enough to make the unwise decision to put herself between the two angry men. Tiger immediately had his hands on her, but she'd planted herself. She supposed his brother stopping short on the rant to register what she'd blasted at him was the only thing that kept Tiger from jerking her out of harm's way.

Which was good, because she didn't want to have to spear her heel through the alligator skin of that boot to tell him she was going to make her point, damn it.

"Stop this. He's deaf. He can't hear you. And you're upsetting your daughter."

Rose was holding Aubrey tight, about ten feet away. Though the little girl's eyes were wide, her hand clutching the one her grandmother had across her chest, what Skye registered in Aubrey's face was a managed fear. Even without her mother's death, she was sadly familiar with borderline violence unfolding in front of her.

Skye had used Sigourney Weaver's Ripley voice, the "get away from her, you bitch" tone. Tiger's back was ramrod straight, he was handling this, but the pain overflowing from him and his brother was a fight itching to happen.

When he'd been talking to Aubrey, and then standing with Skye at the high top, she'd noted him squinting, occasionally rubbing at his temples. He needed to get out of here, and though she'd believed it was right for him to come, there was no reason they had to belabor the point.

When she'd used the voice software, after his initial surprise, Colt had noticed her medical bracelet. Fortunately the side with the word *Mute* was face up. His lip curled.

With a laser stare, she dared him to say one ugly word. His brother's stability obviously concerned Tiger, and she wasn't normally reckless. But watching him take those emotional blows when he was already suffering such deep guilt and pain from what was happening here, the past and present combining to flog him over and over...

No. She wasn't going to sit back and let his brother add barbs to that flogger and tear him to shreds.

But Tiger was his own man, one who didn't hide behind anyone to fight his own battles. When his hands tightened on her, she saw his anger had been leashed, measured resolve taking its place. It was time to step back. Reluctantly. This time when he nudged her to his side, she went.

Tiger met his brother's gaze. "You know why she's dead. Everyone here does. Life is hard. Don't make it harder."

Colt stared at his brother. As the silent moment drew out, another factor entered the picture. Aubrey.

Somehow she'd left Rose's grasp, and stood at her father's side. She touched his hip, drawing his attention. She moved between the two men and touched Tiger's hand, too. She gestured, wanting him to kneel down to her level.

When he did, she lifted her hands to his ears, closing her fingers over them. She looked at Skye's cell phone. "You can hold your phone so he can see what I'm saying?"

Skye nodded and brought the mic close to her again, the screen turned toward Tiger. "Is it hard not to hear, Uncle Tiger?" Aubrey kept her gaze fixed on him. "I'm so sorry."

He gave her a wan smile, a squeeze of her waist in her velvet dress. "Plenty other things are harder, sweetheart. You're the best kid ever." Then he took another breath and looked up at Colt. "I'm sorry about your wife. I'm sorry I didn't see it coming and I couldn't stop it."

He straightened as Rose stretched out a hand, bidding Aubrey return to her. Skye noted her grandmother gave her a sad smile, but also an approving nod.

Tiger's eyes were half closed against the club house lights. He was also turning pale and clammy. Skye gripped his arm. He needed to get out of here.

Fortunately, he recognized the need for an exit himself. When he gestured to her to head toward one, he was ready to follow. However, as they passed a silent, quivering Colt, Tiger dipped his head to say one more thing.

Though Colt stiffened, Tiger had pitched the words so no one else could hear them but Skye. She assumed that was so Colt didn't have to answer the challenge; he could just think about the words, what Tiger intended by saying them.

"Be good to that kid. Do what's best for her. Because at the rock bottom of your soul, you know she's the only proof your life hasn't been a total waste."

CHAPTER TEN

*T*iger didn't go to the truck. Instead, he took Skye toward the farmhouse, heading to a spot behind it. There was a pond there, a swing hanging from a giant oak beside it.

He knew he was moving as if he were made of glass. When he stumbled over a root, it was because his eyes were almost closed. Since he wouldn't willingly deprive himself of any other senses, Skye apparently realized what was happening. She took a firm grip on his arm. He didn't resist her help, and folded down on the swing right when they reached it, rather than offering it to her first. The alternative was passing out, but he'd still apologize to her later.

He dropped his head in his hands, fully expecting his skull to crack open without the support. "Not here, not here." The adrenaline spike was going to make it a self-fulfilling prophecy.

"What happened to me isn't shit." Though he couldn't hear himself, it felt like his words were slurred, mush in his dry mouth. "I hold that little girl and feel all she's lost, and I see Nicole again, who loved her so much. Christ."

Hammers were bouncing off his temples. A pounding storm in silence. Silence versus quiet. He hated silence.

Skye was quiet. Quiet held substance, meaning. Not a sickening void that made him want to throw up his internal organs.

Her hands covered his, pried them away so she could rest her fingertips against his temples, stroke with the right amount of pressure along the sides of his skull. When she directed him there, he rested his head against her breast, his feet braced on either side of hers where she stood in front of him. The swing swayed as she smoothed cool palms over his forehead, threaded her fingers through his hair. It helped. The pain lessened enough he could see through the red haze.

On the way to the swing, he'd dry swallowed a prescription med the doc had given him, in case the headache became full blown. He didn't like taking them, preferred relying on the OTCs alone, but they worked pretty well on these things. He just had to wait it out. It would kick in. Then he could drive her home. Get the hell out of here.

When she shifted on those slim heels, he suspected she was having trouble keeping them from sinking into the sandy ground. He circled her waist and hip with one arm, inviting her to sit on his lap. She settled on his knee, sliding an arm around his shoulders. He used his heels to rock them back and forth on the swing as he squinted at the pond and tried to take some easy breaths.

"How did you lose your voice?" he said abruptly. "Were you born that way?"

When a shadow crossed her startled face, he tightened his hand on her hip. "Sorry. You coming here doesn't give me the right to anything more than I'd expect in a session." He wouldn't pressure her to give him more because he was a fucking mess.

In answer, she slid her hand under his jacket to grip his shoulder, only the dress shirt between skin-to-skin contact. After toeing off her shoes, she adjusted so one foot pressed to his knee, the other resting against his shin. Her toes curled, offering a light caress through the slacks.

She lifted her phone and typed. The dip of her head, the focus of her dark eyes and press of her moist lips, held his attention. He could feel the thin strap of her panties beneath the tailored skirt. With her knee lifted like that, if he'd been a lucky mallard floating on the pond, he'd be gazing at her thighs beneath the skirt. He'd see the color of the panties, the hint of her buttocks pressed against his legs, all the intriguing creases of silk and expanses of skin.

A much better vision to contemplate than the crap in his head.

The nice little jolt of endorphins helped the headache, too. Even if he was a dickhead for using that here and now.

She reviewed what she'd typed, then turned it toward him. He closed his hand over hers and she didn't relinquish the phone. They'd started to make a habit of that, like an indirect way of holding hands.

She settled closer to him, breast pressed against his chest inside the jacket, her breath on his ear and neck. Damn if that didn't help his headache, too. Everything about being with her—just her—made the rest of it go away so he could relax and let the blood flow easier. Her fingers played over the hair on his nape.

As he read her words, that easier feeling increased. As well as introduced other, more serious feelings.

"When I made the decision to go with you to this," she said, "when I let you kiss me, I chose to walk outside the club boundaries with you. I still see us as Mistress and sub, but the lines have room to be redrawn and expand."

He glanced at her. Though she'd offered it to him as truth, her expression suggested she was struggling a little with the decision. He returned to reading.

"You don't ask for help easily. But when things are difficult, you accept having a Mistress in your corner. I respect that. Your question wasn't inappropriate. Just difficult for me to answer. I need to think about it a while."

And she'd apparently decided how she wanted to pass the time during her deliberations. Retrieving her phone, she tucked it in her crossbody bag. Then she gripped his hand and guided it under her skirt, into the opening between her legs provided by the brace of her foot and bend of her knee.

He might not have the mallard's view, but she was inviting him to use an even more pleasurable sense. Touch.

His gaze slid around them, confirming what he suspected she already had. Everyone was at the clubhouse. The occasional perimeter patrols were being done at a distance. Even if they could tell what was going on, they weren't close enough to disrupt their concentration on one another. At Progeny, though they played privately, there was a certain lack of self-consciousness about sex and modesty that trans-lated to how they felt about it in the outside world. Thank God.

Skye had laid his hand high on the inside of her bent thigh. Her lips formed the words slow, so he could follow them. She paired that with a two-hand gesture, as if she was petting the top of her other hand.

Stroke me.

He liked her ASL lessons. "Yes, ma'am."

But as he grazed her panties, he paused. She was wearing some delicate stuff. Skye's hand tightened on his neck, then she typed one-handed, urgent, slightly impatient.

"I don't care if you rough up the silk. I want your roughness."

She was an angel, this Mistress. He let his hand continue on its track. He started by feathering his fingertips over the shallow pocket between her thigh and her sex. He had a fascination with what his touch could do to a woman, particularly when he got it right. Which required asking, listening, waiting, watching. Then acting. Other guys might claim that kind of control meant he had a limp dick, but it was just the opposite. The more he aroused and pleased a woman, did what she wanted, the fucking harder he got.

He craved riding that edge, seeing just how far and high it could take her. Seeing him get stiffer from her desire, yet holding back to stoke her hotter, earned him a lot of perks. Which was great, though the main perk stayed the same.

Her pleasure.

As he stroked oh-so-lightly over the panel of her panties, he watched her lips part and eyes glow with that approval which was almost as damn good as the touch of her hand on his dick. Or reading the words on her screen, which put her voice in his head and told him it wasn't the silence of the grave in there. It was space, filled with stars, galaxies and a whole hell of a lot happening.

He loved the give of a woman's pussy against his work-roughened knuckles, and he played with that feeling for several minutes. She kept her arm curved over his shoulder as he swung them slowly back and forth with his feet, all while watching her face. The movement changed his pressure and rhythm in seemingly good ways.

He kept an eye on their surroundings, pseudo-privacy notwithstanding. A lot of the old ladies here today had started as groupies. Which meant he'd seen most of them suck someone's dick in front of him—or his own. A lot of them had danced naked on the bar that currently held Aubrey's cupcakes.

No matter her openness in the club, Skye hadn't made that choice. He'd protect her dignity and privacy, as relentlessly as he would her life. Every essence of what made her a Mistress.

His Mistress.

The thought gave him pause. Even during his most intense session moments, he didn't really go there. But it had been an emotional day.

He set that aside. He'd been given a command and he needed to devote his full attention to it. Sliding his fingers beneath the elastic band, he discovered slick heat. He painted that moisture over the plush lips, the hair peach-fuzz short. He now knew it was a pale color like the lighter strands of her blond hair.

Her lips parted, and he remembered the sound of her breathy gasps as her body tightened and lifted to the skill in his touch. A skill integrated with the pure emotional desire to give her more pleasure than she could handle. He wanted to be what helped her handle it.

Her nipples were visible against the fabric of her bra. He dipped his head to brush a respectful but inquiring kiss in her cleavage, playing his tongue in that soft crevice. Her grip on his shoulder tightened. When he plucked at the top button of her blouse with his teeth, a mock threat to bite it off, her reaction was caught between a shudder of desire and a breathier laugh. He eased two fingers inside, stroking blood-swollen tissues, seeking a deeper penetration that had her hips jerking up to him.

"So beautiful, Mistress," he muttered against her flesh, rubbing his face against her breasts because his hands were occupied. She had mercy on him then, or increased his torment—for a male sub, they were one and the same. She slipped that button and directed his attention to what was beneath it. Praise Jesus, it was a front clasp bra.

Her hand constricted in his hair, a pull to get him to meet her gaze and see the challenge there. She started to reach for her phone, but they'd played together enough, he arrested the movement with a request for confirmation.

"Get it open with my tongue and teeth without damaging it, and I can have a taste?"

Her eyes darkened with the type of praise he felt down to his balls. Fuck Viagra. A Mistress's approval could keep him piling hard as long as she needed his cock to serve her. Even if that cock never actually got called into service, when its readiness was noted, that appreciation fueled his determination, bringing energy and life to meet her demands.

He wanted to raise her desires by sharing his own. She liked the animal side of him when the time was right. It felt more than right.

"Maybe you want me to take more than a taste. Maybe you want me to suckle them, long slow pulls, until you climax just from that, and my fingers in your cunt."

A feline smile and a tug on his hair, directing his head forward. But as she did that, her lips formed two words.

My tiger.

A startling mirror of the possessive words that had passed through his own mind. They were in the same head space right now. It happened plenty of times for them in their club scenes. Though not to this level of intensity, the potential for it was there, ready to be tapped.

His headache was starting to be a distant memory. Maybe because of the prescription meds. Or because of this, the perfect distraction. If she'd planned that as a way to care for him, he was okay with it. As long as she let him answer in kind.

He put his mouth on the fastener. It broke apart with pressure on the two interlocking pieces, so he used some suction from his mouth, the grip of his teeth, to hold it steady and slid his tongue beneath, against her soft skin. Once he slipped it, the weight of her breasts did the rest, easing the cups apart, the satin cradling them like clouds around the moon.

He traced his tongue over the light blue veins, following them to the left peak. He kept his movements slow, aware of the pounding of her heart under the pressure of his mouth. He looked for her response like he did from an engine he was tuning, detecting where the peak performance sweet spot was.

He'd thought it took his ears to find that spot, but in this case it was far more intuitive than that.

The heavy scent of her arousal, her touch on his head and back, the textures of her clothes and skin, were different but no less welcoming sensations than humming, heated engine components. The cool touch of the breeze off the pond was just enough to give it the right balance.

His knuckles were already brushing her clit with his fingers' penetration, and he passed the pad of his thumb over that responsive center, adding more pressure, but not too much. Sliding over the hood, massaging it, squeezing to match her body's coital rhythm, pumping on his fingers.

As he did that, he nibbled and nuzzled his way toward the taut nipple, brushing his jaw over it, his breath. Her nails bit into his nape, her back arching against the flat of his palm.

He'd put his hand there to guide her through doors, that subtle sign of protection and presence, the message to others that she was with him, and she wasn't to be fucked with. In this company, the message needed to be clear. Now she pressed that part of herself into his hand as if reinforcing her acceptance of that care and support. It filled him with such a need to give to her. Give her... everything.

She'd given him a lot today, and she always had. But now she had him wondering...who gave to her? Who made her their priority? She deserved that kind of cherishing.

He closed his lips on the nipple, making a sound in his throat that would convey primitive need. He couldn't hear it, but he didn't matter. It was for *her*. While he made his initial oral caress easy, gauging her readiness to take it rougher, the deeper bite of her nails, the look in her eyes, filled with the same urgency, unleashed the beast.

He suckled her deep as promised, taking a bite now and then as he kept working her beneath the skirt. Her ass flexed against his thighs, her own legs shifting restlessly. Her arm tightened to a full lock over his shoulders as he teased and tasted the peak. He released it only to impatiently nudge the cup partially covering the other breast out of his way, then gave that one the same attention.

She was rocking against him, making his dick strain against the slacks. He doubled down on his own control. He wasn't going to get a release here. Not the time or place, and his Mistress hadn't put that on the table. He was the rocket shooting *her* into space.

"Fucking love your tits," he muttered against them. Her hands clutched his shoulders, body bending up. When he felt a slight hesitation, saw the dart of her gaze, he took the worry away. "Nobody here but us, Mistress. I'll keep us safe. Let it go. Give your sub what you think he's earned."

He almost said, "Let me hear you come." In this lust-filled

moment, when his brain wasn't as sharp as it needed to be, it came perilously close to his lips.

He managed to amend it, added emphasis in case she sensed what he'd been about to say. "Let me *feel* you come."

She rarely came in club sessions, and when she did, she didn't allow a submissive more than a quick glance, and often not even that. Before, he'd been able to hear her gasp, her breath making the only noise. She might put a hand on his shoulder, clutch him like she was doing now, the rigidity of the grasp, the jerky rock of her body, telling him she was having an orgasm.

A Mistress denying a sub the right to look at her while she came wasn't unusual. But he'd suspected her reasons had less to do with the power exchange, and more with a rare area of vulnerability possessed by an amazing woman who seemed confident in so many other ways.

It wasn't about him hearing it, or her being able to cry out. But without the ability to hear that sweet gasping, that breathlessness, he wanted to use his sight to experience her climax. He'd like to earn her trust so she wouldn't worry that it made a difference to him, her way versus a woman who could cry out her pleasure.

Not today, though. His gaze remained lowered as her fingers dug in and her body stiffened. The climax surged forth and took over. It brought her body up further, pushing her breast deeper into his mouth. Her inner muscles contracted on his hand, her ass rubbing against his cock. She turned her head to his shoulder and bit.

He kept his fingers moving inside her, his mouth on her nipples and breasts, until her body started to come down, until the ripples in her cunt eased. He enjoyed her little jerks as he teased and nuzzled. When the aftershocks ebbed away, he knew he needed to relax his grip, but she was clinging to him too, so it gave him a few extra moments to recall they weren't permanently fused to one another. Slowly, he eased his fingers from her, caressing her, giving the crotch of the soaked panties another lingering touch so he could have the memory in his head going forward, what he'd done for her.

The difference between Dommes and subs boiled down to *To* and *For*. A sub did things *for* his Mistress. A Mistress did things *to* her sub. Took him deeper places in his head, ordered him into service. While he gave her what that service demanded. Did *for* her. Those two words covered it all, why it worked for both of them.

Tiger smoothed the panties in place. Skye had recovered enough to bring the catch of the bra back together. He held her, enjoying the view as she adjusted her beautiful breasts. She gave him a half smile and didn't tell him he had to look away. She was feeling benevolent, then. Maybe because of the memorial and her perception of his more fragile emotional state.

Normally he'd act to correct that, keep his manliness intact, but today he'd let it go. At least for a moment or two. He appreciated she left one extra button open on the blouse so he got a nice eyeful of the cleavage her bra enhanced. With a wink, he shifted her to a more secure position on his lap and curled his hands around the swing chains.

"Hold onto me," he said. "I'll take you flying."

A feline smile suggested she thought he had, but she slid her other arm around his waist, and put her head on his shoulder, her breath on his neck. He pressed his head to hers, just a second.

"Thanks for today."

Before she felt the need to reply, he pushed off and started them swinging. She was comfortable in the cradle of his legs, sure in her hold on him, as they swung up toward the sky. When he felt a warning hint of dizziness on the downward track, he kept his eyes on the sky, his thoughts on her. And then he felt only the right kind of dizzy.

When a trio of Canadian geese landed on the pond, he brought the swing to a gradual stop so they could watch the birds. He couldn't hear them, but it made him smile, watching their beaks move and knowing they were announcing their arrival in the trumpeting way they did.

"It's like watching a silent movie, knowing what sounds need to be dubbed in," he said.

Her hand slipped into his, and he looked down, tightened his fingers over hers. "And things like that, help. When I worry no one can hear my voice because I can't hear it. You show me you hear me, even when I say nothing." He took a breath, smiled at her.

Skye bent her head to her phone. *Tap, tap, tap.*

He was content to wait her out, rocking back and forth in the swing, his thighs shifting under her buttocks. She lifted the screen.

"Take me home. And stay with me tonight."

CHAPTER ELEVEN

iger knew Ros and Abby owned their own homes in the coveted Garden District. TRA was a damn successful business. Skye was top management, and likely could have afforded something in the same location. But she'd gone a different way. The address she gave him took him to New Orleans' warehouse district.

Many of the old buildings that had been factories in the early 19th century were modernized inside and populated by galleries, dance studios and trendy restaurants. Residences were often located on the floors above those businesses.

She directed him to one of those, a four-story, red-bricked edifice that took up a good portion of a whole block. As they approached, she activated a garage door that revealed her Mustang, with a guest spot next to it. As he parked his truck there, she closed the door, the engine rumbling in the small space before he switched it off.

As he circled around to open her door, he noted vintage metal signs mounted on the garage wall, which had been painted dove feather gray. The metal sign in front of her Mustang, placed there like an assigned parking space marker, showed a family in a blue Mustang, happily headed down Route 66, rolling hills and a sunny day ahead of them.

A side door with another key panel led them up three sets of wooden stairs. She went first, the narrow space keeping him from being caught in his thorough perusal of the pendulum movement of her ass. Unless she could crane her neck around like an owl.

When she reached the door at the top and turned, he was contemplating the railing that kept them from plummeting into the eye of those multiple levels of steps. Her faint amusement and narrowed eyes told him he wasn't getting anything past her, but she'd probably let him keep riding the "rough day" pass.

In theory. In his experience, Dommes liked holding punishments in reserve, for the optimal moment to inflict them. And in some cases, to build the sub's anticipation or dread for them.

As he followed her through the door to her place, it looked like she had this entire floor of the building. On the opposite end was the grated gate to a lift, which he expected she used when she had parcels to bring up or was going out on foot.

Pillars mortared with that old red brick braced the high ceiling, crisscrossed with metal beams. A wall of windows looked out over the street and nearby buildings. It was becoming a nighttime view, populated by the lights and skyline of the nearby business district.

Standing screens had been used to create spaces, minimizing the factory floor feeling of such a big area. The back left corner was cordoned off by a curtain of overlapping thick clear strips, like those used on a construction site to contain a work area. They were hung from the rafters, but as they descended toward the floor, the bulk of the strips were hidden by the placement of more mesh screens.

He saw a black marble bar and a good-sized flat screen, plus a kitchen with top-of-the-line stainless steel appliances. Her king-sized bed was on a raised platform, not far from the construction-looking area. A living space closer to where they stood had a cushioned sectional and bunches of pillows, the furniture angled toward the flat screen.

The only walled-off spaces were a couple of spacious bathrooms and closets. Through the open door of the bathroom closer to the king-sized bed, he could see it was big enough to include a Jacuzzi tub.

The bar and big flat screen didn't fit what he knew of her. This place seemed a blend of her tastes and far more masculine ones.

He'd never asked, had he? At the club, it wasn't an issue for him. Up until the past few days, he didn't engage with her sexually outside of it, and he hadn't sought that kind of relationship. Her business was her business.

Yet, looking at those male imprints on her living space, it was feeling very much like his business.

He noted a dozen moving boxes in the shadows near the bed platform. When Skye followed his glance, she started typing. "I haven't been here long. I had a place in Algiers, because I liked the river ferry ride, and I grew up in that neighborhood, but I'd outgrown my place there and I wanted to be closer to work. This place used to be Ben O'Callahan's."

Tiger knew Ben. A Dom sadist at Club Progeny, he was married to a spitfire submissive, Marcie. And completely devoted to her.

"I have plans to make it more my space, but work has been busy. I'm taking my time with it." Skye's gaze coursed over the living area as she continued to type, glancing at Tiger to watch his face as he read the words. "He didn't live here full time. It was mostly a mancave slash private dungeon for his submissives and private parties."

"Why'd he sell it?"

She lifted a shoulder. Typed. "Knowing him, he found another place he liked even better. Gave me a good deal on it and included most of the appliances and all the screens."

She gestured to the construction curtains. "Plus a couple pieces of his equipment. So I have my own private dungeon over there. I haven't used it yet. I've never really brought that part of my life into my home."

When she raised a speculative look to him, taking her time over the terrain, his cock stirred. "But it's been fun to consider ideas for it," she finished.

Now that his hackles had settled over the male roommate question—Christ, he hoped she hadn't noticed that reaction—he saw more evidence that this was her space alone. It also told him what occupied most of her time when she was here. Nearly a third of the area was taken up by a half dozen tables, arranged in a blocky S shape. They were laden with graphic design boards and computer equipment. The horseshoe at one end of the S was her command center. A large computer beneath the table glowed with blue lights, three monitors arranged on the surface above it.

One of the tables held her drones. He expected the high ceiling here made for a good test area. When he moved close enough to touch a toy helicopter next to them, she smiled.

"For Sy's nephew, Butch," she typed. "Remote control communication is glitchy. I told him I would fix it."

Butch wasn't the kid's given name, but Tiger remembered Sy called him that because the eight-year-old was tenacious as a bulldog.

From sessions with Skye, Tiger had already learned communication wasn't limited to the words that came out of a person's mouth. Lately, she'd been showing him just how much of it had not a damn thing to do with words at all.

His gaze fell back to the glitchy remote, whose communication problems she would fix. The irony in her being TRA's IT/Communications manager was starting to seem not so ironical.

Returning his attention to her trio of screens, he noted a bunch of gaming figurines glued to the top of the monitors. "What do you play?"

Going to her keyboard, she tapped in her password so the darkness left the center screen. A game screen came up in its place. The character front and center, ready to be put into action, was a tall warrior woman with a hair style like hers. The sword she was carrying would definitely have been called overcompensating if she was playing a male. He bet she was a kickass gamer.

He glanced at all the technology. "Well, this all makes me feel dumb as a post."

Her expression went flat neutral. She called up a dialogue box on the righthand monitor and typed a question. "Will you teach me how to tune up a motorcycle? I'd like to learn."

He blinked at her. "Sure."

As she straightened, he was surprised to see that neutral look shift into five-alarm, pure ball-busting Mistress. Fuck, he'd stepped into something.

She signed furiously, then typed what he assumed she'd signed. Or she'd cussed him out in ASL before doing the typing bit.

"Never call yourself dumb. Why would you do that?" As she kept going, he could actually see the force going into the thump of her fingertips on the keyboard. Cautiously, he drew closer. When she stiffened, he would have stepped back, but she touched his hand, an imperious command to stay where he was. He took in the words as they scrolled across the screen.

"When I take my car in for a brake check, my life is in the hands of the mechanic, same as if I was going in for brain surgery. Would you want your neurosurgeon working on your brakes?"

Puzzled, he gave her a slow smile. "Would you want your mechanic performing brain surgery?" He lifted a hand as her eyes narrowed. "I hear you, Mistress. And not to rile you, but I didn't say I *was* dumb. I said I felt that way, looking at all your genius tech stuff. It was a temporary thing. I've recovered. Promise."

She gave him another even look. Four more bold taps. "Good."

A pop-up dialogue appeared on the computer screen, an invitation to raid. As she dealt with that, he stepped back to give her the privacy to talk to her online gaming buddies. It allowed him a chance to take a closer look at her space, as well as digest what had just happened.

She was protective of him, of his opinion of himself, and it wasn't the first time he'd seen her react that way. She was quick to leap on him in session if he tore himself down in any way.

But this was the first time he'd thought about why it was such a sore spot with her. His conclusion stirred anger in his gut. He expected even as an adult, there were times she was treated like she was mentally handicapped. Never mind the cruelty of kids when she was growing up. She'd probably been called stupid or dumb a lot.

Which brought the irony back into it. Everything he saw here and knew secondhand from her fellow Mistresses said the woman was brilliant. But she didn't limit herself to that. As he wandered within her view, he saw decently executed paintings with her name on them, pottery, well-arranged flowers, complicated puzzles in process. Fencing swords carefully tucked into an umbrella holder. Roller blades.

When he stopped at the roller blades, she came back to his side, showed him her phone screen. "I like roller blading at night."

In this part of New Orleans? Hopefully she did it with a gun and pepper spray. "That's when I do my five-mile run. Somewhere between eleven to two a.m." Which was when he found it hardest to sleep. "Maybe I'll meet you here one night and we'll see who can keep up."

She made some gestures, signing the words before she typed them.

He liked watching her doing it, even without knowing what they meant. Yet. He glanced at her screen.

"Thinking about your family keeps you awake?" she asked.

"Sometimes. I run it out, and sleep like a baby."

A tight smile at the semi-lie. Then she crooked two of her fingers, dipping them twice, tilting her head toward the bathroom. He lifted his hand to emulate, and she adjusted his fingers for him, mouthing it. "R."

"Oh. Yeah." He pretty much had the sign language alphabet down, but translating it in conversation took longer to process. An R dipped twice. Rest Room.

As she excused herself, he practiced the gesture once or twice. Figuring it was okay to explore what seemed like the "public" spaces in her absence, he stopped at a shelf, studying a photo of a man who had to be her dad, holding a very young Skye on his lap. She looked about three, and she was laughing. He had a guitar propped next to him, his other hand resting on it. Their surroundings looked like a studio.

She was as adorable as Aubrey, which made his heart hurt. When Skye rejoined him, he nodded at the photo. "Is he a professional musician?" he asked.

She spelled it out slow, letting him follow the letters. He spoke them aloud as she signed them.

"W... A... S.... He was. Oh. Sorry."

The ghost pain in her expression said the loss would always hurt, no matter when it had happened. "Mom?" he ventured. He hadn't seen any pictures of her yet.

In answer, she brought him back to the computer screens and parked herself in front of them. She gestured to a rolling stool he could pull up next to her. When she rested her hands on the keyboard, she took a breath, preparation.

He put a light hand on her shoulder. "Don't if it's too hard," he said. "You don't have to do that just because I was curious."

"You didn't ask just because you're curious," she typed. "That's why I'll tell you."

With that cryptic comment, she erased the line and started typing from a blank screen. He brought the stool closer so he could shift his hand to the top of her chair. His fingers rested between her shoulder blades, doing a light stroke. It felt like she needed it. She didn't tell him to stop.

"I don't remember much of what he told me about her, but he wrote a song called "Thank You." It was written to her. About me."

Her fingers slowed, as if she was giving more thought to the words as she typed now. "They weren't married, and she didn't want a pregnancy to slow down her life, her music career. He convinced her to carry me full term rather than getting rid of me. Said he would take total custody and she could leave afterward if she wanted to. She did."

She paused, thinking. He moved his touch to her nape, another easy stroke, and she began typing again. "He did everything. Even arranged for a wet nurse. My aunt told me that. His sister. She took me in after he died. He'd made sure if anything happened to him, I would go to her, not my mother. Not that it mattered. She signed papers before I was born, surrendering me to him completely. She never even held me. Checked out of the hospital and headed to Nashville. Which was fine. Dad figured out how to be a father *and* mother to me, and he knocked it out of the goddamned park."

From her faint but genuine smile when she typed the line, he could tell she meant it. Her love for her dad had eclipsed and left her mother's indifference behind long ago. Which said what a remarkable guy he must have been. And how strong she was.

Skye rose, nodding toward the sectional sofa. A cue that she was done sharing soul-deep stuff. On the way, she pointed toward the bar, tipped a drink to her lips.

"I'll take a beer if you have one," he said, "but I can find it if it's there. Do you want anything?"

When she indicated she wanted a soda, he took care of that. The bar was well-stocked. Apparently, Ben had left her everything, because there was dust on a few of the bottles, including some seriously high-grade alcohol. His Mistress wasn't a home drinker, then, and she didn't apparently have many guests who were. A glass of that scotch would have been good, but he'd told her he'd get a beer, so that was what he grabbed.

When he brought her the soda, she'd slid off her shoes and tucked her feet up under her on the couch. They were still in their memorial clothes, him because that was all he had, though he'd removed the jacket and rolled up the sleeves.

"If you feel like changing, don't stay spiffed up just because I am," he told her. He had a change of clothes in the truck, but he wasn't going to retrieve them until she seemed ready to get that comfortable with his presence in her space.

Setting her soda aside, she reached over to loosen his tie. She slid the knot free, silk slipping through her fingers as she set it aside. Then she opened two buttons of his shirt, resting her fingers on the white tank he'd worn under it. She typed one-handed, the message making him smile.

"This is my favorite suit porn look."

Thanks to the crazy rollercoaster this day had been, a lot of things were moving through him he wasn't sure he wanted to take over. So he went for the same teasing note, glancing at her blouse. "Want me to show you my favorite businesswoman porn look?"

She flicked his chest with a reproving nail and answered his earlier comment. "I'll change in a little while," she typed. "So why did your mother name you Tiger?"

Crap. Right into the swamp of his childhood, though the question was straightforward enough. "I was premature," he said with forced casualness. "She wasn't as careful during the pregnancy as she should have been, but in all fairness, she didn't grow up in an environment where prenatal care was a priority. But once she had me, she cleaned up her act. Never took another drink or any drugs that I remember. She told me, 'You fought like a tiger for your life, so I knew I had to fight the same way to deserve you.'"

He pulled his wallet out of his back pocket, showing Skye the picture he carried, his mother holding an infant Colt while Tiger stood at her hip.

Skye touched the edge of the photo, then spelled out that word "was" again. With a question mark. A poignant way to ask if his mother was still alive. He shook his head. "Both my parents are gone."

He sure as hell didn't want to talk about that. Fortunately, she seemed to figure that out. She put her hand back on his chest to give him a gentle, understanding tap. Then she leaned against him, bending her head over her phone to type something else. As she did, he took the intimacy as a measured invitation and tipped his chin down, inhaling the scent of her hair. Brushed his lips over it.

There'd been a poetry reading at the club one night. Tiger was definitely not a poetry guy. Most of it seemed to be flowery stuff, or lines so confusing he didn't have the patience to sort through what they meant. Authors should write it so people could understand what the fuck they were talking about.

"Yeah, kind of like the lyrics of 'Bohemian Rhapsody,'" Maryshka had pointed out dryly, hearing his grumblings. She knew his Queen albums were his guilty pleasure. Some of his earliest road trips on his first bike had happened with Freddie Mercury belting out "Radio Gaga" in his ears.

But during that poetry night at the club, a big fiftyish guy with a heavy Russian accent had read something he'd written. The stanzas, rough and not flowery, talked about how a man could fuck a woman, squeeze her tits, fondle her ass. Use every inch of her as if he owned her. That was "all good." Yet, what took "good to heaven," overwhelming him, was when his Mistress permitted him the slightest brush of his lips on her hand. Her foot.

"The bliss, unimaginable, of touching her neck, small of back. Holding her as she sleeps. I feel her breath, the bump of her heart against my chest. I am all I ever need to be."

Other subs had been as impressed by the poem as he was. What lay beneath the words was familiar to all of them. Now, as Tiger touched his mouth to Skye's hair, he thought of that poem. At the press of her hand on his thigh, he adjusted to see what she'd typed.

"It bothered you, thinking I live with a man."

He shrugged. "That's not my business."

Her silent look said the answer wasn't acceptable. She wanted a gut-level response.

He sighed. "I don't have any claim on you, and where my head and life's at right now, I sure as hell wouldn't be trying to inflict one on a woman. Let alone one as special as you."

Clearing his throat, he glanced toward the room with the rubber curtains. "Care to share its current state, before it becomes a total girl dungeon?"

He didn't know if he'd get the chance to see that, so he might as well see the front end. He didn't want to talk about the surge of pointless possessiveness. Thankfully, she seemed okay with the distraction. She rose and offered her hand. When he stood to follow her, she brought them around the screens, to the opening in the curtains.

Since he was a step behind, he used his longer arm to reach forward and hold the PVC strip curtains back for her.

She tilted her chin, an acknowledgement of service, the kind of approval that subs fed upon, and she knew it. Though she'd used the alcove near this space for her unopened boxes, she hadn't stored any in here. He suspected she was respecting its intent, keeping it pure.

The first thing he saw made him grin, though. "You really haven't changed anything yet. Or are you a closet switch?"

Her lips parted on that little huff of breath, her version of a chuckle. She moved to the sign, clicked it on so the crimson light flooded the two words that had prompted the question.

Yes, Sir.

A spanking bench and St. Andrew's cross were in the space, the basics for an upscale home dungeon. The third piece of bondage equipment was a cylindrical steel cage topped with a piece of polished wood that made it look like a stool, until one noticed the hole in the seat. It was a stock. When a sub was closed into the cage, his or her throat would be locked inside that opening, keeping the mouth accessible.

The size of the cylinder required them to sit upright, arms and knees folded up against the torso. The bars were narrowly spaced, no putting arms and legs outside of them. A Dom could sit nearby, read his morning paper, have his coffee, and feed his pet treats. Like his cock.

A male Dom came to Tiger's mind because the cage looked sized for a female sub of smaller dimensions. At least he hoped so. "If you want me in that, we're going to have to employ a shrink ray gun. Most Mistresses aren't all that interested in shrinking my parts."

With a smile, Skye moved to the spanking bench and sat down, patting the area next to her. When he braced his ass companionably next to hers, she bent her attention to her phone again.

"Ben told me I could give it away," she typed. "He had no need of it anymore. I just haven't gotten around to it."

"I can put it in my truck and take it to the Progeny warehouse, where they store stuff for the Christmas charity auction. I'll bet it would get some good bids."

She considered that, nodded. Then she glanced toward the neon sign and gave him back the same question he'd asked her. "Is that something that's ever interested you? Switching?"

"You know the answer to that."

Her expression said she agreed with that assessment, but she wanted him to expand on it. And she prompted him with an easier question. "Earliest trigger moment?"

He grinned. "It happened in a strip bar. A dancer had a Domme routine, and she did it damn well. She was catering to a different male fantasy, but she knew her shit."

He shrugged. "From there, it was a lot of things I didn't exactly recognize until they all came together. I'd thought about it, fantasized about it, and one day, I went to a munch and was invited to a play party. I'd left myself open-ended, for the usual reasons. I wanted to see how much shit a guy who looks like me was going to get for preferring the sub side.

"Two Doms walked me through everything, a man and a woman. Darcy was the Domme. After about an hour, she said, 'so, where would you like to start?'"

He remembered how she'd handed him a flogger, one of the thicker, longer ones, after she'd demonstrated how to use it. She offered to let him try it out on one of the more than willing subs. "But as I stood there holding it, all I could think about was how it would feel against my skin, if she was using it on me."

He slanted Skye a glance. "My head went shooting straight from there into her ordering me to stay still and take it. I'd already scoped out my surroundings and realized if she did it in front of this big wall mirror, I could see what it did to her, having me at her command. Being at her command."

Skye closed her hand on his forearm, pleasure in her gaze. She liked hearing him talk about it. "Darcy and I weren't a great fit," he continued, "but enough for me to figure out I wanted to dig deeper. That's where it really started to unfold. It's like…"

He paused, thinking. "Mechanical stuff interested me early, got me tinkering with cars and motorcycles. Then one day you touch the art of it, if that makes sense. You learn how to talk to the machine, and eventually it trusts you enough to start talking back, because you get each other. It took time to get there, and the learning was a maze, trial and error, but the journey was a hell of a fun trip. Nothing

I wanted to rush, because of how much I was learning along the way."

"Did you ever look for it in a relationship before Darcy?"

He grimaced. "I guess we all do, before we recognize what or how strong it is. We just know what we're looking for isn't in the relationships that crash and burn. I also couldn't look for it with the girls who hung with the Fallen Angels. A lot of them are great, but they talk, and stuff gets back. And that... No way in hell my dad would ever have understood that."

She studied him. Typed. "And yet, it sounds like you've never struggled with being a sub. Not the way some alpha males do."

"No." He grunted. "When I walked away from Fallen Angels, I was called a coward, pussy, all the usual. A disgrace. My brother said they should cut off my dick since I obviously didn't have a need for it."

He waved a hand at the anger that crossed her face. "It was a while ago. That kind of shit says more about them than me, we all know that."

She made the gesture of a knife in the chest. *Still hurts.*

"Yeah, maybe, but deciding my own path and ending up where I am now goes a hell of a long way to making it a scar instead of an open wound." He shook his head. "I didn't want to be part of a world where getting a mug shot was a badge of pride. Or like I said, having to stick my head in the sand over the collateral damage our business caused. So one day I made up my mind. I went to a tattoo artist and covered the club ink. Came back to my father's house, collected my stuff, and left my cut on the bed. Then I walked into the clubhouse and told him and Colt I was done."

It had taken him too many years to get there, an inner struggle that had hounded him before and too long after his mother's death. But all along he'd known it wasn't his path, just like he'd known being a sexual submissive was.

He'd always been clear on his hard limits. No heavy restraints he couldn't get out of himself. He'd only granted an exception to that one once, for a session involving Abby's special circumstances.

No blood play, not ever. When he was twelve, he'd been eating breakfast at the bar in the clubhouse. A guy who had broken the MC rules had been brought in, and was taken to the meeting room in back. When it was time to mete out his sentence, he'd bolted.

The struggle had ended up in the bar area, where he was beaten to death. Breaker knew how to use a bat, swift and effectively.

It had happened so fast, blood and brain matter had spattered into Tiger's cereal, including the spoonful he'd been putting in his mouth. It had been too close to stop it from sliding onto his tongue with the Cheerios and milk.

He could still taste that flavor when he thought about it.

By eighteen he was hardened to it. When he left the Fallen Angels, too many years later, he told himself not to think about any of that anymore. But it had come out when Darcy topped him, so he knew right off the things that wouldn't work for him. Learning the things that did...well, that had led him to Mistresses like Skye and Abby.

He shared some of that last part with her, but pushed on to other, better stuff. Things that weren't so much about her original question, but seemed to flow into the conversation.

"I found work as a mechanic, built my way up, saved, and bought a garage from an owner who was retiring. Somewhere in there, Nicole and Colt had Aubrey. I figured Colt never gave a thought to me after I left, except to curse my name. But when Nicole insisted on a relationship between me and Aubrey, I knew she hoped if she could get me and Colt patched up, maybe Colt would eventually do what I'd done and walk away from the life."

His gut tightened over the load of regrets, paths not taken. The shit nobody could do anything about because people were going to make their own choices. He guessed he hadn't entirely circled away from the less pleasant stuff, but the words kept coming. "She refused to see it was like this for him. Something too deep a part of who you are to change it." Rubbing a palm over the spanking bench, he got briefly distracted by the smooth texture, the firmness. Ben didn't fuck around. It was a top-notch bench. But the guy was a fancy corporate lawyer. Probably slept on a mattress filled with Benjamins.

"Colt and I were pretty different people," he continued. "My mother knew it, and that's why I think she gave me glimpses of other paths, whereas Colt clung to my dad. She'd named him Colt because whenever my dad touched her stomach, Colt practically 'galloped' across her womb to get to him."

A tight smile touched Tiger's mouth. "He was born to be a Fallen

Angel. What crawled up into my dad's gut was I was the older one. The firstborn son, the one he expected to take his place."

Skye set the phone aside and offered her hand, a simple gesture. He clasped her hand, and they sat that way, hands knotted on his knee.

He glanced at her. "Care to answer that switch question yourself, Mistress? Because I'm definitely not, but I'd have to be a dead man to not be okay with spanking a beautiful ass if you occasionally wanted that. Behind closed doors, so we don't tarnish your Mistress rep."

He was teasing her, and she obviously knew it. He wouldn't turn down a Mistress request within his own limits, but his heart wasn't into topping. She picked up the phone again, did the slow, thinking-it-over typing thing. As he read the words that appeared, he understood why she was taking her time expressing them.

"Some people might say that me being mute is why I prefer being a Mistress. But Vera told me she doesn't think so. She says it's like being born with a talent. One day a door opens and brings it forth, showing you that you can apply it in a way that fills your soul and spreads that power out to the rest of your life. Which makes you even more sure of your path, and your capabilities."

She swept her gaze over him, lingering on his shoulders, the length of his braced legs. Coming back to his mouth and eyes. "You are not helpless." She emphasized the *not* on her phone. "No healthy submissive is. Finding male submissives I can communicate with, earn their surrender and trust, and hold that control... Initially, it was an avenue that opened up and strengthened a part of me that had been holed up deep inside, waiting." She frowned. Typed again. "It's a circle. Who I am drives me to embrace being a Mistress, and being a Mistress helps expand who I am."

She'd continued to glance at him as she typed. When she concluded, he put a hand on her wrist. "Do you keep looking at me to see if I'm..." He was about to say listening, but amended it to "paying attention."

"Yes and no," she typed. "Some of it is so you can match my expression to what I'm typing. But when I type for a hearing person, the voice app is on, so I'm speaking in a way they're used to. With you, because you're having to read it, it can seem a slower form of communication." A faint smile. "I don't want to get too wordy. And I'd rather shave my eyebrows than be accused of rambling."

He chuckled, but when he met her gaze, he was dead serious. "Doesn't matter how you communicate with me, Mistress. Soon as I know you need to say something to me, you have my attention. Long as it takes you to say it." He nudged her. "If you're doubting that, I haven't done as good a job as I should, proving it."

She gave him a long look, that Mistress light taking over. Sliding off the bench, she moved to the cross bolted to the wall. Ben was straight, but though the cage was sized for a smaller woman, this utilitarian style was built for anyone. Which meant he'd probably used it for the private parties.

She gestured, telling Tiger she wanted to see how he looked against it. Rings for cuffs were on the upper pieces, and he hooked his fingers in them obligingly, aligning his feet with the bottom pieces so she could step back and inspect him.

As she took her time with it, the quiet that came over him was his subconscious—hell, all levels of his consciousness—recognizing those tells. The anticipation locked him into that starting chute for her, rousing his cock and centering him. It was a relief after the surf of volatile emotional terrain.

She moved in and put a palm on his chest, her expression suggesting she was checking on that, keying into the state of his head, the rhythm of his heart. Her gaze slid up to his face.

She signed something he didn't understand. She would translate for him if it was needed, he knew. But the sudden flash of yearning he saw in her expression had him picking up on something for the first time.

Signing was the way she wished she could talk to him. She wouldn't have to take her attention away to type into her phone, like she did now. Especially when what she had to communicate was more complicated.

"You've told me some of what happens to you as a sub," she typed, "and why it went where it went for you. But all of us, Domme and sub, have fantasies of how much deeper we'd take it, if we didn't worry about the bonds of reality or asking too much, crossing lines."

She looked at him, her dark eyes fathomless on his. The ceiling fans moved the wisps of hair on her brow. The thin fabric of her lavender blouse creased against her side as her arm moved, fingers typing. "What do you imagine when you have your hand on yourself? 24/7 sub? Your Mistress putting a collar on you? Or her giving you specific, more extreme commands, to let you prove your devotion, your willingness to serve, out on a knife's edge? Tell me what you'd really look for in a Mistress, if there were no boundaries. In yourself or her."

He moistened his lips, and felt heat when her gaze zeroed in on the reaction. Maybe it was because he was a straightforward guy, or because of what their sessions already gave him, but when he was fantasizing, he was usually just rehashing things that had happened in scene. He might imagine less clothes on her, or her straddling him, since sex and getting fully naked wasn't always on the menu during the club stuff.

He wasn't sure if she'd be impressed by his answer, but she always wanted the truth. So when he opened his mouth, that's what he intended to say. But something else surged out of his heart and overrode it.

"I'd want a Mistress who could dig deep enough to find me. Pull me out of where I live, where I've buried the best parts of me I thought were lost."

CHAPTER TWELVE

*H*ad he really just said that aloud? He spoke it into that vast silence in his head, but the way emotion gathered behind her eyes, lips softening, told him he'd been heard. Maybe she felt some of the WTF he'd just experienced, because he saw a small flash of uncertainty, but then that was replaced by a thoughtful look.

She moved closer. Unbuttoning his dress shirt the rest of the way, she spread it open. She had him lower his arms so she could slide it off and drape it over a chair. The tank followed, her gathering it up then pulling it forward over his head, guiding him to straighten his arms before him so she could pull it off. She would have needed a stepstool if he'd raised his arms straight up. At the very least, she would have had to lean against him, rise on her toes, her body rubbing against his.

When his fuck-with-her teasing side kicked in like that with a Mistress, Skye was one of the best at getting ahead of it. She sent him a look that told him to behave or else. It didn't always work, but it did today, especially when she cupped her hand over the tattoo on his shoulder. She kissed it, pressing her mouth to each animal. Giraffe, lion, tiger. Hermione was last, Skye's lips lingering on the elephant's scarred forehead. The look she sent him in her expressive eyes said she was giving each their due, for representing the life he'd embraced for himself.

As he'd said, he liked the life he currently had—well, at least until recently. But it never hurt to have that reinforced by a friend and Mistress he respected.

She moved her fingers to his throat. As she paused and held him there, she tightened her grip. A faint smile touched her lips as she confirmed and acknowledged his reaction. He loved her touch, loved the feel of the pressure of her hands, and when she got rough with him around his throat, it got him hard. But it wasn't hinting at a collar that did that.

Maybe because he'd grown up feeling shackled and collared to something he wanted to escape, wearing an actual collar wasn't one of his desires. If he ever considered himself owned by a Mistress, it would take a different shape. It would also underscore his active and daily willing submission to that ownership.

She had her leg against his, her hip bone pressed to his upper thigh. His breath stirred the feathers of her hair against her skin. *I am all here. I am all yours. You have my full attention, Mistress.*

He said it in his head. Then he said it with his lips.

She put her mouth on his chest, then the base of his throat, so he tipped his head back. She made him feel like she was drawing him into her in every way possible. Nourishing her. That was a new thought, but every session could go down a new road. Particularly lately, and particularly with her.

Christ, Alan Jackson's "Look at Me" was going through his head, an ode to a woman that pretty much declared the singer's unconditional devotion. *Darlin' can't you see I'd do anything you want me to? / I tell myself I'm in too deep / Then I fall a little farther every time you look at me...*

She stepped back and moved toward a cabinet. Opening it, she showed him she kept some of the things she regularly brought to the club in there. There was other stuff, too, maybe things left by Ben or her own stuff she hadn't used on Tiger before. She removed a flogger with a thick, medium length fall to it. The strands were black, the handle wrapped in purple and an engraved silver band that disappeared under the clasp of her hand.

A typed screen. "Housewarming gift from Ben."

When she came back to him, she trailed the fall over his shoulders and the back of his neck. As she moved it over his chest, she shook it so the tickling feeling teased his nipples and abdomen. Her deft fingers slipped the button of his slacks, opening them so she could play along the waistband of his underwear. Then she took another step back and signaled him to remove all of it.

She wanted him against the cross naked while she remained fully clothed. The gleam of her jewelry, that tiny cross, caught the loft lighting, which also created tiny stars in her intent gaze.

After he complied and put his hands on the rings again, she tilted her chin up. He let the rings go and extended his arms upward on the cross, the back of his wrists against the smooth expanse of the upper pieces. He hooked his fingers behind the top edges to hold the stretch of his upper torso.

Her gaze followed every ripple of muscle. When he shifted his hips to adjust his feet and plant them more solidly, her attention went to his cock, high and hard for her. Her grip on the flogger tightened.

Shit.

Yeah, her first series of slaps were in that area, on his upper thighs, against his cock, but at least she started with easy strokes. She wasn't delivering pain but sensation. Criss cross over his abdomen, the strips falling away like the caress of her fingertips. Then up to his nipples, creating a shiver of reaction across his skin. Back to the navel.

She gestured to her eyes, pointed to his. She wanted them closed. When he complied, despite a frisson of tension in his lower belly, she moved closer then dangled the flogger's thick strips gently over his face, his shoulders, his throat, letting him feel the contact on his cheeks, his jaw.

It was soothing. Erotic. Her pace was slow and easy, and he could sense she was getting as much out of it as he was, taking them from the rougher seas of the day into calmer waters with the leisurely play. A dozen skilled Mistresses had taught him the dangers of anticipation. Everything proceeded at their pace and say-so, including whether a session would end with a climax.

Sometimes Skye was seeking something else for herself and him. A sensual pool where he might drift for hours, being insanely okay with his cock staying hard or semi-erect, wanting that climax, but he'd be fine staying on that edge for her. Enjoying the feeling of wanting. Savoring it.

The flogger descended, and she was back to the slap against his flesh. He remembered the way it sounded, a lush fullness when using a flogger like this, versus the sharper sound of one with thinner, shorter strips. She was increasing her force, delivering a sting as she criss-crossed his chest, his abdomen, back to cock and thighs.

She hadn't given him the tap order to open his eyes. She would when she was ready, but as the sensation and pressure built, he shifted under her touch, a not-right feeling building. He was in the dark, in the silence. He couldn't see her face. Couldn't see her reactions. His hands curled and uncurled on the cross's outer edge. Nothing held him. This wasn't bad enough to be a safeword situation. If she was getting something out of it, all was good, and his erection said he was fine.

Trust. Was it about trust? He didn't know. But as the feeling crested, his safeword broke free.

"Motorcycle."

The flogger stopped, and her palm was on his chest. Waiting. He wet his lips. "Need to open my eyes, Mistress. Need to see you. Sorry."

At a tap of agreement, he opened them. The constriction in his chest immediately eased, though he was feeling foolish over it. Before he'd lost his hearing, he couldn't close his eyes unless she ordered it. Closing the eyes to savor sensation was an earned privilege.

Now keeping them open was a necessity. He couldn't close them. He had to see her.

Her expression said his Mistress wasn't entirely pleased, which tightened him up again, until she showed him her phone. "You waited too long to do that. I was about to do it for you."

"Sorry, Mistress. I thought... I had to work through it. I didn't want to safeword just because it didn't feel right at first."

An acceptable explanation. She set the phone aside and stepped back, but kept her hand on his chest, her arm extended, until he met her gaze again, a confirmation that he was good. Then she started working the flogger again.

With his eyes open.

～

Skye liked how he looked at her. Because he was even more hungry for that visual connection, his blue eyes had a sharper focus.

When she'd had him shut his eyes, she'd intended to order him to open them as soon as she was no longer near his face with the flogger, but she'd wanted to test the theory, see how deep that need and those layers went, and how much he would push it in himself.

She was satisfied; he had handled it like an experienced sub. As he'd said, he wouldn't safeword just because something was unexpected or new. He'd given it enough time to confirm it would truly impact their mutual enjoyment of the session.

Which they could now get back to, with barely an interruption in the flow of energy they were building. His skin was reddening under the repetitive attention of the flogger, and she noted the slight flinches on contact that came with increased sensitivity. He enjoyed some level of discomfort and outright pain, his arousal increased by enduring it for her pleasure.

When she at last set the flogger aside, she put her hands on him to stroke the abraded skin. Playing with him a little, she ran her nails over the same terrain, feeling his muscles tighten. She deliberately didn't look at him, aware of his eyes on her, him absorbing what she was doing, what she was getting out of it.

Her body was as tight as his, just as ready, and she let him feel it in the bite of her claws. Then her teeth, as she scraped them over his shoulder, giving that tattoo another kind of blessing before she moved to his throat, his chest, the left nipple. Her hand dropped to his cock and closed around it to squeeze, her thumb nail probing the slit and earning a jerk of his hips.

Reluctantly she backed off, but it was to retrieve an item from the cabinet she'd never used on him before. A clear gel male masturbator, the opening styled to look like a vulva, the interior textured to give a man a very familiar feel when thrusting into it. She lubed it up generously and then slid it onto his cock. This version had a warming element and could be adjusted to provide a closer fit. As she took advantage of those features, she liked the sparks in his eyes and the ripple through his muscles as he reacted to the slick clutch of the toy. It reminded her of how he responded when she gripped him with her hand.

He gave her a quick nod when it was tight enough. She could tell he wasn't sure about this. She'd had him jerk off into a condom in front of her before. But this gave her all the control. Retrieving a pair of cuffs from the cabinet, she hooked them to the rings and wrapped them around his wrists. As she did, she lifted onto her toes and pressed her breasts against his chest. He nuzzled her hair, her ear. Gave her a nip with the edge of his teeth.

Bad boy. If it hadn't been encased in the masturbator, she would have given his cock a sharp slap to tell him so. When she settled for a flick of her nails against his flank, his eyes flashed at her, lips pressing against a smile. She liked his smile, but she wanted to take the cocky edge out of it.

He could snap out of the cuffs if needed. Their purpose was to tell him she wanted to take over, more than usual. When she backed away, she shot him a wicked look and revealed the final piece. A handheld remote.

His jaw tightened. She noted his testicles below the masturbator convulsed, as if his cock had jumped in reaction. Backing up to the spanking bench, she stretched out on her side on the firm surface, bracing one heel on the lower step. The position enhanced the rise of her breasts, the depth of her cleavage, as she slipped open the next two buttons of her blouse. She'd bent her other knee, bringing it up onto the bench, which had inched up the skirt and revealed her black lace panties. When she slipped a finger beneath and gave herself a stroke, then tasted her arousal, a growl escaped him.

Shooting him a teasing look from beneath her lashes, she turned on the remote. As the masturbator began to ripple and squeeze along his length, that growl became a soft oath. His throat convulsed as he swallowed.

"This doesn't feel like I'm doing anything for you, Mistress," he managed in a strangled voice.

She bumped it up a notch. The vibration could be spread out along the entire shaft, but it had a separate, focused setting for the pulse directly beneath the cock head. If she pushed that up to its highest level, she could yank a climax out of an erect male in a matter of seconds.

She increased the vibration there, that and her intent gaze telling him she didn't want words from him right now. His gaze clung to her as she put her hand back into her panties, inserting her fingers inside her slickness. The movement in and out would tell him how wet she was before she withdrew the glistening fingers to show him, and sucked on them again as he groaned.

The first time she'd had him masturbate in front of her, he'd told her it didn't feel right, seeking his pleasure while a Mistress watched. To answer that concern, she'd made him masturbate to climax. When she straddled his face afterward, pressing her cunt against his mouth and nose, rubbing herself there, she'd nearly drowned him with how wet his show had made her.

The lesson had made an impression, such that he shouldn't have made the same misstep now. But it had been a difficult day, and he liked to lose himself in direct service to a Mistress. She'd give him a pass for his faulty memory, even as she emphatically reminded him of the lesson.

He was trying to stay still, but his hips were rocking in a shallow rhythm from the pull of the massager. She played with the different settings, prompting a lot of intriguing convulsive movements. More creative oaths.

Eventually she had his ass hitting the wall and the crosspieces of the St. Andrew's. He'd lost control of his own body's movements, the rhythm of sex taking over.

He wanted to fuck something, needed to fuck something. His face was rigid, teeth bared, eyes full of crazed, charged, rutting light. When she at last stopped the vibration, it took his body a few seconds to realize it, for him to stop himself.

She came and stood before him. Lifted a flat palm that said *Stay still*.

Two hundred pounds, six feet tall, a tiger wanting to leap on her, take her down. Yet when she leaned in and pressed her tight nipples in her thin bra against his bare chest, he went still. She put her lips on the side of his neck, letting her breath tease him before she bit his collar bone. Pressing her thighs against the massager, she started the vibration again.

"Fucking hell, Mistress..." he muttered, his hands flexing.

She opened the cuffs before she stepped back and gazed at him. He held that look, his dark blue eyes almost black. She pointed to the floor, lifting her arms out to her sides to tell him where she wanted his placed.

His eyes stayed on hers as if he was waiting for her to blink. She didn't.

He dropped to one knee, then to the other. The massager pulsing over his cock caused him some coordination issues, and she stayed close in case his balance posed a problem. However, he managed to put himself onto the floor without assistance, stretching out on his back before her in a magnificent slow-motion display of careful movement.

Standing over him, she gazed her fill at his beautiful, aroused body, the quiver of his thighs and hips, responding involuntarily to the clutch of the toy.

She removed her blouse and skirt, letting the cloth whisper off her flesh, heated by his gaze. Then she placed her feet on either side of his torso, below his outstretched arms. When she squatted, her pussy was close enough he could dip his head and have his mouth on it. *Be still.* She mouthed it, then touched his lips so he'd know what part of his body she particularly meant.

She brought her cunt against his pressed lips and settled herself there, the sheer fabric of her panties between his mouth and her flesh. Then she turned up the vibration and squeeze of the toy, particularly the stimulation just below the head of his cock.

"Fuck...fuck..."

His hands opened and closed, became tight fists. She rubbed herself against his mouth, even as he tried to keep his lips closed and tight, inert as she'd ordered.

It took about eight seconds before the climax seized him, defeating his self-control. As his body bucked, his hands left the floor to clamp tight on her thighs and hips, so he didn't throw her off him.

He bellowed against her damp flesh. Every movement, every hot breath, shuddered through her. She was so close, but she held back, loving his brutal energy, the power of all that sexual release flooding through her senses as he cried out.

As he finished, she didn't ease back on the controls right away. She waited until the masturbator became overwhelming on his hyper-sensitive shaft. He had to endure that for her, the price of the orgasm she'd given him. He rocked and groaned, fighting his movements, trying to control them for her, working to earn her mercy.

She liked that. A Mistress knew the value of being a little cruel to get what they both wanted.

When she finally stopped the massager, relief suffused his features. She moved back and removed it with gentle fingers, giving him an intimate stroke before she set it aside. Then she stood and removed her panties, draping them over the toy before she knelt again.

His eyes followed her as she straddled his tattooed arm. Reaching behind her, she guided him to place his forearm against her buttocks, his palm against her lower back. Then she began to rub herself upon him, the firm biceps and triceps, the rounded part of his broad shoulder.

She painted her arousal over all the colors and images, worked herself against the hard ridges of bone and muscle, until the climax took her. Her hand was braced on his chest, the other by his head. As she rocked, her breasts wobbled above the lace edge of her bra.

While his avid gaze devoured her, he gripped her forearm with his other hand to help steady her. Closing her eyes, she dropped her head back, savoring the final waves of pleasure, all the way to the last tiny quivering aftershock. His spread fingers pressed into her back.

When she was finally done, she let him help her move to straddle his waist, sit on his cock. Which should have been replete, but being Tiger, it was on its way to getting stiff again. She wiggled a little on it just for the pleasure of teasing him, but then, with a more serious feeling in her heart, she leaned forward to touch her lips to his.

His gaze, still filled with heat, held hers. He lifted a hand, pausing to confirm it was allowed before he touched her face, caressing her cheek and throat. As he ran his thumb over her lips, his face held quiet wonder.

Then he said the absolute right thing.

"That is a hell of a toy, Mistress. But coming in that will never be half as good as the privilege of being inside your cunt. Whether or not you ever let me come again."

The aftermath was...unexpected.

Tiger couldn't get it out of his head, her climaxing against the tattoo on his arm, all the intense messages that went with that. But he didn't have to analyze anything right now. She adjusted to sit behind him, putting his head in her lap like she did at the club. While she stroked his hair and shoulders, the planes of his face, he relaxed into her hold. He reached up and touched her face, gazing at it as he played with strands of her hair. She smiled at him, eyes and mouth soft.

After a while, she typed on her phone and showed it to him. "I'll order us some food."

Pushing himself up, he rubbed his five o'clock shadow. "Long as I'm paying for it, Mistress."

She arched a brow, but graciously nodded. As he pulled on his slacks, she took his dress shirt and shrugged into it. She buttoned three of the middle buttons before taking off the bra beneath it, sliding it free through one of the sleeves. Wearing his shirt with nothing under it and only a few buttons done up, he could see random glimpses of a lot of intriguing things as she moved.

"You wear that look for long, you're going to have me ready for another go."

She smiled a very female smile and tilted her head toward her command center. He sat on the stool next to her chair, her elbow propped on his thigh as they decided together what they wanted for dinner.

They went for simple, a pizza loaded with veggies. She seemed surprised he was good with that, but he shrugged. "I like vegetables."

While they were waiting, she pointed him to her guest bathroom to do whatever cleanup he wanted while she went to the master. After retrieving his change of clothes from the truck and smoking a quick cigarette, he came back and cleaned up, donning the jeans and T-shirt. He'd tucked the suit rack into the bag, so he put the slacks and jacket on that, hanging it on a bathroom hook.

When he emerged, the dress shirt was on the doorknob, so he added that to the suit rack. While she'd looked damn good wearing that, he'd almost prefer seeing her in one of his T-shirts. Something with more of his scent on it.

Yeah, he was aware it was a primal male marking thing, but he had no problem with that side of himself.

She'd changed into a pink T-shirt over pajama pants, printed with white fluffy-looking llamas. If the word adorable slipped out of his mouth, he'd get a strip taken off his ass, but he suspected there was no way to avoid it.

Unless he focused above her waist. The loose movement of her breasts under the thin shirt, the jut of her nipples, was absolutely a good distraction from the shitty parts of today. Even the bottoms, clingy and soft, offered the tantalizing shift of her buttocks.

An astute glance told him she was aware of his attention, but as long as he didn't get caught too often, she might let the ogling pass.

When her security cam announced the pizza guy, she headed for the lift. *Oh hell no.* He waved her back. "I told you I'm paying. That includes the tip."

Plus he was the only male getting that view. At least for tonight.

They ate the pizza on the sectional, surfing TV channels, her sitting with one leg drawn up under her. When she was done, she invited him to make himself comfortable, because she needed to do some work.

Though he'd sure thought about it, he hadn't assumed the offer to stay over included sharing her bed. He couldn't remember the last time he'd shared a bed with a woman for more than the time that it took to have sex and share a cigarette or drink afterward. Over time, his relationship needs had narrowed to what he got at Club Progeny. Casual sex was covered by the occasional hookup at MC get-togethers or a biker bar. More social stuff was covered by the garage, bike rallies and extracurricular events Progeny offered.

She didn't seem concerned about having him here while she was working. With the kind of day it had been, him dozing off was expected. The surprise was how easily he was pulled into a much deeper sleep. When he surfaced with an uneasy feeling, the silence was the same, but he wasn't in his own bed, giving him a spike of anxiety until he realized where he was.

She was still sitting at the computer, hands moving with smooth grace over the mouse, touching the three screens, making notes on a tablet. A blanket covered him, a bed pillow under his head, another behind his back. It embarrassed him, her taking care of him, but it also kind of touched him.

Rising, he padded over to her. As he circled the tables and approached her from behind, he saw she was working on the program layout from the art show, doing graphic design stuff to a series of pictures in the middle screen. On the left monitor, a trio of pics caught his attention because the center one was Skye sitting on the edge of his platform, her hand on his leg, gazing up at him as he looked at her.

A casual look would see a woman at a man's feet, and all that could imply. But looking at her face and his own, he saw all the nuances that said otherwise.

As well as some even deeper things.

A dip of her chin to her shoulder told him she was aware of his presence. She pointed to the stool. She hadn't pushed it away when she started working, suggesting she'd left it there for if he woke and wanted to join her. That touched him, too. He'd been thinking of grabbing a quick smoke outside, but he put off the craving and sat down at her side.

Since TRA had been a sponsor of the event, their company logo, a purple, black and silver rose coupled with the New Orleans fleur-de-lis, was on one of the design pages.

When they'd given him his garage logo concept, he'd been initially uncertain about the purple accents. His crew had enthusiastically endorsed the logo, though, Larry getting it on the garage truck as soon as Tiger said okay.

Looking at the TRA logo now, Tiger wondered if the similar color choices had been a subtle brand of ownership. A way of saying the TRA Mistresses had put their mark on him. No matter who he chose at the club, he was one of theirs. He would always be part of their family.

To a guy who'd had to turn his back on his own, that message was valued.

He enjoyed sitting in silence next to Skye as she worked, looking at the other "art" he hadn't been able to view while a canvas himself. Like the girl whose torso had been painted blue and layered with tropical flowers. In the picture he was studying, she had her hair piled on top of her head, her hands holding it up and back arched as the female artist worked on her.

His attention moved to the satisfied smile and intent gaze of the airbrush artist who'd turned a junk car into a horse-drawn chariot. Tiger made a note to tell Larry to visit the corporate centers where those cars were on public display. He handled a lot of the garage's requests for airbrush work.

Skye was clipping additional stills from the drone footage to add to the professional photographers' work. She slid the prints between screens, trying them out, tweaking the quality with a mind-boggling number of layout buttons.

"Is this what you always wanted to do?" he asked. "Or is it what you landed on because it paid the bills?"

She put a hand on his throat, rubbed gently. He could feel that his voice was hoarse. From sleep, yeah, but he'd also smoked a lot this week. "Yeah, sorry. I keep lozenges in my truck."

She called up a dialogue box and typed. "You need to cut back. Not my business or my choice, but I care."

"Yeah, Maryshka says the same. She's the only one in the shop that doesn't smoke."

Her next sentence handed the question back to him, rather than answering it herself. "How about you? What did you want to be?"

In the dead of night, sitting with a woman like this, after the day they'd shared, he was susceptible to saying things he probably shouldn't. But the words came out anyway. "In middle school, I imagined being this kid my brother and I beat up."

At her startled look, he knew he'd roped himself into having to explain. "We only intended to take his lunch from him. It wasn't long after my mom died. Being an angry asshole was my only goal in life. The kid had a note in his lunch. *I'm proud of you –Mom.* That's why I wished to be him. Living a life like that. The note was what made us decide to beat him up. Colt dropped it on his chest after and gave him an extra kick in the nuts. Probably ended his chance of having a family. Good times."

She met his gaze, held a beat, then started typing. "The technology expanded my communication options. Through that, I discovered anything in that field interested me. In middle school, some kids pretended to be my friends so I'd break into the school's computer system and upgrade test scores and report cards, download exams. Find teacher addresses so they could egg the houses of their least favorite ones on Halloween."

She wasn't hesitating, the words flowing across the screen, suggesting it was the same kind of memory as his. A distant pain she'd moved on from, but a significant turning point, even if only in hindsight.

"When a couple of them were caught on the cheating, they sold me out. The principal, Mrs. Standwell, sat me down. Pushed a piece of candy across her desk to me. Let it sit there while she ate one herself. She said, 'When you're standing behind a wall, screaming silently for people to see you, get to know you, become your real friend, you can become desperate enough to accept the ones that most definitely aren't.'"

He laid his hand on her leg. She glanced at him and kept typing. "Just like you, I had the whole I-don't-give-a-shit attitude down, but the way she said it and looked at me, cracked something. She told me if I'd show them how I had gotten into the system and offer some suggestions for improving their security, she wouldn't expel me. She also transferred me into an advanced English class with Mrs. Warren. She said, 'When you communicate differently from others, your command of words is as important as knowing ones and zeroes.'"

A tight smile. "She also told me if I fucked with Mrs. Warren—yes, she used those words—'She will tie you to a chair and read you obscure sonnets until your ears bleed.'"

Tiger grinned as Skye closed the dialogue box and swiveled her chair in his direction. "Did you test that out?" he asked.

She mouthed, "Hell no," confirming that Mrs. Warren had lived up to her terrifying rep.

"If you're still serious about wanting to learn, want to come over to my place next weekend and learn how to tune a bike?"

Crazy, but after he threw it out there, he found himself holding his breath a little until she nodded. He liked the sparkle of interest in her gaze. Then she sobered.

"You haven't asked me again, how I lost my voice." She signed then typed it as well.

"You answer it if you want to, Mistress. I get the feeling it's not an easy one to answer."

She gave him that penetrating look she often had during a session. It made him curious about her intent, until she opened a document she must have typed while he was asleep. She gestured to it, *Read*, then pantomimed a cup of tea or coffee, a question. He shook his head, telling her he was fine.

When she went to get her own, he watched her. The sweet movement of her backside under the llama print, the delicate protrusion of her shoulder blades beneath the thin pink shirt, the tilt of her head.

How she brushed her hair from her forehead as she took a mug from the cabinets.

His gaze slid back to that picture of the two of them. She'd left it up, and it stayed in his peripheral vision as he began to read what she'd pulled up on the screen for him.

"Car crash when I was four. They think it was the result of traumatic brain injury, but the final decision was idiopathic mutism. Meaning they don't really know why my ability to speak never returned, even after everything else healed and seemed fine.

"My father was driving. 'I'll take your voice with me to heaven / I'll listen to you sing every day / You're an angel like no other.' I thought he was singing that to me. I had my hands on his face, in his hair, holding on, but he said, 'keep your eyes closed, baby.'

"The raised bed of the truck in front of us had smashed through our windshield. It took his head off. It had ended up in my lap, where I sat in back in my car seat. They had to pry my fingers off of it."

Jesus Christ. He glanced toward the kitchen. She was steeping her tea, her back to him. She'd typed it the way he suspected she'd thought about it, rough and disjointed, circling around and cutting through, no real flow. That was how you had to talk about something this difficult, cutting it into pieces and scrambling it so the whole cohesive picture didn't crush you. He got that. He returned to reading.

"When I saw *The Little Mermaid*, the part where Ursula took Ariel's voice, I thought it meant I'd get it back when I eventually met my prince and had true love's kiss. I was little when I believed that, but it still went through my mind the first time a boy kissed me.

"After I got over the disappointment of it not being true," —eye roll and silly face emojis that gave him a painful smile—

"I thought, 'if I get my voice back, my father won't have it up in heaven to hear me sing to him.' So I realized I didn't want it back. I'd borrow other voices to create one for myself. He could keep mine."

She was leaning against the brick pillar outside the kitchen, looking at him. He could smell the fragrance of the tea. Rising, he went to her. He took her tea and set it aside, then drew her into his arms. Hers slipped around his back, and her body lifted in a sigh, a letting-it-out. He put his head down over hers.

It was life, wasn't it? All these horrible and wondrous things together. The best way to handle it was to know when you needed to balance it. And who with.

He'd given her a lot of himself today, things he hadn't told anyone. She'd given him back the same. He wanted to give her more. The invitation hadn't been there earlier, but the need was there now. And she looked tired.

"Ready to go to bed, Mistress?"

When she nodded, he could tell he surprised her by picking her up. Moving to the platform that held her bed, he took the short set of steps up to it to sit on the mattress edge. He kept her in his lap, her arms looped around his neck. Leaning over, he drew down the cover. With a smile, he rolled back and deposited her into that spot on the mattress before straightening back up and putting the cover over her. "When she was really little, that was how I'd tuck Aubrey in," he told her, "Whenever Nicole and Colt went on adults-only trips, she'd leave her with me."

Colt of course never acknowledged it, and probably opposed it in theory. However, the indirect indication that his brother trusted him with his daughter, enough not to give Nicole a lot of shit over it, had been a subtle balm on an otherwise trashed family relationship.

Tiger glanced toward the clock. About three a.m. She'd invited him to stay the night, but that had been a while ago. "I should hit the road, but—"

Her hand closed on his. She shook her head and reached over his arm to tug down the covers next to her.

His gut did a roll that probably felt the way that bed move did to Aubrey. A lightness to balance the end of day, the facing of the darkness.

"Sure thing, Mistress."

CHAPTER THIRTEEN

*B*y Thursday, Tiger felt on top of his world. Yeah, things were still silent as fuck in his head, but he was pretty sure outside it the birds were singing. After spending the night with Skye last weekend and getting the memorial thing in his rearview mirror, he felt better than he had in a while. Things were less overwhelming.

He'd skipped the hearing class this week. He was figuring this shit out. He didn't need it, not as a weekly thing. The garage repairs were proceeding with the insurance money. The building inspector had signed off on them using the two bays furthest from the damage. Maybe he'd tell Red to come back next week. Bring in Maryshka and Larry as soon as that third bay was deemed usable.

When he leafed through the mail he'd brought home from the shop, he saw the reminder about a Kentucky rally coming up. Maybe he should go. Maybe he should invite Skye to come with him. Yeah, he had to confirm his balance on the bike first—something that tightened his gut with a little shot of worry, given how badly it had gone last time he'd tried it—but if that was better now, why not?

Some part of himself warned he needed to settle down, not get too confident, but feeling good felt...so damn good. He'd missed being in control of his life. Since Skye was coming over this weekend to learn about bike tuning, he'd hit the grocery store to pick up her drink preferences and replenish his beer supply, plus lay in the fixings for some snacks she might like.

Three hours later, the whole world was shit again.

~

He didn't make it back to the house. The garage was closer. He felt sick to his stomach, he had a tremor in his hands, and the pain and dizziness were a hurricane in his head. He could text the doc about it, but he didn't want another damn doctor appointment. Or to leave his back office. Maybe ever again. There were plenty of grocery delivery services when he ran out of what he'd picked up.

Drama queen shit, but still. What had the slides said in the last hearing class he'd attended? "Don't let yourself hide. Have a safe space, but limit it to thirty minutes. After thirty minutes, get out and do something." The guy who'd taught the class signed everything, but he also used a voice software like Skye that projected words up on a screen.

"Staying in that cave will make the anxiety and bad emotions worse. It will become harder to move forward."

Sure he might know what he was talking about, but who gave a fuck? As stupid as it sounded, Tiger felt like it was him against the world. He thought he could go to a rally? Jesus fucking Christ. Right. There was no point. And not just for that.

He typed in the text, making it quick and casual. *Going to have to cancel this weekend. Sorry. I'll make it up to you.* He sent a dozen rose emojis and followed it with an emoji of two people on a bike, a guy and a girl, one of those animated ones so the girl's hair was streaming out behind her.

It made him imagine what it would have been like, being at the rally, her relaxed on the bike behind him, pointing at things, excited about stuff that was new to her, letting him see it through her fresh eyes. God, he was a pathetic asshole. Damn it. But he was fucked up in his head. No telling how he'd fuck up her day if he had her come over this weekend.

She didn't answer right away. She was at work, so he expected that. She had an important job, a busy life. He was a loser with a burned-out garage, a wobbly head and couldn't even go to the goddamn grocery store without...

He went out to the debris pile he needed to load up and cart away. Chuck was probably getting tired of looking at it.

Tiger picked up a pipe, hefted it. Then he beat the shit out of a half-burned pallet, sending planks flying. He wanted to destroy something, needed to do it. He stepped back, looking for a new target, and tripped over some more pipes. They'd obviously been knocked loose from the pile and rolled behind him, with a jingling metal sound against the asphalt he couldn't hear. He landed on his ass, hand slamming down on a splintered piece of wood. It tore a strip out of his palm.

"Fucking hell." When a deaf man vented his rage, he couldn't hear his howls, the clang as he flung the pipe at the wall of his building.

He wanted to get on his bike and just ride. When things became too much with Colt and his father, with all of it, that was what had brought him back to center and given him peace. As if mocking him and what he wanted, the dizziness overtook him, seized him in the gut with a shot of anxiety and despair. He threw up his toast and coffee.

Shit.

When he glanced up, he saw the shadow as Kat moved away from the back screen door. Chuck replaced her. Tiger held up a hand. *Please, fucking God, leave me alone.*

Chuck's nod was punctuated with a concerned look. But he got it. He followed Kat back deeper inside, though he left the door open. In case.

He didn't deserve friends that good. Tiger retreated to his office, stopping off at the bathroom to rinse out his mouth and wash the cut on his palm. As he stared at himself in the mirror, he couldn't stop the thought. He would have been better off being the dead one, instead of Nicole.

Anything that kicked him over the hearing loss seemed to connect back to that. No pity party was complete without inviting all the available contributors.

Even the stupidest ones, like the grocery store bakery's lack of his favorite morning Danish today. Yeah, put that at the top of his list of traumatic woes.

Disgusted with himself, he tossed the bloody paper towel in the trash. He didn't blame Skye for not answering him. He'd just bailed on her with no real explanation.

He was three cigarettes and two beers into more bullshit wallowing in his office when his screen lit up, and he saw her answering text.

K. I can find another biker with a tight ass to show me how to do a tune-up.

No emoji giving him a hint, no *lol*, which suggested she was serious. Not about looking for another biker, but serious as in pissed. She also didn't ask why he was cancelling.

When a hand came to rest on his shoulder, he started. It had entered his field of vision a few seconds before it landed, and it was a female hand, so he didn't take a swing.

He'd had the hallway door to the outside propped open and the fan on the TV table had been blowing toward him, easing the balmy air of the shop. As a result, he hadn't caught her scent, and he'd been too deep in his head to catch the vibration when she was in the hallway.

Since he'd concluded he wasn't a practical target for the Fallen Angels' shitstorm, he'd become less vigilant about a physical attack. He supposed in this instance that was a good thing, because it meant he was keeping the gun in the drawer instead of on the desk.

It didn't matter. He erupted from the chair and turned on her. "Of all the goddamn people who should know not to sneak up on someone who can't hear. What the fuck?"

An unfortunate déjà vu to the first time she'd come here. He was being large, looming and angry again, something a person his size shouldn't ever be in a small space, particularly with a woman.

"Jesus." He rubbed a hand over his face. "Damn it. I'm sorry. Just... now's not a good time, okay?"

Her eyes had gone wide like that day, but this time, in a blink, that look disappeared and she was up in his grille. Not something many dared to do when his temper was riled. She took two handfuls of his shirt and gave him a little shake. Not hard to interpret. Then she let him go to make some gestures she combined with mouthing the words.

Stop it. Take a breath. She pantomimed that deep breath. When her hand dropped to one of his, he realized they were fists, his body battle ready, as if her presence was a threat. She was looking at him in her quiet way, helping him realign things, no matter how much the rest of him wanted to act like a raging asshole.

He started to speak, to blurt out some lame ass explanation, to say he was sorry again, to say something probably even more idiotic to piss her off, but she put her fingers to her lips and imitated the breathing thing again.

She was handling him. Not something he allowed anyone to do. Yet with her first touch, firm and calm, and that direct look, he knew he'd trust her to handle him, an important difference.

He did notice her pulse beating high in her throat. She covered it well, but it was the sign of someone not sure of the safety of the situation, enough to mark exit options.

Shame swept him. She knew him well enough to be mostly sure he wouldn't hurt her. But that he was behaving badly enough to have her evaluating it, introducing the "mostly" into the thought, put a cap on the total bad of this day.

Well, that was something *he* could handle. He showed her that he was listening, by doing the breathing. He took her hand and put it on his chest to help, dropping his head, letting himself settle before he spoke.

"I'm okay." He met her eyes. "I'd never hurt you. No matter how pissed I get. I'm in the world's shittiest, self-pitying mood and I'm not fit company for anyone, let alone the person I'm the gladdest to see, when I'm not being this complete prick."

A flicker went through her dark eyes, but she lifted her phone. "Sit down and tell me what happened."

As it played through his head, he realized how stupid it was going to sound. But her expression said he wasn't going to be able to weasel out of telling her, especially after he'd been a big enough jerk that he owed her an explanation. Unless he wanted to be a bigger jerk.

He considered it to save male pride, but he hadn't earned that right, either. He sat back down in his chair. Rather than taking the guest chair, she slid onto the desk, pushing his half-drunk beer and ash tray out of the way with a distasteful wrinkle of her pert nose. She did her familiar Mistress attention-getting move, propping her feet, clad in her work heels, against the seat of his chair between his spread legs.

She leaned forward with a forthright stare. The set of her arms pushed her breasts together and up, doing interesting things with the V-neckline of her blue shirt. If he was in the mood to have his eyes scooped out with a melon baller, he should just keep staring.

He lifted his gaze to hers. "It's bullshit stuff," he told her wearily. "I get ready to go to the grocery store this morning, and I can't find my keys. I'd left them on the counter last night. I remembered doing it. But I still looked everywhere, until I could have sworn someone was fucking with me. Instead, I found them stuck in the heat register under the kitchen cabinets. They'd fallen while I was making dinner last night. I'd pushed the placemat to the side, and it took them over the edge."

She said nothing, waiting for all of it. She'd know when he was done. She was good that way. When she and Abby took turns, Skye had always preferred to be the second Mistress, the one that took over. More than any of them, she knew when he'd reached the finish line.

"I couldn't hear them," he told her the obvious conclusion. "That's why I looked everywhere else, not thinking they would have fallen off the counter. Because, hell I would have heard that, right? Like a damn phantom limb. Am I talking too loud?"

She made the measuring gesture—a little. But she also followed it with one he recognized as "Keep going."

He adjusted his tone. "So I get past that and head for the store. In the checkout, this woman comes up with her cart, and she's glaring at me. She starts spouting off. Her teen daughter's with her, looking real nervous about her mom being mad. I didn't know if I'd cut in front of her in line or what, so I just gestured to her to go ahead of me, what the fuck. I didn't say anything because I didn't know what to say, then it just comes out. 'Sorry, whatever I did. I'm deaf.'"

He took a breath. "First time I've said it aloud like that, instead of saying 'I can't hear.' Kind of startled me."

Also kind of crushed him, like the aluminum beer can he picked up, finished the last tepid swallows and tossed into his recycling bin.

"I see her say 'you're deaf?' and I nod. Her daughter has started typing on the phone, just as crazy fast as you." He paused, trying for a smile. "She holds the phone up to tell me what her mom's deal was.

She'd asked me if I could pull something off a top shelf for her. I remembered then that I'd been looking in her general direction, but I wasn't paying any attention to her. She thought I'd looked at her and just walked away. That I was a rude asshole."

He rubbed his hand over his face again. He wanted to put the hand on Skye's knee, but he hadn't been invited. He laid it back down on the arm of the chair. "I told her I'd be happy to do that, if she still needed it, but she shakes her head. Now she insists I go before her in line, looking at me like..."

When he fell silent, his emotions churning, Skye's screen appeared in his field of vision. "Like instead of being a capable adult who can reach top shelves, you're someone she shouldn't expect anything from, because you're handicapped."

"Yeah. I said I forgot something and went back down another aisle until they left. But then I got so pissed. Out of proportion pissed, like there was stuff built up in me that I didn't know was there. I thought the day was going well, you know? And now, all of a sudden, I wanted to grab her and yell, shake her for acting that way. I wanted to drag her back to the aisle get her goddamn Skippy peanut butter or Fruity Oats or toilet bowl cleaner, whatever it was on that top shelf. Just to prove to her that I'm just like her, just as all there, just as... I'm just like her."

He shook his head. "But I'm not. That's what the voice in my head kept hammering me with. I left the cart and headed back to the parking lot. I was worked up, so I step in front of a car coming through, one of those muscle cars I'd hear a mile off, anyone would. Damn, I should have felt it through the asphalt. Guy flips me off, and I guess my expression told him how close he was to being pulled through the window. He takes off while still yelling at me. And rolling it up as fast as the motor can go."

A wry look, one he hadn't been able to summon at the time. "So at that point I feel like I'm in a pinball machine, bouncing from one bat to another to get the shit kicked out of me. I managed not to scurry to the truck like some kind of rodent. That's when the headache and dizzy spell really hit, so I ended up sitting on the running board."

He shook his head. "Managed to clear it up to get back behind the wheel. I come here, and today's mail...there's a card from Aubrey. My brother is refusing to let her go back to Florida. Making her stay at the farmhouse. On the fucking property. She didn't say that. She just said, 'Daddy says he needs me to stay with him a while. I miss grandma.'"

He stared at his hands and turned them over, looking at his callused palms, the skinned place from the splintered board. "This morning, before all of this, I had thought about inviting you to a rally. And then I thought, 'what would have happened if she'd been on a bike with you and you got dizzy like this?' That was the final straw. The idea that I could have screwed up like that and gotten you hurt.

"Shit, Mistress. I thought I was doing good. But that was just because I had a few good days in places I could mostly control. What the hell was I thinking, believing I'm ready for something as crazy as a bike rally, where there'll be a million ways I can get messed up and turned around? And not be able to watch after you like I should? You're not helpless, I know you're not, but...shit."

A long silence. He was looking at her knees, covered by a gauzy skirt printed with that famous blue and white painting of water lilies. Back up to her shirt's ribbon-edged neckline, the hint of her breasts beneath. He wasn't being a jerk. It just helped to rest his eyes on her, and he wasn't ready to look her in the face. The hand holding her phone showed her trimmed polished nails and a gold and pearl ring with a fairy worked into the delicate setting. Helpful aids to swiftly identify her as a woman when she'd touched him.

Her foot shifted, the toe against his testicles under denim, which brought his gaze up to her instantly. She reached forward, her hand out as she sent a pointed look toward the hand he'd cut. Rather than arguing, he laid it in her grasp. Her fingers brushed around the skinned place, a gentle contact.

"Is there anything you can do for Aubrey?" she typed after she let him have his hand back.

"Maybe. Not sure yet. I'd assumed she'd gone back to Florida. I don't know what Colt's long-term plan is, but it's pretty obvious Rose and Bill would take her. Get her as far from that life as they can."

She put a finger to her temple then flipped it up, mouthing the word she was saying. "Smart."

"Yeah. I need to figure out how much contact he'll let me have with her. If he'll even talk to me." The transcription machine worked on the phone itself, not just the answering machine, so they might be able to have a conversation, if he could get Colt to respond to his texts. "Nicole was our go-between for years."

He'd call Rose tomorrow to see where she and Bill were on things. If it came to a custody fight and they needed character witnesses... well, he'd give his brother one more reason to hate him, he guessed. But he knew where Aubrey needed to be.

Skye lifted her phone again. The message she'd put into it was longer than one screen could contain, so he closed his hand over hers to scroll when needed. He was glad for the contact, no matter how neutral it might be. His hand already felt absurdly better, just from the light stroke of her fingers.

"Your ability to ride your bike is an innate skill," she said. "Something you've done for years. Is there a way we can test your balance in a safe place, like a parking lot?"

Practical. Logical. It was what he'd started the morning thinking he would do. It shifted his mind away from some of the heavier things. "Yeah, there is. I have room at my place. A dirt track to test bikes I'm working on."

The gleam in her gaze before she resumed typing should have warned him. She raised the phone again. "Maybe I'll add an element that will help you focus."

Or destroy it, he thought, but wisely kept that thought to himself.

She crooked a finger at him, making him pull in his legs and roll the chair forward a few inches. She shifted, putting the soles of her shoes against his chest, and leaned in.

The semblance of a real smile found its way to his face at the brazen move. She tilted the phone up so he could read it. "I'm going to put a plug up your ass while you practice. If you're nice, it won't vibrate."

He blinked. "What makes you think I won't safeword the hell out of that idea?"

She eased back to type, but one foot dropped down to dig into his thigh. He manfully managed not to wince. She showed him the phone again. "Three reasons. You deserve the punishment, and you need the reminder of how to respect yourself."

The darkness of the thoughts behind the words gripped him, but he managed to keep his voice light. "You said three reasons."

She touched his face, her eyes suddenly serious. She typed again. "You like pleasing me. It's important to you."

He closed his hand over hers, jaw flexing. She one-handed typed her next question, her gaze matching its tone. "Truth? Would a plug make it difficult for you to stay safe in that situation? Or me, if I'm on the bike with you?"

"Probably," he admitted. "Though you know I won't deny you the option when my feet are firmly on the ground." Or his knees. He sighed. "When I was with the Fallen Angels, situational awareness was pretty much life or death. I got out of the habit. The keys, the muscle car, the lady at the grocery store."

"On the flip side," she typed, "that means you don't have to learn it from scratch. You just have to dust off the skills."

"Yeah." He also needed to adapt them, since that earlier honed awareness had included hearing in the mix. "Problem is, I'm not in my teens or twenties anymore. At forty you get a little cantankerous about changing and adapting."

She gave him a solemn look. Showed him her phone. "Can't speak to that. I'm not that old."

"You—"

She grinned and dropped her legs back down, trying to hop off the desk before he came out of the chair to grab her by the waist. When he succeeded in doing so, blocking her escape, she lifted her legs again to lock them over his hips. Not an invitation. Not exactly. One of those heel tips dug into his ass, but she touched his face and gave him a searching look. Signed, then typed.

"Let's go to your place and work on your balance."

No question—there was more than one meaning to that statement.

Did Mistresses routinely carry this kind of thing with them? Tiger eyed the plug she'd laid out on his kitchen table. Guess a Mistress never knew if she might need to whip it out and shove it up some amenable sub's backside.

When they'd arrived at his place, she'd been all business. No chitchat about the house or property. She'd shouldered the bag she'd pulled out of her Mustang, since she'd followed him home, and asked for directions to his guest bathroom.

He was considering all the things she might be doing in there. Including checking her email, meditating, or taking a power nap, if she'd absented herself for psychological effect.

Or because she was giving him time to perform the list of commands she'd left him, typed on his phone and laid out on the table in front of him.

Take care of anything you need to do in the bathroom.

Take off everything and leave it there.

Except your shirt. Leave it by the kitchen sink.

Put your hands on the top of the chair.

Spread your legs shoulder width.

Put your gaze on what's on the table when you get back.

Wait for me.

He'd watched her go down the hallway, hips swaying, head tipped to study the pictures he had on his walls. She might not have made any comments about her surroundings, but she was taking it all in.

It was a decent place, the house a seventies ranch he'd updated. The draw for him had been the barn for his vehicles with an attached three bay garage, plus twenty-five acres with water access.

No question a man lived here. His pictures, whether framed art or photographs, mostly related to cars and motorcycles. His furniture was comfortable and fit his size. She wouldn't look bad curled up, cute as a kitten, in his recliner. In those llama pajamas.

He imagined her napping there on a weekend—if she ever slept. The two of them hanging out, maybe watching TV or taking a hike in the woods. He had a bass boat and could take her out on it.

He liked to do that when he wasn't working on customizing cars or bikes here. He also wasn't averse to spending a Sunday afternoon in his recliner, watching sports, catching a favorite movie or taking a nap after a hard week's work. Particularly in the summer, when New Orleans' heat could make mechanic work especially grueling.

His glance went around the kitchen. A lot of the Fallen Angels he'd grown up around didn't care about cleanliness beyond keeping the coffee table wiped down so nothing sticky fouled their coke lines. He might occasionally have some homey clutter, like a few shirts draped over a kitchen chair to damp dry from the laundry, or change left on his dresser, but everything was blissfully clean. Zero odors of old food, mildewed towels, and sweaty, unwashed men.

No woman had ever lived here. Inhaling Skye's fragrance, he realized that was a scent it lacked. It also gave him a twinge of remembrance, of his mother's light perfume in his childhood home. Before it stopped being a home at all.

Oh fuck, they weren't going there. He was stalling and he didn't really know why. No matter how rarely he'd done it, he knew the house met basic bring-a-girl-in standards. He went to his bedroom and the bathroom there. Though he'd shaved yesterday, he gave his face a quick touch up in the shower. To make himself ready for Mistress standards. They could get dirty on the bike later. He wouldn't mind getting real dirty with her. The thought gave him a grin.

All clothes off, she'd said. *Yes, ma'am.* After he complied, he padded back to the kitchen, and put his shirt by the sink. She was still in his guestroom, but she'd come back while he was gone. That was when he'd seen the plug.

"Shit."

He'd been plugged and pegged before. Until Abby introduced him to being fucked with a strap-on, he'd been resistant to the idea, but now he didn't mind it. The climax could be incredible. So could feeling the Mistress writhe against him, her grip on his waist and hips, nails driving into his flesh. Her breath between his shoulder blades, her body melting against his back, letting him hold her up after the clit stimulator took her to orgasm while thrusting into him.

However, though he would suck on her fingers if she liked that, putting a plug or phallus into his mouth was a hard limit. He had zero interest if what the Mistress wanted was to roleplay a guy fucking him. Inviting a man to join the action was also a no-go. Not his thing. He liked his sexual encounters one hundred percent female.

When Abby had first been overcome by her schizophrenia, they'd done a few sessions to give her a vital shot of normalcy and control, a need Tiger understood way better now.

Those sessions had been done in the presence of Neil, though, a fellow Dominant and now her husband. While Neil had never touched Tiger, unless it was for aftercare help, it wasn't Tiger's thing, having an extra dick in the room. However, he wished Abby all the happiness in the world. She more than fucking deserved it.

Tiger's gaze slid back over the plug. It was bigger than what he usually took. Curiously, there was a black marker on the table next to it. Plus a reassuringly fat tube of lubricant.

Remembering her instructions, he put his hands on the top of the chair, spread his legs, and stared down at the items. He was still carrying the shit from earlier in the day, but this was helping. In or out of the club, this was the same, hearing or no hearing. His mind went to full sub mode, erection thickening as he waited on her pleasure, wondered how she'd let him serve her.

He flexed his hands on the back of the chair. After their last session, he knew he had a new hard limit. No blindfold. No making him keep his eyes closed for too long. Before, he'd liked being blindfolded, hearing the shifts of her body, anticipating where she might touch him next. He wondered if he'd ever again trust anyone enough for that level of sensory deprivation. Swimming in a quiet, dark world, no sight, no hearing, his only awareness the movement of her hands over him.

The vibration through the wood floor told him she'd returned. Though he wanted to see how and if she'd altered her appearance, he kept his gaze where she'd ordered it. His eyes half closed as her hands drifted over his shoulders and down his back. She was wearing gloves, with a satiny smooth feel to them. She'd used them before. They went past her elbows and were incredibly sexy.

She'd always conveyed a deep, erotic appreciation of his body through her touch, as if she was marking every muscle, every inch of skin, every scar, the small hairs on his nape and arms, his chest. The smaller bones of wrists and ankles. She was thorough in her tactile praise. It made him glad to have the kind of body and equipment to please a woman.

To please her specifically.

Her hand slipped through the opening provided between his braced arm and body, and curled around the plug on the table. She used her other hand to put her phone before him and show him what she'd typed.

"I'm going to fuck you with this first, Tiger, for my own pleasure. If I decide to let you come, I'll kiss you between your shoulder blades.

If I don't, I'll leave you aching and hard, a plug up your ass to remind you what behavior you owe your Mistress. And the respect you owe yourself, every day."

She ran a gloved hand over his shoulder, fingers sliding along the tattoo, as she tapped the phone to move to the next screen she'd pre-typed for him.

"You covered this up to send a message. You're no longer part of them. But it's in your heart. It can't be removed. You can never not be connected to them."

Skye had figured out what he had. A trauma could knock you back to fucking childhood. Losing his hearing had returned him to the quicksand where he'd struggled to define himself according to his own expectations, rather than a past that had tried to lock him into theirs.

She hadn't technically asked a question, but he knew the answer she needed.

"Yes, ma'am."

She pressed against him. She was wearing a cotton shirt with nothing under it, the give of her breasts and points of her nipples against his back. True to her threat, she was wearing a harness. While she'd talked to him, she'd fitted that big ass plug into it. It brushed against the back of his thigh.

She put her hand in the middle of his back. She wanted his torso flat on the table. With his height, that meant he had to partially bend his knees, an awkward and vulnerable position.

He wasn't into pain or humiliation, but he suspected this wasn't that. She intended to make this difficult, make him earn her forgiveness. And his own, for the self-flagellation.

He'd taught himself to be in his own corner. Mistresses liked that confidence, a man who didn't have to be constantly reassured, his insecurities stroked.

"You're not a child pretending to be a man while looking for another mommy's tit to suckle."

Cyn had said that. The closest thing to a compliment he'd ever received from her.

He realized that reminder was Skye's intent. While a lot of people wouldn't understand it—men or women—his submissive nature in moments like this was the strongest part of his maleness. Because this was a choice. To serve, to care, to be strong for whatever she needed, because he could be. He could surrender to her as a man, give her whatever she needed, as a man. He'd remember that next time he faltered over something as crazy as a pair of keys falling soundlessly on the floor.

She could expect that from him, that resolve and will. He wasn't too head stuck up his own ass to turn down her help, but she wasn't here to be his caretaker. Just the opposite. She was the Mistress he wanted to care for, to prove himself to. To live up to the expectations she knew he was capable of meeting.

All those overlapping thoughts returned him to himself. Gave him balance, an anchor.

Yes, ma'am. Message received, reinforced, and accompanied by a surge of fierceness that made him feel as if he was standing in a line of fire between her and him. He wouldn't falter on that line.

As he'd suspected, Skye had paid attention to her surroundings. Behind his kitchen trash can he had a folded stool for Aubrey, to reach the dishes in the upper cabinets. Skye brought it over and set it up it beneath his knees, the wood surface cushioned with a dish towel. He had to hold his thighs together to make them fit on the narrow width.

She'd brought her own tie-down strap. Of course. Butt plugs, tie-down straps...like a Domme girl scout. She looped the strap above his knees and ratcheted it closed, snug enough the strap dug into his flesh without cutting off circulation.

She circled the table. She was wearing the thin tank he'd worn under his dress shirt for the memorial. He'd had it hanging up in the guest bath with some other shirts, doing that damp dry thing since he'd done laundry a couple days ago. She wore the tank knotted at her waist over wet latex pants. The harness was buckled over it. The message wasn't sexiness. It was, "I'm ready to work, and the job is to fuck your stupidity right out of your head."

She still looked hot, though.

She stretched out his arms and made him clasp the edges of the table. After guiding his head down until his cheek rested on the flat surface, she squeezed the back of his neck with a pinch of nails, the message clear. *Stay where I put you.*

She showed him her phone. *You can switch from side to side if your neck starts to hurt, but right or left, your face is on this table.*

Picking up the marker, she leaned over to write on the top of his right hand. *Me.* Then she moved to the other. She caressed his side with gloved knuckles as he turned his head to see what she'd written there. *Trust.*

Trust me.

The words could mean her. They could mean himself. Whatever worked. He'd be staring at each of the words in turn, having time to think about them, as she shoved that plug into him. Until he couldn't think any more.

She was behind him again, and had taken the lube off the table. When she replaced it and put the business side of the plug up against him, it was reassuringly slick. Gripping his hips, she parted his cheeks with her thumbs. She rubbed the head of the plug against his rim, adding more oil there to further tease those nerve endings. It sent a jump start cable jolt to his cock, already jutting hard and tight below the table edge. Because of his thighs being strapped close together, his balls were likely bulging out behind, between them.

She confirmed it, her gloved fingertips whispering over them, then giving them a little slap. It didn't take much for that to hurt, not like that, and the sting startled him, but not enough to safeword. He wondered how it would feel when she was thrusting into him and pushing against them. A torment and pleasure both. *Christ.*

She was easing into his ass, taking her time, but it was a lot. She clasped his hips, adjusting him to help her with the angle. Then she was sliding in.

She tapped his back, a request for status. He had his right cheek to the table, staring at the left hand. *Trust.* He chose to respond in alphabet sign. *O* and *K*, left and right hands. He kept them that way until she stroked the middle of his back, showing approval that he'd chosen to do it that way.

Reaching beneath the table, she pushed a lubricated rubber cock ring over the head, all the way down to where she gripped his cock at the base. The ring had studs on the inside. And she didn't have just one ring. She had three, which she put on his cock, evenly spaced.

She pulled out of his backside, slow. All the way out. Fuck. She was going to have to get all the way into there all over again. Her fingertips slid away, and he couldn't see what she was doing, until she ran her tongue along his testicles. She teased that tender, stretched connection point, then went back down, playing over them, sucking one into her mouth. It wrenched a groan from him as his cock tried to stiffen further and those studs dug in.

Another tap for status. Another O and K. He shifted his head to the other side, glimpsed white-blond hair, a set mouth, the hint of dark eyes. The tank was so thin the color of her nipples had been visible beneath its stretch when she circled the table. A nightmarish wet dream.

She eased in, came partway out, eased in again. Then she started to pick up the pace. Holding him steady, his knees on the stool. With his legs bound together, the feeling of her having all the control was increased. She'd let him free if he safeworded, but he was at her mercy otherwise.

He'd always had an ironclad opinion on a Mistress's mercy.

You didn't ask for it.

You earned it.

It was all sensation, discomfort, arousal, a climax building with nowhere to go. She leaned over him, thighs pressed flush against his, weighted pressure against his balls, and gripped his hair, tight enough it pulled against his scalp. She bit the back of his neck, his shoulder blade, and the muscle flexing below that.

Then she was pinching his ass with sharp nails as she kept hitting the right spot dead on with that plug. He was gasping, groaning, hands in tight fists. Her palms covered his forearms, fingers stretching out to tap and point toward the words. *Trust. Me. Trust. Me.*

"I do, Mistress. I do. But this...is hard. Tearing me open..."

But that was the goal. Not the physical discomfort, not the stress, not the punishment. She was kicking in the door to his head, to the anger and frustration, to things that were even older than what had happened today. A good Mistress knew how to do that, but until his hearing loss she'd stayed away from it, respecting that door because he hadn't needed that incursion. She was crossing that line because she thought now he did.

She must be right, because he was letting her.

Her hand rested on his back, acknowledging his words. Another tap, tap. A pause. His hands once again formed OK.

She resumed. His balls were going to explode, and his cock was an aching, pulsing weight between his legs. He wasn't a sub who begged, and she never asked that of him. But things were hurting in his gut and chest. He could handle the abuse to his ass and balls, his manacled cock. But if she made him cry, he'd just have to kill himself. After he killed her and hid her body so there were no witnesses.

His throat was aching. "Mistress...please. Don't. Don't."

She laid down upon him again, and thank God, she'd removed the shirt, giving him the pleasure of round flesh and firm nipples. Reaching below, she slid off the cock rings and let them fall. Stroked her gloved fingertips along his length, up and down, and put her cheek on his shoulder. They both looked at that one word, *Trust*, as she kept working him.

"Please...please..." he was murmuring it, out of his head. When she shifted to plant a tender, significant kiss between his shoulder blades, above the tattoo he had on his back, the climax boiled out of his balls and jerked him hard against the table. She held on as he snarled, maybe even yelled at the strength of it. It was like she was riding him, the friction between their bodies adding to the intensity. Fuck, coming with his legs tied like that, it had him feeling like a worm jerking on a hook. A hook she had embedded in his ass.

When he at last came to a stop, she was moving her hand up and down his arm, over the tattoo, slow. She brought the glove to his mouth, and he understood. He gripped the finger ends with his teeth as she slipped her hand free of it, then removed it from his grasp, touching his mouth. As she moved her bare hand to his side, everything was so sensitive he shuddered at the contact. She scraped her nails over the gooseflesh.

At length, she pushed herself up, easing out of him. When she removed the harness, he watched her walk to the sink, gaze lingering on her naked back, the nip of her waist above the low ride of the pants. He wanted to put his hands there. The latex curved lovingly over her ass, shaped the cleft between. She dropped the phallus into the sink, leaving the harness on the counter. She removed the other glove, the one on her dominant hand, and left it with the harness.

She'd brought his T-shirt with her. With her back to him, she put it on again, but left it unknotted and removed the latex from beneath it, exposing her legs. She did it efficiently, barely giving him a glimpse of what hid beneath the shirt. A reminder he wasn't being rewarded. Her goal had been helping extract his head from where he'd shoved it up his ass.

But that meant he had another imperative, and when she came back to him, he asked for the privilege. "Let me serve you, Mistress," he told her. "Please."

Because she hadn't climaxed, and had left him no option to hold back for her. For him, that, too, was its own kind of punishment, and she knew it.

Without answering, she undid the tie strap and rubbed his thighs to help his circulation. She had a hand on him as he pushed himself up. He swayed, damn it. Yeah, it might be because of the intense climax. It didn't have to be his hearing. He had a Mistress to serve, if she'd let him. No time for babying himself.

She pulled a cushion off the seat of a chair and dropped it in front of the stool, gesturing him to kneel on it. When he complied, she made an up motion, telling him she didn't want him sitting on his heels yet. Instead, she went behind him and looped the tie strap around his ankles. She ran it to his wrists, a standing hog tie. She positioned the buckle within reach of his fingers, so he could break it loose at any time. Then she slid onto the table, propping her feet on the stool before him. The T-shirt was long enough to reach her mid-thighs, continuing to deny him the view beneath. For now.

Leaning over, she reached into her bag, which she'd left on one of the chairs. His jaw flexed as she brought forth a vibrator that looked modeled after a fucking horse. She gave him a level stare and pointed to his eyes, then downward, between her legs. As he put his attention there, she gathered the shirt to her waist, showing him her soft thighs, trimmed pussy, and the dent of her navel.

His gaze was to stay on her cunt as she did whatever she was going to do with that thing. Probably putting it inside her, her fingers working her clit and labia around it as she pumped it in and out, the shaft getting slick with her juices.

He'd sit on his heels, hands flexing inside the straps, and stare at her taking care of herself. All while she had his cock and mouth at her disposal. Watching her fuck herself with that would get him hard as a rock again, only this time he knew there'd be no release forthcoming. Oh, and she'd do it all in his shirt, her lush body writhing, inanimate cotton getting all the joy out of that.

Yeah, full punishment, all the fixings. He ached, he wanted, he watched. When she played the head of the dildo against her cunt, getting it wet, he bit back an oath at how slick she was. His spent cock throbbed, reaching for blood, wanting to show he had the hardness to satisfy her. Even if she denied him the honor.

Looking at that beautiful pussy was a gift, but he wanted to see other things, too. The focus of her eyes, the set of her mouth. As she arched back, he knew her breasts would be straining against cotton. He imagined holding that shirt later, putting his mouth on it where those nipples had been, moistening the fabric with his breath as he thought about the chance to suckle the firm points again.

She was killing him.

Her thumb lightly caressed and rubbed her clit as the dildo slid in slow, out slow. It shone with her arousal.

Her pace picked up. As she fucked herself, her ass lifted and pressed back against the table. She'd moved one foot to the chair on her right, keeping the other on the stool. Spreading her legs wider. Thank God it was a sturdy table; otherwise it might have scraped the floor, moving out of his range as her rocking increased in strength and urgency.

He thought about the sound of her breath, her self-consciousness about climaxing, because she couldn't moan or make cries like other women. Did she think a lover missed that with her? He didn't, because she expressed herself in ways just as captivating. Her facial features tightening, body writhing like a tribal queen dancing by firelight. God, there'd be a whole symphony in her eyes as the climax took hold of her. He wanted to see it.

For that, he would beg.

Looking at someone's face, particularly a lover's, had become far more critical to him, a deeper need, when he couldn't hear anything. She knew that, but with her reluctance about subs seeing her face during release, he wasn't sure if denying him that now was punishment or preference. Or if one served the purpose of the other.

He saw the trembling and locking of her leg muscles. The smooth movements on her flesh had become jerkier, her fingers on her clit more random. Her foot was up on its toes on the stool, going rigid. He wanted to look, fuck, he needed to look, but he kept staring at her hand, her wet cunt, the flushed, swollen clit.

"Please let me look at you, Mistress." He whispered it, because she was caught in the rush toward climax and he wouldn't interrupt that, but he had to throw his wish into that void. "Please."

Her hand, braced on the table, moved. She tapped her fingers against the wood. Not her usual graceful move, but she'd heard him. And had decided to give him what she never had before.

The permission flooded him with a surge of feeling almost as strong as an orgasm. It might be the first time in history a man had wanted to see a woman's face more than a close up of her climaxing cunt.

As his gaze rose, her eyes locked with his, her lips parting. Her breath would be rasping out as she rode that crest. "You are so beautiful," he told her. "The most fucking beautiful thing in the world. Thank you, Mistress."

Her eyes softened and her face tightened, her mouth stretching open wider, the arch of her neck more extreme. If he'd been free, he would have surged up, cradled her neck with his hand, held her so she had support as that powerful wave took her. As it was, his hands strained against the bonds. He could get free, he could do it, but this was how she'd left him, and he would honor that.

He relished every expression, every time her wild eyes met his and saw his pleasure and desire, his appreciation of the gift. When at last her climax ebbed away, it did so in that warm, poignant sunset kind of way. Something unforgettable, the punctuation at the end of a good day, a reminder that day might always end, but a nighttime of dreams lay ahead.

Her feet slipped off the stool as she straightened, then leaned forward, clasping his shoulder for balance. When she brushed her cheek against his, he nuzzled her face in return. He couldn't keep the urgency out of it, because she had his cock fully erect again. It would take time for that to settle down. She touched his face, warm eyes telling him she didn't mind the roughness. Or his aching hard state.

She left the table, bending over his shoulder to take off his bindings. He put his cheek to her hip and brushed his lips over a buttock. Yeah, he'd probably get hell for that, but he made it reverent. It felt good, just resting his mouth there. After she released the strap, she took a seat on the stool in front of him, spreading her knees. She guided him to sit on his ass on the cushion, his head to her thigh, his back against the other one.

Punishment was over and done. That was the end of it.

To distract himself from things he wasn't going to be offered right now, he thought about the sounds she'd be hearing in his kitchen. Ticking clock. The refrigerator motor. The various languages a house spoke, the same way a body did. Shifts and rustles, like the hum of a note spoken under one's breath, a murmur to oneself. The absence of it still rattled him, if he let it get under his skin.

She'd retrieved her phone and showed it to him. "I assume it's a little late for testing your balance on the bike. I can come back tomorrow."

He hadn't noticed the time, but it was later in the day than he'd thought. "If you want to stay the night, you're welcome to," he offered. "We could get some dinner. There's a good diner nearby that does takeout. I can give you the fifty-cent tour of my place if you want one, and we can find some stuff on TV. Watch a movie."

You don't have to let me fuck you like a damn animal, though if that gets put on the table, glory fucking hallelujah.

She arched a knowing brow, touched the curve of his lips with her fingertips. "You also have a shelf of board games in the guest room," she typed. She sent him a haughty look. "I can totally whip your ass at Candyland."

"No you can't. I've had way more practice. Those games are Aubrey's," he informed her.

"How about the puzzle?"

"The one with a thousand freaking pieces? She gave me that for my birthday. Picked it out herself, according to...Nicole." He pushed himself past the hitch over the name.

The picture was a black and silver Harley cruising bike, set against the background of an American flag. He'd planned to set it up one night on a card table in the living room so when he was hanging out with Aubrey, they could work on it, an ongoing project. When done, he'd brush it with glue and have it framed.

Skye hadn't given him her answer about staying the night, but was looking around his kitchen. A black, red and silver 1950s diner theme had evolved in here. It worked with his essential cooking appliances, the pots hung up above the butcher block center island. Red mugs beside the Keurig, a TV mounted on the wall. Flour cloth towels were printed with Harleys, matching the framed canvases of bikes mounted on the wall behind the six-seater kitchen table. A table he'd never view the same way, now that she'd brought herself to climax on it.

"I have coffee and tea. And I cook a mean breakfast." He crossed his loosely fisted hands in front of him so she could see the *Trust. Me.*

She smiled and uncrossed his wrists, making him realize the way he'd done it had presented the words backwards. But that was all right, because then she did with her hands what he'd done with his earlier.

She made the alphabet sign for *O* and *K*.

CHAPTER FOURTEEN

$\mathcal{H}$e showed her his shop slash garage, and the half-dozen customized bikes he had, including the Harley Dyna Street Bob he had for in-town use and going to the club. It was also his favored ride for opening up on the NOLA backroads. He had a silver Harley Street Glide for when he wanted to take longer, more comfortable trips on a bike. He'd ridden it to the last Sturgis rally in South Dakota.

She asked him questions about all of his rides, wandering through their ranks with keen-eyed interest. What customizations he'd added and why, what he liked about one kind of bike versus another. After that, she wanted to see some of the property; the water access, the dirt track, and the cows that lived on the other side of his property line fence. Charmingly, she was intensely interested but a little wary of them. His Mistress was a city girl.

She let him ask questions about her, too. They stayed away from sensitive stuff, just kept it to the fun and interesting.

By the time they came back to the house, it was nightfall. They picked up the takeout, and after dinner she had him dig out the card table so they could get the puzzle going. After separating out all the edge pieces, they did the frame.

She was right. She kicked his ass at Candyland, but he learned some new strategies to hold his own against Aubrey. He didn't know when or if Aubrey would ever be here again, but Skye didn't let him dwell on that.

She was a night owl, but as a guy who was usually at his garage by seven in the mornings and had pretty labor-intensive days, his gas started to run out around ten o'clock. Unless he was involved in working on a project in the barn, and then time stopped meaning anything.

Today was not one of those days. Getting along in a hearing world was really fucking tiring. Way more than he'd realized. He wondered how long it had taken her to build up endurance for it, from the speaking side of things.

He managed to suppress the yawning until they sat down on the couch to channel surf, her leaning against his side. One moment, he was watching; the next, he was coming awake and realizing he'd been out for a while. He was starting to make a habit of that around her. He hoped he hadn't snored, or worse, drooled.

She'd moved to the floor to sit at the coffee table, and was working on a laptop she'd brought. Closing down her work, she gave him a smile and pointed to the hallway. A question. *Bedtime?* He nodded.

He had a king-sized bed, a no-brainer for a guy of his dimensions. She was welcome in it, but he wouldn't assume. He saw her pause in the hallway and consider her options. Take a left into the guest room and its queen-sized bed, or walk a few more paces down the hall to the master?

"You can have my room if you prefer the bigger bed. I can take the guest room." When she turned toward him, he added, "Can't have a Mistress in the house and not offer her the best room."

She pointed to him, to herself, then toward the master bedroom. She did a questioning thumbs up.

"Yeah, sure, if you prefer that. That would be great."

That would be fucking fantastic.

He didn't anticipate any sex happening, but being in the same room made it far more likely. He had no agenda; he'd simply have to be dead or dickless not to think of it. However, if she wasn't taking it in that direction, just having her that close and lying with him made him better than okay with that.

He cleared his throat. "You're welcome to use my shirt to sleep in."

She'd kept it on through dinner, wearing only panties beneath it. Something difficult not to think about.

She cocked her head and glanced down at the shirt. Coming to him, she picked up his hand and put it on her breast. He was smart enough not to move the hand, her grasp an implicit command to keep it still. However, his palm and fingers itched to close around that generous curve, to squeeze and fondle the nipple. Especially when it peaked against his touch.

He had to tear his gaze from her fathomless dark eyes to look at her phone when she held it up. "Do you prefer me to wear your shirt?"

"Yeah. You better believe it."

Her lips curved, and she pivoted, drawing away from his touch but leading the way to his bedroom. He'd brought her bag for her. As he thought of its contents, he sent her an amused look and set it on the dresser.

"Next time I have to secure a load in my pickup, I'm calling you. You handle tie-downs like a pro. Do you always carry Monster Bob in your bag?" At her blank look, he shot her a grin and clarified. "The battery-operated boyfriend modeled after Mr. Ed's junk?"

She mouthed a chuckle, typed. "Cyn has one stamped with the letters BTU."

"Like British thermal units?" His brow furrowed.

Her grin deepened. Tap, tap, tap. "Better than you."

"Ouch. That is one mean woman."

While she went to make use of his master bathroom, he stripped down to his boxer briefs and turned down the bed, plumped the pillows. So he wouldn't take her side preference, he waited until she returned. He'd never shared his bed, so he usually gravitated toward the middle. He could accommodate a change in habit for tonight. Maybe longer, if it was for her.

He was in a marshmallow mood, for sure. Might be a good idea for him to be the one to embrace some silence, rather than risk saying things aloud he shouldn't.

She emerged with her hair brushed out, her face soft and younger-looking without makeup. She slid into the right side, but moved to take part of the middle. The smile she had when she gestured for him to join her there said she understood. "So, never been married or lived with anyone either, hunh?"

She shook her head as he slid into the bed and came to her. He wasn't sure how she'd feel about being held in his arms, but she relaxed into his hold with a sigh that lowered her body more deeply into the angles of his.

Sometimes the word *wow* was the only one that fit. He wasn't sharing that incredibly idiotic thought, but it sure felt true, with her in his embrace. "You like the TV off or on?"

She motioned that she kept it off to sleep. And glanced at the lamp on the night table. He was closest to it.

Shit. He'd forgotten. So caught up in the pleasure of her sleeping with him, he'd ignored the reasons it would be better for them to sleep in separate rooms.

No, he could do it. He turned toward it, put his hand on the switch. Then he couldn't go further. He dropped his palm to the night table, his heart rate suddenly elevating.

He was not going to do this. Not in front of her. Not in front of anyone. She touched his shoulder, a question. He tried again, failed again. Then he spoke gruffly. "I've been keeping it on."

Like a child.

The pressure of her hand brought him back to lie next to her. No judgment in her eyes, only understanding, as she settled back in his arms.

It didn't seem to bug her. She closed her eyes, her breath soft on his chest. But it was going to be difficult for her to sleep like that. She'd have to eventually turn away from him, and though he was pleased to spoon, she seemed to want to lie like this.

He wanted it to be her choice, not a requirement because she had a light shining in her eyes. He could leave on the bathroom light. Or switch on the TV and leave it on mute. But the flickering might bug her.

Screw it. He tightened his arm around her back, reached over and switched off the lamp, so abruptly he almost knocked the damn thing off the table. Fortunately he could see enough of the silhouette to confirm it rocked in place and then steadied. He told his thundering heart he could switch it back on anytime. And to stop being such a pussy.

Her touch drifted over his chest, back and forth, her breath on his neck. He wasn't alone in the silent darkness. She was here, resting against him the way a woman did when she felt secure and safe.

His heart rate evened out. He could handle this. She put a hand on his face, her lips brushing his jaw. Approval. When she did turn over, she nestled her bottom against his dick with a few teasing strokes, enough to get him going again, and went peacefully to sleep. A true Mistress.

～

Was there anything more pleasurable than waking up and finding the gorgeous man who'd satisfied her sexually—without even putting his cock inside her—was making her breakfast?

"In the kitchen, barefoot and pregnant" might be considered sexist thinking, male-to-female, but "in the kitchen, barefoot and wearing nothing but jeans," was a suitable female-to-male answer for it.

Blinking sleepily, she came to stand at his side at the stove. He was making fried green tomatoes, transferring the finished pieces to a metal rack over a paper towel. He'd already finished the bacon, laid out on a separate paper towel. When she glanced at the tomatoes, he gestured with the spatula. "Go ahead and try one, but be careful. They're probably still hot."

She nibbled a breaded tomato, and her brows lifted. "Good," she mouthed, then typed. "I've tried making these from tomatoes Vera brought from her garden. They're always soggy or the breading is too thick."

"It takes practice. You're probably giving it too much flour. It requires a really light coating to keep it crisp, not soggy. See, like this." He dropped one into the flour, turned it over and then lifted it smoothly out of the white stuff with a near translucent covering. "Now the egg wash, then the corn meal."

When he laid the prepared tomato slice in the pan, it sizzled and increased the familiar Southern fried breakfast scents in the kitchen.

"You're very self-sufficient," she typed. "And you take good care of a guest."

He nudged her, smiled. "I've been taking care of myself for a long time."

Me, too.

They held gazes, then he slid his arm around her waist. "If you don't mind, Mistress, I've gotta kiss you."

Her lips curved as his pressed to them. She still wore his shirt, nothing beneath it but her panties, so when she leaned into him, his fingers trailed along her bare thigh. He lifted his head. "And taking care of you is part of what works for me. Thanks for letting me do it. Makes it even more of a gift. How do you say bacon in sign language?"

She held up forefinger and middle fingers for both hands, brought them together in a point and then wiggled them apart in a horizontal line. His brows raised. "Is that wiggling supposed to be the pigs running away from the farmer?"

She grimaced, but shook her head and mouthed *sizzle.*

"Oh, the oil jumping in the pan. Got it. Fuck, I swear everything you do and say could make me think of sex. No matter how you say it." He pointed to the skillet. "Form the word skillet with your lips like you just did. Then show me the sign for it."

When she did, he slid his arm around her to cup her ass again, pulling her against his side, her legs brushing his thigh. "Yep, totally thinking about sex."

She gave him a light thump with a fist for the teasing, but then she smoothed her hands over his chest, enjoying the feel of it as he cocked a brow at her, an expression of waiting. To see what she wanted. What he could do for her.

Oh, so, so much. But she wanted breakfast. And to help him with his balance on his bike. Followed hopefully by a ride. First the bike, then the man.

∽

On the way to his place last night, she'd detoured to her house to grab a couple things for an overnight bag. He'd suggested she include a pair of heavier weight jeans and a long-sleeve T-shirt, if she had one. "In case the balance stuff goes well, and you want to join me on a ride on some of the backroads around my place."

She liked that idea. He'd also suggested boots to protect her ankles and calves from the heat of the bike's exhaust.

"The rule is you dress for the slide, not the ride," he told her. "At rallies and in states they don't require helmets, even us more experienced bikers get slack about our protective gear, I won't lie, but I'm not taking any chances with you."

Fortunately motorcycle and Goth boots were remarkably similar, complete with thick tread and buckles. She'd gone through an alternative rock phase in her twenties, and then the boots had been repurposed for occasional role play with subs. His brow had raised when he saw them, but his slow sexy smile told her he approved.

Now he'd pulled a pewter-gray Harley he'd called a two-seater bobber out of the barn and guided it to the dirt track, walking side by side with her. The bike seemed more dinged up than his other two bikes, and he confirmed it was one he considered more of a workhorse, for off road or rougher terrain.

"This old girl's a good choice for balance stuff around this dirt track, nothing too fast."

When she passed her hand over the seat, he smiled. "Want to get on, get a feel for it?"

At her eager nod, he held her hand as she swung a leg over and settled on the driver's seat. The steadiness of the bike was surprising. Her legs weren't long enough for her to reach the ground on both sides at once, but there were small platforms on either side for her to rest her feet upon.

"This one weighs just under six hundred, but when they're parked, they're sturdy. Long as you recognize it's got a bit of a left lean because of the single kickstand." He nodded to the ground, where he'd put a flat piece of wood under the stand. "Because the ground here at the track isn't asphalt, I use that to increase the stability."

He squeezed her hand. "If you want to stay seated on it while I spread out the cones, that's fine. Just don't move around too much when I'm not close by."

As she watched him pick up a stack of cones and stride off onto the track, she thought of him sitting where she was now, his ass snugged down on the padded cushion, his legs straddling the bike. The vibration through his testicles when the engine was running.

A motorcycle seemed designed to make a sexy man look even sexier. She could easily call to mind the way his backside flexed as he mounted and dismounted, imagine the ripple across his shoulders as he gave the bike gas or leaned into a turn.

Carefully, making sure the bike stayed still, she leaned back on an elbow, tossed her hair and arched her spine. She was being playful, but she guessed it made women look sexy, too.

His wolf whistle confirmed it—and that he was keeping a close eye on her. She flashed a smile his way, which became something a little more serious at the look in his eyes.

When she typed into her phone, he came back. He always stayed aware of that, never making her wait when she wanted to "talk." He bent to brush a kiss on her knee, laying a hand on her thigh, an intimacy she permitted. While they weren't in session, she liked how he gravitated toward those gestures. She also liked his touch.

She handed him the phone. "I wouldn't mind laying you out on the seat, your hands tied to the back. I'd suck on you until your thighs trembled and you got that fierce look in your eyes. Like you want to beg for mercy, but you never will, wanting me to test you as far as I like."

His expression tightened as he read the words, eyes sparking with flame. "I'd ask for the privilege of switching places," he responded. "Letting me eat your cunt until you screamed, grinding yourself against my face and ripping up my shoulders with your nails."

His deep blue eyes came back to hers, and she saw the hunger he'd had to bank after she brought herself to climax on his kitchen table. "It's a hard limit because I've seen too much blood drawn in my lifetime, for the wrong reasons. But it's different when it's with you."

It was a significant declaration, one she wouldn't gloss over. She trailed her fingers along her denim-covered thigh, rocked her knee outward. With a pointed gaze downward, she mouthed the words. "Kiss me."

She moved her fingers to the button of the jeans, slipped it and pushed down the zipper. He steadied the bike as she lifted her feet to the handlebars so she could raise her hips and slide the jeans down over her knees. She wanted him to see the silk panel between her thighs.

One kiss. A raised finger she pressed to her mouth. Shook her head when she touched it to her tongue and teeth.

Just a kiss. No tongue or teeth.

"Time limit?" he asked, gleam in his gaze.

She used her phone for that. "If you lift your mouth from my skin, that's one kiss."

He smiled, a destructive weapon to a woman's defenses when coupled with those hot, dangerous eyes and firm mouth. But as he shifted his gaze to what she'd revealed, she could see him thinking it through, a careful man weighing his options to make the most of them. He gripped her thigh, his palm warm, and lowered his head.

One lingering, pressed kiss on the fabric between her legs, and her body dampened for him. She heard the shift in his breathing as he inhaled her scent. A long, thorough, slow-moving pressure of his lips ensued as they slid along her flesh with that thin barrier between. No break in contact. His mouth explored every contour and crease.

Oh, he was so damn good at this. Good enough to keep. An unsettling thought, and one that led to another one. What were Tiger's thoughts on relationships, a commitment to one Mistress alone?

She knew the answer. He'd always rotated between two or three. He hadn't indicated a desire for anything different, even with his changed circumstances.

Whereas ever since Ros had teased her about Abby, her desire for exclusivity was only growing stronger. She didn't want him doing sessions with other Mistresses.

He increased pressure and tempo, and she decided not to think any more about it, swimming out of the troubling waters into ones churning for far different reasons.

A long time later, when her stomach was quivering and she thought she could have come from the slightest touch of his tongue, if she'd permitted that, he lifted his head and gazed at her.

He was challenging her, knowing just how much he'd stirred her. Balance, she reminded herself. For both of them.

She gave him an even look and put her clothes back together. Then offered him her hand, regal as a queen, to help her straighten. His erection was visible against his jeans, and following her glance, he shot her a smile.

"Seems you managed to distract me anyway, Mistress. Even without a plug up my ass."

That concerned her, because she really didn't want to mess with his focus, but Tiger reassured her. "If anything, it might help. I won't get so tense about screwing this up if I'm feeling an endorphin rush."

He sent her a wink. With an easier heart though no less of a raging libido than his, she eyed the cones. When he'd taken them to the track to spread them out, he'd also carried a tin bucket of golf balls. The balls were on the tips of the cones. The bucket, which he'd left near the bike, was printed with cartoonish tigers against a bright green background.

"Aubrey gave it to me one Easter," he explained. "Filled with painted eggs. When I was talking to the doc, I mentioned a lot of the games they do at rallies are balance tests. She suggested using them to help."

He nodded to the cones. "The goal is to maneuver close enough that you or your passenger can pick up the ball and put it in the bucket. No feet on the ground. If a foot touches the ground, you've lost." He pointed to the final cone of the course, smaller than the others. "An extra challenge, since you have to lean down further."

"They do this at rallies?" she typed.

"Oh yeah. They do serious stuff like races, but there are also competitions for everyone. It's like a big festival or fair." He sent her a teasing look. "Some of them have rowdier events. Like hanging a hot dog from a stick, and the passenger takes a bite as you go past. No hands allowed."

She narrowed her gaze. Typed. "Why am I fairly certain the passenger is always female?"

"Sometimes they also slather mayonnaise on it. To make it more difficult. Slipperiness, you know."

"I'm sure. You made the right choice with the cones."

"Are you sure? I probably have a pack of Oscar Meyer in the fridge." He laughed and caught her arm as she got off the bike, pivoted in a mock show of heading for her car.

"Let me get on and then you swing on behind me. This game can be done solo, but I figure I'll focus on keeping the bike steady and getting close to the cones. Let you handle the balls." He winked at her. "If that works out, I'll try it on my own."

That ass flexing was front and center for her viewing pleasure as he swung on and settled. She knew she wouldn't hesitate to join him on the bike. He'd already made it clear he wouldn't let her ride with him if he thought he was putting her in any danger.

Even so, she typed one last question. "Anything I should know about being a good passenger for this?"

"Pretty common sense stuff. Don't do any big acrobatics that might upset the bike's stability. As I said yesterday, if this goes well and you're up for it, we can go for a ride on the backroads. I'll give you more advanced tips on being a passenger then." He sent her a warm look. "There's a lot of trust involved, both in taking a passenger and being one. But to my way of thinking, it's similar to the trust we've developed doing scenes together."

He handed her a half-sized helmet he'd hung on the handlebar, what he called a skull cap. "While we're in my dirt track area moving at slow speeds, there's no need to make you sweat inside a full helmet. But I want you to wear this, so if I do lay it down, it will keep you safer."

When he'd verified she'd secured the helmet properly, he gave her the go ahead to get on behind him.

She grasped his shoulder to do so, settling onto the seat and finding the foot pegs for the passenger seat. "We might have to make a few passes," he said. "Don't lean out any farther than you feel comfortable doing."

She slid her arm under his, giving him a thumbs up sign. He started the bike, and the engine made a sharp roar that settled into a growl. Resting her hand at his hip, she watched him release the clutch on the left handlebar. The bike started to chug forward.

He did his first passes through the course without attempting to get close to the cones, just feeling the way of it. The tension in his shoulders translated to his back, those muscles rigid as a board when she laid her palm there. She suspected he hadn't been on a bike since he'd recognized how the balance issues would affect his riding. Which meant however he'd confirmed that must have been unnerving. And what unnerved a veteran biker wouldn't be something minor.

When he came to a halt to take a break, putting his boots to the ground, she had typed the question. She slid her hand under his arm and showed him the screen. "How did it go the last time you tried to ride?"

He grunted. "Better than the first time. Threw my leg over, got dizzy and puked before I even started the engine. In all fairness, it was about a week after I got out of the hospital, three weeks before the doc told me it was a good idea to even try. Next time, I could get on without any problem, but when I tried to go faster than what a snail could beat, I leaned into a curve and my head swam like I had gone over a waterfall."

He grimaced. "I panicked and braked mid-turn, a total rookie move. I dumped speed off the bike and upset my stability, even without the head-fuck happening. Me and this old girl skidded into a roadside ditch. Luckily, she landed upright, resting against the side bank of the ditch. Made it easier to walk her out, once I found some planks to help me do that. She took the beating and was fine."

She was more concerned about the beating he'd taken, but he put his hand on her knee, pointedly gazing at her jeans, boots and the long-sleeved T. "I was smart enough to be fully geared in leathers that day, anticipating that shit happening. Got bruised but I was okay."

He reached up and rapped her helmet with light knuckles. "I've been feeling steadier since then, but that's why I wanted you to wear this."

In response, she rapped his bare head and tossed him a significant look. He shook his head. "If I can't ride my bike in my backyard without gear at little more than idling speed, it'll feel more hopeless than I can stand. Don't tell me how stupid that is. I'm aware."

Skye squeezed both his shoulders, then gave him a pinch on his ass that won a stronger grin. She tapped him on the shoulder. *Let's do this.*

"Okay. I've won this golf ball competition three times at the rallies, by the way."

"Big talk. Let's see if you can do it without puking."

He laughed when she typed that, and the set of his shoulders eased. Then they were off again.

They did several more passes, during which he relaxed further, and agreed they could start to come in close enough she could try for the golf balls. With the tension slipping away, and no balance issues appearing to hamper his maneuvering ability, she quickly figured out why he'd excelled at what might seem like a frivolous game.

He rode as if he was part of the bike. Eventually, she was able to collect all the balls, then put them back again on another pass, holding onto his shoulder as she leaned out to retrieve or place. He was balanced in the seat, no sign of dizziness, no need to put his feet down to keep the bike on a straight, upright path.

Relief and gladness had started to come off of him in waves, making his dark blue eyes sparkle. She felt so glad *for* him, she put her arms around his shoulders and gave him a hard squeeze. He reached back and gripped her thigh.

When they'd done three more rounds, he wanted to try it solo. As she got off the bike, he kissed her hand, squeezed her waist, before he took the bucket and headed back onto the dirt track. Balls on, balls off, his hands moving easily between the cone and the bucket he carried. When he came to a stop next to her, the engine idling with its chug, chug, chug rumble, the triumphant expression on his face made her reach out and touch his jaw. Then lean in and give him a congratulatory kiss. *Well done.*

His smile was shy, almost boyish, but then he shook it off and laughed, her badass biker man again. "Want to take a ride with me?" he asked.

Hell yes.

"Okay, wait here." He put down the kickstand and left the bike, headed for the barn. When he returned, he had a full helmet for her, and a skull cap in his size for himself. He fitted the helmet over her head and showed her how to do the chin strap.

"It's one of Maryshka's. She does some of the custom work and testing out here with me. If you find you like riding, we can get you one that fits you specifically."

She thought she might. After she got on behind him again, she continued to pay close attention to how he operated the motorcycle, the shift between clutch and throttle, the movement of his feet on the pedals.

But as they left the property and headed down one of the mildly curving backroads in this area outside New Orleans, the experience itself swept her away.

Whoa. As his confidence built, so did his speed. He didn't exceed the limit, but it was more than fast enough for her first ever motorcycle ride. The engine was much louder, but it didn't bother her in the wide-open space. The road was flanked by forest and occasional marsh. Bayou waterways in the distance were populated by lone kayakers or small boat fishermen.

He'd told her she should move with him, so on the curved roads, she held onto him, her front pressed to his back, while on the straightaways she would relax against the bar behind her, resting her hands on his hips. She tipped her head back, watching the sky and clouds, then looked to either side, the wind touching her features. He'd left the helmet's face shield off, telling her she'd enjoy the ride more without it.

The miles slipped away as she saw what he'd meant, that their ability to trust and anticipate one another, developed over so many sessions together, worked for this in a way that had her falling in love with being on a bike.

Or maybe just being on a bike with him, like this.

When he finally pulled them over, it was at an overlook with a picnic table and large trees, branches spreading over the area to create shade. The tree was occupied by an army of white and black ibises. Since they were fluffy and round, they looked like a real-life Dr. Seuss Truffula tree.

She shared that with Tiger, and he chuckled, squeezing her fingers where they rested on his chest. He'd taken her helmet and hung it on the bars with his, but they'd remained on the bike, his feet on the ground, hers on the pegs. She rested her chin on his shoulder, her arms around his waist as she watched the birds, the water, the floating of the clouds across the sky. His jaw brushed her face.

He had his long legs braced, hand stroking hers as his other rested loose and relaxed on his thigh. He was in his element here, even without being able to hear anything.

She put the phone on his leg beside his resting hand, using it as a typing surface. "It's nice, just riding. I thought the noise would bother me, or there'd be exhaust fumes, but on the backroads, it feels very"— she paused, then typed—"freeing."

"That's the best part of it," he agreed. "The rallies are popular because it's the chance to enjoy your bike around people who get it, who live life a different way, at a different pace, when they're on them. Like camping."

She'd seen a couple of postcards about those rallies pinned up in his office, before the attack. She remembered he'd thought about inviting her to one, and was about to broach the subject again when he shifted it in a surprising direction.

"When you were taking over our scenes, you sometimes used sign language with Abby. I assumed it was Mistress secret code, to tell each other how I was doing and where my head was at. Or what diabolical things you were planning to do next, without giving me a heads up to prepare for it." A smile. "That kind of thing."

She nodded against his back. He glanced over his shoulder. "I'm glad you use the phone to tell me what you say. But I really like the way your hands move, the expressions you make when you sign. Would you mind continuing to do that, if it doesn't bug you? I, uh, enrolled in a signing class at the hearing center."

At her neutral expression, he continued. "It's Signing in English, where you learn grammar and how to say basic things. 'I would like to order now,' that kind of thing. But you can advance to classes where you learn ASL as a language, not just phrases and how to spell the alphabet. Though I'm getting that down pretty good." He spelled out Tiger for her, making her smile, though her chest was tight.

"Anyhow." He shrugged. "I thought, if you were willing to show me some things, that would be cool."

She spell-signed *Why?*

He rested a hand on her knee again. "I'd like to be able to talk to you, without you always having to use the phone. If that's something you'd like, too."

Most people didn't understand the level of effort it took, to communicate with a world who could speak, or hear. They didn't seek to make it easier for someone who couldn't, not because they were assholes, but because there was no reason to learn a different language when most of the people around you spoke yours.

But he liked the idea of being able to communicate in the easiest way for her. He wanted that intimacy, the message it sent to her. She told herself she shouldn't be surprised. It came from that core of him, which was about serving a Mistress. Caring for her. He was in a position now to understand deeper ways to do that.

That he'd picked that up, had thought beyond his own challenges to think of hers... It moved her. So much that she was still staring at him and he was looking concerned, because she hadn't responded. She broke out of the stupor and spelled out "ok."

"Good. Thanks." He sobered. "Do you ever get frustrated with it? I know that's a stupid question—of course you do."

She typed. "Yes. But I've realized that's not a useful perspective. I focus on the things that end up working even better than if I could 'talk' like other people."

At his curious look, she paused, thinking of how to word it. "Because you don't focus on words coming out of my mouth, you pay much closer attention to what I want, from my body language and expressions. And you build on it. Like after I told you what I was thinking about doing to you on your bike, you attached your own fantasies to it. Made it more, with my nonverbal input and your imaginings. It doesn't always work out that way, but when it does, it makes up for the times it doesn't."

As they gazed at one another a few minutes, his smile slipped away. He brushed her face with his knuckles.

"I'd like to make love to you in my bed. Would you like that, Mistress?"

She dipped her head. Spelled her response against his thigh. *Y.E.S.* But since that might take their relationship down the road to a fatal crash and burn, she typed a caveat on her screen. *One day.*

"Okay." Disappointment was in his gaze, but he didn't let it turn into a sulk. He was too good a sub for that. "Want to move to the picnic table and sit there, enjoy the closer view?"

She had no problem with the idea. As they left the bike, she started toward the water's edge first, intending to peer into the lapping depths. Tiger clasped her hand, drawing her toward the picnic table. "Not a good idea. There are some pretty sizeable gators in these waters. People aren't their preferred food, but unfortunately, too many idiots feed them, so they associate people with a food source. They might drag you into the water before they figure out you don't have anything."

A prudent warning. She took a seat next to him on the top of the picnic table, hip to hip, feet braced on the bench. It was nice to lean against him, her arm linked through his, with one set of hands clasped together.

He glanced toward the marsh. For a second, his dark blue eyes rested on a large white egret doing an elegant walk through the grass, the bird's attention trained on the current as he looked for fish.

"Am I difficult to trust, Mistress?"

The question twisted in her. Tiger's mind was still on her response about the making love thing. She didn't want emotion to guide her, though her emphatic signing probably telegraphed her feelings. She translated the gestures on her phone.

"When I make you wait in session, why do I do that?"

He lifted a shoulder, the answer obvious enough not to be voiced, but he latched onto a different aspect of her response. "Yeah, that's the problem, isn't it? Being outside of a session with you."

The words stung, but when she would have pulled back, he held onto her hand, refusing to let her have it. His alpha side showed in the act, his eyes steady on hers. "Shit. Wrong word choice. It's not a problem. What I meant is that in a scene, you denying me doesn't get tangled up with other assumptions, other shit happening. It's harder to keep it clear out here."

She settled down again, considered. Then typed. "In session, when you're not sure, when it gets fuzzy, you use me for guidance. You don't assume where I'm going with a question. You answer it." She gave him a stare. "So, when I make you wait in session, what does it mean?"

His jaw flexed. "You're expecting me to trust your timing, where you're taking us. Where you want to go."

He slid his gaze back to the water. She could see him digesting it, trying to accept it. She bit her lip. If she demanded that kind of honesty from him, he deserved the same. She touched his arm, bringing his attention back to her and the screen.

"Part of it is what you think. I'm protecting myself. The look of our relationship has changed because of an unexpected event in your life. It's making our friendship evolve, but I want to be careful about thinking it's more than it is. For either of us."

The words were truthful, weren't they? Yet from his expression, they didn't sit well with him. They didn't sit great with her either. But it underscored her point. He'd said himself he was at a crappy time of his life to take on a relationship. And she didn't want to corner him into something he might not need when he clawed his way out of it. Ruining what they already had as Mistress and sub.

All of it made sense, even if it irritated her. Or both of them. He must have reached the same conclusion, because slowly, he gave her a nod and offered his hand again. When she took it, their fingers formed a knot on his braced knee.

He slid off the table, keeping that hold. "Let's ride some more. I'm a big fan of finding out what's waiting farther down the road." He met her gaze. "Because the road and what it brings is endless. If we could just do that, the rest of the shit...I don't think it could hold onto us the way it does."

She knew what he meant. Even as she knew the benefits of staying still and seeing what came to her through patience.

Though that was also a great way to get left on the side of that road.

CHAPTER FIFTEEN

*W*hen they returned from the ride, she told him she was ready to learn how to tune a bike. But he didn't want to see that nicely clingy gray shirt tossed in a trash bin thanks to an oil stain. So he retrieved a thick black T-shirt from the barn, one of his extras, and offered it to her. "No reason for you to ruin a shirt when I have plenty. If you want, you can change in the barn. I also put some of that soda you like in the fridge I keep in there."

She looked surprised and pleased by his consideration. When she removed her crossbody bag that held her phone, he realized she was going to change the shirt here. No neighbors around to see, so Tiger guessed it made sense. He sure as hell wasn't objecting, even as he shifted his gaze to the bobber he'd parked on the concrete pad outside the barn. It was due for a tune up, so he'd use it to teach her how it was done.

She touched his arm. Pointed to his eyes, herself, question mark.

Would you like to look?

Was he breathing? "Yes Mistress, I would."

She grasped the hem and, with a lithe move of her upper body, removed the shirt. It might have been designed for getting a little dirty, but what was beneath it was not. The silver-gray satin bra with a darker ribbon border had cups split low and deep, giving her breasts plenty of exposure to his appreciative gaze.

He'd never done a bike tune up with a hard-on, but the experience was inevitable, especially with her standing before him in bra and jeans. The loose waistband made him want to slide his fingertips along smooth skin and the band of whatever panties she wore beneath. He cleared his throat before she donned his shirt. "I'd lose the bra."

The imperious angle of her brow made him chuckle. "Yeah, I know how it sounds. I have coveralls for dirty work that don't let anything soak through, but since it's a typical humid New Orleans day, I don't want to give you heat stroke. Plus they're too big to be practical. Maryshka hasn't left a set here, so I don't have anything smaller."

He was almost glad he couldn't hear himself talk, because pinned by that Mistress look, he probably sounded like a stammering teen explaining how he "accidentally" ended up hiding in the girls' locker room.

With a twist of her lips, she laid her shirt on his shoulder. She smoothed the fabric with her hand, a stroke that included him, before she pivoted and presented her back to him. She tilted her chin to her shoulder, a clear directive. Those strands of blond hair curved over her brow and caught on her lashes. Her sweet lips had a kissable quirk to them.

She had a single tattoo on her back, inside the left shoulder blade. He'd registered it before, but this was his first close look at it. A series of musical notes, tumbling down. Maybe from that song her dad had written about her?

His hands weren't steady. What was up with that? He unhooked the bra, then, after a pause, he took the straps off her shoulders, absorbing soft skin and delicate bones through his palms. Her nearness, the intimacy of it, flooded him with contentment.

Between that and how well the bike riding had gone, he couldn't ask for a better day. No other problems could touch him right now.

She took the bra the rest of the way off and turned in his arm span, laying it over his shoulder on top of her shirt. With that enigmatic smile, she put on his T-shirt.

Her braless in a tight T-shirt—wet from a sudden devil-blessed rainstorm—would have been a biker's dream. However, her breasts moving beneath the loose fit of his shirt, giving him the hint of a nipple as she shifted and turned, was just as distracting. He'd always appreciated more subtle pleasures.

He'd set two footstools next to the bike. She perched on one, listening closely as he went over the basics of a tune-up—oil change, filter check, et cetera—and then he showed her the tools they'd need, explaining their uses. She was familiar with some of them, which confirmed his theory that she got into the guts of her hardware when needed and had probably even tinkered with her Mustang in the past. Mechanical stuff didn't put her off. Even so...

"You surprised me," he observed. "Asking how to tune the bike before learning to ride. That's usually what people want to do first."

She pursed her full lips. Typed. "I like to know how a powerful beast works, how to care for it, before I ride him."

He grinned. "How long you work on that one?"

Her gaze twinkled. Tap, tap, tap. "That's not the right question. How does it work on you?"

"Remember the skillet thing? Everything you do and say works for me." He gave her a mock look of alarm. "Unless you want me to wear stilettos. Those scare me. Plus a man's got to draw the line some-where, or a woman will think he'll jump off a bridge for her."

She leaned forward and laid her lips on his, just a brush of contact. When she drew back and dipped her head to her phone, her response took a little longer. That was okay. He liked having the time to look at her.

"No stilettos. No bridge. Unless we're jumping together, and there's a cool, deep creek below with a nearby bank. One to make love on, getting coated with that soft, sticky clay we could rinse off when we're done. Know a place like that?"

Yeah. A perfect one. He finished reading the provocative words and lifted his gaze to hers. It was a place he'd stayed on the way to the South Dakota rally. The creek had run by the motel, and he'd followed it up into the woods, finding where it was wide and deep enough for swimming. The motel had a porch built along its entire rear length, a wooden swing mounted outside the back door of every room. It had been a great place to enjoy a beer at the end of a good day's ride. Order a pizza. Watch the sunset.

He went to several long distance rallies every year, depending on how busy the garage was. Rubbing elbows with other MC enthusiasts in that environment was his idea of a vacation. The semblance to the kinship he'd lost when he left the Fallen Angels helped him recharge his batteries and leveled him out.

That local rally in Kentucky was a reasonable option. He'd talked himself out of it, but today he'd proven he could ride again, at least for shorter distances. And a dark-eyed Mistress was talking about making love on creek banks. It made unwise things come out of his mouth.

"That rally I mentioned before. Would you be interested in going? It's a long weekend kind of thing. I'd trailer my bike down with my truck. Riding a bike for a few hours when you're not used to it isn't fun. Gotta build up to that."

"Wouldn't that make it less enjoyable for you?" she typed.

Any loss of enjoyment would be more than compensated by her presence. But he gave her the less pleasant truth. "With these headaches and the dizziness coming and going, I was going to play it safe and trailer it anyway. Once I get there, I'd use the bike to see the sights and do rally stuff."

She considered that. Typed. "We'll see. Let's do the tune up. Then I'll badger you into teaching me how to ride one solo." She tossed him a challenging look.

"You go with me to the rally, I'll make that happen."

Her eyes narrowed at the blatant carrot and stick offer. Tap, tap, tap. "I'll have to review my offers from other hot, fine-assed bikers."

"I am the only biker with a fine ass," he informed her. "All the rest are tubs of greasy lard with long, unwashed beards."

Her eyes twinkled, but she pointed to the bike. *Show me.*

Not a yes, but not a no. For a guy who only a few hours ago was sure he wasn't going to go, he was hoping for that *yes* way more than was smart. But a man getting his head and heart tangled up with a woman wasn't all that interested in smart.

No surprise, soon after he started explaining and demonstrating the oil change process, she wanted to take over, get hands-on while following his direction. She picked up on things fast.

Typical for a first-timer, she did get her shirt dirty, so he was glad he'd told her to remove that pretty bra. The day continued to go well, enough breeze and sunshine to make things feel hopeful and good. As requested, she did mixed communication with him, signing as well as typing. She told him that, like most languages, ASL could have different signs for the same expression. The man who taught the intro signing class had said friends and family who signed regularly might develop shorthand versions of phrases only known to them.

He copied her gestures. To internalize them, he resolved to start signing when he knew a word. Like if he asked her if she wanted bacon for breakfast, he'd say it, but also make the gesture for bacon. That sizzle sign that looked more like a pig running away.

He needed to learn it. He might never hear again. He forced the words into his brain pan. But watching her eyes light up when he signed back and asked to learn more, helped take his mind off that. Whether he could hear or not, he liked talking to her like this. Maybe he'd get good enough they'd develop their own phrases, known to just the two of them.

When they were done with the bike, he brought out two folding chairs. The concrete pad was under a tree, so the shade was good. They sat companionably, taking in the day as she drank her soda and he finished his beer. He'd chosen the downwind chair so he could smoke a cigarette, but he hadn't lit it. Not until she posed a question that put a small cloud over his mood.

"Will your brother be at the rally? Any of the Fallen Angels?"

"No." He lit the end, drew on it as he dropped the lighter and pack into the mesh pocket of the chair. "It's outside their territory, and they don't get along great with the one-percenters who hold it. Though those guys aren't likely to be there anyway. This one is a smaller, more regional event, heavily family-oriented, the wilder stuff discouraged. Though some of that always happens, particularly in the more partying campgrounds and at the night spots."

She made a querying gesture, and mouthed *one-percenter?*

"OMG members. Outlaw motorcycle gang," he explained. "Most bikers, they're enthusiasts. Part of legit motorcycle clubs, a lot of them formed around a common theme. Clubs where you get a membership because you own a particular brand of ride, like Harley-Davidson. Veterans clubs, Christian groups, or locals who just form a club and create a cut for themselves. For those groups, belonging is usually as simple as 'Hey, you're interested in joining? Great, pay your fee and let's ride!'"

He tilted a half-smile at her. "In those clubs you'll find some like me and my crew, those who customize or work on bikes. But most are just people who love to ride, who like experiencing the world like that. Lawyers, doctors, retired couples. It crosses all the lines, blue collar, white collar, black, brown, white. Men and now a lot more women, on their own rides instead of straddling a pussy pad."

He stopped at her amused look. "Sorry, less PC term there, Mistress. But MCs have every kind of person you can imagine, hopping on their bike for a rally getaway, or just a ride after work to remind themselves life is more than the grind."

He flicked ash off the cigarette and took another draw, his eyes going back to the horizon. "Somewhere along the way, when those clubs kept pointing out that the OMGs make up less than one percent of bikers, the term caught on. To MCs like the Fallen Angels, it's a badge of honor, being called one-percenters."

He grimaced. "Almost all of them started riding for the same reasons as the ninety-nine percent. The freedom and feel of the ride, the life. That's why you'll see them at the rallies. They enjoy them, same as anyone. Plenty of them can be decent guys, when they're not having to do and be what they signed up to be."

Men who had been as close to him as his own brother.

He crushed the cigarette into his empty beer can and put it down on the concrete. "The bond is different in a group like that. Taking off the cut, walking away from them...it was hard." The world's biggest understatement. "Before then, the circles I ran in, everywhere I went, that cut was recognized and got respect. You're part of something strong. But that respect, too much of it came out of fear, because of what happened to people who didn't respect it. That wasn't how I wanted to earn or hold respect."

He glanced at his arm tattoo. "When I was growing up, my mom read to me from a book about jungle animals. I liked the cover. So I gave it to the artist as a guide."

She touched his tense arm. He tilted his head toward her, an acknowledgment, but he'd already reached for the second cigarette. She didn't say anything as he lit it. He wished she would put her fingers into a typing frenzy, to stop his damn mouth from moving.

"I worked hard as hell to sever the connection, took the hits, even encouraged them, to make that severing as public as possible. It didn't matter a good goddamn. If I hadn't been the brother of the Fallen Angels president, they wouldn't have targeted her there. They knew the police wouldn't pursue it much, but because I was separate from the club, I didn't have the defenses a club business would have had."

He shouldn't have gone down that road. Should have stopped with "No, Colt probably won't be at the rally."

Fuck, Nicole's death had ripped off that scar and turned it into an infected wound. "People like Rose can say it's not my fault," he continued, his chest tight with the ache. "But it's not about blame or guilt. That's just what you use to give something like this a target, a poison arrow to dig in and make something shitty feel even worse, because you feel like you should have been able to do *something*. Be born as someone else. Or not be born at all."

He left the chair with an abrupt movement and moved a few steps away, sucking hard on the cigarette. He wanted to feel the burn. "They fucking shot her when she was a foot away from me. I saw the van coming. But why..."

He shook his head, a hard snap. The words could bang around in his head, but he spoke them into a void of silence as absolute as God's absence that day.

"Why didn't I tell her and Aubrey to stay the fuck away from me? Why didn't I act like an asshole and scare her off? I was sure as hell raised to be a mean bastard, one no woman with any sense would want her kid around."

She'd started to rise, but he made a sharp gesture. Moving to the bike, he picked up the toolbox and put it on the seat. "Sorry, Mistress. Just... Fuck. I'll be back."

He didn't look at her as he said it, so no gesture she made would stop him, short of throwing herself in his path. He returned the bike to the barn, but when he emerged, he didn't return to her right away. He headed for the house, shoulders set as though a rod had been driven across their span. She could see the headache propelled by that flood of anger.

She hadn't known he'd been that close to Nicole when she was shot. No wonder it was haunting him. She could imagine the blood on his hands, a limp woman's body in his arms, beyond his ability to help her.

Though she had no conscious memory of it, sometimes she dreamed about her father, his hair wet with blood, the deceptive solidity of his head under her touch. Like when he carried her on his hip and she'd curled her hands against his neck, in his shaggy hair. A far better memory.

Barely into her thirties, she was the youngest of the TRA executive team. Life had required a maturity from her that far exceeded her age, but she was now older than he'd been when he'd died.

She thought of the bobber, all tuned up and running smoothly. Now she knew more about the beast.

She was ready to ride.

She could follow him into the house, but instead, she went to the barn, stepping through the double doors he'd latched into an open position. Thanks to the large trees draped over the tin-roofed building, it was a cool space. In addition to his collection of bikes, there was a nice trailer plus a hulking Dodge Ram pickup, probably what he used to haul his rides to the rallies and custom bike shows. Beside the Dodge was the antique truck he'd driven to Dale and Athena's.

Everything clean, no rust. Tools organized on pegboards above several sturdy workbenches.

She stopped by the customized Harley Dyna Street Bob he rode to the club. She thought of his gentle behavior toward the female subs. He was protective toward a Domme, too, in a different way. One was like watching over tiger cubs, the other like caring for their powerful adult mother. It might take more to hurt the mother, but it could be done. She deserved just as much of his protection and care. Maybe more, because she was far more likely to risk herself intentionally.

With Nicole and Aubrey, it was clear he felt he'd failed both mother and cub. It would take time for that to heal, but she'd just witnessed how the silence in his head could ambush him. It reached out of the abyss and dragged him down, gave him thoughts she wouldn't tolerate, no matter how natural they might be to the grieving process.

Shouldn't have been born at all.

She was angry for him, for what he'd been through, for the guilt it had put inside him. For an asshole brother who would keep twisting that knife and dig it in deeper, when Tiger contacted him to secure Aubrey's future.

She returned to the barn door. Good timing. He was returning with more sodas, as if that was his reason for going into the house.

She suspected it had been for pain meds for the headache. She'd deal with that, plus him deliberately using his inability to hear to ignore or avoid any communication she'd been willing to offer.

He'd provided her with an opportunity, the way a sub did when he or she really needed something from their Dominant. He'd obviously gotten a better handle on his feelings, but she wanted to do a full purge of that pain and keep the headache she still saw behind his eyes from taking over.

She returned to the recesses of the barn, expecting him to come find her. They'd gone down this road yesterday, somewhat, but sometimes a lesson needed reinforcement, like a wound needing repeated treatments to heal.

She had pieces. Nicole and Aubrey, his brother, his father, his mother, but she sensed she was missing a key piece that kept this wound festering, like hidden shrapnel. She didn't know the question to ask to reveal it, but she could keep sifting through the complicated layers of his emotional anatomy until she found it.

She heard the scuff of his shoes on the barn floor and turned toward him. She could tell he wasn't sure of his mood, if he could give her what she might be wanting or needing. She was going to show him she knew how to call forth the part of him that would respond and serve her, no matter what mood he was in. She knew how strong that part of him was. It just needed a strong woman to call it forth.

She would smash the fingers of that darkness holding him, and tell it to back the fuck off.

She pointed to the tuned-up bobber, the one he'd aptly called a workhorse. She made the gestures and word spell combination he'd recognize.

Go there. Or safeword.

Despite the steel-edged resolve in her thoughts, she delivered the command with a different tone in her expression. The choice was always his. She knew what would help, knew what she wanted from him. She could handle both things. But if he couldn't align his mind to it, if he had to safeword, she wouldn't punish him with disappointment.

Last night had been about punishment, for him doubting himself and his own strengths. This was about grief, her desire to help him find a better way to handle it.

After a long moment, he made his decision. He came to her, dropped to a knee and kissed her hand. She'd never tire of that gesture of obeisance, one he'd spontaneously worked into the beginning of their sessions together. It told her he was with her, on board to trust what she had in mind. The deliberateness he put into it, the obvious forethought, took care of her concerns that he might push himself too hard for her, for the wrong reasons.

This time he also brushed his jaw against her knuckles, holding there a second.

Words were used far too much. Touch and expression said and did so much more, especially when strong emotion was involved. Her fingers slid along his skin, offering cool, even strokes. She nodded to the bike. A reminder.

He went to it, and she followed, showing him she wanted him to brace his hands on the seat and spread his legs. When he complied, he put himself on the bike's right side, pushing into the more stable and supportive left lean of the bike on the kickstand. Because of the outward angle of the lower parts of the bike, his body was even more stretched out.

She didn't flirt or tease. She went behind him, took a two-handed hold of his ass and gripped hard, even as she leaned in and used her teeth on his shoulder blade, nipping him through his shirt. She crowded him, one leg braced between his spread ones as she reached around, opened his jeans, dipped in and found him.

This is mine, her firm clamp said. *To jerk off, to play with, to use how I want.* She used her other hand to squeeze his ass again. *This too. All of it. Your mind, heart and soul, centered on me and what I want.*

She let go of his ass to shift to his side, flexing her hand on his cock as she tapped his temple, two light beats. *Nothing in your head but what your Mistress wants there.*

He knew the gesture's meaning, as well as how to respond to it. "Yes, ma'am." His voice was rough, his eyes stormy. Too much of the wrong kind of fight still going on in his body. Including his hands, digging into the bike seat.

Those hands belonged to a man with the patience to figure out how to make a broken engine run again, purr and perform at its best.

She had that, too. With man and machine. She worked his cock, a slow pump, thumb playing over the head, scraping the slit, alternating hard squeezes with lingering strokes. A prostitute or girlfriend might jerk a man off for his pleasure. A Mistress took her time, enjoyed having his cock stiffen and build toward climax at her pace, giving her time to relish the build to savage urgency. Knowing he'd better hold it all back until she said differently.

She pushed his jeans and underwear to his thighs, and then indicated she wanted all of it off, including the shirt. She released his cock to allow him to take off his shoes, a necessary step to comply with her wishes, but then reclaimed its heat in her damp palm as soon as he returned his hands to the bike seat. Now nothing impeded her exploration of his ass with her free hand. Grasping, pinching, running a finger along the crease to make a shiver run across his broad back. Those capable hands dug into the bike seat for a different reason now.

When he was in a particularly challenging mood, she'd strapped his ass with his own belt. There was something about putting marks on what belonged to you. Marks that hurt, that could be remembered long after the skin healed. It wasn't in her like it was in Cyn, but Skye could feel the urge in a different way.

"Mistress..." His voice had that hoarseness, a warning, a question with a touch of desperation. She knew what she was doing, where she wanted to take him, and she wasn't allowing him any room to resist. Having left him aching with a hard-on since last night, she'd put him on the cliff edge fast.

He'd still kill himself waiting for her permission. It was a glorious kind of power, but one that she'd never abuse. She put a hand on the center of his back, one tap. *Come.*

It took him a second, because his emotions and his head got in the way. Not all of it was about the other things he was dealing with. No matter how much she reinforced it, she knew he'd never become completely comfortable with her simply jerking him off. He thought it took away the service element for him. One of these days, if she worked with him more often, more deeply...more exclusively, she'd prove to him that it didn't take that away at all. It deepened that element and proved his service reached beyond his own definitions of it to trust hers.

When she dropped her hand again to play against his rim, he lost his hold on that conflict. Thoughts disappeared in the surge of response, the jetting of his cock.

She had a condom in her phone bag, but she'd purposefully not rolled it on him, wanting to see his release spurt from him. Abby had told Skye she'd once threatened to have Tiger do this over the seat of the bike he brought to the club.

Abby had issued the threat. Skye had made it a reality.

But she'd chosen the right bike to use for it. If she'd ordered him to come against his gleaming Harley Dyna Street Bob in its place of pride in the corner of the barn—he even had a special spotlight for it, the crazy man—he'd have safeworded faster than if she'd pulled out a piling-sized phallus.

Or stilettos for him to wear.

Though the thought gave her an inner smile, the rest of her was tight and needy, caught up in watching him finish, the cords standing out in his neck and shoulders, the ripple of muscle along his back, ass and thighs.

Without the type of service element he embraced, with the emotions he'd been struggling with, he was in danger of subdrop, a bleak feeling she didn't want to touch him. So as the climax finished, she squeezed his side, a nonverbal order to stay where he was.

She retrieved the hose he had attached to the utility sink and turned on the spigot. The sprayer was on a light setting, the water cool but not cold. She ran that light spray over his nape, watching his shoulders tighten and muscles jerk as they adjusted to the temperature. Drops ran over curves and angles, the infinity tattoo on his back, down to the intriguing cleft of his ass and quivering buttocks.

Easy, she crooned through her touch, following the flow of the water. He wasn't alone on this journey. She was with him in the silence, and she was pleased with him. Her every touch said so.

Slowly, as intended, she saw him level out, not take that darker plunge. He had his head down, sides heaving. She kept her hand moving, stroking his nape, his back, down to his trembling flank and upper thigh.

Her touch also said *it's okay*, but she mouthed it, too, no matter that he couldn't see her.

She turned off the hose and set it aside. As she shifted to his right, still behind him, her glance fell onto the seat. She leaned against him, typing a message on her phone. Her free hand rested on the curve of his hip and ass as she brought the phone into his field of vision.

"I expect you to clean that seat and all parts of this bike thoroughly. Its owner takes care of the things he cherishes."

Tiger lifted his head, turned it to lock gazes with her. Suddenly that post-coital daze, that satisfying exhaustion, was replaced by something else. That famous second wind he could get before being worked over by the next Mistress. Where something just as sharp and needy as when they'd started came back to life. Only this time, instead of being driven by the state she'd put his cock in, the leap in her pulse said this was driven by deeper parts of him. Like his heart.

"Damn right. Let me cherish you first, Mistress. Take care of you."

Several pleasurable options came to mind to grant him that wish. "How strong are you?"

"Strong as you need." She expected the cocky male response, but knowing the strength she herself had felt from him, she thought he was telling the truth.

She pointed to the bike. Mouthed, *Get on.*

His eyes glittered. "Yes, ma'am." Then he obeyed.

Holy Mother. She'd seen an erect man naked on a motorcycle. Easy enough to find on the Internet. When she'd started doing sessions with Tiger, she'd indulged a little biker porn on occasion, to flavor her dreams or fuel an intense self-pleasuring session in her bedroom.

But to see it right in front of her, within reach... She held his gaze as she slid out of all of her clothes but his shirt. It had the scent of the oil she'd gotten on it, but he was in the threads as well.

He always smelled like what kept an engine running. At the club it was mixed with his soap and that cucumber, bergamot and pomegranate shampoo scent. She liked that combination, any element of those aromas bringing him to mind when she encountered them.

She fished the condom from her phone bag and tucked it into the pocket of the shirt. Then she came to his side. What she wanted was clear. She wouldn't dwell on how he knew the smoothest way to help her on, facing him, sliding her thighs over his, bringing their bodies in close lock. He was already semi-erect, that stamina and endurance serving her now. He kept his feet braced on the concrete, holding the bike on its stand, his thigh muscles tight.

She gave him the condom to handle. After he did so, she pulled the shirt over her head, arching against the grip of his hands on her waist, watching his gaze follow her breasts as they bobbed free, tipped by taut nipples.

His length thickened and stirred further against her cunt.

She gripped his shoulders and glanced down at her breasts. An order for him to put his mouth to work. He wet his lips, eyes dark blue flame, and closed the distance.

As he suckled her, teased and caressed, her eyes half closed. She rubbed herself slow against his length, letting him feel her slickness, covering him with it. He caressed her sensitive skin with his clever mouth, hands strong and sure on her waist, flexing. Subtle signs he was ready to help when she wanted to mount his cock.

All in good time, because the man had a mouth meant to be enjoyed. She stretched further against his hold, secure in his strength, waves of pleasure building.

She had left her phone in its bag on the pile of clothing, so she touched his face, caressed the mouth tasting the top curve of her left breast. She drew his attention to the start button of the bike. She wanted to feel the vibration. Have him rev the engine as he drove into her.

Her arousal was taking her up and up, making her want all the trappings of primitive power and sexual heat.

He understood. He looped her arm over his shoulder, an unspoken direction to hold on as he started the bike up. As he settled back onto the seat, her gaze met his. He clasped her waist and lifted her up, angling himself so she slid down his full length, that excruciatingly wonderful slow descent. She clenched her muscles on him, feeling every point of friction possible until she was fully seated.

The chug-chug-chug idling of the engine, the heat coming off of it, gave her the pleasure she'd hoped. She could tell the vibration and that heat brought him the memory of the sound, how it made him feel.

She pushed herself up, came back down. Bless the man's intuition, he'd put his hand on the throttle, keeping his other at her waist as he revved the engine for her. The noise level increased like the crashing of her heart as she rose and fell, her arousal rising on the same power surge. God, it was incredible.

She held onto his shoulders as his head dipped back to her breasts. Her desire spurted at the heated, wet touch of his mouth, his teeth, the sexual possession and devouring of her flesh. His one hand remained tight on her hip, and she reached out blindly, grasping his other forearm, letting him know she wanted both hands back on her.

He put them to good use, curving them over her ass to drive her down, bring her up, helping them both. She let go of Mistress and sub, and they became one in their intent, in mindless animal pleasure as it was meant to be experienced.

As the climax roared over her, she dug her nails into his jaw, capturing his attention, giving him the cue that told him she wanted his release again. No matter that he'd offered that a short time ago, she had no doubt he could find more to give her. It took some extra minutes, time she used to ride him through her aftershocks. As his orgasm jetted forth at last, she savored his groans. Her body reacted to them as if he'd shot his seed into her without the condom, sending sensations through her cunt, thighs, and lower belly, a whole-body tingling.

The engine's idling matched the hum through her blood. When he finally switched it off, he held her close, his arms around her back, face pressed into her throat, nuzzling her there. The engine ticked as it cooled, as his hands swept over her spine, waist and hips. Gripped and held. They were still rocking, she realized, like they rested in a cradle being pushed by the universe of feelings they were experiencing.

It wasn't a moment for declarations. They were mature enough to know that. But that seed that she'd planted in her head was growing, spreading throughout her like the sensation of that orgasm. If it was there the next time she was calm and rational, both of them fully clothed, she would eventually say the words.

She didn't want to share him with anyone. She wanted him to be hers.

CHAPTER SIXTEEN

Six boxes of cookies. That was what happened when a man was accosted by a Girl Scout troop stationed outside the grocery store.

He'd gone to stock up for the rally. Though he'd shopped there since that earlier disastrous trip, refusing to be defeated by a damn grocery run, he'd still been uptight about it. He decided he was tired of that shit. This time, he was ready to take the bull by the horns.

When the little girl jabbering at him from behind her stacks of cookies stopped to take a breath, he spoke. "Hey. I'd like to buy some, but I'm deaf and I don't read lips. Can you use your phone to talk with me?"

Wasn't he hot shit? Like a damn PSA for the hearing-impaired. Yeah, he'd felt a little too proud of himself, but it was his private moment and he'd enjoy it.

The girls had been enthusiastic, and excessively helpful. Apparently there was a merit badge for assisting the disabled, and he'd given them a primo chance to earn it.

He didn't get too riled about that, since he was busy enough managing his unmanly terror at being eyed like romance cover candy by giggling pre-teens. Thankfully, the supervising mother curbed their attempts at flirtation, which he indulged in a hopefully *very* appropriate adult man way.

It all went so well he bought the half dozen boxes. Plus gave Mom a parting wink that made her blush and laugh before he headed for the parking lot with the cookies and his groceries.

Life hadn't ended because he couldn't hear. He had three bays open. Regulars were returning for service and repairs, because Red, Larry and Maryshka were working alongside him again. He was also letting them do more in the front office, and he'd told them what kind of communication help he needed—and what he didn't.

He'd never been so tired at the end of a workday, because communicating with people he couldn't hear took as much energy as working on an engine. But he was doing it.

He'd sat out and shared an afterwork beer with Chuck, who couldn't type on his phone worth a damn with his big fingers, but he could scribble all day long on a pad of paper. Tiger had shown him a couple sign language phrases. Including the dirty ones, of course. Skye had rolled her eyes when he asked her to show him those, but she'd done it.

Reaching out to Colt hadn't gone as well. His dickhead brother wasn't willing to let him see Aubrey. He probably suspected Tiger would be more on Rose and Bill's side about where she should live. However, he'd grudgingly told Tiger he could write to Aubrey and send her stuff. So Tiger had mailed her a care package that included her favorite homemade cookies, a funny card and letter from her loving uncle.

Skye surprised him by contributing to it, with a bracelet and matching charm for her school backpack. The trinkets had beads that looked like animal faces, elephants, giraffes and tigers. Stones were also strung on them that Vera had told Skye represented comfort during loss, a healing of mind and spirit, plus a boatload of protection and courage.

Yeah, the kid needed that. He was worried as shit about her. Rose and Bill were talking to a lawyer and trying to get things moving as fast as they could to sue for custody. It was all they could do for now. Tiger still hoped Colt would pull his head out of his ass, though. Maybe that was why Tiger had baked the cookies from their mom's recipe. They'd been Colt's favorite, too.

Skye had helped him get to this better headspace, helped him do it for himself. While his memories of Nicole and worries for Aubrey, plus the occasional anxiety about the hearing shit and headaches still kept him up too many nights, he was back on track.

Proving it, none of his worries were strong enough to make him change his mind. He was taking his Mistress to her first rally.

~

Though Tiger had offered to get them a hotel room, Skye's online surfing of rally footage told her most bikers like him preferred to stay at campsites.

Skye would never offend his pride, but she could guess his current financial constraints. With him owning a business and property, and being a motorcycle enthusiast with a half-dozen bikes of value, she had no doubt he was financially comfortable. However, when business or personal needs shifted, cash poor periods could happen. His loss of time during the weeks after the attack, plus things his insurance might not have covered on his medical or to make the garage operational again, were two prime examples.

She was also almost certain he'd funneled extra money to the garage owners who'd taken on his employees during that transition. Taking care of his people.

Beyond those concerns, she suspected a big part of the rally experience was staying where a lot of the other bikers were. When she attended Dragon Con in Atlanta, she always stayed in one of the hotels that hosted the event, since it would be fully booked by attendees.

When she shared that thought with him, he informed her that no "geek" festival could be comparable to a bike rally. In response, she'd pulled up a Dragon Con montage video. Though he'd seemed a little dazed by the visual hordes of costumed attendees at panels, parades and social events, the camaraderie, the passion of a shared interest, was obvious enough he conceded her point.

So here they were, on their way to a rally campsite, a few hours' drive from New Orleans. His mind was apparently on a track akin to hers, because he reached out and touched her knee, a concerned look on his face.

"If we get there and you change your mind about camping, we can still book a hotel. Since this is a small rally, relatively speaking, they shouldn't all be sold out."

"I have camped," she informed him, typing it out.

He shot her a dubious look. "Yeah? When? Where?"

"When I was little," she responded with dignity. She held up the screen beside the steering wheel so he didn't have to shift his attention fully from the road. "My father made a tent in the backyard using blankets and clothesline. I don't remember it, but there are pictures."

She got his slow smile in response, his blue eyes flickering from the sunlight coming through the driver's side window. "Forgive me," he said gravely. "I didn't realize you were such a seasoned outdoorswoman."

He laughed as she gave him a rude gesture. "I did date a guy in college who took me camping," she added. Why she'd brought that up, she didn't know, but his laughter loosened her hold on things she normally didn't talk about.

"That so? Where did you go?"

While she typed the response, he took a sip from his coffee travel mug and changed the GPS's suggested route to keep them on the rural highways. "Just one of the national parks," she showed him the screen. "He only took me once, but not because I wasn't willing to do more."

Tiger glanced her way. "There's more to that story."

She lifted a shoulder. She'd wanted Brit to take her on more adventurous hikes, the ones that went into deeper terrain. He'd balked.

"What if you got lost? You couldn't call out for help. And what if your phone gets broken or the battery goes dead?"

She'd pointed out multiple ways to handle his concerns. She did carry a panic whistle. Plus, unless she'd broken both her legs, she could track her way to him using the sound of his voice, if he or other campers were calling out.

He'd hedged and made excuses. She'd been young, not yet experienced enough in recognizing the signs. Dating a mute girl had been a novelty, something that won him praise and admiration. Even some sympathy. But over time, the luster of that died and what he'd seen as intriguing and self-congratulatory, putting up with a mute girl, became burdensome.

The intrigue part wasn't a dealbreaker. Every man, even every woman friend, had that at first. It was what the intrigue evolved into that mattered.

From the beginning, Tiger had taken everything about her in stride, even learning how to navigate communication with her differently than with Abby as if it was no big deal. Rather than answering his implied question about Brit, she shared that last thought with Tiger and how much she appreciated it.

"It was easy." The weathered skin creased around his eyes and mouth as he smiled. "I liked you. And the more I got to know you, the more I liked your style, how you didn't make a big deal of it, didn't get uptight. You put me at ease over doing the wrong thing, so I didn't worry as much about making things harder for you."

That was what had worried him. Making things harder for her. Which was why he'd offered the hotel setup.

"You going to tell me more about the camping prick? Because I can tell he was a prick."

She relented with a half-smile, though she kept it high level. Tiger pursed his lips after he read it. He didn't say anything for the next few miles, then he fished out a pad and pen from his center console, handing them to her.

"Do me a favor. Start making a list of guys who treated you like that, so I can go kick their asses."

That deepened her smile, though she picked up the paper notebook with two fingers as if it was an alien object, looking at it from all angles and comparing it to her hi-tech phone.

Throughout the trip, she and Tiger talked about a wide variety of things. Travel and work experiences, opinions on movies and music. The challenges of supervising employees, since they had that in common. What it was like living in New Orleans. They teased one another a lot. Most all of it was light-hearted, but not because they were avoiding the heavy stuff. They were simply enjoying one another's company.

No matter how long it took to type her responses, Tiger made her feel like they had all the time in the world. She couldn't remember the last time she'd "talked" this much with anyone, even the TRA women.

She also showed him more sign language. He asked her to correct his shaping of letters and gestures, so she had plenty of excuses to touch him, putting her hands on his free one to help him adjust his fingers. Like she had for the RR for restroom.

"I have that one down," he said, when the gesture came up. "Figured it was important for traveling with a female passenger."

He had an endless amount of travel anecdotes he was willing to share, like riding the "Tail of the Dragon," a two lane, eleven-mile stretch of road in western North Carolina. "It's about an hour from Pigeon Forge, Tennessee. Dollywood." He shot her a grin. "Over three hundred curves in those eleven miles. I have the 'Done the Dragon' shirt. Riding it with other experienced riders is a hell of a rush."

He'd done scavenger hunt poker runs, where riders picked up playing cards on the way to the sponsoring rally. "One of them was at this roadside tourist trap in the middle of fucking nowhere, a huge metal bull standing by the road. When you picked up your card, the husband and wife who ran the place gave every biker the best loaf of banana bread you've ever tasted. They were retired bikers, because he'd cracked his spine from a crash a few years back."

He also told her more about the rallies he'd attended, and the events she could expect at this one. Races, as well as games like he'd shown her, and backroad rides to local attractions. Lots of vendor goods and bikes to look at.

When they pulled into the RV park, the few hours of travel almost seemed too short. She recognized the desire to keep him to herself, not to have to deal with communicating with anyone else. A thought she immediately pushed away. She had left that kind of thinking behind a long time ago, and it certainly wouldn't help Tiger, either.

Another important reason for staying at the campsite was wanting him to experience the rally as normally as possible. He needed to navigate the challenges in that environment, rather than having the choice of retreating to a hotel room offsite.

If he could get through this one, and she could help him make it a good experience, it would be another way for him to see that he wasn't being denied the life he had before; he was developing skills to reclaim his enjoyment of it.

The RV park was as he'd described it on the way down. It had a large bathhouse, a big pool and amenity center. There were power and water hookups, an outdoor grill and a concrete patio at each of the sites.

"Geek girl will be able to charge all her devices and keep running the world," he'd told her. "Plus do her gaming dailies to keep up with her online crew." He gave her a hopeful look. "Do you dress up at any of those cons? Blue-skinned alien princess in a tiny outfit?"

"I shouldn't have shown you those YouTube videos," she'd typed. "Keep it up, and you'll experience my Red Sonja topping Conan role-playing fantasies."

He'd chuckled. She liked hearing him laugh. Now, as he went into the main office to check in, she watched a bunch of kids playing on the slide at the pool. The park seemed to have a decent crowd of campers, most appearing to be here for the motorcycle rally, but it wasn't at full capacity. Tiger confirmed it when he returned to the driver's seat.

"I think you'll like the spot I picked. But if you don't, they've got a few left."

The site he'd picked was on the border of the property, beneath a pair of large old oaks. It offered shade and privacy and a concrete pad long enough to accommodate truck and trailer. A seasoned camper, he started setting up with a relaxed expertise. He attached an awning to the side of the trailer, and placed two camping chairs beneath it, adding a pillow to the seat of hers. He'd also brought a collapsible table in case she needed to do some work on her laptop, though Paula had things well in hand for the next few days. She'd keep Skye informed via text and email.

She hadn't requested any of those comforts, and so was touched that he'd thought of them. After she helped him put up a roomy tent, something he did with impressive efficiency, he unloaded and carried two cots into it. She untied the straps on the two foam mattresses for them.

"No double wide cot?" she typed.

He nudged the long sides of the cots against one another, and sent her a significant look that had her smiling. He'd put a cooler between the chairs under the awning, a convenient table, and went there to pull a beer out and offer her her preference. When she chose a hard cider, he twisted off the cap for her.

He reached for the cigarettes and lighter he'd left in a chair seat, but she was faster, grabbing and holding the pack away from him—as if she had a chance against those long arms. He grinned, recapturing it, but dropped the cigarettes back on the chair, choosing to put his hands on her instead, leaning down to kiss her. They were being playful, like a couple of kids.

She eased back at the sound of Tiger's name being called. She tapped his hip, drawing his attention to it.

"Hey, boy! Good to see you." The sixtyish year old man who'd called out was in a white Ford F150 pickup. His T-shirt was printed with Old Glory and a Live Free motto. A bandanna held back his hair, which fell to his shoulders and tangled with his brown and gray beard. The familiarity with which the thick-waisted woman in the passenger seat leaned over him suggested husband and wife. She had freckles and a thick red braid that lay along her ample bosom.

"We're heading out for a backroad ride in an hour to see the falls," the man continued. "You and your lady friend want to go?"

The woman gave Skye a friendly wave. Skye answered it, even as she typed swiftly on her phone and showed the screen to Tiger. "Backroads ride, waterfalls. One hour."

He gave them a thumbs up and a smile. "Sounds good, Brian. Hey, Greta. Great to see you both here."

"We're running out to the food mart to get some things for grilling out," Greta said. "You're welcome to join us for dinner. I know you like Brian's burgers. Need anything?"

When Skye showed him that, Greta and Brian exchanged a look, but this time she waited on Tiger to explain. She wouldn't take the lead away from him here on his turf. Things could get awkward and frustrating, or not. It all depended on how he chose to react.

Tiger stepped closer to their window, drawing Skye with him. "I had an injury a while back. Can't hear a damn thing. She uses her phone to tell me what you're saying if I can't pick up on it."

"Oh, heavens, son." Greta put a hand on Brian's shoulder.

Responding to her sympathetic but kind expression, Tiger shook his head. "I'm alive and here. Hey, yeah, I could use something. Grab me some of that McCormick's seasoning. I'm about out, and I packed steaks for a romantic dinner with my 'lady friend,' one of the nights we're here. This is Skye, by the way. Don't tell her any bad stories about me."

"Like when you dumped your bike because of Harvey?"

"Harvey," Skye typed.

Tiger jabbed a finger at Brian. "That fucking rabbit did exist. I saved his life."

"And risked Brian's." Greta winked at Skye. "Helping Tiger get that bike back up was the first time he'd experienced cardio since the eighties."

"No animal crossed that road," Brian told Skye in a stage whisper, putting his hand to the side of his mouth. "Someone oversteered the curve, showing off."

He laughed when he got flipped off, Tiger obviously having picked up the gist of what he'd told her.

As they drove away with another friendly wave, Skye saw the speculation in their gazes. But they hadn't made excuses to take off or acted awkward. When she saw Tiger's mouth tighten at those looks, she typed, "It's good to have friends who care."

"Yeah." He shook it off. "Yeah, you're right. Let's finish getting set up and go for that ride."

~

He'd brought the Harley Street Glide, since he said that was more comfortable for longer rides, especially for a passenger. While she doubted his bikes had ever been put away with any dirt on them, the bike had been given an extra shine before being loaded for transport. As he took out the Street Glide and put down the kickstand, she noticed a smaller bike in the trailer, and made a questioning gesture.

"You said you wanted to learn to ride. There'll be a couple places around here I can show you the basics. That's the bike we'll be doing it with. It's an old Honda Nighthawk, which is a great learner bike. Sturdy and not over-powered, plus low enough to the ground to fit your height better. Though truth, when you're learning a smaller engine is more important than a smaller bike. When you twist that throttle, you don't want it to have too much power."

She sent a pointed glance at his larger bike. He gave her an unapologetically male laugh—practically a scoff. "No way, baby. No one drives this one but me. And it's way too much bike for a...." He paused significantly, while she put her hand on her hip and pointed a finger gun at him.

He chuckled. "Beginner. I was *not* about to say woman. Just yanking your chain, Mistress. You'll see plenty of women on bikes like mine. But they're also experienced riders. This bike," he patted the smaller one, "is about three hundred pounds. Mine is around seven hundred. You got to be able to hold that bike once you take up the kickstand, and if you dump it, getting it back up is a total bitch."

"Like for imaginary rabbits?" She typed it, while making a bunny ear gesture.

He bared his teeth at her as she grinned. Then she cocked a brow and typed, "Did you just call me baby?"

"No. Absolutely not. I didn't hear me call you baby, so it didn't happen."

When she punched his side, he caught her wrist and drew her to him, and then his mouth was on hers. It was spontaneous, no thought to it. She could have stopped and called him on it, but she wasn't in the mood to tell him he'd overstepped.

She didn't want him to stop, period.

She put her hands up to his throat, fingers sliding into his hair and tugging as he pulled her closer with a noise of hunger. Turning, he lifted her up against the inside wall of the trailer. It brought their bodies into more advantageous alignment as their mouths explored and tasted. His body was firm and hers soft, fitting together just right, setting off a spiraling pleasure that increased the longer they kept moving against one another. Fusing together as if they were two things meant to be one.

When he drew back, they were both out of breath. He let her down but gripped her upper arms, almost keeping her on her toes as his burning gaze stayed fixed on hers. "I always want to fucking eat you alive, but here, in this place... I might get a little out of control with you, Mistress. Not be as well-mannered."

She made two gestures, then typed, so he understood what she'd said. "Warning? Or promise?"

His eyes flashed. "Show me how you signed 'promise.'"

When she did, he repeated it, his gaze locked with hers.
Promise.

～

About a dozen bikes were going on the ride, over half carrying passengers. When Tiger fell into their ranks, Skye on the seat behind him, the group rumbled out of the park. She noted the engines were a mix of sounds due to the different styles of bikes being ridden, everything from powerful cruisers like Tiger's, to classics, choppers, dual purpose bikes, and three-wheelers, Harley "trikes."

Brian and Greta were on one of those. When explaining the different models of bikes, Tiger had said riding a trike on twisty backroads was actually more dangerous than riding them "on the slab," the interstates and straighter highways. Three-wheelers, those with the two wheels in back, were more apt to tip. Excessive speed, or a jerky, unstable line through the curve, could make the rider lose control and possibly lift a tire or flip. However, Tiger told her Brian had ridden and shown choppers for years. He was an experienced biker who knew how to handle the trike, and it better fit his current health.

The national park with the waterfall was about fifteen miles away. While that sounded good, Skye quickly realized the ride, and riding together like this, was as much the reason for going as the destination.

They passed through the section of town where the main rally site was. Pavilion tents were already set up, vendors plying their wares to bikers here a day ahead of the rally's official start. And there were plenty of them, visiting the tents and milling around, drinks in hand, their rides parked in shining rows.

When Brian hollered out their destination, some headed for their bikes. As such, by the time they turned onto the route out of town, their ranks had swelled to sixty riders. In town, that noise was indescribable. Added to that was the startling immediacy of car engines growling so close nearby as they rejoined town traffic, the groan of a dump truck starting up, or screech of tires when someone had to brake faster than expected. The heat of so many bikes and vehicles pressed upon Skye, including from the engine below her. Tiger's T-shirt was damp with sweat under her palms.

But on the two-lane road, the sound died off some and a breeze picked up. The road curved through forest and open fields. The houses set back from the road were old farms and outbuildings, shotgun houses and the occasional new build or small subdivisions, city people bringing their money to seek a slower pace of life.

She was glad Tiger had taken her on the backroads near his own property to help her learn how to be a good passenger. She liked leaning into the turns with him and wasn't worried about the tilting feeling. He'd told her, "Put your chin in the direction we're curving, and keep your eyes where we need to go, not on the road surface. That way you don't overexaggerate the lean, or stiffen up and lean to the opposite side."

Watching him do that made doing it with him even easier. The confidence he had in the bike's movement, the way he understood and anticipated what it would do, reassured her. He was solid and steady, no sign of uncertainty or tension under her hands. He was home, she realized. A person could have several homes during their life, and this environment, with these people, was one of them for him.

The line of riders stretched out, some of them ramping up into higher gears, enjoying the chance to open up and go faster. Tiger stuck to the leisurely pace, though, staying in rough alignment with Brian and Greta. It gave Skye time to look around.

She knew some riders called people in cars "cagers." They saw them as stuck in a prison, not able to get the full sensory input this provided. She suspected people in cars thought riders had to be crazy, especially when caught out in bad weather, or in tricky situations where they had so little protection. But right now, there was no question in her mind why the people around her preferred this.

On the wall of his bedroom, Tiger had a framed picture of what he'd told her had been his first bike. A quote was handwritten beneath it. "Motorcycles tell us a more useful truth: we are small and exposed, and probably moving too fast for our own good, but that's no reason not to enjoy every minute of the ride."

The quote was written on cardstock. Tiger said it was from a birthday card given to him by his parents when he'd received the bike. He'd cut it out and put it in the frame. His mother had written the words, a quote from "Season of the Bike" by Dave Karlotski.

Skye had looked it up. After reading the whole essay and experiencing this with him, she understood better what Tiger was seeking on his bike, what about riding had called to him. Especially during the life he'd lived, and the battles he'd fought to leave it.

That he still fought, especially now, after the violence that had come to his garage and taken Nicole.

She had a convertible because she liked the open feeling, but she admitted she felt even closer to the surrounding world like this, as if all walls had been removed. Moving around curves, up and down hills, reminded her of the excitement of a rollercoaster ride.

The bike engines drowned out any other noise. Based on that and what she'd just experienced in town, she might have made the mistake of assuming Tiger wouldn't feel his deafness so keenly in this environment. Yet to a person who appreciated engine noise like music, it could only deepen the sense of loss.

Fortunately, at the moment, he looked like he was getting enough from this experience to make up for that.

While it might not be in her blood and bone the way it was in his, she sure as hell could enjoy and appreciate the ride. As they passed families sitting on their front porches, most waved at the riders. The bikers gestured to each other, drawing attention to the sights. Looking over, she saw Greta toss her a big smile, saying she knew what Skye might be feeling. Greta stretched her arms out to either side, tipped her head back and gave a whoop, one that was picked up and echoed by other passengers on the backs of the bikes moving together.

It was like a bonded pack. A family. Skye slid her arms under Tiger's, around his chest, and saw the corner of his mouth tilt in a smile.

When they reached the park and dismounted to take the trail to the falls, she was glad she'd purchased multi-purpose boots for the trip, ones that worked for motorcycle riding and hiking. The signage indicated it was about a half mile hike to the waterfalls. She quickly found that trail had a lot of uneven ground, thanks to the twists and turns, and the roots of the forest trees.

The boots handled that terrain well. Plus had the advantage of being kind of sexy, with their silver buckles and a thin decorative chain at the ankles. Ros, the Queen of Footwear, had helped her find them.

The walk was more than worth it. A swift-rushing creek passed beneath the wooden bridge that provided the best view of the beautiful forty-foot-tall falls. As they wandered over the bridge, she captured a dozen photos for the vast library of images she was always augmenting for design work, and for her own pleasure in recalling the moment later.

Which meant she took a few of Tiger as well, and then a fun selfie of them, giving him the phone so he could use his longer arm to position the phone for the best shot. She texted that one to Ros and the others, including Bastion.

When they stopped at the mid-point of the bridge to gaze at the rushing water, Tiger slid his arm over her shoulders, a gesture as natural as hers going around his waist.

In session, every touch was negotiated, part of a protocol, until it became more intuitive. There were fewer lines out here, and she wasn't minding it. It had been a long time since she'd had the pleasure of that informality with a man.

Tiger had hinted at the occasional hookup outside the club, some brief, casual relationships, but she hadn't had anything like that for a really long time.

Teenagers at the base of the falls were stripped down to shorts or swimsuits to wade into the creek. One boy and girl came together, arms twining, to kiss and play. Skye tightened her arm around Tiger's waist. She expected that kiss was like riding the motorcycle, a rush that started in the vitals and spread joy through every part of a person. When she looked over at Brian and Greta, holding hands, she couldn't think of a better way for a couple to remind themselves of that. No matter the years they'd been together, they seemed to be proof that the feeling never stopped being accessible.

She was thinking forever-couple thoughts. Not applying it to herself, no, but she wasn't an idiot. A woman didn't go down those roads if she wasn't starting to think about it. Which was a great way to set her heart up to be pummeled into kindling, like a boat dropped from the edge and landing at the bottom of those falls.

Sliding away from Tiger with a smile, she continued across the bridge to explore the hiking trails. They were here together, enjoying themselves.

Leave it at that.

～

The next morning they attended a handful of rally events. One of the games she watched was similar to their cone and golf ball exercise, only it was done with raw eggs. Other riders competed to roll kegs toward a finish line. There was a "slowest" bike race, to see who could keep their bike balanced at the slowest pace. She was impressed when one contestant managed to do it so well he seemed to not be moving at all. Brian hollered out to his losing competitor, a bearded giant who couldn't keep his feet from touching the ground at the snail's pace. "If this is too tough for you, Roscoe, I'll race you anytime."

"Big talk from a fat old geezer on a tricycle," Roscoe retorted, making everyone laugh, including Brian.

"The day will come, boy, when you'll like planting your ass on that three-wheeler. Just you wait."

After the games, they walked around the pavilions, visiting bike part and accessory vendors. Stunning motorcycles were on display everywhere. She could tell the ones Tiger liked most from the look in his eyes, the way he talked to the owners and then explained to her what it was about them that made them exceptional.

Despite his obvious enthusiasm, he frequently checked to make sure she wasn't bored, thirsty or hungry, or too hot on the asphalt. On the contrary, she was having a great time, and watching him in his element, a world of leather, metal and powerful machines, amused and aroused her.

They stayed busy enough through the afternoon she didn't find time to indulge the latter, but she could tell he picked up on it. Or maybe he was feeling the same way. Most of the time they had their hands on one another. Her fingers were hooked in his belt loop or jeans pocket, while his arm was crooked over her neck. His firm biceps rested against her shoulder as his hand clasped hers over her breast, close enough his fingertips occasionally trailed across the curve.

That night they ate dinner at the campground with Greta and Brian again. Since a bigger group joined them, Tiger and Brian manned the grill and got everyone fed. After dinner, she and Tiger settled into the camp chairs they'd brought over and enjoyed the conversation. She translated for him on her phone, well enough for him to keep up with things.

Eventually though, she felt him studying her more closely than her phone screen. Proving it, his hand closed over it, and he leaned over to brush his lips over her ear. "You've worked hard enough for one night, Mistress. How about I work hard for you for a while?"

The firelight licked his intent gaze with flame. All that sexual need she'd banked throughout the day responded. Her reaction needed no translation.

His jaw flexed, firm lips pressing together. Rising from the chair, he offered her his hand. His grip was strong, transmitting the same objective as his gaze.

He made their good nights, raising his free hand in a friendly farewell that nevertheless discouraged further conversation. Skye saw Brian's knowing grin, but also Greta's soft smile. She felt oddly glad about that sign of approval. They liked the way she looked with Tiger.

As soon as they broke away from the others and the night closed around them, those softer feelings were replaced by something else. Tiger had warned her that he might be more out of control with her here at the rally, and the feeling was contagious.

When they reached the tent, and he held open the flap for her, she tugged him in behind her by his shirt front. Though a faint smile touched his serious mouth, it didn't detract from the matching urgency she felt pulsing from him. She pushed him down on the cot, rough enough to tell him the mood she was in. She wanted to take control, here and now.

Being a Dom or sub didn't require elaborate settings or props. She used the cues they both craved to take over. She tossed a condom on his chest as she got rid of her jeans and panties. A bare second after he'd opened his jeans and rolled it on, she straddled him. With nothing but her hand on his chest and throat, and the lock of her eyes, she slid down on his length and held there, her lips parted, eyes glowing upon him.

"Fuck," he murmured. "Oh, fuck." His body quivered as she tightened on him, slid up, then down. His fingers were clamped over her hips. Though he didn't break her control or try to resist it, his savage need was a wave of energy that covered and wrapped her up, binding her to him.

She remembered him putting her against the wall of the trailer, letting her feel his need to take. The leash a Domme held on a powerful alpha sub wasn't about its weight or thickness, but what it was made of. Every moment he obeyed her sent the intoxicating message he was surrendering to her restraint.

The contrast pushed her up to the climax, and she gave him a jerky nod just as she went over. She wanted to feel him come with her.

She'd like to feel it without the damn condom. But that would require the exclusivity conversation. And she wasn't going down that road. *Stay away from all the warning signs, girl.*

He groaned out his release softly. No one was close, but the wind carried. At the club, hearing his groans tearing from him honored her control and reinforced it. Here, muffling his response showed his respect for her.

She tipped her head back, gasping through her climax and relying on him to hold her until she'd milked the very last sensation from them both.

Wow. It took some time to get their breath back, but when at last they did, she was ready for a different kind of aftermath. She had him turn over so she could lie upon him, her arms overlapping his, breasts against his back. They had the tent flap back to allow the screen mesh layer and a battery-operated fan to pull in air and cool the perspiration on their skin. Pressing her mons against his buttocks, she thought about his motorcycle beneath him, between his legs, all that heat and power, carrying him wherever he wanted to go.

She understood the appeal.

"Next full moon, I'll take you out for a night ride," he said. His voice was a rumble in the dense space.

She liked the idea. She shifted so he could turn over. When he did, she leaned down and touched her mouth to his, a soft intimacy. They held gazes, him lifting his hand to stroke back her hair. She nuzzled his hand, and his gaze flickered. Then she settled into his arms, her head tucked against his neck.

They fell asleep that way.

CHAPTER SEVENTEEN

The next morning, they headed for a local track to see the bike races. Sitting next to Tiger on the bleachers, Skye learned who was demonstrating good bike handling skills and why. People around them jumped in to add their own opinions to Tiger's and Brian's, turning it into a small community forum.

It was a little tricky, keeping her attention moving between him, them and the track. When someone else was speaking and Tiger didn't notice, she put his hand on his wrist, a cue so he wouldn't throw a comment of his own in the middle of someone else's.

Since there was too much noise to use her transcription recorder, she typed what they were saying, the basics, as there was a lot of information going back and forth. Tiger was missing about half, but he appeared pleased she was being pulled into the dialogue.

Then one man directed an engine question at Tiger. He had a shaved head, a trim gray goatee, and a tattoo on his arm that said he'd served in the Iraq war. Skye typed in his question.

"I'm deaf, man," Tiger explained at the veteran's curious look. "But she can tell me what you're saying."

Tiger was getting a lot of practice explaining his circumstances, but it wasn't always easy for him. Especially when he faced the reaction she knew happened far too often. The question was the type that would naturally lead to further conversation on the topic, but once Tiger answered it, the vet grunted a general agreement and returned to watching the race—and talking to his companions on his other side.

Tiger's expression stayed mild, though she detected the slight tightening of his lips. He slid his arm behind her, bracing it on the bleacher by her hip, and offered her a half smile. "Guess the upside is being able to focus on the race with fewer interruptions."

She pressed her shoulder into his side, but when he returned to watching the race, she drew back and lifted her phone.

She'd taken so many pictures this weekend, which wasn't unusual for her being somewhere with a lot of graphic design material. But she'd taken a lot more personal ones than the norm. Like now, when she captured Tiger's profile.

His gaze turned toward her and held. His expression became more intent, as if her attention alone was what held him still for the camera.

She took that picture too, then touched his face. He pressed his lips to her fingers. A cheer from the crowd, people jumping up around them as an underdog took the lead, drew their attention back to the track. But he took her hand and held onto it. A firm grip that offered her strength. He'd noted her worrying about him, and was letting her know he was okay.

She thought he also wanted to let her know she could count on that. Could count on him for anything.

Message received. Clearly enough that it was getting pretty difficult to deny how much she wanted to do so.

Though porta-potties were not her first choice for a bathroom, too many people were lined up at the raceway restrooms. Outside the entrance to the track, she located the line of orange plastic boxes. They'd been put at a reasonable distance from the food vendors, and at least were roomy and clean. Portable sinks with soap and paper towels were set up outside them.

After she took care of that, she walked up a hill where people sat out on blankets watching the races. Though being outside the bleacher area meant a portion of the track view was obstructed by them, the far side curves were visible. She zoomed in and acquired some good shots of the racers coming around them.

She imagined blurring their movement into multi-colored streaks, working taglines for a product into the impressions of air flow. She typed a note and appended it to the pic, then saved it in her pending design file.

As she headed down the slope and back toward the entrance to the track, she noted a group of bikers clustered beneath a section of the bleachers. They had their motorcycles with them, though there'd been yellow tape there before, specifically prohibiting parking in those areas.

All the riders were men, except for a woman in a thong, tank top and leathers, leaning against the back of one bike. Though as Tiger had said, this was a more family-oriented event, Skye had seen a few blatantly sexual outfits like this woman's at the pavilions in town.

It didn't put her off. When she'd researched the bigger rallies online, she'd recognized a comfort with sexual displays similar to that in a BDSM environment. And just like it, various sizes and ages embraced those displays. However, this girl was in her early twenties, with an eye-catching figure and long dark hair.

The large man straddling the bike had one leg stretched out, a hand hooked in his jeans pocket, the other clasping a beer. He wore a black leather cut, but she couldn't see what MC affiliation patch was on the back of it.

She'd seen plenty of them these past two days, ranging from the whimsical to the badass. Brian's was the Old Mud Dogs, a Texas MC group mostly in his age and interest group.

Two additional men leaned against their bikes, while a third sat on a crate. From the nonverbal cues of their conversation, she thought the man on the bike was the leader of the group, unofficially or officially.

The Harley he rode was beautiful, a deep red enhanced by the gleaming silver of the engine and wheel spokes. His powerful body was angled so that the shadows and light sculpted the planes of his face, enhancing the depth of his eyes. All of that, coupled to the attractive woman in provocative clothing, her glance periodically moving his way in an obvious *I'm his* manner, presented story elements that could catch attention and draw interest.

A custom jewelry shop had recently become a client, and they wanted to approach a more eclectic clientele. Based on the preliminary information Cyn had given her, Skye could see the possibilities in this material. She'd rework the identifying features, using the rest to mock up some concepts.

She'd taken several pictures when one of the bikers leaning against his ride noticed her. After he said something to the large man strad-dling the bike, he twisted around, shooting a look her way. When he spoke, the one on the cooler and the man who'd first noticed her headed her way.

No problem. It wasn't the first time she'd had to explain what she was doing and why, and assure someone she was using design elements, not actual identities, in her work.

Yet as they advanced, she experienced a trickle of unease. Their expressions were neither friendly nor unfriendly, and the dispassion gave them the look of hunters.

She thought of dashing for the track entrance, but she was only standing a few feet from it. People on the bleacher ends flanking it could look down and see her.

If they weren't too distracted by the race.

But she just didn't like the idea of retreating without explaining how she intended to use the material. That would be unprofessional. She could handle this. She started typing as they drew closer, and engaged the audio. Helen Mirren was always a good choice. Her voice carried, and a British accent tended to catch attention. "Hello. I work for—"

A roar from the crowd swallowed the sound, and one of the men plucked the phone from her grasp, capturing her wrist with the other. His hold on the phone disappeared the screen and muted the audio.

"Why are you taking our picture?"

Being grabbed startled her, but when she tried to yank free, he anticipated her resistance. He moved further into her personal space, tossing her phone to his buddy, and gripped her hair.

The shock of it told her too late she should have run. This was a man used to resistance and violence. She was in trouble.

He smelled of beer and sweat, but his gaze was flat, faculties fully intact. Golden-blond hair was tied back from his bearded face, and he had remarkably attractive gray eyes, no matter that they looked chill-ingly cold. While not as large as the man on the bike, he was far bigger than Skye. The other man had a shaved head like the Iraq vet and a tattoo of a tower of skulls on his forearm. So did the one holding her, along with "Ride or Die," ink around his biceps.

His meaty hand was digging her ID bracelet into her wrist, concealing it. She tried to sign with one hand, knowing he wouldn't understand, but at least he might comprehend she couldn't speak to him.

Instead, he interpreted the motion as her flailing, so he gave her a quick shake to settle her down. It was rough enough to snap her teeth together and leave no doubt how easy it would be to snap other parts of her. "Answer the fucking question. You don't look like a biker's bitch."

His apathetic expression told her it wasn't personal. She had the harrowing thought that his job was to hurt anyone the large man on the bike told him he wanted hurt. The dead eyes told her he was long past getting into a moral quandary over it.

In only a few seconds, they'd pulled her further under the bleachers. The third man had moved to block the view from the vending and bathroom foot traffic. His posture clearly said, "not your business and keep moving."

Though Skye wasn't as much into the self-defense stuff and going to the MMA gym as the others, Cyn had made sure she knew the basics. But she hadn't practiced them as much as she should have. And she'd done exactly what Cyn had told her never to do. Second guess herself, rather than risking embarrassment with an overreaction. Like bolting and blowing her panic whistle. Which was back in the tent.

If she survived this, Cyn would kick her ass.

Cyn had also told her controlling her fear was more important than anything else, but Skye had never been at someone's mercy like this, someone ready to hurt her. Panic fought to take control, because she couldn't communicate. She couldn't call out for help.

But someone had heard her anyway.

"That's my girl, Warthog."

Tiger's voice was calm. When her captor shifted around, Tiger's tall, broad-shouldered form sent relief shooting through her. She wasn't alone. He was here.

He stood beside the third man who'd been blocking the view of passers-by. Though Tiger had one hand hooked in his jeans pocket, the other loose at his side, the casual posture wasn't casual at all.

When she'd confronted him in his office, he'd betrayed a temper that could cross the line when he was pushed too far. But the look in his eyes now was one she'd never seen before. It was every bit as cold, flat and dangerous as what she saw in the face of the man holding her.

Brian stood at Tiger's right. In the older man's fixed expression, Skye didn't see the amiable retiree hanging out, shooting the shit with lawyers on six-figure Harleys. She saw the chopper guy who'd rubbed shoulders with bikers most of his life.

A determined-looking Greta stood a hovering step behind her husband. She might be as worried as Skye was, but she was hiding it well. She looked full mama bear, ready to throw down and kick some ass.

Tiger didn't seem worried at all. Navigating this kind of violence might not be his preference, but it appeared to be familiar territory. She wasn't sure if that was reassuring or alarming.

He hadn't been calling her captor names. As her glance fell on his burly chest, she saw the name patch. *Warthog*. Tiger couldn't see that from his position, so that meant they knew one another.

Thankfully, Warthog let go of her hair, the most unsettling of his holds, but he kept a tight grip on her wrist. She wanted to shove away from him, but Tiger's gaze shifted to her, and what she saw there was clear. *Follow my lead.*

"Let her go and tell me what the fuck the problem is."

Warthog grunted. "Bitch took pictures of us. Of Rock."

"This is her first rally. She's been taking a lot of pictures." Brian delivered the comment in a similar, what-the-fuck tone. "We didn't know you were here, so we didn't know she needed the warning."

As he spoke, he gestured to Skye's phone and sent Tiger a significant look, cuing him into the problem.

Warthog shrugged. "We were in the area on other business. Decided to stop in, check out the races and the food. We like the chili cook off."

Despite the unexpectedly casual comment, his focus on Skye remained unwavering. His attention passed over her body, noting her breasts, her mouth. It was an impersonal yet invasive evaluation, as if judging how well she'd suck dick, or look stripped down to her skin.

He was obviously used to being around women expecting that kind of appraisal. "She won't tell us why she took them."

"She's mute. Grinder there is holding the way she talks." Brian pointed to Warthog's grip. "That thing you're digging into her wrist is her medical bracelet."

Warthog's I'm-going-to-fuck-you-up look changed to curiosity. He shifted his hold and pulled her arm up to examine the bracelet. "Well, hunh." Releasing her, he shot Skye an intrigued look. "You can do all that sign language shit?"

The signs she made in response were impossible to misinterpret. Being afraid always pissed her off. She shoved at the male's chest and glared.

Warthog laughed and grinned at his buddies. Even Rock's lips curled in a tight smile. The girl gave Skye a speculative look and tossed her long hair over one shoulder.

Tiger's muscles had tightened, but she saw approval in his expression. That also helped. She held out a demanding hand for her phone.

After a confirming glance at Rock, Warthog jerked his head at Grinder and he handed it to her. Under Warthog's watchful gaze, she called up the photos, showing him that she'd taken four.

"Shit, you might want to see these, Rock. She made you look not so ugly." Warthog took the phone from her again, though at least this time he didn't put his hands on her.

As soon as his attention turned to their leader, and before Skye could make a grab for the phone, Tiger reached out and pulled her to his side. He was right, of course. The phone wasn't as important as putting space between them. Her gut was churning, her limbs trying to shake. She didn't want to give these assholes the satisfaction of seeing it, so having his solid form to lean against helped mask it.

She still wanted her goddamn phone back.

Rather than making him bring it over, Rock swung off the bike and strode their way. He was every bit as big as Tiger. He grunted as he took the phone and looked at the shots, but he didn't seem to agree with Warthog. Instead he held the phone out to Tiger, a pointed gesture as he sent Skye a warning look, telling her she better not reach for it, much as she wanted to.

Tiger had pressed her slightly behind him. He held the phone out so Warthog and Rock could see while he deleted the shots, going into her trash folder to finish the act.

When Rock nodded, Tiger returned the phone to her, their fingers brushing and his eyes meeting hers for a brief but significant contact. Skye tucked the phone into her crossbody bag and shot Rock a venomous look. He ignored her, responding to Tiger's questioning brow.

"Yeah, we're good. How you been doing, Tiger?"

The greeting wasn't friendly. Rock's gaze was measuring threat and response, like the leader of a pack crossing paths with a lone wolf.

Tiger had glanced toward Skye, a question. She signed it, "How are you?" because he had a good grasp of the basics from his Signing in English class. Like *How are you, My name is,* and *Would you like my foot up your ass?*

"Hell, boy. Is that how you hooked up with good-looking special ed here? That hit on your place and Colt's old lady left you deaf?" Rock tapped his own ears.

Skye wished she knew how to kick him in the nuts hard enough to end his chance to reproduce. Or walk. She made a note to have Cyn show her how to do that.

She was glad Tiger didn't catch the first part, though. While he still seemed like a flat sea, a maelstrom was brewing beneath those waters. Fortunately, Rock's ear tap was enough that Tiger didn't require further translation from her.

Tiger nodded, a noncommittal response. "We'll go back to the race now. Sorry for the trouble." His tone said he couldn't give a shit what Rock felt about any of it, as long as it took them out of his path.

Brian was drawing Greta away, picking up on Tiger's cue, but the way Brian hung back warned Skye it wasn't done until the others walked. Tiger and Rock hadn't moved out of their squared-off position. Rock studied Tiger like a schoolyard bully, thinking he needed to take a swing at a defiant kid to prove who was boss.

"Wasn't a surprise when you bailed," he murmured, eyes sharpening like a drawn knife. Brian and Greta couldn't hear him, but Skye could. "Since your momma was fucking someone else, you're probably not even his son. Maybe Big Mac should have taken you out with that same trash. Clean slate."

People, particularly strangers, tended to say things in front of a mute person as if they thought they were neurologically impaired. Though she tried hard to mask her expression, everything inside her froze at the implication. Rock shifted a look toward Skye. "You tell him that, special ed. I'm going to look to make sure you said it word for word."

All the turmoil she was feeling surged into anger, mixed with a healthy dose of fear. But not for herself. If Tiger realized what Rock had said...

She lifted her chin and met Rock's gaze. *Fuck. You.* She mouthed it, then signed it.

Though she'd had a lifetime of studying body language, Tiger registered the change in Rock's before she did. In a blink, he'd moved fully between the two of them, blocking Skye from Rock's view.

Violence shimmered in the air. She was sure Rock and his crew were armed. Tiger traveled with a gun, but he'd left it at the camp, locked in the trailer.

She was sure Cyn would have something to say about that, too. *"Yeah, just as useful as that panic whistle. Why have a carry permit if he's not going to fucking carry?"*

Their face-off was attracting attention, a knot of race attendees standing at a curious but careful distance. Not all of them looked boozed up and hoping for a brawl. Some looked poised to call the cops if it didn't defuse.

Or maybe they already had. Off-duty cops hired for security had appeared, heading their way.

Tiger spoke. "We took care of the problem, Rock. We have no fight. This rally's for old timers and families. People not part of your world."

"Like you." Rock spat the two words.

Tiger understood that. But instead of making him rise to the bait, the words seemed to drop an extra blanket of calm over him. One Skye expected had been woven from long, painful experience.

"Since I was the one who walked away, I think I sent that message pretty clearly myself. Have a good time. We're going to go do that ourselves."

He took Skye's arm. Brian and Greta preceded them as Tiger led her away from the bikers.

"Tell me if you hear anything that could be a problem," Tiger told her quietly.

She could tell how difficult it was for him not to turn around and track that himself, but she appreciated the trust. It gave her something to focus on other than her roiling emotions and the trembling low in her abdomen.

Tiger offered the two officers a courteous nod and a lifted hand of thanks for their presence, and kept going.

A glance over her shoulder a minute later showed Rock and his buddies back under the bleachers with their bikes. The cops were talking to Warthog. Rock was monitoring the conversation, but he was still watching Tiger.

The look held disgust, but also bitter confusion. A reaction that suggested Tiger had once been a respected part of his world, no matter what Rock had implied.

He spat on the ground at last, and straddled his bike next to the girl. She was scrolling through her phone again, the poster girl for "too pretty to be bothered by much."

Brian had noted what Skye had, because he let out a relieved breath. "Fuck, been a while since I've been that close to a brawl. Not as fun as it once was." He sent a fond look toward his wife. "Sorry you didn't get a chance to crack a beer bottle over someone's head, Mama."

There was a twinkle in the somber brown eyes when he looked toward Skye. "God knows, you don't want women involved in a biker fight. I had a cocktail waitress jump on my back once, like a cat on a pit bull's head. Not a whole lot the pit bull can do but howl and run."

"He's not telling you about the double D mud wrestler who practically handed him his balls," Greta said dryly. "The night I met him, he was telling that story. Said he'd never been happier to have his ass kicked."

"Until I met you, baby," he assured her.

Greta punched him lightly in the side. "Those brawls were different. Nine times out of ten, both sides bought each other drinks afterward. They didn't involve people like that. I'm just glad it turned out okay."

She glanced at Skye. "At the bigger events, they usually come in the kind of numbers where you notice the cut early on and can steer clear of them. They can be good guys, but that's the problem. One moment, they're bikers who love the life, just like you, sharing a beer. The next, that one-percenter side kicks in and you find yourself knee-deep in their bullshit."

Skye had recovered her composure enough to have her phone recorder out, capturing their conversation on the screen for Tiger. He watched the words scroll, but didn't smile. His expression was oddly blank.

"Your lady handled herself well," Brian said carefully, gauging his mood the same way Skye was. "Why don't you take her over to the playground, get an ice cream and cool off? They won't pull any of that shit near the kids. Now that they're on the cops' radar, they'll likely head on down the road."

Tiger read his words. "We'll see you back at the camp," he said. His tone was flat, but the follow-up was sincere. "Thanks for the back-up. Both of you."

Skye reinforced it with a nod. She had her hand on Tiger's arm, and he shifted it to drop her hand into the clasp of his. She tightened her grip, tucking her phone away. He met her gaze. "Let's go," he said.

The place Brian had suggested was a park a few hundred yards away from the track, a place for kids bored by the races. There was also a soccer field, but today it was occupied by food and craft vendors. Earlier, when they'd arrived, Tiger had said they could stroll through them, if she was interested.

Unlike most other men, he hadn't suggested she go do that on her own while he watched the race. Thinking of it, she realized Tiger had stayed pretty close at the rally events. Even when not right at her side, he'd been marking her whereabouts, as this incident proved.

For the most part, it was a friendly environment where help was as close as reaching for it. But he'd known the potential for a different element. She'd eventually give him hell for not giving her a heads up, because ignorance was the worst protection strategy there was. But that aside, Tiger had proven he could navigate a dangerous, tricky situation without one of his key senses. Since tension was thrumming through him like lightning, she wondered if he realized the significance of that.

She brought him to a stop by one of the playground benches. "You did good," she typed. "You handled yourself really well. Thank you."

His hand closed over hers on the phone, covering it, and squeezed hard. Anger flashed in his gaze, and something deeper. "That could have gone to shit," he said. "You were right in the middle of it. I couldn't...I didn't know what he was saying..."

"And I couldn't communicate with him." She typed it, then put her free hand on his face. Used her lips to mouth the next words, emphatically. *You. Kept. Me. Safe. Thank you.*

As he stared down at her, she dipped her head, typed and held up the screen with an expectant look. "Now go buy me a damn Sno-Cone. Cherry-flavor."

His jaw eased, his lips twitching. But instead of immediately obeying her, he pulled her into his arms and held her close. But they were okay. It was all right. Life went on, and getting bogged down in the drama meant missing better things.

She eased back, trying to give him that with her expression. He stroked her hair from her face. "I'm sorry, Mistress," he said. "I forgot what a badass you are."

She poked him in the chest, a don't-you-forget-it move, but she couldn't be less than honest with him, softening it with a smile that trembled on the edges. He cupped her face.

"You're okay," he echoed her own thoughts. "This is a good event. Something like that...it's the exception here. Like Brian said, they'll bug out soon. The cops will stick pretty close until they take off. This isn't their usual scene."

He bent and brushed her lips with his, then nipped the lower one. He rested his forehead on hers before drawing back. "One cherry Sno-Cone, coming up."

They ate the frozen treat on a park bench while watching the kids play. The raspberry one he'd chosen turned his lips and tongue blue. Something he brought to mingle with the cherry red on hers, teasing. By the time they finished eating them, he'd eased her onto his lap, holding her there.

The intimacy was needed more than she wanted to admit, a way to lessen the anxiety and anger the near miss had caused. She suspected he felt the same. When they were done, he tossed their empty cone wrappers into a nearby can and then sat back, his arms clasped loosely around her. He had his palm against her hip, fingers resting on the top of her buttock as she kept her arm looped around his neck, playing with that thick wave of brown hair that went to a point at his nape.

"So what did Rock say that you refused to tell me? Was it about my mother?"

When he met her surprised gaze, he kept his tone mild, though the words weren't. "I'm not a kid, Mistress. Don't you ever fucking treat me like one. I assume you know better than most what that feels like."

He was right. She did know. "Before I answer that," she typed, "were you doing the same? Keeping an eye out for trouble and steering me clear of it?"

He lifted a shoulder, his dark blue eyes troubled. "I wanted you to enjoy the rally without giving you unnecessary crap to worry about. If I had known Rock and his crew were here, yeah, I would have steered you clear, but I'd sure as hell have told you why and let you know what cut to look for. Promise."

She could take issue with him shielding her from any of it, but that was a conversation for another time. He was still waiting on her response. Reluctantly, she typed what Rock had said and showed him.

His gaze flickered and he looked away from the screen. "Yeah. I figured it was something like that."

She lowered the phone and stayed still, letting him know if he wanted to talk about it, she'd listen.

He didn't look like he did. A darkness gripped his expression, his gaze tracking the kids on the playground as if they were birds in a far distant sky. But then he spoke.

"My dad...he took us into the bedroom where he'd laid out her body. We'd just gotten home from school. I'd made an A on a history test, and I wanted to tell Mama about it, because she'd helped me study. I wasn't good at any subject that didn't involve an engine. He said, 'Say goodbye to your mama. She didn't do right by me, but she was good to you boys. You're old enough not to need a mama anymore, anyhow. It's a father's job to teach his son what a man is.'"

Tiger's hand was a fist on Skye's hip. His lip curled, but the blue eyes were glassy. "He shot her in the head. A quick kill. He loved her enough to make sure she never saw it coming. He told us that."

Oh God...

No matter how Rock had phrased it, she'd assumed Tiger's mother had been killed like Nicole had. A casualty of their violent world. But by his own father...the father who had raised him through his teens, whose right hand he'd been into his adult years, until he walked away because he couldn't take any more.

Her stomach had plummeted, her chest tight. She wanted to hold him, wanted to smash something. But what was vibrating in him had her settling her hand on his shoulder, a simple contact, telling him she was here. Listening. He was still staring into the distance, now far past the kids on the monkey bars and swings.

"I never told my dad, but I'd met him once, the guy. Zayn, a convenience store employee who slipped her candy bars and made her laugh. He was studying to be a teacher. She took me to a carnival with him. On the way back home, she told me, 'I wanted you to meet him. Colt wouldn't understand, but I think you do. Or you will. I love your father very much. But to keep my heart from splitting, I spend time with Zayn. It seals up the cracks.'"

Tiger shook his head. "The year after she was gone, I recalled those words so many times, and what my dad said in the bedroom. They're in my head like this tattoo is in my skin. She could have left my dad at any time, but she was telling the truth. He was the love of her life. She just didn't know how to live with him, and those few moments of difference with Zayn eased the pain, spilled some of it off, so she could keep being my dad's old lady."

At her look, he lifted a shoulder. "People are always trying to say what's normal, but really, in the billions of lives going on in this world, what manual exists to tell you what's normal and what's not?"

He sighed. "The other part of it was us. She knew Dad wouldn't let us go, not without a fight, and she couldn't abandon us to the life he was pulling us into. She kept thinking she could convince us in little subtle ways to take a different path, no matter that my father's will on it was like a tidal wave. She was going to get hit by it, no matter why. Just like Nicole."

He was silent for a few moments. "Colt...accepted it. He always accepted things in a way I didn't, wanted Dad's approval in a way I didn't. He was my little brother. I couldn't stop loving him. Never have, even though I want to tear him apart for what happened to Nicole. I wanted to love my dad, but he made it so fucking hard, I kept falling short. I probably should have kept trying to hold onto the hope for it, because it was when I let it go that it moved into gut-eating hatred. My brother and I fought until the wedge between us became a wall. I took my mom's name, Roseland, and left McAlister behind."

He lifted his gaze to her. "I wasn't lying. That kid whose lunch money we stole? It kept coming back into my head, again and again. Somehow it was the tip of the knife that sliced through, showing me the way out. Not because I wanted to be some white-bread kid in the suburbs, but because it reminded me there was more out there.

"By the time I was in my early twenties, I'd seen plenty of guys in the club get killed, badly hurt or put in prison. Colt got nabbed for a felony and served a couple years. That was when I knew I had to break free or that was my future, too. It was a fucking miracle it hadn't already happened, but my dad always said my brains were what he valued. He'd throw Colt into shit with the other guys but hold me back, keeping me learning. Because I was the one he thought should take his place. But in the end, it's like Rock said. Colt belonged in that world. I didn't."

She drew his attention to what she typed next. "I'm glad you're not part of that world. So are people like Brian and Greta, Maryshka, Red and Larry. Your friends. Your family. The one you built yourself."

He nodded. Took her phone and set it aside. She let out a little gasp when he slid his arms around her to hold her rib-crushingly tight.

He put his head against the side of hers. "So glad you're okay, Mistress. Maybe I shouldn't have brought you here, but I wanted you to be part of this world with me, while I tried to figure out how to fit into it now. I didn't have company the first time around."

She knew that feeling. She also recognized what was gripping his soul, and so she held him with the answering embrace of someone who'd also had a family member taken from her, way too brutally and abruptly.

They stayed that way a while. Then something bounced off her back.

When they drew apart, she saw a colorful ball rolling away, the kind sold in big bins at dollar stores. A boy waved his apologies with a big grin on his face. He scampered past to retrieve it.

Tiger managed a half-smile. "Fucking kids." He ran his hands up and down her arms. "So, want to go check out the craft booths? Do some girl shopping while I hold your purse and pretend to look interested, when all I'm really doing is looking at you and that fantastic smile when you find something you like?"

Charmer. She would like to check out the booths, maybe bring back a souvenir for the TRA women. Afterward, though...

She typed it out and showed him. "You promised to teach me how to ride."

CHAPTER EIGHTEEN

They trailered the motorcycles to a nearby high school parking lot he said was a good place to practice on a weekend day.

Though he'd told her it was best for teaching, when they climbed into the trailer and she was looking at the smaller motorcycle again, she gave him a look. "You're sure this isn't a 'girl' bike?" she typed and signed.

"Have you ridden a horse before?" At her nod, he pointed to the bike. "The first time you rode, did they give you a gentle mount, or the one breathing fire out of his nostrils?"

He ran an affectionate hand over the chrome of the Street Glide. No question which kind of horse he saw in it. "Even on that gentle horse, the first time you mounted was probably unnerving, seeing how far away the ground was. Plus you realized what was between your legs had its own mind and propulsion system."

He rolled his eyes at her pointed look between his. "No argument there, but don't make me smack your ass, Mistress. Need you to focus here. This smaller bike can kill you as easy as a big hog like mine if you don't know what you're doing."

He was teasing her about the smack, but his serious tone reinforced the admonishment. He went over the controls and the order of their use, the relationship of clutch, throttle, gears and braking. Key, ignition, kill switch. When she'd ridden with him, he'd pointed out those basics, but now he went over them again, far more thoroughly.

"We're going to keep it simple, because none of this is simple at first. You'll make squares, like a city block. Follow the perimeter of the parking lot, all right turns. Then turn around and do left turns. Followed by a few figure eights. As my passenger, you've learned to trust the tilt of the bike in the turns, but when you're the driver, you'll be worried you're going to tip over."

He kicked the back tire with the toe of his riding boot. "You can trust your tires. They'll hold you, long as you don't do any fancy low turn trick riding. Do me a favor and don't get that cocky your first time out." He smiled at her. "Ready to get on?"

Following his direction, she turned the handlebars toward her, giving the bike a lower set to throw her leg over. He held onto the bike as she did it, something she found she needed. "You have to learn to balance yourself on a bike, same as when you learned to balance yourself on a bicycle, only there's a lot more weight involved." He touched her chin, bringing her eyes up. "And don't forget, if you focus on the ground in front of you, you're going to screw with your balance. You scan ahead and keep your chin and eyes up."

How often had she touched his jaw to bring his eyes up, or tell him to lower them, to trust the direction she was taking him? A faint smile touched his face, as if his thoughts had gone to the same place, then he was back to his instructions.

"When you get started, remember, ease off the clutch, let that pull you forward. You don't need to give it gas or change the gears right away. Just work with that and get a feel for the brakes. Then, once you feel comfortable with all that, we'll go onto the other things." He touched her knee. "I'm right here, and we're all good."

He was right. It didn't matter that it was a smaller bike. It was different when she was the driver, and not entirely sure what would happen or what she was doing. Taking a breath, feeling the anticipation as well as the nervousness, she eased forward on the clutch. Thrillingly, the bike rumbled into motion. She wobbled a little, but then she steadied.

He was jogging next to her, but when the bike outpaced him, he moved to the center of the lot area, gesturing to her to turn, calling out instructions in a booming voice that penetrated the helmet and overrode the engine noise.

She was glad for that direction, needing it more than she'd expected. She'd listened closely as he explained where all the bike's controls were, but that knowledge wasn't instinctive. Clutch on the left, front brakes on the right, rear brakes on the right foot. Really? Shift with left foot...what? Down for first, halfway up for neutral, and where was neutral again? Then there was the 'push, don't pull' counterintuitive instruction on the handlebars, which was nothing like riding a bicycle. Oh and for fuck's sake...

"Keep your chin up," he boomed for the fifth time.

Her pulse was beating high in her throat, but somewhere in the middle of it, she realized she was smiling, even as she was slightly terrified. Every turn was a victory. She wobbled a couple times, and once or twice she had to put her feet down and stop. When she forgot to use the clutch on her left, because she was trying to figure out the mix and amount of brakes to apply on her right, the bike also stalled. Each time those things happened, Tiger was watching and anticipating, well enough that he'd already closed the distance between them, ready to help if she tipped. He gave her more instructions and encouragement, and off she went again.

She lost count of the right turn loops around the lot she did, but eventually she switched directions and did some left ones. Then the figure eight. After she did five of those, enough to feel dizzy, she obeyed his gesture to bring the bike to a stop and hit the kill switch.

When she did, she would have thrown her fist up in a victory pump, but her arms were shaking too much. That smile was still on her face, though, and the thrill of the ride was enough to ignore the shaking of her limbs. As he approached, she made the emphatic sign for *more*. Tiger laughed.

"You can do more. I just wanted to touch base, give you a few more tips and see how you're doing." He grinned. "You're doing great, by the way. I'm not saying my ass isn't puckered, but you're doing fine."

She wasn't wearing a face shield with the helmet, so he ran a light knuckle over her cheekbone. "You're flushed and your eyes are dancing. This little Honda's not so bad now, is it?"

In answer, she gave it an affectionate pat. He chuckled. "Growing up, any ride that wasn't a Harley, Indian or custom chopper was sneered at. No Fallen Angel would ride a 'Jap bike,' as my dad would have called this one. Shame, because there's a lot of good engineering in these bikes." Tiger winked. "I can appreciate that without feeling like I'm cheating on my Harleys."

He put his hand over hers on the handlebar. "On that note, you should talk to the other women riders here. They'll tell you the stuff about riding that works for them that the guys don't think about. When we get back home, you can practice on my dirt track, and then some of the back roads around my place. If you think you're ready for more after that, you can take the motorcycle safety course to get your license."

She pointed at him and made the question sign to ask if he'd taken one.

"Eventually." He winked. "I was on a motorcycle long before I could reach the pegs. But having a license keeps the cops from hassling you over it if you're stopped without one. You'll find plenty of backroad weekend warriors who don't keep theirs current, which is part of why they like the backroads. That, and it's a great way to ride."

She agreed. She was seriously considering a side-by-side ride with him on those backroads, her on her own bike.

"Careful. Once the passion gets into you, it's hard to shake." His gaze had the same light she expected hers did. Since she'd relinquished her death hold on the bike, their fingers were twisted together in a clasp on the left grip. Tiger's gaze lingered on that point of contact as he added, "To a lot of us, the M stamp on the license says who and what we are."

He brushed his mouth over hers, then pressed his lips together, his eyes lit with warmth. "Yep, tastes like a biker chick."

In answer, she straightened in the seat, poised to start the bike up again. Tiger laughed. "Yeah, go do some more. First gear only for now, though." He stroked a hand over her shoulder. "My heart's had enough strain for one day, watching you shove Warthog and shoot Rock that *fuck you*."

"You gave me an approving look," she typed.

"Yeah. Doesn't mean it didn't give me a bad moment." He held out his hand and made a show of examining it. "If it had turned into a fight, it would have ruined the manicure I had done special for the rally."

He grinned as she slugged him, capturing her fist to kiss it. She held up two fingers on the other hand, then pointed one at the Honda. "Let's see how it goes," he said, with a stern look that would have sent a wild flutter through any of the Progeny female submissives. Skye admitted it actually did the same to her, even if she had a different angle of appreciation.

"Impress me and I'll let you take it up to second gear. Though I'm pretty much already fucked on that, because you always impress me."

He softened the kiss, teased her knuckles with his tongue. She straightened her fingers to touch his rough jaw. Then she mouthed her response.

Same goes.

On the evening before they went home, he grilled her the steak dinner he'd promised. Even with the limitations of a campsite, the man delivered on his cooking skills. Which had been evident in his kitchen at home, with its assortment of appliances. Mixer, sous-vide cooker, air fryer and bread maker. Pantry stocked with spices, plus a kitchen garden outside the back door that included bright peppers, pungent rosemary, basil and thyme.

He offered her samples from the seasoned baked potatoes and green beans he'd made as sides. On the way back from the school, they'd picked up some peaches from a roadside vendor. He used a Dutch oven over their fire pit to create a peach cobbler, a heavenly aroma wafting from the pot's bubbling contents.

He'd moved the chairs to the upwind side of the fire pit and set up a borrowed folding table between them. He charmingly created a centerpiece for it with a handful of wildflowers placed in a rally souvenir cup.

He'd told her he'd learned early how to take care of himself. But somewhere along the way, he'd also learned how to take true care of a woman, making her feel special in a way that was genuine, because it took time and thought.

One-percenters might be romanticized, but he was the real deal.

He'd learned how to be a good man, his character rising from a life of complicated choices. It was in the details—the quiet care and attention to others in his life.

He was the type of man a woman would want, not just for a quick ride, but as her companion on a much longer journey.

As she watched him cook while purportedly checking her email on her laptop, Skye thought back to when he'd first caught the attention of the TRA women. His reputation at the club had been in troubled waters. At the end of a full session, he was just revving up. Still antsy. That hadn't worked for anyone, and he'd known it. No Mistress liked to give her all and find the sub was ready to do it all over again right afterward. A lot of them had started to pass on him.

Abby had invited him to sit down with the five of them one night, and asked him what was happening. Fortunately, he'd been frustrated enough to tell them.

"The Mistresses here, they bring it all to the table, and I love every minute of it." Though he glanced around the table, including everyone in the conversation, they remained silent, letting Abby taking the lead, which meant his self-consciousness dropped, revealing an intriguing depth of need in his body language.

He liked smart Dommes. He'd never disrespect one by trying to lie to her. There was just no way to hide that he had tons more to give, even after she'd gone as far as she intended to go.

"They get this disappointed look in their eyes. Like they think they've been alone during the whole thing, that I didn't take the journey with them. But I did. I really did. I can't explain it to her, though. Not in a way that doesn't come off as a lame-ass, 'It's not you, it's me.'"

He'd sighed and rubbed a hand over his neck. "Maybe I should hire myself out as a sub. A Mistress has less expectations. It doesn't bug her to see a hired sub doing multiple sessions in the same night."

It was clear he didn't want to be a hired sub, though. "I'm asking too much, I know it," he told Abby suddenly. "But in a session, I give her my all. Maybe that doesn't feel special to her when I do it more than once in the same night. But that's how I go home with an easier mind and gut." He shot her a miserable look. "No win situation, right?"

"I wouldn't say that." Abby had glanced around the table. "How about you try it with us? I'll be your first Mistress of the night. One of our group will be the second. And the third, if you need it. No starting each session from scratch. Continuous session, one Mistress handing you off to the next."

Not only did the TRA Mistresses have the kind of bond that could make that happen, it had been the perfect solution for Abby herself. Because of what had been going on in her head, hints of what would come later, the starting session worked best for her. Ros, Vera, and even Cyn had taken that second slot once or twice, but it had been a couple months before Skye took her turn.

She liked Tiger, and what she'd heard of him from the others, seen in him herself, had deepened that liking. She didn't want to lose that, if he turned out to be one of the male subs who saw her communication style as a limitation.

During her first solo session with any submissive, she had a process. She would use noise-cancelling headphones to help him focus on the nonverbal cues. If that worked, in subsequent scenes, she'd transition to foam earplugs, where sound could still get through, but it was muted. Eventually, if he became one of her small handful of regulars, he no longer needed that.

She remembered the first time she'd done a session with him after Abby slid from the room. He'd had his head down, a waiting submissive posture. Yet when Skye put her hand on him, there was a recognition between their flesh, and she'd known she wouldn't be disappointed by him.

From that point forward, it was almost always her and Abby who had sessions with him. If he needed a third Mistress, Vera or Ros stepped in, at least until she and Lawrence had gotten together.

Cyn could do it, but she had to curtail her preferences, since they fell well within his hard limits. Tiger didn't want to leave her unsatisfied.

One night, when he was invited to join them at the group table for a post-session drink, he'd raised his beer in a toast. "Thank you, ladies," he'd said. "I no longer go home feeling like a dick."

"Well, at least not for that reason," Sy had said, grinning at him from his spot next to Vera.

Vera had elbowed him. "Your honesty with Abby, your integrity, the type of person you are, meant the solution was just waiting for you to find it," she'd told Tiger. Her gaze slid over the club, the play areas, the lounge, the people at the bar, all in various stages of prep, play or aftercare. "You don't ever have to doubt this world. As soon as you think you're asking for something that isn't there, it will prove it had way more to offer than you ever knew."

Prophetic words, since that world had brought Skye a man who was starting to seem like a match for her, as much in the outside world as inside the club. Though she wouldn't have wished for him to be deaf, it was undeniably helpful that he could now understand many of the communication challenges that permeated her own life.

She surfaced from those thoughts to find Tiger had taken a seat next to her, legs stretched out and beer in hand as the steaks cooked. He'd recognized her head was elsewhere, and hadn't interrupted. His hand was on her chair, though, fingertips brushing her shoulder, as he looked up at the sky. The sun had set a little while ago, clouds turning smoky gray against a sky tinged with orange and deep blue.

Though he could have just been enjoying the look of it, he seemed to be seeking something in particular, turning his head to scan the firmament. Closing down her laptop and setting it aside, Skye drew his attention to her typed question. "What are you looking for?"

"The moon," he said. "I have this theory that when she appears while the sky is still lit up some, she's watching the sun painting it all these twilight colors. Same for the sunrise, when you can still see the moon in the sky. I tell Aubrey the sun puts a little extra effort into those sunrises and sunsets, using every last bit of time to impress her."

When she gazed at him, she was tenderly amused to see his ears get a little red. But when he reached for a cigarette to cover it, she closed her hand on his, stopping him.

"I like that," she typed. "Do you think riding brings out your poet side?"

He chuckled. "I wouldn't call it that, but yeah, I think it unlocks something inside you. Riding a bike in the middle of the night on an empty road, the moon over the fields. Or at sunrise, or even in a rainstorm, feeling the water trickling down the back of your neck. You're just closer to all of it, you know?"

He shrugged. "Quid pro quo. What were you thinking about? You seemed to be staring into space more than doing email."

"How we started, our earlier sessions," she typed. "Your need for more than one Mistress a night. That has to do with the MC, doesn't it?"

He grimaced. "Yeah, somewhat. I was given a cut and told 'this is who you are.' I believed it enough, was enough of that person, that leaving the Fallen Angels was the hardest decision I ever made. When you kick an addiction, you discover that helplessness they talk about, the power it has over you. I thought nothing would ever feel like the high of being part of them, but that was false. I had to figure that out. When I got free of it, I found out who I truly wanted to be. I *chose* who I am now."

His jaw set. "What's real and true may not take me to the same place, give me the same feeling, but that drop into hell after the high isn't there, either. I had to give that power to something else, give it a chance to grow into something just as strong. That's what I stumbled into with the submission."

He lit a cigarette and drew on it thoughtfully. "What Rock said, about me never being a part of it. That was trash talk, but remembering being part of the club is like thinking about an old girlfriend. You remember how you met, fell in love, and the good times you had. The potential. What you felt when you thought it would be forever. But then you remember what drove you apart."

He sent her a rueful grin. "How she cheated on you, tried to stab you in your sleep, and slashed the tires on your bike. You could let the first two go, but touching your bike? That's fucking crossing the line."

He rose to check the steaks. He pronounced them ready and started setting things on the table, asking her what she wanted to drink. He didn't let her do anything, making it clear he wanted to wait on her and let her relax. In the darkness beyond the firepit's light, she could hear the sounds of other groups laughing and talking, music being played. It was a comfortable background, not intrusive.

As she'd watched him throughout the day, there'd been times his head had been at a slight cock, as if he was trying to hear it, wanting to hear it. She'd heard other deaf adults talk about that, a phantom pain of sorts.

It made her think of her earlier thoughts. When she moved to sit at the table, responding to his invitation to do so, she typed the words, looking for confirmation. "It was an important part of this, wasn't it? Hearing the engines, the music. The people."

"Yeah." He smiled, though. "Sometimes it'll rattle the fillings out of your head. It can get overwhelming for non-bikers, which is why I told you to let me know whenever you're in the mood to get some 'wind therapy.' I've picked up the vibrations at least." An odd look crossed his face, but at her questioning expression, he shook his head. "Nothing. Just digesting the day."

When he sat down across from her, she looked at the plate of appetizing food and the wildflowers, the trouble he'd taken to give her this. She curled her hand on top of her other hand, pinky extended, and made a leisurely circle on top. She pointed to him then herself, before typing out what she'd just signed. "You're spoiling me."

"You deserve spoiling. You willingly came to a rally, rode on the back of my bike in choking exhaust and ball-sweating heat, all while having your eardrums pummeled." He opened the tin foil around her potato for her and nudged more salt and butter her way if she wanted it. "You handled helmet hair with good grace, looked at a million bikes and endured fuck knows how many conversations about them. Plus got into it with surly photo-shy one-percenters."

She considered, then typed. "You're right. I deserve *a lot* of spoiling. And most of the peach cobbler."

He laughed. "I'll give you the bigger spoon."

The table was small enough he spread his feet apart so hers could rest between them. As she picked up her fork, she noted he'd paused. At her glance, he shook his head.

"It's nothing. I was just thinking about Aubrey. When we put together a dinner at my place, she won't let me eat until she says grace."

"You're letting a six-year-old Domme you," she typed.

"Yeah, probably. But I don't argue when she's right." He looked up at the sky, all around them, then settled his gaze on her. "Suddenly, I'm realizing just how grateful I am for a lot of things. Especially for the company I'm keeping, and how much you've helped me."

The reminder of the basis for their current relationship—her expanding his comfort zone and communication skills—gave her an uncomfortable twinge. But she set that aside and typed a simple truth on her phone, pushing the screen over where he could see it.

"I'm feeling grateful myself. It's been a good day. Say grace for us."

He did, a simple prayer thanking God for the food and the

company, and for all the blessings of the day. When he raised his head, she had an additional thought waiting for him to read.

"Thank you for making the trip so enjoyable for me. It's been noted. And your efforts will be amply rewarded." She had followed that with several imperious queen emojis that curved his lips.

"Oh yeah? You trying to make me rush through this steak?"

"You can rush through it all you like. I plan on savoring every bite," she typed and signed. "Slowly. Exactly how I plan on enjoying you later."

Putting her phone aside, she cut a piece of the steak and placed it in her mouth. As he met her gaze, she chewed it at the pace she'd described, licking the juice off her lips when she finally swallowed the bite. Muttering an amused oath, he took another pull from his beer.

"I'm yours to command, Mistress. At whatever pace that pleases you."

～

She might think he was blowing smoke up her ass about wanting to spoil her, but nothing was further from the truth. Her thinking about their early sessions had turned Tiger's mind in that direction, too.

Ever since Skye and Abby had started doing the two sessions with him, it had dramatically cut down on how often he needed a third session. Yet lately when he'd had a third session, he thought there was a different reason he'd done it. He'd made the choice to keep it contained to the club, to expend it all there, but sometimes after that second round with Skye, there was an unresolved feeling...an ache.

Everything a Mistress wanted from a male sub within the club walls, reaching that moment where she realized he wanted to offer that level of service, and in a way that met her needs and exceeded them; that was what he had always been after. When that shift happened, the Mistress stepped inside the circle with him and time stopped. They were ready to explore what they could give each other.

That ache in his gut that remained afterward had been indefinable but manageable. At least until he sat here tonight, looking across the table and thinking how much he liked pleasing *her*.

Not a Mistress. Her. Skye.

The fire pit illuminated her face, sculpting the shadows while it cast light on her eyes and lips, and turned the white strands of her hair more golden. As they listened to one another, using his voice and her phone, her signing, he thought he could sit and do this for hours. It was a full-body style of communication, a total involvement of the heightened senses they both had available to them.

Somewhere along the way he'd decided a Mistress wasn't an option for him in the real world, not as a long-term relationship. But what would it be like to be with Skye? Live with her? Be hers permanently?

Whoa. They'd only recently started seeing one another outside the club, and that had been due to his circumstances, not a conscious decision in that direction.

Plus he didn't know what she wanted. And she'd never seemed shy about telling him that, so it was something she had to take the lead on. Right?

Maybe not. In the club she took the lead. Out in the world, if he wanted to take it further and deeper, he would tell her. Put it out there, let her decide how she felt about it.

While he sure as hell wasn't going to do something like that tonight, he had no qualms about showing her how much he wanted her, right here and now. He'd brought her a glass of wine to enjoy by the fire as he cleared things away. He watched her as he did, her profile, those sweet strands of hair caressing her cheek, her lips. Then she turned her head and looked at him.

She set the wine aside and reached out a hand to him. When he came to her, she tugged, and he understood. He dropped to his knees before her. She kept looking at him a long time, giving weight to the drawn-out moment. Their hands were in a knot together. She traced his cheek and jaw, then put her fingers on his lips. He remained utterly still, feeling the command for it in her touch.

Be still, until I give you life. Until I order you to live, to move, to serve my desires. Poetic stuff he'd never say aloud to anyone. He had told her riding put his head in that kind of space, but so did she.

Sound isn't significant. Words can be merely words. He'd read that in the materials from the hearing center. A summary of something said by a philosopher who'd lived a few hundred years ago, but he'd struck a chord in Tiger's present.

While he missed the hell out of hearing so many things, he understood what the passage meant. Words couldn't convey the things that mattered the most. Those things were beyond that. It was her hand on his face, the look in her eyes, the closeness of her body, their surroundings, a place he felt at home, as he was touched by the woman...who was his home. The home he'd wanted all his life. That he'd missed ever since the last time his mother touched his face.

Not that he'd sought his mother in a Mistress. But what had been so cruelly wrested from him so young was a connection forged in the act of creation itself. In a love that could be tested, wounded, broken...but never destroyed.

Skye leaned in and pressed her mouth to his brow, to his nose, his cheeks and jaw, moving to his throat and back to his lips. Holding his throat in her feminine hand to keep him still, she sipped, tasted and nibbled. His hands had landed on the arms of her chair as she scooted forward, her knees pressed to either side of him.

Someone was playing GooGoo Dolls. *Past is never far... Did you lose yourself somewhere out there... Grew up way too fast... Nothing to believe... I won't tell them your name.*

She knew him. Who he was. And he knew her. As she drew him in, he slid his arm around her back, his other hand cupping her head.

She eased back to fish in that small crossbody purse she wore for her phone. When she produced the dark marker she also usually had with her, she turned his arm over and wrote on the smooth side of his forearm.

Fuck me like there is no tomorrow. Fuck me like tonight will last an eternity. That is my command.

She capped the marker and her dark eyes captured him, a sorceress bringing him into her service, now and forever. He rose, drawing her up with him, and turned to the tent. He held the flap for her, pausing to cast a gaze toward the heavens. Stars dotted the sky with the sliver of a moon.

It felt like a night with that kind of magic to it. A night that *could* last forever, and yet be the perfect night to be the last night on earth.

～

He gave her everything she wanted. When he was done, she was curled in his arms. She gave him a triple tap that told him she was pleased. A tap to his head, to his heart, a playful one to his spent, damp cock, lying against his thigh.

Stand down, soldier. At ease.

He was content as she drifted off to sleep. How easily she managed it told him the camp sounds were dying down as the hour grew late. A massive difference from the rally campsites where people partied and drank through the night. To sleep at one of those, a person had to be wearing industrial ear plugs or be conditioned to sleep through anything, like a soldier in a war zone.

Or be a deaf person.

He did miss the sounds of the rally, keenly enough the thought had jagged edges, pushing into his chest and throat. Fuck, he missed hearing anything.

He expected it got easier as time went on. If he could accept that it wasn't coming back, would that help? Like when you knew a family member really was dead and gone.

Yeah, like that got easier. How long had it taken him to wake in the morning and not expect to find his mother in the kitchen? Hear her voice in his dreams and realize she wasn't calling him to get up?

That kind of acceptance was difficult, and the longing for it to be otherwise could play cruel tricks.

Apparently, the desire to hear again had the same problem.

He woke about four in the morning. The vibration through the cot and tent walls told him someone had started up a bike for an early morning ride or departure.

Shit, that guy needs to check on that valve rattle. They're either loose or out of adjustment.

He stilled, his arm around Skye tightening. She shifted, but didn't wake, her breathing even against his chest. He was surprised, but she was a deep sleeper. Probably because she didn't sleep much, so when she did, she went to the bottom of the ocean for it.

In contrast, he was abruptly wide awake, infused with an urgency that had him gingerly sliding out of their pushed-together cots. He adjusted the blanket around her before he ducked out of the tent opening.

Two rows over, a bike was leaving the park. He could still hear what he thought he'd heard in his head, and it seemed to match the bike's rhythm, its movement.

But he could be doing that, making it fit. The sound was drifting out of his mind, like smoke. Or the way a forest absorbed a bird call, here then gone.

His hand went into a tight fist against the side of his trailer as he tried to grab for it, but all he got for his trouble was a warning pounding in his temples, aided by the thundering of his heart in his throat.

A staticky white noise was buzzing around in his head that hadn't been there when he'd gone to sleep. That was new, but the headache meant he was trying too hard to hear something he might not have heard at all. Like his mother's voice, it was probably something he'd registered in his dreams, in a place where things so familiar to him could be picked up at subconscious levels.

Because Tiger had lost his hearing after a lifetime of having it, the doc had told him he'd have "auditory sensations" in his dreams. It had happened a few times, and man, it sucked. Hearing things in his sleep and then waking to tomb silence, realizing it was only a dream, hooked his gut like a damn chain hoist.

This was no exception. Fortunately he had a few moments to breathe through it and settle, before he felt her touch on his arm. It must have still been in his face, though, because Skye was looking up at him, concern marking her brow. She had donned his shirt, but was barefoot. He slid an arm around her. "Nothing. Just a weird dream."

She made a gesture. "No, I don't need to talk about it. Just need to shake it off. I didn't mean to wake you."

She made a shivery gesture. "Oh, sorry. Your human heater left, hunh? I can make you some coffee. Or we can head back to bed."

He brushed a kiss over her mouth, using the pleasure of it to banish his personal mind fuck. "Your sub could go down on you and give you a hell of an early morning orgasm."

She pushed at him, amused, but a spark in that sleepy look said he'd made an impression. Proving it, she slid the heel of her hand against his morning erection. It hadn't diminished in the slightest, thanks to the shot of pure adrenaline when he thought he'd heard that engine.

The shift in attention helped ease the pain of knowing he hadn't. He wasn't lying to her or hiding the truth, because he had no idea what the hell had just happened. If the white noise crap didn't go away, he'd let the hearing doc take a look. He had another checkup coming when he got back.

Skye curved an arm around his neck to lift herself on her toes. It pressed her against him, so he dropped a hand to grip her ass and hold her closer, trying to lose himself in the deep kiss she offered. When she drew back, she put her hands on his temples, telling him she could see the headache. Could probably also tell he was a little spun up. He shook his head, confirming he was fine. He hiked her up so she wrapped her legs around him.

When she signed, the two words he picked up replaced a pointless wish with a far better reality.

Coffee. After.

CHAPTER NINETEEN

*A*fter he left the doc's office, Tiger stood by his truck for a while. Then he started walking. He didn't have a destination in mind, just needed to think, but an hour and several miles later, he stood in front of the TRA offices.

He texted Skye, but after a few minutes with no response, he realized she was probably still in her Monday staff meeting. He should go. Instead, he called the general office number and watched the transcription scroll across his screen as Bastion picked up. "Thomas Rose Associates. This is Bastion. How can I help you?"

"Hey. This is Tiger. Is Skye available? If she's not, it's not a problem. She's not expecting me. I was just in the neighborhood."

Before his hearing loss, he'd only talked directly with Bastion a couple times, but he could easily recall the deep baritone. Bastion made an impression with his football player build, waist-long locs and a sexuality that resisted instant classification. He might address a male as "honey" or "baby" one moment, then offer him a beer and shift to "dude" or "bro" in the next, depending on his mood or the person.

The gate buzzer blinked. Since he had his hand on the wrought iron bar between the finials, Tiger felt the vibration when the lock disengaged. As he pushed it open and stepped through, Bastion responded. "She'll be out of her meeting in about twenty minutes. Come on in and we'll get you set up with coffee and a pastry."

"If it's all right, I'd like to wait for her out here."

A pause, then the screen bloomed with words again. "Sure thing. I can have the coffee brought out to you."

"Oh hell, no, but thanks. I'm not a client. Don't worry about me. If it gets past a half-hour, I'll leave and catch her another time. But if she gets out...I'm here."

"You don't have to be a client to be treated like a welcome guest. We have a good coffee blend Cyn likes, a minor step up from motor oil. I'm guessing it will suit your palate."

The transcription turned that into "pallet," which, along with the words, gave Tiger a tight smile. "Seriously, I'm good. But thanks for that, man. And yeah, I do prefer it strong and black."

"Don't tease me, honey. I'm at work."

That did make him chuckle.

The guy was a Dom, something Tiger had found out because Bastion came to Progeny as Ros's guest several times. On one of those nights, he'd chosen two subs for play, a man and a woman, handling them together with skill and memorable creativity.

Progeny wasn't his usual venue, either because he preferred to play elsewhere, or couldn't afford the membership. TRA offered above average salaries, Tiger was sure, but Bastion had expensive taste in clothes. He was also partial to jewelry. That night he'd worn a dark gold ring on his forefinger. The setting had been a snarling lion, a ruby resting in the grip of his jaws. Tiger remembered how Bastion had caressed his female sub's cheek with the sculpted metal and glittering stone. Letting her feel a taste of the cold and unyielding over the warmth and gentleness she might earn...if she was good.

Tiger moved toward a concrete bench that kept him within sight of the front door. The gardens were a mix of native favorites with fancier flowers and shrubs. Statuary placed among the greenery ranged from classical to sensual or whimsical. A good reflection of the women who ran the business.

This section had the classical type, a woman with her abundant hair piled on top of her head, face tilted as if listening to something. The statue reminded him of Skye, her posture when using all her senses to take everything in.

Butterflies flitted over the flowers, a baby praying mantis crawling along the edge of his bench, the bug smaller than his thumbnail. Near the base of the statue, a writing spider created a full novel on her web.

A frog, perched on a birdbath framed by wispy white flowers, had his eye on a juvenile Eastern garter snake, ribboning through the azaleas.

Sitting on this bench, a person would witness the opening of blooms in summer and the dropping of leaves from the live oaks in fall and spring, before they became winter mulch. Birds and squirrels hopping from branch to branch would persevere through the changing of the seasons.

He'd expected to miss conversation and engine noise. But how much he'd missed the background noise of life had been the real surprise. Birdsong, traffic, voices in the grocery store, that current of noise was something that made a person feel like they were in it, included in the rise and fall, the changes and cycles. Without it, he stood apart.

When he'd first been struggling with the hearing loss, the crazy silence in his head and his inability to hear himself talk, he'd woken in a sweat too many damn times from the same nightmare. In it, he was shouting, and realizing that not only could he not hear himself, no one else could either.

The teacher of his Total Communication class had talked about how the newly deaf struggled with depression and loneliness, exacerbated by lack of information. Tiger had had his struggles, but he'd also had Skye. She'd helped build a bridge and kept him out of the worst of that.

But had she ever had nightmares like that? Considering it now had his brow creasing. He rose from the bench and moved to stand in front of the statue. Her lips were parted. What would she say, if she could?

The doctor had done her tests. Confirmed some significantly different readings from his last visit. But amid all that technical talk was the one statement that had made his heart leap, his stomach doing a flipflop.

Yes. He likely *had* heard that valve rattle.

"Whatever needed repairing appears to be repairing itself, Mr. Roseland. How much of your hearing you'll get back, only time will tell. We can't predict the rate. It could happen quickly, in short leaps. Or gradually, over weeks."

"What if I get stuck somewhere in the middle?" The ability to hear people, yet having their voices muffled and unintelligible like the adults in a Charlie Brown cartoon, might be worse than being fully deaf. The static he'd been dealing with since the rally was like an out of tune radio.

"It's possible," the doc said. "But for that, we have some options. Implants, hearing aids. During the transition, you may hear things most people can't, sounds outside their normal range. That normal range drowns out those sounds. Which will also happen to you, if and when your hearing moves back toward baseline. Be patient and keep me posted."

His nose was still working at heightened capacity, because he inhaled Skye's fragrance a full five seconds before her touch landed on his arm. Her expression was concerned, and he realized it had only been about ten minutes. "I'm sorry. I told him it wasn't urgent. I hope he didn't pull you out of your meeting."

She pointed to him, touched her throat and creased her brow. Bastion had heard something in Tiger's voice that concerned him. Figured. Those damn Dom vibes.

Tiger took her hand. Her head was tilted, taking in the details, just like that statue. It *wasn't* urgent, but he guessed he seemed strung like a wire. Even so, she was busy, and he needed to tell her what had brought him here.

She was the first person he'd wanted to tell. Only her. He didn't want anyone overreacting, or jinxing it, or...whatever the hell reason he was hesitant to tell the world. Hope was fragile, and came with a lot of mixed emotions. Even more now that he faced her. Neither of them had acknowledged it outright, but their relationship had changed because of his hearing loss. How would it change if he got it back?

Didn't matter if the thought gave him pause, though. Change happened. It was a tank that would run your ass over and leave you flattened if you tried to stop it.

"The last day at the rally, when I got up so early. Do you remember that?"

She nodded.

"Someone started up their bike. That's why I got up. I heard it."

Shock crossed her face, her hand tightening on his. "Yeah. At first, I thought I was feeling the vibration and turning it into something else, but then I realized I was picking up a valve rattle. Muffled, but I could tell they needed adjusting."

Her face transformed, reflecting delight on his behalf. With her free hand, she made the sign for doctor, a question.

"I just came from there. She did a bunch of tests." He relayed what the doc had said. "I'd prefer to keep it between you and me until I can do more than hear engines and stuff so jumbled I can't tell if it's real or made up in my head."

She had some questions she posed through her phone. As he answered them, her smile for him, the light in her eyes, was genuine. She took both his hands in hers and squeezed. Mouthed, "Are you okay?"

"Yeah. Lot of maybes and ifs and whens. But...sorry, I should have told you when it happened. I know I was a little distracted on the way back from the rally. I just wasn't sure if it was what I thought it was."

She shook her head and turned her phone back toward herself to type. It took an extra few seconds, but then she lifted it for him to read. "It's a lot to take in. You deserve time to process. I'm very glad for you." She signed that last statement, then typed some more. "Are you headed back to the garage?"

"Yeah. We've got a full day. The crew's probably cursing my name. On the plus side, once the lift repair is done on the final bay, we're back at full capacity. Just cosmetic shit left, like painting, sign replacement, repaving the parking area. Crazy week here?"

Her phone buzzed. She glanced at it, then finger-spelled *Ros* for him.

"Guess that answers that. You need to get back to it."

She gripped his arm and typed one-handed. "We'll figure out a time to get together and celebrate."

Before he could respond, she closed the distance and wrapped her arms around him. She held him tight enough he lifted her off her feet, pressing his face into her hair. Cupping the back of his head, she put her lips to the spot under his ear. She held there a lingering moment, then gave him another squeeze that told him she was ready to be let down.

When he put her gently on her feet, she stepped back. He managed to catch one of her hands and hold onto it.

"Skye...Mistress. Thanks."

"Before long, you'll be able to hear everyone again." She gave him a smile as she typed it, her eyes glistening. "Everyone but me."

She pivoted and hurried back to the front porch, turning once she reached it to do a short happy dance with a lot of intriguing hip action. Then she tossed him a thumbs up he returned with a grin. She disappeared into the building.

But something about it...he sent her a text.

I've always been able to hear you, Mistress.

About thirty minutes later, during his walk back to his truck, he got a heart emoji response. Nothing else, which should have been enough. But as her words stayed in his mind, so did an odd feeling of disconnection.

~

On the curved staircase to the second level, Skye stopped as her phone chimed. She read what was on her screen. Seemed to read it two or three times, her hand tightening on the device.

Bastion noted she seemed...lost, as she stared at the words. Then she snapped out of it and headed up.

He glanced at the message on his screen she'd sent him a few minutes ago. *Shoot me a text that Ros needs me.*

What had happened in the garden that she needed an excuse to leave Tiger's company? Bastion watched the tall man walk to the gate and buzzed him out without making him call it in. Tiger turned toward the front door to wave an acknowledging hand. While he looked okay, there was a pensiveness to him, as if he'd picked up on Skye's mood.

Bastion frowned. Doms often forgot that subs could be every bit as intuitive as they were. Particularly a sub who'd had multiple sessions with the same Master or Mistress, like Tiger had with Skye. Bastion didn't know what was going on, but he hoped whatever it was would work out. Skye had looked happy during the weeks she'd been with Tiger.

She'd never been an unhappy person, but she was intensely self-contained. As if she took the lead on handling every bump in her life because she was afraid to get out of the habit.

Yet when someone took hold of a person's heart, there was a

300

change in gear. She'd definitely had a change in gear, an opening up, these past few weeks. It had made her closest friends consider she hadn't been as happy as they'd always assumed. True happiness gave her a very different look.

Enough for them to notice when it had taken a hit, or vanished altogether into the void of status quo. Where life went from good to good enough.

Bastion frowned and glanced up the staircase. Skye had reached the third level and disappeared. He made a mental note to clue Ros in if it seemed necessary.

Skye had a family here that could find her if she got lost, tend to her hurts, and help her up when she fell down. Even if she could handle every damn thing in her life, she didn't have to. She always had a hand to grasp within reach, and people at her back.

Those born into that support system often didn't recognize how precious it was until they saw how much someone they loved needed it. That would be Ros and maybe Vera.

Those who'd never had it took time to trust it, but once they did, they would protect that family like mindless savage animals. That would be Cyn, no question.

Because she'd always walked on quicksand, Abby valued love and friendship, and all its precious moments. She'd known they could slip through her fingers and disappear into an abyss, from one moment to the next.

Then there was Bastion. A mix of all of those things, he reflected, and the guardian at the gate. Ready to hold the line between the circle of women he loved and anyone who tried to hurt one of them.

He didn't think Tiger was one of those. On the contrary, Bastion had suspected Tiger was close to stepping inside the circle and giving himself over to its binding with no regrets. Like Lawrence and Neil.

Life liked to fuck with happily-ever-afters, but he and the Mistresses here had an arsenal of skills to put it on *its* ass if it messed with them.

Bastion pursed his lips. Now if it was Skye herself who'd fucked with it...well, that required a different kind of family response. He might clue Ros in sooner rather than later.

$\sim$

301

Over the next couple weeks, sounds notably sharpened. Tiger had some nasty headaches, but each time they passed, he had more of his hearing back. He accepted the tradeoff. By the time the final bay was repaired, he could hear like his grandfather. Since Gramps had been too stubborn to wear a hearing aid, they'd had to shout at him, but he'd pick up enough from that to get by.

The doc was a champ. Tiger couldn't shell out thousands of dollars for a hearing aid, especially one he hoped would be temporary, so she'd fitted him with a 30-day trial pair. Gramps should have been less stubborn. Suddenly Tiger could hear most of what the doc said, and she only had to raise her voice an octave or two. He'd sent Skye a text, telling her. She'd returned a thumbs up with cheerleader emojis.

He missed her. They hadn't had their "celebration" get-together, but in their text exchanges over those first few days after his visit to her office, she'd hinted things were getting crazy at work. A rollout for some big account. Busy, like she'd said. Over these two weeks, she'd stayed in touch, texting him for status with the doc, seeing how his day was going, how things were going at the garage, but she also made it clear she wasn't in a position to meet yet.

Two weeks wasn't an eternity, no matter that it felt kind of like it. He'd been seriously considering another drop-in at her office, even if she was only available for a few moments, when she sent him a text he didn't expect.

Usual session day coming up. Nine o'clock. Ready to get back to that?

Made sense, right? They were friends, she'd helped him through a hard time, and things were getting back on track. In that efficient Mistress way, she was paving a return path to the life he'd had before. A life he'd enjoyed a lot—going to the club, working in his garage and taking care of his own business. Every level of it.

Hell, it was hard to believe all of it had started only a handful of months ago. In his head, it had been so much longer, dealing with Nicole's death, the shit with his family, losing his hearing, and working with Skye to deal with that. While digging into parts of his psyche he hadn't even known were there, he'd gone from denying he was deaf, to facing it might be permanent, to finding out it wasn't.

Skye had taken a big part of that rocky journey with him, so yeah, it felt like a bunch of things had changed with her. But most people wouldn't consider it long enough to be true, permanent change. Right?

He'd had that moment of hesitation before he told her about the return of his hearing, wondering how it would change things. Now he was thinking harder about that, and why he'd so readily accepted her not seeing him these two weeks without pushing it.

Was he supposed to feel guilty that the other night he'd stood on his back porch, grinning like a fool when he could hear the trumpeting of a flock of geese going over the house?

Or that the first time he heard Maryshka calling out to Red, giving him shit about something and getting a shouted *fuck you* in response, his chest had gotten tight? He'd had to stand with his back to them, pretending to look for a tool, until he pulled his shit together.

No, he shouldn't feel guilty. Of course not. But why hadn't he shared things like that with Skye, when he'd shared so much with her?

She'd looked nothing but interested and pleased for him when he'd told her his hearing was coming back. Like a Mistress would look. Like the Mistress with whom he'd shared scheduled sessions every other week for the past year. A Mistress who'd gone back to communicating with him the same way she had before the accident. Why did that feel off to him?

Maybe that was his problem to deal with, what it meant. He'd think about it some, but he could also talk to her about it. Right?

Sure, he texted. *See you there.*

He took the Street Glide. Rumbling into the parking lot felt good, seeing familiar people getting out of their vehicles and heading into the world they all knew. As he put his gloves away, shouldered his bag and strode toward the entrance, he nodded to a few of them. He pulled out his phone and adjusted the hearing aids for restaurant mode, figuring that was the best setting for a BDSM club. The static sound was dying down, but sometimes it got together with white noise in a busy environment and turned his head into a beehive.

Inside, he went to the locker room, did a fist and shoulder bump with Sy, and caught up on things. Then he came to a full stop when Sy told him something he didn't expect. Tiger closed his locker carefully, turned around and faced him. "Care to repeat that?"

Sy gave him a curious look. "I said, there's a new sub tonight stirring up the Mistresses. Good looking, decent-seeming bloke. Friend of Lil Bit and Charlie, up from Florida."

"Yeah, I got that. What was the part about Skye?"

"Skye and Vera tag-teamed him, finished up about a half hour ago. They did it private, but he said they put him through his paces. He liked Vera, but couldn't get into having a Mistress that couldn't talk. I told him if he trusts Skye, learns how to go with it, she'll rock his world. Doubt he will, though. You know it takes a sub with a particular mindset to appreciate her approach." Sy shrugged.

Tiger scowled. "Did the asshole say that to her?"

"Probably didn't have to. She always knows. Seen it happen plenty of times to her before. You have, too."

No. He hadn't. Because he mostly hung with subs who appreciated her as he did. Those who saw their sessions with a Mistress as a chance to push the boundaries of what they expected or knew.

He struggled with his anger that anyone couldn't value that. On top of that was a snarled tangle of feelings about her having a session with someone else.

That was when it clicked. What was before was...before. She'd steered them back toward who they'd been, and he wasn't sure he wanted that.

They should have met before tonight and had an in-depth conversation about it. He would have liked to be asked how he felt about it before she made that decision. As a Mistress to him in these walls, maybe she had the right to make that decision. If they were more, outside these walls, then no. No, she didn't have the right to be that unilateral.

Walls were an artificial construct. Feelings were real. And he could tear those walls down with what he was feeling right now.

"You okay?" Sy asked.

Tiger thought about that quick flick of the fingers she could do, spelling *O* and *K*. Or how she asked if he was all right, with that forward and back tip of the side of her hand against her other palm before she pointed to him.

"Yeah," he said. And slammed the locker door.

He went to the room she'd reserved for them. He usually stripped down to his shorts before he knelt on the mat she left for him. She always made sure that was there, to protect his knees. He would put his fist to the floor, bow his head, make that mental shift. Once she joined him, they'd take a journey together.

He'd never had a problem connecting with her. Understanding what she wanted. His first time in a room with her, she and Abby had done the session together. Abby had handled a lot of the communication, but as the session progressed, she'd turned even more of it over to Skye. They'd been testing his responsiveness to her, how he handled her way of communicating. Like she and Vera had done tonight with the other sub. The other Mistresses helped Skye vet the subs and see how open they were to how she did things.

How had he never paid attention to that? Realized how many of the subs took a pass?

Probably a good idea he hadn't noticed, because now he wanted to take the shallow prick from Florida out in the parking lot and beat his ass for not realizing what he was missing. Oh, and finish it up with a good head pound on the pavement to say that's not yours, and don't fucking forget it.

In a club, Doms and subs clicked or they didn't, due to personality, limits, and preferences, that kind of thing. Everyone was required to be mature about it, be courteous and kind, but clear and firm, too. She would put those subs' rejection in that category, but it still pissed him off.

She could handle her own shit, and did it well. She probably saw herself as having left the hurt of such stumbling blocks behind. She just took it in stride and considered it an efficient elimination process, so she didn't waste her time on someone she couldn't connect with.

He thought of the veteran at the races, avoiding further conversation with Tiger because it made him uncomfortable or was too inconvenient. She'd learned a long time ago to accept that, deal with it and move on.

But he knew firsthand now that it didn't erase the gut punch reminder that silence cut you off from a lot of things.

He felt that anger on her behalf, yet when she opened the door, he realized he was also pissed at her. Maybe he should call this off. He hadn't expected to be in this kind of emotional turmoil, but finding out she'd been in a session earlier had boiled forth some of his conflicted feelings about how she was treating this and what it meant.

He hadn't changed clothes yet, but he moved forward to the mat she'd left for him and dropped to one knee. Bowed his head. If he focused, maybe he could make the shift and push that shit out of the room. The clothes could come off later.

She had a lemon cake scent tonight, mingled with something else he couldn't quite place until he recalled the lavender Chuck's wife grew in a pot by their back door. She'd said it worked great at calming the nerves.

What was working up his Mistress's nerves?

She's not yours.

The fuck she's not.

Had the Florida sub been allowed to touch her?

He needed to stop the session before it started. Instead, when she tapped his shoulder, the signal he could look up at her, he let his gaze pass over a pair of sexy black heels she'd paired with thin jeans. His cock enthusiastically approved of the fit over her thighs and hips, and wanted to see her bending over in straining denim.

The jeans were artfully faded and marked with white lace appliques of roses on the right thigh. The waist was hidden by an off-the-shoulder black shirt that molded to her breasts and the nip of her waist. The strapless bra she wore beneath pushed up her curves so they teased him over the wide ribbon of neckline.

Her silver necklace had an infinity symbol, one side of the chain threaded through it. At the end of it dangled a tiny charm, a closed hand with thumb, forefinger and pinky lifted. In ASL, it meant *I love you.*

Wrap the thumb over the other two fingers, and it meant the universal *rock on* gesture. Knowing her personality, and since he'd seen heavy metal heads do that one without wrapping the thumb, the pendant could mean either one. But coupling it with the infinity symbol suggested the ASL version, and that it meant something special to her. Like the lavender, maybe it helped steady her. He was betting it had been a gift from the TRA sisterhood, a reinforcement of their backup.

He lifted his gaze to her face. He'd seen sheets of blank paper with more expression. Yeah. Something was wrong. A lot of things were wrong.

"Mistress." He touched her knee. She didn't move, but her gaze went to the contact. "Tell me what's going on."

She made a gesture that had his lips twisting. Even in sign language, when a woman said *I'm fine*, a guy knew he was fucked.

He sat back on his heels. "No games, Mistress. Why are you pulling back from me? It's not your style to act like this."

She started to type into the screen and hesitated, glancing at his right ear. The light had likely made the tiny hearing aid tube glint, which meant she'd remembered she could use audio and let him hear one of her voices as she was typing, rather than making him wait to look at the screen. He would miss how she came close enough to press her shoulder to his chest, leaning against him as he looked at the screen past the delicate shell of her ear and fall of her hair.

"Don't use one of the other voices. Use yours."

Her face went wooden, but her fingers started flying in their usual way, the words coming out in that musical Southern accent. "It's going to seem a little awkward at first, going back to how we did this before. That's all."

"You want to go back to how we did this before."

She nodded.

He was impressed with himself for keeping his tone even, for suppressing the spurt of panic and what-the-fuck that decisive gesture gave him.

"Okay. Why? Where we took it for the past few weeks seemed good for both of us. Why shouldn't we keep going that way?"

When she started typing again, she dipped her head over her screen. He couldn't see her eyes. He'd gotten used to her making sure he could see her face, so he could interpret her expressions. Not just hear spoken words.

Words that hit him like a nail gun fired into his chest.

"You had a need, and I helped out with that need. I'm glad, because I'm your friend, and you needed the kind of friend I could be for what you were going through. I was a safe shelter, because I understood. But you don't have that need anymore. We can be Mistress and sub like this, here. Again."

Okay. Apparently there was a line he wouldn't tolerate. He rose to his feet and came toward her. Her eyes widened as he crossed the personal space barrier, until he was staring right down at her. She'd backed up to the door, and he put a palm flat on the wall next to her. "Who the fuck do you think you're talking to?" he said quietly.

Her pulse jumped in her throat. It only took her a second to switch to offense mode. He wouldn't have expected anything less. Crazy temper moments at his garage aside, when she'd tapped into his more volatile side in sessions, she'd never backed down from it. She knew how to channel that out of him, into more positive places for both of them. He had no worries that she couldn't handle what he could dish out.

But for this, he wasn't going to be fucking handled.

"I believe I was clear enough. Do you want to do a session or not?" She'd switched to her frosty Helen Mirren.

He straightened and gazed down at her a long moment. "Okay." He signed the next word, same as she had. "Fine."

He backed off a step, forcing his expression to neutral. He let the curl of his lip show, though, and sparked a challenging light in her eyes. Good. That was what he was hoping to see. She wasn't as settled as she was trying to appear. With her lavender scent, and her girl power jewelry.

He went to the corner where he'd left his bag and took off his shirt. Maybe he put a little extra stretch into it, knowing her eyes would be on him. Then the shoes, followed by the jeans. As he shoved them off his ass, he revealed the snug black cotton boxer briefs he usually wore.

He turned to face her, well aware the right kind of anger was good for an impressive hard-on. "The usual position to start, Mistress?"

She pointed to it, confirming the location but then pantomimed lacing hands behind his head. She wanted his ass on his heels. Eyes forward. She was going a little more edgy on him. He was fucking fine with that. If the Florida prick couldn't test her skills, he sure as hell knew how to do it.

He was perfect. Over the next nineteen minutes and twenty-four seconds, he did everything exactly as she ordered it, mirroring her behavior, letting nothing through, but giving her nothing to complain about. And with every minute that passed, the atmosphere in the room became toxic enough to choke them.

They were both too stubborn to break. She pointed him toward the spanking bench. When he braced his hands on the seat, she shook her head and gestured. All the way down, chest to the bench, arms out to the sides.

She yanked a collar from the wall and put it on him, attaching a chain to it she clipped to a ring on the bench. It kept him bent over as she cuffed his hands to either side of the equipment. She used an insistent foot to spread his legs out wider. Blood was pounding in his cock like a hammer. He wanted to use it, wanted to fuck her back into being his Mistress, the Mistress she was holding out of reach.

She was pissed, but she never forgot his limits. He could reach the cuff attachment points, free himself if needed. He wanted to circumvent that civilized shit, bust them free with a shriek of wrenching metal.

Picking up a dragontail, she tested it with a sharp snap in the air. Hell. She and Abby both liked that damn thing. He could tolerate the stinging type of pain, especially if the Mistress got into it, and Skye sometimes did. Apparently, this was one of those times.

She held onto the dragontail, but also picked up a flogger. She started with it, warming him up with easier strokes. As they gained in force, he suspected she was trying to break out of the wrong feeling gripping her by immersing them in things that had brought them pleasure in the past.

It worked, somewhat. She'd always been able to get into his head and take him there with her. She'd said it, hadn't she? They might have some awkward starts, but they'd walk it back to where she wanted it.

Except he didn't think that was where she wanted it at all. He knew he sure as hell didn't.

She dumped the flogger and brought the dragontail into it. If done right, bringing him gradually up to a more intense pain level could take him to the edge of climax. In the past, she'd rubbed his ass between the stinging strikes, sometimes with that sexy satin gloved hand. She'd lean over his back, her grip on his testicles, her breath whispering over his neck and spine, letting him know she was there. That they were together.

That was the only way pain worked for him, combining it with the more intimate shit, the sense she was right *there*, standing in his heart and head.

He unsnapped the right cuff and used that hand to do the same to the chain attached to the collar, then turned. He'd done it so fast, she couldn't pull the dragontail back in time. It didn't matter. He caught it over his forearm, took the sting with a grimace and yanked her to him.

"Stop this shit," he told her. "Just stop it."

Before she could say anything, he'd freed himself from the left cuff and was kissing her. It was a dumb move, he knew it was, but he couldn't stand her remoteness, and he gave her what he was feeling in the anger of the kiss, the need of it. The plea in it. Yeah, he wasn't going to deny it. He could fight anyone, tear down walls, but this was a door only she could open. He'd lay himself down on the threshold like her fucking dog, guarding the entry way, even as he'd wait there until the end of time to be let in.

She shoved back from him, though it was a good, hot, wet and angry twenty seconds before she did. She slapped him, her eyes fiery. Keeping his gaze on her, the handprint throbbing against his jaw, he dropped to his knees.

"Be my Mistress, Skye. The way I know you know how."

She stared at him. The moments ticked away, an eternity before her hand went to his shoulder. It settled there as tentatively as a wild bird. Then she moved her touch to his shoulder, his hair at his nape. She gave it a brief tug. This was a touch he knew, the Mistress he knew.

That blank paper expression was curling away, burned away by emotions, but what he saw in that turmoil made hope falter. She wouldn't open the door.

She shook her head and made a motion that said they were done. She was done. She couldn't do this.

She backed away and strode for the door. Before she reached it, he was there, his hand on it, his body against hers, his arm sliding around her waist. "I know. I know you couldn't do it. I needed you to know it, to prove it to yourself, because you're a damn Mistress, and you won't be told what's right or wrong for you. I was a bastard about it, but I have faith in what's inside you, that it's more and stronger than what you're acting like is possible."

She trembled, and his arm tightened, his mouth against the back of her neck. "You're so in control, Mistress. So compassionate. You're the level one, the one who talks without talking. But underneath, you keep it here, at this club. You think about outfitting that sex room at your new place, but you don't. Why risk it? Guys never reach far enough past the silence to find you."

She hit his arm with a weak fist and moved against his grip, shaking her head, but he couldn't let her go. Not yet.

"Trust only within the boundaries of this room isn't trust," he told her. "Trust is walking outside those lines and still knowing you have my devotion. My desire to serve. And that it will grow stronger every fucking day."

He loosened his grip, enough to let her face him. The bleakness pierced him, an emotion he'd never seen in her face before. She was letting the façade drop, letting him see all of it. The pain, the loneliness, the past and present, how she had to envision her future. She put her hand on his face and held it there a long moment. Then she dipped her head and typed. She didn't use any voices, so he had to look at the screen. But she leaned against him in that way he liked. It made his heart under the press of her body ache harder as he read the words.

You are perfect. You always have been. But we're done. I'm sorry.

She turned and slipped out of the room.

～

She should have left, but Skye needed to be sure he was okay. She wouldn't leave that to someone else. She put herself in the booth with Vera, Cyn and Ros. Abby was home with Neil tonight.

When Skye switched places with her boss so Ros was on the outside, she refused to be ashamed of welcoming the fortification. Ros's gaze was on her. All of them were looking at her. She shook her head. She didn't want to talk, just needed to be here. Understanding, they resumed their conversation.

A few minutes later, Sy joined them, sliding into the opposite side of the booth, next to Vera. Relaxed conversation, banter, and more drinks. A normal night. She picked up that Lawrence wasn't here because he had a field trip with kids at the center where he worked as a coach and counselor. Ros was expecting him back tonight, though, so she'd leave soon, bringing the sexual energy she'd collected here home to him. No matter how demanding his day had been, it would help Lawrence to decompress, having his Mistress demand his service before they ended the day in bed together.

Skye thought of Tiger's arms around her as she slept. And hurt.

She tensed when he emerged onto the public floor. Since he hadn't needed to do more than put his clothes back on, she expected the time it had taken him to appear had been spent figuring out his next move. Hence her tension.

He looked calm, but it was the lethal kind he'd shown when he'd faced down Rock. He was looking for someone, and it wasn't her. She gripped the edge of the table as his gaze lighted on his target.

Shit.

She was about to vault her way over Ros, but she was already too late. He'd reached Little John, the sub she and Vera had scened with earlier in the evening. True to the scene name, the man was tall and broad, even more so than Tiger. But Tiger's force of will seemed to diminish Little John as Tiger leaned in, got in his face and said something. He waited until he'd received the other man's wary nod. Then he thankfully walked away.

She hoped he was headed for the exit, but he wasn't done strangling her with her emotions.

Near the bar, navy blue chalkboards covered two sides of a corner. Each panel was six feet tall and eight feet wide. Whenever she walked past them, she smelled that powdery chalk scent. Those who used the boards sometimes carried the faint dust on their fingertips.

People could put anything they wished on them, whatever they felt. They were erased at closing each night, though it was one of the few places in the club where people were allowed to take pictures. No one ever signed them, anonymous offerings of their most personal thoughts and imaginings. They drew things, wrote poetry, made simple statements, declarations, or jotted random thoughts. Another way of expressing oneself, in a place with so many to offer.

Tiger put down his bag and picked up a piece of chalk. Then he began to write, in broad, uneven strokes.

Afraid.

Alone in my head.

I didn't understand until I was in the silence, and realized what your silence had given me. What it meant. What was there.

I want to be yours. I am yours.

I feel like you're mine. Are you? Will you be? Is it too much to ask?
I've always been able to hear you. Always.

He underlined the last word twice, with enough strength to break the chalk. He put the two pieces in the tray and picked up his bag. He headed for the exit without looking around at anyone.

Including her.

Skye stared at the words. She could feel the others' attention upon her. Ros had already slid out of the booth, so nothing was in her way as Skye rose. She walked across the lounge, down the short series of steps and past the bar. She stood before the board. He'd used lavender chalk, and she knew he'd done so because he detected the scent on her. Another potent message.

She touched the words and marked them with her fingertips. The word *Mine. Yours. Silence.* She stroked that word until the dust was on her fingertips and the word was streaked to illegibility.

"Why did you come to work for me?"

Ros had joined her and was standing at her shoulder. When Skye looked at her, surprised by the question, Ros continued. "You were excellent at doing what you did. You didn't have to put yourself out there, become part of a company where you had to deal with bigger communication hurdles every day."

Skye had thought about it herself, often enough to know the answer. It didn't make it any easier to admit it, not when it pointed right at the issue she was facing now.

"I'd become invisible," she signed. Not her work. Her. It had become too easy to stay that way. When she stood before her bathroom mirror, she'd sometimes thought her image was fading away, like a ghost. "I was cutting myself off from what life has to offer." The things that were only accessible when she connected with others.

Skye stared broodily at those words again. Sighed. Ros put a hand on her shoulder.

"The rest of us can only guess how difficult it is to interact with a world that communicates a different way," she said. "You and Abby both live that truth. But he's said it right here. He was given a glimpse of it, which let him get past that gate and go deeper into who you are."

Ros touched the word *Alone*. "Every one of us struggles with isolation, because we're stuck inside our own heads with whatever bullshit is happening there. Vera says the mind is a fortress that has to be opened up to let in light, air, and meaning. I can't say I disagree." Her eyes darkened with remembered losses. "You had the courage to figure out that it makes life more worth living. Not everyone does."

Skye knew who Ros was remembering, and she put a hand on her boss's arm, a comfort for an old pain. But Ros shook off the feeling, squeezing her hand.

"Don't let him get away for the wrong reasons." Her blue eyes sparkled. "Though plenty other Dommes wouldn't mind it a bit if you did."

When Skye narrowed her gaze, Ros tossed her an unrepentant bitch smile. Then she sobered. "Be the Mistress you want to be, to the sub you know is yours. No matter what happens, you won't regret risking your heart with him."

Emotions swamped Skye as she shifted her gaze once more to the words on the wall. Abruptly, she turned on a heel and headed for the exit.

Cyn glanced at Ros as she returned to the booth. Sy had his arm stretched behind Vera in companionable intimacy as he took a swallow of his drink. "I figured Tiger was about to set his sights on someone," he commented. "He had that feel to him, ever since he and Skye started doing sessions together. Dumb bastard just didn't realize it until someone tried to blow him up."

Vera looked amused, but nodded in agreement. "Love is as inevitable as life and death. It finds us all eventually."

"And skewers you," Cyn noted. "There's a reason Cupid carries those fucking arrows."

Sy sent Cyn a fond glance. "You must love me, Mistress. You skewer me regularly."

"I'll love you into an early grave," Cyn promised, her dark eyes reflecting the light like a cat's. "Dismembered and disemboweled. And castrated. Once I'm done with your dick."

Sy winced and grinned at Ros. "When they find bodies at her place and the news crews show up, I'll pay a hundred bucks to the first one of you who can say 'she was a quiet person and everyone seemed to like her' with a straight face."

"I'm okay with being the psycho bitch everyone's too scared of to look under her house," Cyn said. "Go big or go home."

Skye wasn't certain of her intent when she reached the parking lot. Tiger might already be gone, but she could go to his place. Or his garage.

Instead, she saw him with his Harley, hips propped on the seat as he watched the door. He'd been waiting to see what, if anything, she would do.

As she approached him, her stride slowed, and she tapped into her phone. She used the generic Southern one he'd called "her voice."

"How long would you have waited?"

He glanced up at the sky as it rumbled with distant thunder. Lightning flashed on the horizon. She smelled the heat of an impending storm front. Her weather app had said it would move in tonight, which would be welcome, since things had been dry.

"Until I felt like it was time to leave," he replied. "I didn't write it to force you into anything, Mistress."

The chalkboard statements were often open ended. But the look he gave her was full of things that could tangle a person up. Bind them to another.

"It's your move, and I'll abide by it," he said. "Maybe not gracefully. If you don't want to move forward together, I'll stay away from Progeny a while. You'll need a new mechanic, and I can recommend one. But before you decide, there's one more thing I need to say to you. You remember that day at TRA, when you said I'd be able to hear everyone again? Everyone but you."

"Yes. You texted me. Told me you've always been able to hear me." He'd put it on the board, too, in case she'd missed how much he meant the message.

His gaze intensified as he took it even further. "From Day One. Because I wanted to, because I knew you had things to say that mattered, that spoke to me and made me want to serve you. First in that club, and now in a whole hell of a lot bigger world. That's what losing my hearing gave me. Getting it back isn't going to change that truth. Unless me being deaf is what made me more appealing to you."

As she flinched, he shook his head. "I'm not saying that to piss you off. Or to judge you. I go to motorcycle rallies because I like being around people I connect with, because we share a passion for something and speak a language we all get. At the end of a tough day, I go to the club, or a biker bar, because those are my people, too. Where I'm connected and accepted. That's the way people are. Greeting cards can say love bridges those gaps, and it does, but..."

He ran a hand over his face. "Fuck, Mistress. I love you. I want to find out how deep and far that goes, how many bridges we can build between who we are and who we want to be with one another. But I also want you to be happy. You're content, you're accomplished, you're amazing, but I'm not so sure you're happy. I want to be something that makes you happy. If I can't be that anymore, because I can hear again, well, I can't."

Pain flashed across his face, but mixed with it was what he'd just told her was in his heart. Love. "Who we can love or not love isn't about fair or right or any of that shit. It's finding a home that speaks to you, same as the rest. But I sure as fuck would like you to give it a chance with me."

He was a plain-speaking man. He'd gone right to the heart of the matter and left her facing a mirror of herself that wasn't entirely comfortable. But Ros had said it. As life was lived and desires and needs went down new paths, finding one's real home sometimes meant finding the courage to leave one behind and go to another.

She signed, one hand closed with the thumb up, did the same with the other hand and brought them together, before gesturing at herself with one of them. Then she took her hand up to her cheek, near her mouth, and made another gesture.

"What does that mean?" he asked.

She lifted her phone, typing in three words.

"Follow me home."

His phone started buzzing as he smiled at her, though it was a tense thing. They had things to work out, but for the first time tonight, she didn't feel like a knife had been jammed up into her heart.

Little John hadn't connected with her because of her inability to communicate with him in the manner he expected. Even so, she'd known from the moment she'd stepped into the room with Vera that he wasn't who she wanted to be with. She'd been determined to soldier through it and get back to status quo. She'd told herself it would start feeling right eventually.

When Vera had picked up on her mood, that was what Skye had

told her. Vera had given her a look that called serious bullshit. Skye had ignored it. Until now.

Tiger's brow had creased at the caller ID. Nodding apologetically to Skye, he answered. "Colt?"

When his expression whitened, she put her hand on his arm, everything else forgotten.

"Who took her?" he demanded.

CHAPTER TWENTY

$\mathcal{A}$s he gathered details, Skye was able to do so as well, because Tiger was still using the transcription feature on his phone to clarify what he received through the hearing aids. She stood at his side, her hand on his tense arm. While she couldn't hear Colt clearly, she picked up his mood in what syllables she did catch, and in how fast and garbled the words came up on the screen.

Aubrey was supposed to be picked up at a friend's evening pizza-and-movie birthday party, but when the Fallen Angels prospect had arrived to do that, she was nowhere to be found. The party had been in the backyard, which was flanked by a wooded area. With twenty-five kids running around, no one had seen when she disappeared. Since the woods were just a patch of trees, a common area in a subdivision, and the backyard had been lit up for a bouncy house and the movie screen, no one had anticipated the risk.

"What can I do?" Tiger asked.

"Come with me. Help me find her, and get these fuckers."

Tiger's expression tightened. "You know where they're holed up? You think they took her there?"

It went without saying that what Colt was proposing was off the grid, no police involvement. The harsh look on Tiger's face said he knew exactly what Colt was asking of him.

No matter that he'd left that life behind, she knew he'd go, for Aubrey. In the space of a few minutes, he'd donned the mantle of the

Fallen Angels brother who would cross any line to get his niece back safely.

Skye pulled up the app on her phone, her heart in her throat. *Please, please, please...*

The two dots were not together. They were an alarming distance apart, one inside New Orleans and one well on the outskirts. But they were there, which she hoped was good. She thrust the phone screen at him, and his gaze locked on the Find app, particularly the Friend name at the top of the screen.

Aubrey.

"Hold on, Colt." Tiger gripped Skye's wrist to hold the screen still, his gaze fierce enough to bore into it.

She gestured to her wrist, a reinforcement of the label over one of the dots. *Bracelet.*

A hundred thoughts moved through his eyes, but he only spoke the one that mattered right now. "This one, *Charm*, that's the one for her backpack?"

At her nod, Tiger put his phone on speaker. "Colt, did they find her backpack?"

"It was still at the friend's house."

"What was the address?"

As Colt told him, Skye verified that it was the location of the tracker inside the city limits.

"Okay. It looks like my Mistress put a tracker on your kid in that bracelet and charm I sent."

"What the fuck? You—"

"Was she wearing the bracelet?" Tiger snapped.

"She doesn't take the damn thing off. She's named all the animals on it." Colt's voice roughened.

"Okay. Soon as I can figure out where we're headed, I'll call you back." Tiger disconnected. Skye was zooming in on the more remote dot. Her heart moved to her throat, but she showed it to him. He looked at it, looked at her. The hand overlapping hers on the phone clenched to bruising.

"That's fucking bayou. Swampland. Jesus Christ..."

His face spoke the words as if he'd said them. The perfect place to dispose of a body. Skye took his phone and typed so she didn't have to switch from the tracking screen on her own. "We head that way. Stop at my place and get one of my drones to help us search." Though the ball of nerves in her stomach already knew the answer, she asked. "Can we call the police?"

"I'm pretty sure the crew that took her did this as an intimidation ploy against the Fallen Angels. Trying to get them to back off of the drug trade. If they're laying a trap for Colt and his boys and they hear sirens..." His jaw tightened. "You know where she is, and have the tools to get us there. The police can't do what we can do. Kill these bastards if they've hurt her, and leave them in the goddamn swamp."

She had police officer friends who could call resources to the area quicker than she and Tiger could get there, but he was right. If they were already in the swamp...the chances of anyone, biker or cop, reaching them before they did what they intended to do to Aubrey, were slim.

But they had another option. She typed it as Tiger read the screen. "Neil."

Abby's husband, the active Navy SEAL. At Tiger's look, she continued to type. "If the signals crap out in the swamp, Neil is a hell of a tracker."

That skill had been honed as much by the bayou as being a SEAL, since he'd had a house there for years before marrying Abby. They still stayed there a lot of times when he wasn't sent off on missions, though Skye knew tonight he was at Abby's place in the Garden District.

"Get him," Tiger said. "Where's the Mustang? I'll follow you to your place."

She'd ridden with Vera tonight, so she pointed to his bike. He nodded, and retrieved his phone from her to type out a text to Colt. *Have potential location and backup. Pursue your own leads while we're confirming. I'll keep you in the loop.*

The phone immediately started buzzing with Colt's name on the screen, but Tiger silenced it and stuck it in his pocket. "I'm not losing my niece to stray gunfire as these assholes fight it out with each other. We'll call them in if we have to do it. Let's talk to Neil first and get a game plan."

He gave her his helmet, adjusted it as much as possible to make up for the bigger size, and found the spare skull cap he carried in his saddle bags. Without the high possibility of being stopped for not wearing one, she expected he wouldn't have even bothered with it for himself.

After she got on behind him, he glanced back at her. "Hold on tight, so I know you're there. Move as I move, just like at the rally, only we're going to go a hell of a lot faster. When we have to stop for an intersection or stop sign, brace yourself by leaning back some and pushing against your foot pegs to keep yourself from being thrown against me."

She wrapped her arms around him as he roared out of the parking lot. When he'd given her those lessons at the rally, he'd told her an experienced rider developed a sixth sense about traffic, anticipating the unexpected. She saw that now, as he seemed to adjust a beat before a vehicle pulled in front of him, or changed lanes as if oblivious to their presence.

His highly developed awareness of details in sessions as a sub had come from this, she suspected. Coordinating the operation of the bike, scanning his surroundings, staying aware of potholes, pedestrians, other vehicles, anything that would affect the balance of the bike or his destination.

Or the maximum speed he could reach to get there.

When he skimmed low on the curves, she had to remind herself what he'd said about trusting the tires. In this case, she put her trust in him. She made her body relax into the movements of his, though it was hard and tight. His eyes would be the same. Hard and still. Under her palms, she could feel his heart pounding with the bone-deep rage that fear could bring.

And under that, a cold-stone ache that they were already too late.

As soon as they arrived at her place, Skye ran up the stairs and put together the drones and associated tech she'd need. Tiger prowled around her place, staying out of the way but obviously not in the mood to sit. He received and sent a couple more texts, she assumed to Colt, but nothing that changed their course or added information, since he didn't comment on them.

Within ten minutes of their arrival, her call for help had arrived.

Neil stepped out of the elevator, Lawrence at his side. He'd arrived home in time for Neil to pull him in.

Skye felt relief at the sight of them. Though Lawrence was a former SEAL, he still had that edge to him, and it became even more evident in a situation like this, his sharp green eyes focused.

A tall, rangy male with a steady gray gaze and an imperturbable demeanor, Neil had a limitless well of patience and uncanny intuition. Those traits had made him the perfect match for a Mistress with schizophrenia.

A Dom himself, his unlikely pairing with Abby had resulted in a match indescribable in its complexity; Vera called it proof of miracles. Ros said it showed the angels looked out for those in desperate straits, giving them a route to love and a life worth living.

A good thought for right now.

In her text to Neil, she'd said, *child missing, need your help. Tiger's niece. No police.* Skye had resisted the urge to text others, like Athena's husband Dale, also a retired SEAL, or Max, a mutual friend and former SEAL who now worked security for Kensington & Associates. K&A was a New Orleans manufacturing company whose top management were friends and clients of TRA.

Max and Dale had both served with Neil and Lawrence. However, because of that, she'd trust Neil and Lawrence to make the call if they thought more backup was needed.

As Tiger explained the situation to them, she understood why his father had resented losing Tiger. And why Colt, despite their estrangement, had called him during such a desperate time. Whereas Colt's rage was on the surface, Tiger's was deep, the hand on the trigger ready to pull, but only when it was time. Though Tiger had worked to distance himself from a life of violence, she saw plenty of evidence that the well had always been there if he chose to drink from it.

As long as he stayed with her, she would assume those skills could be put to good use. She didn't know what she'd do to stop him if he decided to join Colt for a potential blood bath, but using a stun gun that could take down an elephant was an option.

Neil had Skye put up a map on her largest monitor of the area around the tracker. "What are the chances they left her there alive, deep enough they knew the swamp would take care of her? Cleaner, less forensics."

Lawrence and Neil had been doing their own assessment of Tiger's ability to hold it together. Since Neil didn't waste time softening his question, he must have reached the same conclusion as Skye, though she expected Tiger felt the same clench in his gut she did as he asked it.

"If this is the group associated with the Mexican cartel, we're looking at two scenarios. Best case is the one you just pointed out. It was a scare tactic, showing Colt how easy it is to grab his family. They dumped her because the mission was accomplished. If she dies in the bayou—" Tiger's voice hitched briefly, but he continued, "that would be a stronger message than they intended, but they won't lose much sleep over it."

He didn't say the worst-case scenario aloud and Neil didn't ask for it. They could all see the tracker hadn't moved, not since Skye had called it up at Progeny.

Neil pointed to an area about a mile from the dot. "We could take a boat, but we'd be further away, slowed down by the limitations of getting the boat through that area at night. There's a good access point here, a park. No barriers to entry. We go in on foot. I have night vision goggles to help with visibility and keep us from telegraphing our presence to anyone waiting for us. That storm moving in is going to be over that area by the time we get there."

Neil glanced at Tiger. "Take the Mustang and we'll follow you. The bike won't give you any advantage in the storm."

"We can get my truck. The garage is on the way, and she can drop me off there." Tiger shifted his gaze to Skye. "Show me how to use the drone, and put what I need on my phone."

She shook her head. Typed, using her Southern female voice. "We can take the truck if you prefer it, but I'm going with you. My drone has night vision and is waterproof, but storm conditions will be tricky. You'll need an experienced operator. Once the storm hits, the tracker signal might get spotty. I have a better chance of holding onto it."

At his stony expression, she punched out the words with enough force to mistype them, but he got the gist. "She's a child. She's all that matters. Either we go together, or I follow and call the cops to come with me."

His gaze went cold. But she wasn't one of his employees, like Maryshka, or the Fallen Angels he used to lead with his brother and father. He took a step closer to her, but she matched him. Neil and Lawrence's attention sharpened, attuned to the near combustible emotions suppressed within him.

But so was she. She didn't back down.

"It's not all that matters." He spoke softly, surprising her. His eyes reflected harsh emotions. "Once we reach that park access, you don't get out of the truck. Not for goddamn anything. You keep it locked and the engine running if you have to bolt. You have a gun you know how to use?

At her nod, he spoke shortly. "You bring it. The people who took her make Rock and Warthog look like pissant schoolyard bullies. Got it?"

Neil and Lawrence's expressions said they were on the same page as Tiger. "You'll do a hell of a lot more for us, working your tech magic in the truck," Lawrence said. "And he's right. If the bad guys show up, haul ass. We'll be in a far better position to handle them if you're not in the mix."

She wasn't an idiot. This was a world they knew far better than she did. But she would stay as close to Tiger as circumstances allowed.

"We're trained for combat and tracking in uncertain terrain," Neil said to Tiger. "You're not. Once we get there, your job will be coordinating with Skye and getting to wherever Aubrey is. Keep your focus on that."

He tilted his head toward Lawrence. "Ours will be to take care of anything standing between you and that goal. Delegation of duties. Best way to get the job done. And we're good at our job."

"What will you do if she's not alone?" Tiger asked. "These assholes aren't the type to give up and let you zip tie them."

"We'll put down anyone executing lethal force," Lawrence responded. "But we'll use other options if we can."

He directed that to Skye. Probably because he could see as well as she could that Tiger had no problems with killing anyone associated with Aubrey's kidnapping and letting the bayou have the bodies. And if they were too late...

While Lawrence was talking to Tiger, discussing other logistics, she made a subtle motion to Neil. As he put his arm around her, a gesture that looked as if he was offering her reassurance, she showed him what she'd typed, muting audio.

"If you find her body, do not let him out of your sight. Knock him unconscious if needed."

She didn't know exactly what Tiger would do, but she would suffer his wrath if it saved him from being sent to prison with his brother or worse, being killed in a firefight with a rival gang. He'd worked most of his life to leave this behind. She wouldn't stand by and let the anguish of losing his niece throw him back into that abyss.

Neil understood. "Roger that," he said.

The drive took almost an hour, though it seemed much longer, every minute crawling by. Skye kept her attention on the tracker. She'd put the phone on the truck's dashboard mount so Tiger could keep his eye on it, too.

It still didn't move.

They could have her tied up somewhere, she told herself. Guarding her. She held onto that thought, even though her mind told her that scenario would have made more sense in a building, a defensible place to get out of the weather.

As they drove, she went through the tracker's history on her tablet to confirm Aubrey had been taken at the common area. They'd carried her through it to a vehicle waiting on another street. Once she'd been driven to the bayou, the tracker seemed to loop around, stop, move slow, then stop again. Then it had moved again, once more, before it came to its current resting place. All along waterways, as if they'd had her in a boat. Or were on foot, traveling along the banks.

Aubrey could have done that same track if she was lost. She was six, but she'd seemed smart enough to stick by a waterway that could keep her from moving in circles. Until she got tired and found a place to sit down. Maybe fall asleep.

Or someone had followed that same pattern to locate an optimal place for a shallow grave, or to weigh a body down and leave it in the water.

Fuck, those thoughts weren't doing her any good. Skye put the tracker app on Tiger's phone and sent it to Lawrence and Neil's as well. They had different carriers, so that might help with keeping at least one of them connected with the signal. She turned her attention to making some adjustments to the two drones she'd brought.

The second one was a backup. She would be sending the drone into a swamp with a lot of canopy cover. Even with collision avoidance, a variety of things could knock one out of commission. She was damn good with it, though, so she'd do what she could to keep it flying.

Just as Neil had warned, they drove into the storm. When the light shower pattering the windshield started to strengthen and pelt the glass, she heard Tiger mutter a fierce oath. He'd increased his speed. He was a more than competent driver, and he was aware of what was at stake, so she wasn't worried he'd risk a wreck on the wet roads. She kept her attention on what she was doing, but she reached out and touched his thigh, gripping it briefly. He glanced at her, his expression grim, but he gave her a nod.

When they pulled into the park, the two SEALs pulled in behind them and emerged from Neil's truck. They were in foul weather gear, night goggles strapped to their heads. Lawrence had given Tiger the same gear, along with a short lesson on how to use the goggles.

Before Tiger exited the truck to join them, he turned to face her. "Get on the driver's side after I get out. Be ready to leave, like we said." Reaching over to the glove box where she'd put her Walther nine-millimeter, he pulled it out, putting it on the console. "You keep this close," he told her.

She touched his face. "Be careful," she mouthed.

"Okay." He brushed a knuckle over her cheek and gave her a grim smile she thought he had to dig deep to find, but he had, for her. Even in this situation, he hadn't forgotten she was going through it with him.

"Whatever happens...thanks for putting that tracker on her. We'll have a chat about why you didn't tell me later. But for now...thanks."

With his rocky relationship with his brother, she hadn't wanted him to struggle with the morality of the decision. Yet knowing how worried he was about Aubrey being at the Fallen Angels' compound, she'd wanted to do what she could to help.

But he was right, that discussion was for later. For now, she typed him what was important.

"Whatever you find, I'm here. We'll get through it."

He met her gaze. "If she's dead, I'll be a dumpster fire, Skye."

Then she'd be a firefighter. One who refused to let what mattered to her become ash. She put all of that in her expression and kissed him, a fierce battle of lips. Then he'd pulled away and was out of the truck.

He gave the other two men a thumbs up. She had a momentary hitch when she saw Lawrence was carrying an assault rifle, Neil checking his own pistol. She didn't know what to hope for. If there were men with Aubrey, it meant she was alive. But if there were men with Aubrey, it meant they'd have to fight to get her back.

If Aubrey was alone... Her gaze went to the seemingly impenetrable thicket of woods. Abby had once been lost in the bayou, and Neil's worry over it had made it clear just how dangerous the environment was for someone who didn't know it.

Tiger had pulled down the goggles, as had Neil and Lawrence. She could see nothing but the hard set of Tiger's mouth. He didn't look back as they disappeared into the trees. Neil led the way, Lawrence watching their six with that big gun.

She'd received a brief text from Ros. *Standing by. Praying. Keep us posted.* The brevity of the message said Ros, Vera, Cyn and Abby knew it was best to let them focus on the mission at hand. No time for handholding, but she expected Ros and Abby were as tense as she was, with their men in a situation that could become far more dangerous than it already was.

Her gut twisted at the thought. Abby's schizophrenic episodes could be triggered by stress. However, Neil was an active SEAL still, and Abby had learned ways to manage that worry when he was gone, tactics that the TRA women helped her with routinely. Skye was willing to bet they were all together now, for that very reason.

It helped, to imagine them over at Abby's house, sharing a glass of wine and waiting for news. Supporting one another. Being ready to support Skye, in whatever way she needed it, for herself or Tiger.

On the day Abby had been lost in the bayou, Vera, the most spiritual of their group, had said overwhelming situations called for simple prayers. Ones focused on results.

Please let her be safe, Skye prayed. *Let them all get out of this safe.* And because it felt right, she added one more. *Nicole, Dad, Tiger's mom...if you're where you can help, please guide them.*

Because even beyond the grave, no one would fight harder to protect a child than the parent who loved them. Who'd done their best to prove that during their lives.

She turned her attention back to her job. Neil had told her she was tactical command, and when it came to anything involving the word "command," she was on it.

∼

The demons of hell had been unleashed to fuck with them. Tiger pushed down the helpless anger and frustration as the storm's force increased. Wind lashed through the cypresses, white oaks and palms, their fronds looking like clashing sword blades through the goggles.

The goggle lens streamed with pelting rain, but the thick lacing of the maritime canopy gave them some protection from the deluge. Rainwater peppered the swamp and marsh.

He'd taken off the hearing aids because the roar of the weather made them mostly useless. The three of them were having to shout right up against one another to be heard, though they mostly went by hand signals. At least they were getting closer to the tracker. His phone was in a waterproof sleeve that shed the water enough that he could still see it.

However, the tracker's continued stubborn refusal to move, and how deep they were getting into a place no one would go unless they were trying to hide something they didn't want found, was expanding that cold dread in his gut. It was squeezing his chest and making it hard to breathe.

He'd handled some bad shit in his life. Never the death of a child. Never someone who'd stayed at his house in her *Tangled* princess pajamas and done puzzles with him. Who'd told him she wanted to be a zoologist and in the same breath told him she'd make sure all the zoo animals were taken back to the wild and taught how to be free again. She'd live in a pink camouflage tent among them and feed them good stuff, like ice cream and candy corn.

This wasn't helping. He shoved it away, called back the man he'd once been to survive. Everything strapped down, the only thing to do being the task ahead of him. Just a task, no matter how unpleasant the outcome.

He was with two men who understood that. While he hadn't spent much time with Lawrence, the same wasn't true for Neil. When Abby's mental illness had manifested, and Neil had been a quiet, watchful presence during her sessions with Tiger, he'd gained a sense of the man's character.

Anyone the TRA Mistresses trusted, particularly Skye, he knew he could trust. But getting the direct evidence of it in the competent behavior of both men now helped steady him.

For a lot of their walking in this mess, Neil had them follow in his tracks. He had the best experience on where the terrain would get more treacherous. So far, there'd been no sign of anyone lying in wait for them.

That was one plus. Another was their additional backup. Way closer than he wanted her to be to this, but she had to be making deals with the devil to keep giving them as much intel as she was in crap weather conditions like this.

Eventually, however, that deal ran out. A flicker, and the screen went dark. No signal. The intense weather and the thick foliage of their surroundings had likely killed it.

Skye's last text had read, "you're within a thousand feet, SE." Close to a quarter of a mile on open ground shouldn't be anything. But this was different. Neil and Lawrence had a compass to stay on target, and he followed them, but after they moved forward another few hundred feet, he realized they'd reached a spot where there was nothing but water on three sides. A forest of cypress knees grew in the slow-moving current.

Despair gripped him, a cold fear. He imagined an alligator storing that small body in its cache for eating later. He didn't know if that made sense, if the tracking signal would even transmit from such a place, but his imagination was starting to resist any attempts to suppress the worst of his nightmares coming true.

Tiger closed his eyes, water running down his neck and back. His jeans were plastered to him, because the poncho only sheltered the top half. But he felt none of it. The cold he felt came from the heart outward.

Nicole had died in his arms. Nicole, who'd tried to convince him to help pull Colt out. He'd been lucky to get himself out, and he'd known Colt wouldn't leave until their father died. When Colt became President, it went from unlikely to not a chance in hell. But there were other things he could have done. To help Nicole and Aubrey. If he'd known it would end here, like this, what more could he have done?

No, fuck it. No. Help me, Nicole. Help me. I will make sure she stays safe. Just help me.

Neil moved to his side. Though the weather and goggles made it impossible to see his face, Tiger figured his thoughts weren't far from Tiger's own. The grim set of his mouth said so. He was looking, though, head turning in a slow back and forth, scanning to see if the conclusion they were being forced to face was as hopeless as it seemed.

Tiger's hand shot up, grabbed Neil's shoulder. In an instant, Neil's gun was up, and Lawrence had likewise gone to combat-ready. He was standing a few yards away on Tiger's right, on a stretch of ground Neil had confirmed was stable.

Tiger shook his head, his best way of telling them it wasn't a threat he'd detected. He bent his head to the wind, continuing to grip Neil's shoulder. "I think...I thought..." He waited, willing his heart to stop thumping so fast, holding his breath. There, just a faint...something.

"I can hear her."

"What?"

Tiger held up his other hand for silence. He stood, drops continuing to run down the sides of the poncho's visor, over the goggles and his lips. He willed all competing noises to shut the hell up. *Don't strain to hear things.* The hearing doc, reminding him. *You'll just frustrate yourself. Let the sounds come, log them down for our next appointment...*

There, on the wind...it blew in waves, up, down...there. A thin cry. A wavering note. He took a step in that direction. Then another, and another.

His mind could play tricks on him, and would do so. But the doc had also said he might be able to hear what other people couldn't. *Please, please...*

Neil and Lawrence fell in, following his lead, but adjusted left and right to increase the range of their view as he kept moving forward. Neil grabbed his arm, stopping him from walking straight into a section of marsh that would have plunged him up to his waist in the water. The goggles caught the gleam of a surfacing gator's eyes as they adjusted to walk parallel to the water.

A few minutes later, Neil brought him to a halt again and gestured. They'd been skirting the cypress swamp, staying close to the edge because what Tiger was hearing was coming from somewhere across it. Now Tiger saw why.

About fifty yards away, in the middle of the water, was a sand bar built up with debris and thick grasses.

Tiger squinted to bring an unexpected assortment of straight edges into focus. A fucking shack, the size of an outhouse, probably somebody's hunting shelter. Infrequently used, because even in this visibility it looked like nothing more than a ramshackle assortment of rotting boards. But it had walls and a roof.

Lawrence and Neil pressed against his sides to stop him from jumping into the water and trying to swim across. Neil motioned to them to stay where they were and moved off into the rain-soaked darkness.

Lawrence spoke loudly in Tiger's ear. "If the hunters using it come in on foot from the park, they might keep a craft covered up somewhere to get to it. He's checking."

He'd kept a grip on Tiger's arm, so Lawrence must have felt what was going through him. "You okay, man?"

No. Fuck snakes, gators, or anything else in that water, Tiger needed to plunge in and start swimming. That thin cry had expanded. It wasn't a bird, or the whistle of the wind, playing tricks with him as he'd feared. He could hear *her*. Hear Aubrey.

She was crying. Calling for him, in between choking sobs. *Uncle... Tiger. Mommy... Grandma...help. Please help. I'm so scared...*

Thunder clapped above and he flinched as the last syllable became a piercing shriek. She didn't like thunder. He'd told her he'd take her on his motorcycle one day, show her with a roaring engine that thunder was nothing at all to be scared of. Just the opposite.

"Hang on," Lawrence said, and Tiger realized he was straining against his hold. "He's coming back."

Neil was returning along the water's edge, holding a rope to a small raft that looked like it belonged to fucking Huckleberry Finn. Something a hunter wouldn't worry about leaving tied up to the cypress knees and concealed under a layer of debris. The platform was big enough for two men to precariously pole themselves across. For deeper waters, an oar was lashed next to the pole.

As he and Lawrence joined Neil down on the bank, Neil called out over the wind, holding up a hand to clarify his intent, in case Tiger couldn't make out all the words. "Let me get on first. Do it exactly like I do it."

"Unless his ass falls in, and then don't do it that way," Lawrence shouted in Tiger's other ear.

Neil shot him an eat-shit look, but handed him the rope before stepping onto the raft, testing its stability. He went to one knee to free the pole from the rope securing it.

"Almost everything in the world worth do ing can be accomplished from a kneeling position. My Mistress tells me that all the time."

Startled, Tiger looked toward Lawrence. Despite the roar of the storm, and everything else going on, Lawrence had spoken as if they were at the club, sharing a drink after a long, hard session. When the mind, while exhausted, was the clearest on the things that mattered.

He hadn't removed his night vision goggles, but Tiger felt like he could see the green eyes meeting his. Whatever was ahead, Lawrence had just jogged him out of the tunnel vision groove, opening up his senses to better prepare him for what lay ahead.

Tiger gave him a nod, and held onto the most important thing. She might be scared, she might need him, but Aubrey was *alive*.

At Neil's gesture, Tiger got on the raft and accepted control of the pole. Neil showed him how to use it to guide the raft forward, then pointed to the oar, a cue to use it when the pole could no longer reach bottom.

When Tiger gave him a thumbs up, Neil took up watch, his gun drawn as they started toward the island. The shack wasn't big, but at least two other people could fit in there with Aubrey. Lawrence staying watchful on the bank took care of the possibility that they could have left backup hidden in the woods.

They reached the island, and Neil directed Tiger to tie the raft up to a branch protruding from the island's foundation of debris. Then Neil pointed to the door.

A board had been nailed over it. Which meant there was no one in the shed but who they'd trapped in there.

Rage flooded Tiger. He managed to wait for Neil's go ahead, but once he had it, he'd crossed the ground and was at the door. With Neil's reminder in his head, that Tiger's job was to get to his niece and theirs was to keep everything out of his way, he ignored anything but getting that door open. And letting her know he was there.

"Aubrey, it's me. It's Uncle Tiger. It's okay, honey, we're here. It's all right."

Fuck, he needed something to get that fucking board loose. Neil tossed him a pry bar he'd pulled from his kit, saving him from doing it with his bare hands. Tiger wrenched the board off with one screeching yank.

The five-by-five space was more a crate than a shed. Aubrey was huddled on the floor, knees drawn up, hair snarled, face scratched and dirty. But when she saw him, she sprang up like a cricket, meeting Tiger halfway to be swallowed in his arms as he went to his knees for her.

Lawrence was right.

Her sobs were hoarse, caught in a throat exhausted from crying and calling out. But she'd kept doing it, trying to believe they were looking for her, would find her, even in the middle of a storm.

If they hadn't found her, there was no telling how long she would have survived here. He wanted to kill every one of the bastards who'd put her through this, but now that he'd found her, that would be Colt's area, not his. He had one priority.

Remembering Nicole bleeding out in his parking lot, looking at the child who had his brother's eyes and her mother's brown hair, Tiger knew exactly what that priority was.

He'd make it happen, even if he had to kill Colt to do it.

CHAPTER TWENTY-ONE

*W*e got her.

Tiger's text made Skye's heart start beating again. The signal had been coming in and out, enough to tell her the men were headed back in her direction.

When they came out of the woods, Tiger was carrying Aubrey. She was covered by his poncho, but her thin arms and legs were clamped around him like a vise. Her head was on his shoulder.

In the truck, she seemed disoriented and unresponsive, but Tiger told her it was a post trauma reaction, not an injury or shock. With their field combat medical training, Neil and Lawrence had checked her for anything serious, so hadn't needed to immediately use the first aid kit they'd carried with them. However, before he got back into his own vehicle, Neil told Skye to follow him and Lawrence; he'd take them somewhere close by to get out of the wet and do a more thorough exam.

Tiger got into the passenger seat holding Aubrey, but he freed one hand long enough to squeeze Skye's hand hard and to exchange a look with her that had too many things in it to say. *Words can't cover it, Mistress.*

He also sent a short text to Colt, telling him his daughter was safe, and Tiger would call him soon with more details.

Skye drove. While him holding Aubrey in the front might not

meet child safety seat requirements, the best place for her was in her uncle's arms. Skye drove carefully with their precious cargo.

Neil brought them to a small house that looked like a fisherman's weekend retreat. Obviously familiar with the place, he went around back and returned with a key to get them inside. The place had a bed, kitchenette and, most importantly, a bathroom with a shower.

Neil's gentle but more thorough exam confirmed Aubrey had nothing physically worse than scratches and bruises. Skye went into the bathroom to get her out of her wet clothes and into the large sweatshirt Lawrence found in the closet. As Skye helped Aubrey pull the sleeves up, her hand closed over the bracelet on the thin arm. A deep quiver went through Skye as she thought of how this day might have gone if she hadn't been wearing it. Or if they'd taken it off...

When they emerged, Neil and Lawrence had changed into dry clothes they'd brought in their go-bags. In the same closet as the sweatshirt, Tiger had found an XL T-shirt, socks and jeans that were baggy and a little short, but fit well enough. He'd also put his hearing aids back in, though Skye noted he'd done well enough with her voice software in the truck without them. His hearing had improved so much since she'd seen him last. She ignored the conflicting emotions that thought gave her, and how it took her back to their unfinished conversation at the club.

Nothing mattered right now but Aubrey.

She needed fluids and carbs, so Skye sat with her on the bed, encouraging her to take sips from a bottle of water until Tiger brought in a package of Fig Newtons from his glove box. "I carry them for her," he told Skye. "They've been in there a while, since before... but they should still be okay."

The fisherman either had kids or liked juice boxes, because he had a six pack of them. Lawrence brought one to her. Even the tough SEALs were having trouble not hovering over Aubrey, who looked so frail in the big sweatshirt.

Skye stroked the girl's hair. She only looked up from her charge when Tiger placed a blanket around her own shoulders. She hadn't realized she was damp herself, enough to be shivering, but he had noticed. Tiger squeezed her shoulder and waited for her nod, the brief touch of her hand, to confirm she was okay. As okay as any of them.

She wrapped both her and Aubrey in the blanket, so Aubrey was getting direct body heat from her. The girl rested her head on Skye's breast as she chewed the Fig Newton. Then she spoke, her voice shaking.

"Do you need me to tell you...what h-happened? S-so Daddy can get the bad g-guys?"

Tiger didn't look surprised as the rest of them by the question, but he knew what it was to be raised in the outlaw motorcycle gang world. While a girl might be sheltered more than a boy, Aubrey had likely already seen more violence than most kids did, even beyond the worst thing, her mother's death. Aubrey's serious expression was like Tiger's when he was determined to protect someone he cared about.

"You don't have to do that right now," Tiger said.

"T-two men t-took me," she said in answer. She worried the bracelet with her fingers, rotating it around her wrist. "One was really mean. He kept telling me to shut up, and cursing at me, keeping me scared. The other...he told the other man he'd take me into the swamp and leave me. The mean man wanted him to...throw me in the water. So the alligators..."

She paused, a shudder gripping her.

"You really don't have to do this, honey." Though Tiger murmured it gently, Skye saw the brief flash of murderous fury in his dark blue eyes. He'd pulled a chair close and leaned forward to clasp Aubrey's hand. "You've been brave enough for one day."

Lawrence and Neil's expressions were fixed and cold. All of them feeling the same surge of emotions.

Aubrey just shook her head. "The mean man stayed in the car. The other man put me in a boat they had. He took me to the shed. Said he hunted there. Said he'd come back in a day or two to make sure I got home to Daddy. But then the storm came up, and I was too scared to stay quiet, like he told me to do."

"You did just what you should have," Tiger told her.

Her chin wobbled, but she looked at Skye. "I need to go to the bathroom. I'm a big girl, and can do it myself, but..."

"I'd be happy to go with you." Skye typed it one-handed. She used her Angela Lansbury voice, the most reassuring one on her phone. "Grown-up girls go to the bathroom together all the time." She winked at Aubrey. "It's where we talk about how silly boys are."

After they disappeared into the bathroom, Tiger turned his attention to Neil and Lawrence.

"Most MC guys don't have an appetite for killing kids outright. They do it indirectly. Sell drugs to the guys who sell it to kids, or form alliances with gangs into sex trafficking, turning a blind eye to what they do in favor of the money. But killing a kid straight up—that's not in their repertoire."

He didn't have any warm feelings toward the man who'd put Aubrey in the shed, but he would get more of a description from Aubrey and tell Colt. Colt could decide if he'd earned a measure of mercy. At least a quicker death.

He picked up his phone. Time to give Colt that more detailed update. And do what he was resolved to do. But first, he glanced at Neil for one more reassurance on a different topic. "So she doesn't need a hospital?"

"No. Vitals are good, she's eating and drinking normally. Communicating clearly. It wouldn't hurt, but it would raise a lot of questions, and you said that could cause problems."

"Yeah."

The two SEALs exchanged a look. They'd taken a seat at the kitchenette table. Lawrence and Skye had both sent communications to Ros, letting her know their status. "What do you want to do next?" Neil said to Tiger.

"It's not what I want to do. It's what I'm going to do." He met their somber looks. "You mind being my backup for one more meeting? A family one."

"Family meetings are more dangerous than insurgents," Lawrence observed. "But throw in the promise of a good bottle of whiskey and we're your guys."

Tiger nodded. "I'll make it two."

～

Tiger told Colt to meet him at a rest area outside New Orleans, off the interstate heading for Florida. Though that was a good enough reason for the location, Tiger chose it as a not-obvious place to those who'd taken her in the first place.

On the way, they stopped at a Family Dollar to get Aubrey colorful and soft kid clothes. Skye helped her pick out a blue shirt with an ice-skating penguin and sequins on it, paired with a ruffled white cotton skirt. Tiger found a pack of little girl underwear, plus socks and generic white sneakers.

When he revealed there were blue sneakers, too, he was immediately dispatched by his niece to switch out the white sneakers for ones that matched the penguin shirt. It choked him up in a way he had to hide. Then Skye mouthed "Domme'd by a six-year-old," and tears he hadn't spilled in two decades nearly escaped. Fuck, at some point in the near future, he was going to do some serious drinking.

Skye bought her a stuffed elephant, which Aubrey clutched when she was back in Skye's lap, both of them occupying the passenger seat of Tiger's truck.

"When are we going home, Uncle Tiger?"

"Soon, baby. You hungry again?"

She shrugged, but her eyes were deep set in her pale face. Though he knew that was more the emotional toll of the day, they still rolled around a drive-thru to get her a Happy Meal. She ate a little but then fell asleep, her head against Skye's soft bosom again. When she adjusted in her slumber, her legs ended up over the truck console, feet resting on Tiger's thigh. He kept his hand over them, thumb passing over the tops of the sneakers. He drove one-handed as the rain cleared up and road conditions improved.

Skye dozed a little herself, but as she roused and noted the difference between Tiger's large hand and Aubrey's small feet, her throat got thick and tears threatened. The same reaction she knew Tiger had experienced, doing something as normal as picking out shoes for his niece.

But that moment had passed. From his profile, Skye could see he had too many things left to handle to let anything else in. Like recapping what had happened, or what could have happened. She didn't want her mind to go there, either. Not until thinking about it wouldn't make her whole body shake hard enough to rattle her teeth.

She remembered Tiger putting the blanket around her shoulders. Taking the time to care for both of his girls. She reached out and stroked his shoulder. He glanced her way and nodded. A reinforcement that they were okay, and the things that weren't okay, he was going to fix.

She knew the misguided theory that submissive men were just looking for someone to take care of them. No question, there was that subset, in male and female submissives, just as there were the matching Dominants who wanted to provide that care, because it satisfied their topping needs.

But there were men who had an unshakable stance on what being a man meant, no matter the situation. She thought of what his father had said, that it was his job to teach his sons that. Tiger would probably say that was the job of any parent. So would she. But if they did their job right, teaching him to stand on his own two feet and think and care for himself, ultimately the son himself decided what being a man meant.

Tiger surrendered in session because he liked to take care of a woman. Craved it. Was satisfied by being allowed to serve her desires. Out in the world, Tiger didn't consider it anyone else's job to do what he was supposed to do. Care for those in his family, blood related or otherwise. Be someone others could look to for leadership, character. Someone who didn't hesitate when a stand had to be taken.

Her hand was still on him, her fingers caressing his biceps under the sleeve, following the slash of the scar across the elephant's ear. He glanced her way again. She made a gesture, a thumb following her sternum up toward her throat, then pointed to him.

I'm proud of you.

He didn't know what it meant, but he read her expression as approval and care. "I'm glad you're here," he said.

She felt the unspoken words between them. The question. Did she want to always be here? At his side?

She put that in the same box as other things she wasn't prepared to handle tonight. Plus there was no time to do so. As they pulled into the rest area, Neil and Lawrence right behind them, she saw Colt was already there. Along with five Fallen Angels.

They had enough to handle.

"Stay here with her," Tiger said in a low voice, glancing at the sleeping Aubrey. He pointed to the keys he'd left in the ignition. "If things go bad, get her the hell out of here, and call 911 if anyone tries to chase you down."

He pulled out his phone and called up his address book. Her phone chimed. "I just sent you Rose and Bill's contact info."

He pocketed the phone and removed his sizeable nine-millimeter from beneath his seat. As he tucked it into his back waist band, pulling his shirt down over it, he gave her a long look.

Then he eased Aubrey's feet to the seat and slid out of the truck.

~

A light drizzle was falling again. Tiger met Neil's gaze as the SEAL emerged from his vehicle, Lawrence coming out of the passenger side. They'd talked about the plan back at the cottage, the possible ways this could go. They'd be ready.

Two of the Fallen Angels were on their bikes. Colt had come in an Escalade, one club member driving, two in the back.

If their father had still been alive, Tiger knew he wouldn't have come with Colt. He'd have been strategizing their response toward those who'd taken her. Dad had never had much use for a girl. He loved Aubrey, but in a distant, Sunday picnic, hold her on his lap for a few minutes and then send her off kind of way. She was simply a possession no one was allowed to fuck with.

His father's open casket funeral had been the first time Tiger had seen him in five years. He hadn't felt much. The cauldron of poison feelings had been dumped out some time ago, drained with the expectations and hopes of the kid he no longer was. Though he'd had her in his life a far shorter time, it was his mother he still missed the most.

The Colt he'd grown up with was a different matter. He still saw that kid in his adult brother. Not just the few times he and Tiger had crossed paths, like at the funeral and memorial. When Nicole or Aubrey had talked about him, those memories were kept alive. He and his brother had stayed connected through that female bridge.

Their father was gone, but his influence on Colt was strong, even beyond the grave. Tiger needed to find the brother he'd once known inside the man he was now.

Tiger waited in front of his truck as Colt came toward them. The grim urgency and strain in his face told Tiger that Colt's feelings toward his daughter, while not enough of what Tiger thought they should be, far exceeded what her grandfather's had been.

He bypassed Tiger for now, making a beeline for that passenger side. At Tiger's slight nod, Skye had the window down by the time he got there, though she didn't get out. Colt's face tightened further, but then he noted his daughter was sleeping. It at least gave the impression they weren't denying him his daughter's embrace.

When his brother leaned in and gazed at Aubrey, the way Skye's face became softer and less guarded confirmed the depth of the emotions Colt revealed.

Colt reached in carefully to touch Aubrey's hair. His shoulders eased down as he expelled a rough sigh. He gazed at her another moment, then adjusted the blanket over her shoulder before he backed off and turned toward Tiger.

When he closed the few steps between them, the club president hardass expression was back in place. The Fallen Angels on bikes had moved under one of the picnic shelters to their left. Neil and Lawrence had responded in kind, positioning themselves to the right, where they had an equal vantage response point. Everyone seemingly casual, but most definitely not.

Colt's gaze slid toward the SEALs, who were studying the Fallen Angels backup as impassively as they were being measured. The way two opposing forces had done it, ever since the first two armies faced one another across a field.

Colt's dark blue eyes came back to Tiger's. "So your hearing's back."

"Mostly." Tiger tapped the hearing aids.

Colt's shoulders were stiff. "You're going to try and keep me from taking her home."

"My hope is you're not going to try to stop me from doing it. Her home's with her grandparents."

Colt's jaw went hard. "That's not happening."

"You willing to kill me to keep me from it?"

"What kind of bullshit question is that?"

"The kind I'm dead serious about." But Tiger injected a calmer note into his voice. "I'm not going to turn this into a battlefield, though. Not with Aubrey and Skye here. But what I'm showing you is my resolve. Let's go under the other shelter over there, away from our backup, and talk about it. Get out of the rain. You willing to do that, little brother?"

Colt's brow rose. "You haven't called me that in a long time. It still pisses me off."

"I only called you that because you went through your growth spurt first and it made me mad that you were an inch taller than me for a year."

"It was fun jerking your chain about it." They gazed at one another, then Colt dipped his head toward the second shelter. When they got there, Colt sat down on a table, boots braced on the bench. Tiger took a similar position on the table next to it, facing him.

"There are two ways to do this. The first way, the best way, is you agree to let her live with Rose and Bill. Give them permanent custody without a fight. The second way, I throw whatever weight I've got behind them to win that in court."

As Colt's gaze flashed, Tiger pressed onward. "That's not what I want to do. You're her dad. You love her. You need to be a part of her life. But be as much a part of your life as you can as a long-distance dad. Let her grow up without the Fallen Angels in her life."

"If I give them full custody, they'll never let me see her again."

"I will do everything I can to convince them not to do that. And if you don't fight them, you'll already be halfway to winning that argument. Let them have her, and ask them if it's okay to come be a part of her life, on their turf, whenever you can get away. Prove that you intend to keep her as far from your world as possible. Let Nicole have that peace and honor her memory. She was about to leave you, wasn't she?"

Colt shot him an angry look, but there was a helpless despair beneath it. "Fuck her," he said. "Fuck that bitch. She knew what she was getting into."

"Yeah, she did. But Aubrey changed it for her."

Colt's mouth went to a thin line, but before he could respond, Tiger sighed. "Let's tell the truth, Colt. You love her, you loved Nicole, but you love the club and what dad wanted more. You always have. With her grandparents, she *will* be the most important thing in the world. And she'll have her uncle to watch out for her. While you do what you do in a world no kid should ever be a part of."

Colt stared at him, his face granite. Tiger stared back.

"Would you kill me over her, Tiger? If it was her or me?"

"Yeah. Absolutely. If you feel the way about her you should, you'd want me to do it, if it was in her best interest."

The sound of the truck door opening had them both looking that way. Aubrey had woken up and seen her dad. She wanted to come to him. Skye was holding her back with gentle hands, but Colt gestured to her, that it was okay, and Tiger reinforced it with a nod. Fortunately outside of Colt's view, so it didn't aggravate him.

"Come here, baby," Colt called.

Even knowing it should be okay, Tiger tensed as Aubrey came toward them. His eyes were on the waiting Fallen Angels. So were Neil and Lawrence's.

Neil had told him the same rules applied as in the swamp. They'd watch his back while he focused on the part of the mission only he could accomplish.

"Unless things go bad," Tiger had told him. *"Then the most important thing is you guys protecting Skye and Aubrey and getting them out of there. I'll slow them down and watch your six. You don't worry about me."*

Aubrey looked okay, but even after the store stop, the stress showed. She needed to be somewhere she felt completely safe. They weren't there yet, and she knew it.

Skye stood next to Neil and Lawrence. Her expression was strained, but her eyes were laser sharp. His emphatic direction to her, to keep Aubrey safe, would take them both out of the crossfire if anything went south here, thank God. Otherwise, if his brother tried to shoot him, Tiger had no doubt Skye would get right into the middle of things.

As Colt noted the direction of his gaze, he spoke, voice oddly neutral. "You've called her Mistress a couple times. Not a pet name, is it?"

"No, it's not. I'm proud to call her that. Don't give me any shit about it. It's been too fucking long of a day, and she's a big part of the reason we found Aubrey."

A muscle twitched in Colt's jaw, but he spat. "You trust a woman too much."

"Maybe you trust them too little. Mom fucked up, but she loved Dad, Colt. You know she did. Maybe if you had let yourself surrender your will to your own woman now and then, you'd understand a lot of things better."

Nicole might be alive. Tiger didn't say that, but he guessed the implication was impossible to avoid. Colt might have had a retort for that, but then Aubrey was there. When Colt reached for her, Aubrey's response was tentative, her gaze moving to Tiger for his slight nod before she went into her father's arms. Colt saw it, tension thrumming through him, but he ran a hand down her back and tousled her hair. "I'm glad you're okay," he told her roughly. "You know I love you, right? And I loved your mom."

"She's in heaven. Do you still love her, even though she's there?"

"Yeah. I do. I'll always love her."

Colt paused a long moment. The girl was tired enough that she moved into his touch, adjusting to lean against him, nestling her face under his chin as she got easier with the contact. Colt squeezed his eyes shut, then spoke roughly. "I probably didn't do the right things to make her happy. Not sure if I'm made that way. But...I'm going to do right by you, so maybe that will help make up for some of that."

Colt's gaze went to Tiger's. Anger was there, anguish, frustration, a million different emotions. But the words that came out of his mouth were quiet. "Would you like to go live with your grandparents? Tell me the truth, baby." He cleared his throat. "I won't be mad."

Aubrey pushed herself back to look up into his face, her own uncertain. "Would you come visit me? For things like bring-your-dad-to-school day? And the daddy-daughter dance?"

What went through Colt's expression this time had Tiger looking away. He knew Colt loved her, but that love got mucked up with so much other shit. Seeing Colt realize it was heartrending, and clawed at Tiger's gut. "We'll see," Colt said.

"Can Uncle Tiger visit, too?"

Colt looked up at him and tilted his head. Not exactly a nod, but close enough. "Yeah. Okay."

Tiger moved close enough to stroke a gentle hand over her hair. "Anytime."

"Will the two of you come together sometime?" She looked between them. "Mommy would like that. She told me."

"She did, hunh?" Colt touched her shoulder. "You still haven't answered the question."

Her eyes welled up with tears. "Yes. I would like to live with Grandma Rose and Grandpa Bill. I'm so sorry, Daddy. I do love you."

"No. It's okay. It's okay." Colt held her close as she let out a little sob then put her fist against her mouth, as if to hold it back and bring herself under control. Something no kid her age should know how to do, but Tiger knew exactly where she'd learned to pull it back in that way.

So did Colt. He swallowed, his eyes wet as he looked toward the trees. Then he had himself under control, and eased back from her, touching her face once more. "All right then," he said gruffly. "Uncle Tiger's going to take you to them. Road trip. Lots of good snacks, I'll bet. Pork rinds, right?"

Aubrey made a face. "You like those. I think they're gross."

"If I poured chocolate over them, you'd be fine with them. I'll send you some chocolate-covered pork rinds."

She giggled a little, a weak sound, but genuine enough to give Tiger a relieved feeling. Kids were always heartbreakingly tougher than adults realized.

He and Colt were proof of that. So was Skye.

Colt had dropped his attention to Aubrey's bracelet. He ran his thumb over it, squeezing his daughter's arm. Then he lifted his head and met Skye's gaze square. Skye answered his short nod with one of her own, as well as a follow up gesture, a rounded sweep of her hand from beneath her chin to her mid-section. Colt sent Tiger a questioning look.

"She said you're welcome."

Colt nodded thoughtfully, then touched Aubrey's face. "I want you to go back to Skye while your uncle and I talk."

"Okay, Daddy. If you promise you won't fight."

Colt stroked her hair again. "No, baby. We won't fight. Uncle Tiger knows I'd whip his butt."

Tiger scoffed, but smiled when Aubrey looked toward him, confirming all was good. She let out a little sigh, part relief, part weariness, with just a touch of worry for the future. It was such an adult response it was startling.

Especially when she sounded just like her mother.

Pain gripped Colt's features. As Aubrey headed her way, Skye reached out a hand, clasping the child's to guide her to the truck, tucking them both safely inside again.

Tiger looked at Colt. "I know you're going to seek retribution for this. But try not to get killed doing it."

"Yeah." Colt's fingers pressed into the top of the picnic table, his expression as wooden as the slats. "When Rose and Bill draw up the papers on the custody thing... make sure they put you as the person who gets her if they kick off before she grows up."

Tiger's brow creased. "What are you talking about, man?"

"It's nice to think about, me coming to visit her...but no. We're not doing that." Colt's half-laugh was bitter. "Shit, you know how likely I am to live to see her be eighteen, Tiger. She doesn't need to go through that twice."

Tiger closed the distance between them then, gripping the edge of his brother's cut. He gave him a sharp shake. "You prove that wrong. Be her father when it counts. Be there to scare the shit out of her prom date. Wipe away her tears when she gets her first broken heart."

"Too late on that one. She has nightmares about losing her mom." Colt's expression became even more brittle. "Did she...was it fast?"

It was the first time he'd asked anything about Nicole. Just like his feelings about his daughter, they were buried so deep people didn't think he had them. Tiger had always known better. Maybe because of the minefield between them, he'd let himself forget that.

"Yeah. It was fast. I think—I think she was already gone when we went down together. And swear to God, her last words to me were about you. Loving you. She just didn't know how to live with you."

His own mother's words, echoing in his mind.

Colt digested that, his eyes bleak. "Yeah. So you be the one who scares the shit out of Aubrey's prom date, okay? Go to Florida whenever you can. Take her to Animal Kingdom. All right?"

"You're just going to walk away from her? Your own daughter?"

Colt's expression hardened, the Fallen Angels president coming to the top. But not just that; the man who knew what choices he'd made, and where that put him. Tiger's gut twisted at the inarguable truth in his brother's eyes.

"The best way to keep her safe is to sever all ties," Colt said. "I'll send you money to give to Rose and Bill. Far as the club goes, you're not part of it. I haven't reinforced it the way I should. That stops now. If my enemies think I don't give a shit about you, could care less if you live or die, they leave you alone. And anyone connected to you." Colt's gaze went to the truck, touching on Skye, then came back to him.

"Colt..."

"No. You know it, same as I do. You were always good enough to be President. Better than me. Dad knew it. It was why it stuck in his craw so bad that you walked away." Colt had moved back a few feet. To his men, his body language would appear indifferent, on guard, in control, but his eyes said something different. "I love you, big brother. You take care of Aubrey, okay?"

Before Tiger could say anything else, he walked away, back to the waiting bikers, a saunter, a leader sure of himself. Tiger watched him go, fighting that same feeling he'd carried for so long. And would keep carrying, probably long after he was told his brother was dead. Or sentenced to life in prison.

On the path he was walking, it wasn't an if. It was a when.

Tiger had told him to be the best dad he could be for Aubrey. With the life he lived, Colt had decided that meant walking away.

Agreeing with him didn't make it any easier to watch.

Especially when Tiger didn't see the president of the Fallen Angels walking away, but the younger brother he'd fished and gotten into trouble with. Who he'd held carefully in his arms when he was born. Tiger remembered his mother's touch on his face, her protective hand on his arms, helping his younger self cradle the precious burden.

"This is your little brother. I'll need your help looking after him."

He couldn't look after Colt anymore. Or their mother. But he'd sure as hell look after Aubrey.

CHAPTER TWENTY-TWO

*S*kye rode with him to Florida. They drove through the rest of the night, and arrived early afternoon. Rose and Bill opened the front door as soon as they pulled into their driveway. Bill, a sturdy seventy-something with military-short gray hair and a rugged face, carried his granddaughter into the house, to the bedroom that had been hers for some time. Skye and Rose went with them while Tiger stood on the back porch, looking at the boat dock and marsh behind their place. He was so fucking tired. But he still had more to do.

When he came back inside, he sat on the couch, tipping his head back on the head rest. He was dozing when Skye touched his shoulder. Bill and she had returned. "Rose is sitting with her," Bill said grimly. "Aubrey said she couldn't wear a nightgown during the day, but Rose told her today was special. She fell asleep while Rose was getting it on her."

"She slept off and on in the truck, but it's not the same as being in her own bed. This is home to her."

At Bill's wary look of surprise, Tiger brought him up to date on everything. He told him Colt's decision, and that Tiger would coordinate getting the guardianship papers finalized with Colt, be the go-between.

Rose came down during the last part of the explanation, so he rehashed some of it for her and answered both of their questions.

When he at last rose to leave, telling them they needed to go, Skye at his side, Rose hugged him, hard. Bill shook his hand. "I wish you would stay for a day or two at least," Rose said. "It's a long drive."

"Skye needs to get back to work, and I have the garage waiting. We'll trade off driving. It'll be fine. I'll try to come down at least once a month, and Aubrey can call or text me anytime." Tiger paused. "We'll need to help her understand why her dad's not going to be reaching out to her. He'll give me money for her. I know you don't need it, but let him do it. It'll be important to him."

Bill's expression hardened. "Our daughter made her own decisions. We've tried to accept that. I know he's your brother, but..."

Tiger shook his head. "He loved Nicole, even if he was shitty at it. He made the right decision tonight, Bill. Her daughter, your grand-child, is safe. That's all that matters, going forward. He's paid the cost for the life he's living."

The words shoved glass shards into his chest, but Tiger got the rest out. "He's my little brother. Still is and will always be. The club has a way of swallowing your best intentions to do anything other than the club. It's why I got out of it."

Bill gripped his shoulder. "Thank God you did. You come back soon, son." He glanced at Skye. "You're welcome to come with him. Anytime. Tiger has always had a strong compass. If it led him to you, then you're good for him."

～

"Sure you don't want to stop at a hotel tonight?" she typed. Skye had volunteered to take the first shift on the driving, because Tiger looked...she wasn't sure. But he'd taken the wheel, saying he wanted to stop somewhere on the way.

He shook his head and didn't say much else, not until he reached that somewhere. It was a state park, with hiking trails and a scenic marsh overlook. Egrets fished in the tall grasses, with their careful long-legged strides, and a shrimp trawler was sailing up the distant waterway.

There was something about daytime when a person had been up over twenty-four hours, facing crises that were now in the rearview mirror. The exhaustion and relief made the sunlight softer, the edges of everything fuzzy.

He put the truck into park. Stared through the windshield, but she didn't think he was looking at the view. Glancing down abruptly, he retrieved the McDonald's bag and an empty gummy bear candy mini-pack, one of the snacks they'd gotten for Aubrey. He got out, tossed all of it in the trash can. Then he started walking.

She slid out of the truck. Because he was obviously seeking space, she didn't chase him, but she kept him within sight. He took a path that led to the overlook, a wooden walkway over the marsh. Several steps across the bridge, he stopped and turned, waiting on her so he could offer her a hand. "Boards are a little slippery," he said.

He stopped them halfway across the walkway and braced his hands on the rail. Gazing at his profile, her heart was in her throat. He'd dealt with a lot over the past day, and he'd handled all of it like a hero. She didn't give a lot of thought to those kinds of things, but she liked video games for reasons beyond the strategy and tech—heroism called to any heart that had room for the notion.

She slid an arm around his waist and rested her head on his shoulder. He had his chin dipped to his chest. His energy pulled hers in, and she felt it rise up in him. What they both had kept pushing down, all these long hours.

All that could have gone wrong.

How close to the edge it had been.

Aubrey's capture, her father's willingness to let her go.

Tiger's arms were around her, hers around him, holding onto one another. Drawing strength and stability. But then he pushed back. He still had his hands on her upper arms, his grip suddenly tighter. He stared down into her face. "Use that voice you use for yourself. The Southern girl one. No celebrity shit."

"What do you want me to say?" she typed, turning it on.

"I wanted to confirm how wrong I was. What I said to you in the club, when I asked you to use 'your' voice. That's not your voice. It never has been. People associate it with you, because it's how they can connect to you. I connected to you when you used a different kind of communication. That's what I hear...feel, as your voice."

He stepped back, the act of letting her go a visible effort. She didn't want him to stop touching her, but the deliberate way he did it told her he had an important reason for establishing the space between them.

"I'm a grown man, Skye. I know how to handle my own shit, my own heartbreak, and not take it out on the woman who doesn't want what I want. But I need to know where I stand with you. Was all of it just because I was a guy who'd lost his hearing, and you had the skillset to help me get through it?"

He put a hand over hers before she could start typing. "I'm not saying you were faking anything. I think it got deep for you, too, and bigger than you were expecting. I'm saying if you're swimming for the edge of the pool, intending to return to dry land because you don't want to stay in those waters and see how deep they can go, I need to know that. As I said, I'm not going to judge you for your reasons for that. It will hurt like hell, no lie. And before you cut me off at the knees, I would, respectfully," a muscle twitched in his jaw, "like to request a fucking reason for you doing it."

She turned toward the rail, her hand clutching the phone. Her mind was turning, rolling over things to say to answer the question. But her heart was churning, making it hard to think.

She could say they'd been through too much, their emotions too worn out, to do this now. But maybe that was exactly why it needed to be now. When there was no strength for defenses.

"You say it's done, it's done," he said after a long moment, his voice heavy. Her silence had provided him her answer. "As I said, I'll spend time at another club for a while, to make it easier for both of us. Maybe that smaller place that Dale and Athena use. There's a mechanic in Algiers who can take good care of your Mustang..."

She slapped her hand down on the rail and then did what she never did.

She lost her grip on the phone.

It bounced against the wood, flipping up and outward. She lunged for it, and the rail hit her hip, stopping her. The phone was already well beyond her reach, twisting and flipping to plop into the murky water and sink to the silty bottom.

Tiger had grabbed her waist when she lunged, probably thinking she might dive after it. He was holding her tight, his front against her back. She closed her hand on the air, made it a fist and brought it down on the rail before she turned and gazed up at him.

He ran his knuckles down her cheek, a lingering touch. There was frustration in his eyes, but also tenderness. A care. Love. In its early stages, but undeniable in its presence. It made that churning get worse, threatening to drown her as if she'd fallen and been sucked into the water below, like her phone.

"It's not your voice," he reminded her. "Talk to me, Mistress. Tell me you don't want me. Tell me why you won't let me all the way inside, when I can goddamn tell you're falling for me the way I am for you. Why can't we take that ride together?"

She swallowed. He tried to do that stepping back thing, probably employing the unlikely logic that being stabbed with rejection was better when you weren't being intimately touched by your assailant. She screwed her hand into the front of his shirt and held him in place.

She had a backup phone in her overnight bag. She always did. Everything on the phone was backed up daily. But she didn't go get it. She stood with him, closed her eyes, let it all in. And told him the simple truth.

She released him to put her hands in front of herself, one hand positioned above the other, fingers spread, and then jerked them horizontally, short, choppy movements. She did it twice, looking up at him. Three times. Each time, her heart cracked open further, shoving the emotion fully into her expression, out between them. It made her want to run as it took hold of her in a way she didn't permit. Never.

He put his hands back on her shoulders, thumbs against her throat. "You're scared," he said quietly.

She nodded and began to sign. She tried to break it down in gestures he'd be able to understand with his basic knowledge. With signals they'd worked out in session. That had applied to very different things, but he was proving he could make the leaps in logic.

"Scared...do it again. Same. Repeat." He studied her hands and face, tracking both. "Your other relationships. You thought...you're scared it'll turn out the same way."

"And I can't handle that. Not with you. Because as much as I thought they mattered...you matter so much more. You're inside me already. No one ever got there. Not that deep."

She signed all of that, knowing he would only get some of it, but then she pantomimed stabbing herself in the heart, and his hand closed over her wrist. He pried open her fingers and brought them to his lips, pressing them to her palm as he always did. "It will hurt too much if it happens again," he said, breaking it down to the one sentence that covered it all.

Yes. And, much as she hadn't wanted to admit it, when his hearing had started to return, she'd felt as if he was leaving her alone in a place she'd gotten used to him being.

He dropped to one knee, the way he did, and kissed her palm again. A sob choked her. He put a hand on her face. She liked that he was tall enough to do that, touch her cheek while on his knees. Connect with her.

"I'm not a kid," he said. "I've been in relationships that lasted long enough to consider marriage, or moving in together. They ran their course and didn't work out. When I look at you, there's something different there. We connected in a way I've never experienced. You know the day Nicole died? Right before it happened, I was thinking about the session you and I had at Progeny. Do you remember it? Really remember it?"

She did. When he saw how quickly she recalled it, he gave her a satisfied, tense nod.

"What I'm saying is it wasn't my hearing loss, Skye. We had already stepped onto that road together. It just got delayed. Or maybe what I went through, that helped move it along even faster, what was opening up. Abby could have been the Mistress to come see me after-ward, but she wasn't. It was you. But I don't really give a fuck if that meant anything significant or not. Things happen in the world, and whatever gets thrown in your path as a result, you grab it if it's worth holding onto."

When she kept looking at him, all those thoughts whirling in her brain, he pressed on. Tiger wasn't the type of man who did lengthy conversations, but she could feel his determination to break through, to answer her fear and give her something to replace it. Something real. Terrifyingly real.

"Before, if I pleased a Mistress and was what she needed, that meant a lot. But as you and I got deeper into it, I was doing more than that with you. Pleasing *you* was what mattered, digging into myself to give you everything you needed, learning more about you so I could do that. And every time you gave me more of who you are, I felt like I'd found treasure."

He gave her a painful half smile. "Somewhere along the way, it hit me in the head. 'Dumbass, you fell in love with her. You *are* in love with her.' And that sense that we're all alone in the world, that no one will ever get deep enough inside us to make that feeling go away? I don't feel that way with you. I think it's because you let me inside, too. It has to go two ways for that feeling to disappear."

He took a breath. "I'll make you a deal. If we don't work out, it won't be because I can hear, or you don't talk the way most people do. It'll be because I pissed you off to the point you need to end it or murder me. And if you don't mind, I'd prefer you to give me the choice, because I might just decide killing me would be easier than giving you up. It sure feels that way now."

Tears were sliding down her cheeks. He stood, bent and kissed them, finding his way to her lips. Then he lifted his head and gazed down at her, his eyes so full of determined resolve, the sexy alpha male she knew, that her legs actually felt a little weak.

"Do you know, when I lost my hearing, I had this fucking awful coffin feeling, of being shut in with the silence. Then being with you, your help, made it into a cocoon instead. When I was with just you, it was a world all our own. I should have seen that it became that for you, too."

His hands tightened on her. "You're so good at handling your world. I forget we all can be vulnerable. And yeah, Mistress and sub, it's my job to recognize it, but I got pissed because you were pulling away. I didn't look at why. You weren't pulling away. You were shoring yourself up, reinforcing the fortress. Getting ready to handle it alone again." Those eyes became fierce. "I can be your fortress, Mistress. Let me. Just let me."

Skye held his gaze. Lifted her hands. Formed the *O* and *K*. Then she slid her arms under his and held on. For the first time in her life, she let herself be held the way her father had held her.

With a strength and surety that told her she'd never have to doubt the depth of the love being offered in those arms.

CHAPTER TWENTY-THREE

A month or so later

*S*he'd been in Spokane, Washington for a week, helping with a marketing system implementation that was not going smoothly. The IT manager was determined to prove they hadn't needed any help getting it set up. Which they did; else she wouldn't have been called in.

The only thing saving the idiot from bodily harm was the regular texts Tiger sent her, making her smile. Each night, she video chatted with him in her hotel room because she wanted to hear his voice and see him.

Before she left, he'd driven her to the airport. She'd thought about telling him he didn't need to do that, but since he was either sleeping at her place or her at his most of the time, it seemed natural to let his desire to care for her evolve that way.

His hearing had returned almost a hundred percent. No more hearing aids. She wouldn't have held him to any goals he'd set himself before that, but his determination to learn signing had only increased.

Though she'd threatened to tie his hands so he'd stop asking her to show him more words and phrases, the message his commitment sent was impossible for her to ignore. Her quiet joy over it set up a small place in her heart, growing in strength each day. Her ability to talk to him only with her hands, her body, her expression, was growing. One day, it would be all organic, no tech involved.

When they video chatted, she did a mix, signing and typing, but mostly she liked watching and listening to him. He usually called from his office garage, which told her that he was sleeping on that cigarette smoke saturated couch.

Part of it was him working needed hours to make up for time and income lost. But when she looked for confirmation on that, he told her, "My bed feels too empty."

He had a knack for connecting heartstring-pulling thoughts like those to easier, arousing ones. Like he had during a chat earlier in the week.

"You once asked me my ultimate Mistress fantasy. What's your sub one? No judgment, no constraints. You know who I am. I won't feel like you're asking it of me. Just gives me the chance to follow where your mind goes when you dream of possibilities."

She hadn't answered him right away, wanting to think about it through the next day. Then the first part of her morning had driven everything out of her head but frustration, when she discovered the IT manager had mucked up the programming she'd done yesterday, not knowing what the fuck he was doing.

She straightened it out, but came back to her hotel room that evening with a pounding head, an aching back and neck, and a desire to do nothing but face plant on the bed.

Eventually, though, she rolled over on her back, stared at the ceiling and recalled Tiger's question. She lifted her phone and started to type.

She did have a fantasy. It wasn't something she needed from Tiger, but she liked the idea of sharing it with him, seeing what he did with it. How he reacted.

"I come home to a sub...my sub, at the door. Kneeling for me. He wears a cock harness with a cuff under the head that vibrates, keeping him hard. He's wearing nipple clamps, a chain between."

She could see the way the steel would look against his flesh. His birthday had been a couple weeks ago, and she'd gotten him a leather cut with the tiger logo on the back, Roseland Garage Crew circling it. The cut had metal studs on the front, over the pockets. She liked the way it looked on him. Particularly when he didn't wear a shirt under it. Just low-riding jeans and his boots.

"He holds a collar in his hands. If I put it on him, I've accepted his submission to me. Every day it's his choice, to offer that to me.

"It has metal studs on the inside so when I tighten it, it leaves marks on his skin. Over time, they get callused and remain there. The cock ring also has studs at the base, so when I grip him, he has to tell me, trust me, when the pain is too much.

"I put on his collar and from there forward he attends me however I need him to do. Starting with a neck and back massage." A faint smile crossed her face. Tiger was familiar with her body aches from computer work. He'd picked up on it one night when her neck was tight, and had been learning how to give her massages, his strong hands cradling her head.

The kneeling sub she'd fantasized about would be ordered to clean up her place before she arrived home—make the bed, wash the dishes, maybe a little dusting and vacuuming. Ooh, window cleaning. There'd be a webcam where she could watch him do it, in nothing but that cock harness. When she arrived home, she'd watch the footage while she ate her dinner, as he knelt by her feet. Then she'd make him kneel between her legs while she sat on the couch. He'd hold a vibrator for her as she brought herself to climax against it.

"He'll remain hard and aching, unreleased, because that's how I want him. I'll go to bed, have him kneel in the corner next to a sleeping mat. He has to stay that way until I fall asleep, so every time I open my eyes, I see him waiting to serve me until I call for him.

"In the morning, I'll shower, take his collar off as I leave. Go back to work. That night, it starts all over again."

She reviewed the words, then hit send. He wasn't a fast reader, but his response was worth the wait. She had her arm over her face, reducing the dim light in the room further, managing her headache, when the phone chimed.

Two words on her screen. *Holy shit.*

She wanted to laugh, but closed her hand on her empty throat instead. She gazed at the wall of text she'd sent, and felt strangely bereft. But then she thought of the phrase he often sent her. *I hear you, Mistress.*

God, she missed him.

The Francis Bacon paraphrased quote she'd seen on his hearing class materials went through her mind. *Sound isn't significant.*

Neither was the fantasy. It was about the underlying things. The trust, the marking. The service. Her imaginings were just different scenes that could change to fit the mood, the man. Her heart and soul.

The rest was merely window dressing for what mattered.

~

The system was set up, but if she ever had to work with that condescending little prick again, she'd return to private contracting. The client was a good one, so they wouldn't end the relationship based on that. Her job had been to implement the system and train the sales department how to use the software effectively. She'd done it, while keeping her temper and courtesy, but the IT manager had pushed it, and she'd finally had to act.

He'd been trying to talk over her—again—because he could. At least with his vocal cords. In mid-sentence, she leaned over his shoulder. He'd parked himself at the terminal she should have been occupying to better demonstrate the features they now had at their disposal.

She called up a dialogue box and began to type, cutting him off and drawing his attention.

"You have a choice. Learn to listen, or explain to your boss why your need to compare dicks with me means you can't operate a quarter-million-dollar marketing system overhaul that will triple your profits."

His gaze had snapped up to her face. She'd held the lock with it until he'd pushed back from the desk and let her take over, with a muttered insult that she'd forced herself to ignore. It helped to see the obvious relief from his staff, who'd known he was the obstacle on successful implementation.

She would let Ros know about it, not to complain but because he might try to sabotage her work and say TRA had delivered an inferior product. Ros could stay ahead of that. Skye suspected she'd have a frank talk with the client and suggest they groom one of his staff to take his place. Skye would recommend the slim twenty-three-year-old with bad acne who'd been intensely attentive, wanting to learn everything she was willing to share. His tech skills needed work, but he was obviously eager to grow those.

On the plane ride back to New Orleans, she thought longingly of Tiger's hands, his mouth, and the simple pleasure of his company. She also thought of riding him mercilessly for the catharsis of a mind-blowing series of orgasms, his cock filling her.

He didn't deserve her in this mood, though. She texted him that it had been a shitty couple of days. Even though she really wanted to see him, she'd reach out to him tomorrow, after she had time to get her head right and be better company.

She received a thumbs up, the brief acknowledgement telling her he had his head under the hood of a car, a place she never wanted him distracted, so she didn't ask for more.

When she came out of the gate, there he was.

He leaned against the rail, arms crossed over a Sturgis, South Dakota bike rally T-shirt, his long denim-clad legs hooked at the ankles of his black motorcycle boots. Dark shades emphasized his stubbled jaw.

The number of women casting him sidelong glances could have qualified him as a tourist attraction, but his focus was all on the gate. As she emerged from it, he was already headed for her.

He relieved her of her carry-on and laptop bag, and then slid an arm around her, bringing her close to brush his mouth over hers. He even lifted her off her feet as he did it, secretly thrilling her, though she gave him a mock frown when he put her down. He grinned, meeting her gaze with a dark blue one that told her how much he'd missed her. Just as much as she'd missed him.

"Respectfully, Mistress," he said mildly, "I think we're past the 'I only want to see you when you're in a good mood' part of the relationship. I'm here for you. That's the beginning and end of it."

She rested her hands on his biceps. *Same goes.*

"You already proved that to me," he answered that look. "You've seen me growly and at my worst and didn't have the sense to leave me alone." His eyes twinkled. "But just in case..."

He fished in his pocket, bringing out a cookies and cream Hershey bar. "I brought chocolate in case you were pissed at me for ignoring your direction. It's a little melted, but I remember that doesn't bug you much." His wicked glint recalled the last time she'd sucked warm chocolate off his skin.

She was so glad to be home.

As they walked toward the airport exit, she had her hand on his elbow. He shot her a sidelong glance. "That 24/7 sub fantasy you sent me? Kneeling until you fell asleep would be a bitch on my knees, because I know just how long it takes you to fall asleep."

She poked him in the side, earning another chuckle. Through the wide bank of windows, the gray and orange smoky streaks in the darkening sky showed twilight was talking hold over the city. When he brought her to the exit doors, he added, "But I can rub your feet, make you dinner, and hold you on the couch. Best of all, I can take you on sunset motorcycle rides."

Anticipation flooded her. It was a lovely night for it, the humid air flirting with the light breeze through the covered passenger drop off area.

Maryshka was pulling up in her tricked-out bright blue Corolla. She leaned over and spoke through the open window. "Hey, Skye. Welcome home. I'm the taxi for your luggage."

"I figured she could leave your stuff at the garage," Tiger told Skye. "We can pick it up when we're on the way to your place."

Skye signed a thank you to Maryshka. The girl smiled, but as Tiger put the luggage in the backseat, Maryshka mouthed a "thank *you*," taking Skye back to how this had all started.

"Love you, boss," Maryshka said impulsively as Tiger straightened and gave her a look. She blinked back tears. "You guys look great together, you know that?"

"You scare me when you act female," Tiger informed her, though he looked a little moved by her unexpected admission. "Get the fuck out of here."

Maryshka shot him a grin, waved and pulled out. Her navigation through the cabs and other vehicles was as smooth and harrowing as if she'd done stunt work for the *Fast and Furious* franchise. Tiger offered Skye a hand. "Come with me?"

Always. She grasped his hand, and he escorted her to short-term parking, where his bike was waiting, dark, gleaming and dangerous. And tempting. Much like the man.

Tiger had brought her boots and a jacket to go over her thin blouse, pulling them out of one of the saddle bags. As she switched out her heels for the boots, he steadied her, his hand sure and warm on hers. Fortunately, she'd worn jeans on the plane. Though they weren't the same weight as what she'd normally wear for a ride, it was a balmy night and Tiger determined they'd be enough for what he had in mind. He handed her the helmet with another flash of his sexy smile.

The moment she swung on behind him, her tensions from her trip started to ebb. When he started the bike, put it in gear and left the parking lot, he called over his shoulder. "Hold on, Mistress. I want to open her up."

Yes, please. She gripped his waist, pressing up against him. The bike roared its approval as he gave it more throttle and took it into higher gear. As they sped along the airport road, leaning into the curves, the wind on her body, the rush of being on the powerful machine, open to the elements, made everything even better.

He used the service roads to connect to other rural roads, and after a blissful thirty-minute ride, brought her to a Cajun-style restaurant nestled up against the bayou. There was an outdoor seating area on a deck over the water, illuminated by string lights and lanterns on the wooden tables. Like most New Orleans venues that looked like holes in the wall, the food was exceptional and had several of her favorites offered on the menu.

It was late for dinner, especially at this location on the outskirts of the city, so their corner was quiet, making it easy to catch each other up. He offered more details on what had been going on at the garage this week, and prompted her with the right questions, ultimately getting her to share the irritations she'd glossed over in their phone calls. She hadn't wanted their evening calls spoiled with that kind of bullshit.

He got her laughing about some of it, threatened to beat up the IT guy for her, and then she was able to let it go. The world had assholes. Big deal. It also had this.

At length they sat together, comfortable and quiet. She moved to sit beside him, and they adjusted their chairs so they could brace their feet on the cable lines strung below the deck railings. She shared her candy bar with him, putting the chocolate on his lips so she could taste her two favorites together.

In time, he straightened and squeezed her leg. "Stay here a minute."

Assuming he was heading to the facilities, she was surprised when he used the side exit steps from the deck to go to his bike, which he'd parked in view of their table. He withdrew something from the saddle bag she couldn't identify, since his back was to her. When he came back, he put it on the table surface next to her and sat back down in his chair on her other side.

He met her gaze, his expression hard to read, but she detected a slight tension. "I want to give you something, Mistress. There's nothing about it that obligates you to anything. I may not be the kind of sub who kneels at your door after work every day, but I can be just as committed to meeting your needs. That's what this says."

It was a hard-shell silver box, the top engraved with the outline of a tiger and a rose, the bloom near the tiger's head, the stem twined around the front paws.

Glancing at him, she cracked it open. The interior top was lined with black satin, the bottom black velvet. Resting on the velvet was a silver cuff bracelet. Stamped on the metal was a finger-spelled word. *Yours.* Next to it was a cursive word. *Mistress.*

Yours, Mistress.

"When I'm working, I can't wear any jewelry," he told her. "But if you decide you want me to wear it, anytime I'm not working it will be on. It's my promise to you, Mistress. I'm yours until you tell me I'm not."

She could feel his concern that he'd presumed too much. She put her other hand on him and gripped his forearm hard, so he knew he hadn't. Then he paused, giving her a long look. That tension from him increased as he reached in his pocket to draw out something else. A much smaller box.

Her heart jumped, her breath drawing in.

She heard the nerves in his voice as he spoke. "I don't know your thoughts on this kind of thing, but...if it's something you want, I wanted you to know it's a hundred percent on the table for me."

He leaned over, putting the box next to the bracelet box. As he straightened, his dark blue eyes held hers. "You can keep it and put it away. Or wear it for the rest of our lives and never have to do anything people consider official. It's what you keeping or wearing it means to me, to us, that matters to me. It tells me you consider yourself mine, too."

She licked her lips. She could untangle code that looked like string pounced on by an army of cats, but that tangle was what her mind felt like right now.

This box was velvet on the outside, a dark blue. It reminded her of his eyes. When she opened it, she gazed at the ring a full moment, taking it all in. The center stone was an opal, its colors a sunrise mix of golds and pinks, with touches of green and silver. She suspected in daylight there'd be even more variations to the shades. The stone was flanked by two smaller diamonds, the band embedded with diamond chips in a silver border.

"The opal reminded me of you, all those colors, changing, never just the one thing. The lady at the jewelry store told me the opal actually means change of colors, like changing the way you look at things. Which you did for me. And when I changed the way I looked at relationships, I found you."

He stopped, cleared his throat again. Put his hand next to the box. Giving her the choice. He'd take it away if she wanted him to do so.

After a few long minutes, she closed the box. She didn't know how she felt about it, but she did know one thing. She slid the box away from him and put it in her crossbody purse.

She wanted to keep it.

A half-smile managed to curve her lips as he let out the breath he'd been holding. But she reached out and gripped his shirt, stopping him from doing anything else for a minute. After a weighted dozen beats of her heart, she signed the words that had been in her heart for a while. Afraid to be spoken, in any language available to her.

His hand closed over hers, and he dipped his head, detaching her from his shirt so he could press his lips to her knuckles. He signed it back, while still holding her hand. Then he spoke it aloud.

"I love you, too, Skye. More than anything in the fucking world."

~

He drove her to her place. She opened up the garage so he could put his bike in there, a confirmation that she wanted him to stay.

As they entered the loft from the stairwell door, she came to a stop. The room was dark, except for a spotlight on a small table that had been placed near the entry. A bouquet of flowers was on it, along with a remote control and a card.

We did this because he's yours now. In every way that matters.

No signature, just a purple rose stamped beneath the words. Telling her it was from Ros, Vera, Cyn and Abby.

As Tiger read it over her shoulder, she looked up at him with the question. He shook his head. "What I gave you was between you and me, Mistress."

Ros and the others hadn't needed to be told. They'd already known, with that exceptional intuition they possessed. Even before Ros had said straight out that Lawrence was it, the rest of them had known. When Neil had proposed to Abby, they'd all been present as witnesses, sure it was meant to be.

Skye wasn't into making an announcement like Ros, and she didn't know what she felt about marriage. As Mistress and sub, she and Tiger were on safer, more familiar ground. But her sisters understood her silence the way Tiger was learning to do, the nature of their relationship meaning he had found his way onto ground even they hadn't reached.

And with the surprise they'd left her here, they'd given her their blessing.

Because of their shared past, and how closely they embraced their Domme side, that blessing had a different shape from a bridesmaid toast. It was a validation, a claim and an assurance, all in one. Both for the man and the Mistress who'd decided he was the one she wanted to keep.

It also contained a warning, against anyone who would threaten or disrupt what Mistress and sub promised one another. The TRA women would be part of her defense, to eradicate the threat. Stand against its influence and remind and verify what the two of them were to one another, so they themselves never doubted it.

Skye picked up the remote and opened the page folded beneath it, scanning the intriguing step-by-step instructions.

Press green button first.

As she pressed it, an oscillating projection ball attached to her center light fixture came to life. It cast a moving mural of shapes along an expanse of solid black curtains covering her bank of windows. It was a man and woman, moving in the various dances of Mistress and sub. Him on his knees to her, kissing her foot as she stood in a hip-cocked stance, stilettos braced. Her throwing a whip as he was restrained on a cross, cock fully erect, seemingly longing for the touch of the lash. Him kissing her hands before she put them on his face and they began to turn in an actual dance, her skirt flowing out.

The images flowed in a direction drawing the eye toward the unfinished "dungeon room." When she'd left, it had still been cordoned off by the rubber strip construction curtains. No more.

A free-standing wall screened it now. A door-sized space between the windowed loft wall and the newly constructed one made it look as if the flowing images disappeared into the room beyond it.

Her sectional sofa was against the new wall, several of her paintings in an attractive arrangement above it. Since the wall only went two-thirds of the way to the ceiling, purple string lights were draped over its top edge. Width-wise, the wall ended at the mid-point of the loft space, terminating at one of the brick pillars that braced the ceiling over her open living quarters. It left the right-hand view to her platform bed open.

The wall had been to formalize the space behind it, not to enclose it. The brick pillar had a neon sign mounted on it, the words stacked in a tantalizing pink glow. *Love. Cherish. Kneel. Serve.*

With her hand in Tiger's, Skye circled around the pillar and sign to view the room beyond. Once there, she paused, gripped by a wealth of emotions.

"Damn," Tiger murmured.

She agreed. Her sisters knew her well. It was everything she could want in a play space.

There was a webcam for her to watch him, if she chose to step out of his view, leaving him wondering and anticipating. A mounted screen meant no matter where Tiger was in the room, restrained or otherwise, he could see what she wanted. She could sync it from any monitor or device. *Lie down. Spread your legs. Wait for me.*

But the crowning piece of the room was a spanking bench that looked like a motorcycle. Instead of legs, it had silver and black fixed wheels. The bench's seat was a Sybian stimulator, complete with attachment options. Useful for a male or female rider.

A half-dozen riding "gloves" were draped over the silver handlebars. Vampire gloves, velvet gloves, waterproof gloves. Plus starlet satin elbow-length gloves. As they approached the bench, Tiger picked them up.

"These are from your dresser," he said, gazing at her with heated eyes. "I like them. A lot."

She trailed a hand down his arm, resting her fingertips there as she continued to absorb. A chain was draped over the rafters, close enough to the bench to reinforce the motorcycle theme. It connected to hardpoints for restraints.

The loft wall behind the bike now had a brick covering like her pillars, only these bricks had been painted black and then overlaid with green strands of code, raining down the wall in straight lines. Like the opening to the Matrix, one of her favorite films. These lines also looked like bars, caging the silhouette of a kneeling male. Head down, shoulders tense in a waiting posture. A woman's silhouette was painted in front of the bars, to the right, reaching for him between two lines of code.

Skye glanced down at her instructions. *Once you're in the playroom, press the blue button.*

A ripple of green light started flowing along those lines of text. Silver sparks touched the shoulders and eyes of the kneeling male, the silhouette of the Mistress, her heels.

She loved it. Absolutely loved it.

Who had set all this up? Her sisters knew she'd be curious, so they'd satisfied that question with an explanation at the bottom of the paper, handwritten in Ros's crisp cursive. *We pulled in Jon Forte from Kensington & Associates, the only person as smart as you about this stuff.*

Jon routinely brought erotic toys and gadgets to Progeny that impressed Skye. They'd swapped ideas before. Being a Dom himself, he'd obviously known what subtle touches would kindle a Mistress's pleasure.

A medicine-sized cabinet had been mounted on the wall. The bronze handle looked like a naked kneeling male from the back. Her fingers curled around his waist and hips to open the door, and she inhaled a silent chuckle as the tip of her finger brushed over a blunt but noticeable erection inside the curve of his body.

Inside the cabinet were lubricants, first aid supplies and snips. On a round glass table beneath it a tall vase contained purple and silver carbon canes and several floggers. A bottle of whiskey, two shot glasses and a trio of frosted glass dildos were also on the table. Tiger's firm lips quirked at the arrangement, then he shook his head with further amusement as she pointed out the cabinet handle's lifelike anatomy.

There was more. A contoured couch would allow her to ride her biker in different positions. On a strip of wall next to the Matrix design, they'd mounted some of her favorite toy choices. Paddles, more floggers and restraints, plus one of Tiger's belts. They must have retrieved it from her room, since she had him keeping some clothes here. It just so happened it was the belt she'd used on him during the first session where she'd learned how well he responded to impact play, particularly when it came from leather.

She'd be using it on him again for sure.

The carefully chosen equipment still left her ample space to create the scenarios she wanted, with the perfect props to enhance them. The final section of her new space had a mat laid out next to a low table. Colorful candle wax options and supplies were arranged on it. Wax play was something she hadn't yet investigated to her satisfaction, but they'd known it interested her.

As she imagined marking Tiger's skin with the hot drips, creating designs inspired by wherever her mind took her, she noted a card had been left on the low table. A bow with gauzy ribbon ends flowing from the ceiling fan currents had been attached to it, so she wouldn't miss it.

She picked it up and began to read.

This is all for you, but each of us left a specific gift for Tiger.

The Matrix wallpaper with the suggestion of him behind the bars of code, willingly your captive, was Cyn's idea.

The monitor, so he could easily see what you want and demand, was Abby's.

The bike was mine. Self-explanatory.

Vera's was the mats and candle wax, so he can serve you in new ways.

Their validation and claim, just as she'd thought, to reinforce the one she had on him. One he'd just confirmed himself, by giving her a symbol for a collar. Plus the ring she had tucked in her phone bag.

We all helped pick out the toys. Enjoy, celebrate, and know we love you.

As she looked at all of it, at the things her sisters had left her, at all they'd done for her, knowing what he meant to her, her gaze came back to him. This space was theirs, to share. Accepting that, understanding it, meant she was brave enough to share a lot more with him.

She drew the ring box out of her bag. Tiger had been studying their surroundings, as pleased as she was with all of it. But as soon as she did that, his attention was on her. She offered the box to him.

He took it, his expression carefully neutral, honoring his declaration not to pressure or judge her decision on it. But before he could tuck it back in his pocket, she extended her hand. Palm down, fingers spread out.

She wasn't giving it back.

That neutral look dropped instantly, replaced by an exultant joy that had her smiling, feeling giddy and delighted...all the things she never thought she'd feel about such a moment.

Tiger took the ring from the box and slid it on her finger. Then he dropped to his knee, still gripping her hand, and pressed a kiss high on her thigh. His arms circled her and held.

Touching his face, she drew his attention to her. She gestured to the room. To the beginning of where the journey would take them from here. She lifted both hands, freeing them only for the time it took to make the sign. Thumb and pinky lifted, rest of fingers closed, a quick flick of them forward and back. A smile crossed her face.

"Let's play."

∽

WANT MORE MISTRESSES OF THE BOARD ROOM?

Ten years ago, Mick should have arrested the drunk, angry woman vandalizing a cemetery. Instead, on that cold night, he yielded to her pain and rage, and let her go. Now a former cop, he's come to New Orleans on business, which brings him face to face with the woman he never forgot.

Cynbad Marigold is a successful businesswoman and a formidable Domme, a Mistress who chooses subs who need enough pain to appease her limitless craving to give it. Most subs safeword before she goes too deep, but when Mick reappears in her life, he doesn't want safety.

In uncovering the shocking depths of his own darkness, Cyn realizes the pleasure she takes in giving pain is matched only by how much she wants to give him the home he needs...safe in the shadows of her soul.

Whose darkness will take them deeper—and will their bond keep them from going too far?

**CLICK HERE TO READ NOW
AT HER PLEASURE**

Reading this in print format?
Look for it at your favorite book vendor!

ABOUT THE AUTHOR

Having penned over fifty acclaimed BDSM contemporary and paranormal titles, which includes six award-winning series, *Joey W. Hill* has been awarded the RT Book Reviews Career Achievement Award for Erotic Romance. A submissive herself, Hill brings authenticity to her intensely emotional love stories.

She is grateful for the support of a wonderful and enthusiastic readership, which allows her to live on her beloved Carolina coast with her even more beloved husband and menagerie of animals.

- On the Web: https://storywitch.com
- Twitter: https://twitter.com/JoeyWHill
- Facebook: https://facebook.com/JoeyWHillAuthor
- Facebook Fan Forum: https://facebook.com/groups/JWHMembersOnly
- MeWe: https://mewe.com/i/joeywhill
- GoodReads: https://www.goodreads.com/author/show/103359.Joey_W_Hill
- BookBub: https://bookbub.com/authors/joey-w-hill
- Amazon: https://amazon.com/Joey-W-Hill/e/B001JSCIW0

ALSO BY JOEY W. HILL

Arcane Shot Series

Arcane Shot

Arcane Madame

Arcane Chaos

Arcane Knight

Daughters of Arianne Series

A Mermaid's Kiss

A Witch's Beauty

A Mermaid's Ransom

Knights of the Board Room Series

Board Resolution

Controlled Response

Honor Bound

Afterlife

Hostile Takeover

Willing Sacrifice

Soul Rest

Knight Nostalgia *(Anthology)*

Mistresses of the Board Room Series

At Her Command

At Her Service

At Her Call

At Her Pleasure

Nature of Desire Series

Holding the Cards

Natural Law

Ice Queen

Mirror of My Soul

Mistress of Redemption

Rough Canvas

Branded Sanctuary

Divine Solace

Worth The Wait

Truly Helpless

In His Arms

Ignition Sequence

Naughty Bits Series

Naughty Bits

Naughty Wishes

Vampire Queen Series

Vampire Queen's Servant

Mark of the Vampire Queen

Vampire's Claim

Beloved Vampire

Vampire Mistress *(VQS: Club Atlantis)*

Vampire Trinity *(VQS: Club Atlantis)*

Vampire Instinct

Bound by the Vampire Queen

Taken by a Vampire

The Scientific Method

Nightfall

Elusive Hero

Night's Templar

Vampire's Soul

Vampire's Embrace

Vampire Master *(VQS: Club Atlantis)*

Vampire Guardian *(VQS: Club Atlantis)*

Vampire's Choice

www.ingramcontent.com/pod-product-compliance
Lightning Source LLC
Chambersburg PA
CBHW071647260626
47170CB00001B/265